SCHOLARSHIP:
DEATH BEFORE DEFAULT
BOOK TWO OF THE FRONTIERS

David Alan Jones

Seventh Seal Press
Virginia Beach, VA

Chris Kennedy/Seventh Seal Press
2052 Bierce Dr.
Virginia Beach, VA 23454
http://chriskennedypublishing.com/

Publisher's Note: This is a work of fiction. Names, characters, places, and incidents are a product of the author's imagination. Locales and public names are sometimes used for atmospheric purposes. Any resemblance to actual people, living or dead, or to businesses, companies, events, institu-tions, or locales is completely coincidental.

Ordering Information:
Quantity sales. Special discounts are available on quantity purchases by cor-porations, associations, and others. For details, contact the "Special Sales Department" at the address above.

Cover Design by Brenda Mihalko
Art by Ricky Ryan

Scholarship/David Alan Jones -- 1st ed.
ISBN 978-1950420377

This book is dedicated to all those who find social interaction as easy as hopscotching through a minefield while juggling chainsaws.

I'm with you.

Chapter One

They were supposed to catch the smugglers in space. That had been the plan. But sometimes plans turned out as useless as wishes, or so Cadet Major Colt Maier had learned in his nearly four years at Fulcrum Mercenary Training.

And sometimes wishes turned out worse.

Colt forced his taut muscles to relax inside his Combat Assault System, Personal. The CASPer, an armored suit which stood more than seven feet tall, shuddered in its deployment cradle as the sound of atmosphere screaming across the dropship's hull reverberated through its steel alloy and polymer chassis. Pinplants, a set of ports surgically installed at the base of Colt's skull, interfaced with the suit to give him constant feedback about his surroundings, both inside and outside the CASPer. Twenty more suits like his filled the dropship's hold, each piloted by one of his fellow cadets. Bristling with weapons from accelerator cannons and lasers to simple blades half as long as Colt was tall, they all bore the bright yellow "E" for Echo Company, except the one directly to Colt's right. He turned his viewer in that direction, the holographic Tri-V monitors inside his suit panning to follow his gaze. That CASPer wore a gold chevron on its shoulder, meaning it held a fellow cadet member of the command staff.

"You ready, Yard?" Colt sent his voice over an encrypted channel shared only with Cadet Lieutenant Colonel Stephen Yardley, the school's battalion commander. Yardley tended to get nervous before any mission, even guard duty during their freshman year.

"Ready as I'm going to get." Yard's voice, crystal clear over the digitized channel, sounded strained.

"I'm right here. Things get hairy with these guys, we'll handle it together."

"You mean you'll handle it."

Colt said nothing. He didn't know what to say. Yard was right, but he probably didn't want to hear that. Or maybe he did? Who could say?

At sixteen, Colt had mostly come to terms with what he thought of as his social anchor. He had Asperger's, a condition neurological science hadn't managed to conquer despite nearly one hundred and fifty years of study and the advent of alien tech. Having it meant Colt was on the autism spectrum. Not so far along the line he couldn't fend for himself—he had left his parents back home in Stanford, California to join FMT after all—but far enough to make other people something of a riddle for him. Or maybe it was the other way around. He was the riddle, one few of them could solve.

Fortunately, his anxiety and fear melted away inside a CASPer, at least when it came to talking to Yardley. The big commander needed Colt's help, and Colt was glad to give it.

"Fifty seconds to drop." The voice, female and confident, broadcast over the common channel from the cockpit.

Colt reopened the private link with Yardley and sent a message via his pinplants.

"Ready, Kit," Yardley said, repeating Colt's words. "Captain Butler, Captain Onishi, prepare your people to disembark. We're about two kilometers from the downed smuggler craft. Looks like they had to ditch because of our pursuit. Our task is recovery. You are not to fire unless given direct orders to do so. Acknowledge those orders."

"Company Alpha, acknowledged," Captain Terrell Butler said.

"Echo, acknowledged." Captain Alice Onishi's voice rang over the common channel.

Though FMT boasted five companies, only the first four ran at the optimal regulation strength of one hundred and fifty cadets. The fifth, Onishi's Echo Company, also known as Shortfall, was made up of a mere ninety-two troopers. That meant Shortfall usually dropped with a mix of other companies, and today's mission was no exception. Colt had elected to bring forty of their best people with an additional forty from Alpha as a supplement. He figured that would easily suffice should their quarry decide to fight. Yardley had signed the order without question.

Things hadn't begun this way, with Colt feeding Yardley commands. The two had set out as freshman cadets bent on forging themselves into the best mercenaries they could. Both had hopes of hiring on with one of the bigger companies, maybe even one of the Four Horsemen, after graduation. Big, boisterous, and outgoing, Yardley made the perfect cadet officer. Granted, his Voluntary Off-World assessment scores wouldn't set the world on fire, but he had squeaked by to land a spot on the school's officers' track. And once in, he was set. Everyone loved Yardley. He got on well with the cadets and the school's staff. He seemed to know all the right buttons to press and all the right words to say to make people follow him.

Too bad he sucked as a commander.

Given a choice between an ice cream and a candy bar, Yard probably would be stumped for hours. Decision making and he got along about as well as Colt and public speaking. But if you wanted a flag planted somewhere, and you placed Stephen Yardley at the front of your unit, that flag would rise. Yard just needed someone to tell him where to put it.

And that someone was Colt.

They hadn't discovered their unique dynamic until their sophomore year when, during a field exercise, a then-Cadet Lieutenant Yardley had nearly killed his platoon in a simulated fortress defense game. Colt had made a few simple—to him anyway—suggestions to Yard that had sent him from bumbling to winning in minutes. From that point on, Yardley had led with the quiet Colt at his side.

A resounding boom shook the dropship as it touched down. Its rear door opened to harsh daylight, causing Colt's Tri-V monitors to darken. The clamp fitted around each CASPer split open and retracted into the wall, and Echo Company, Platoon One surged forward onto a rock-strewn, red plain covered in thick sand. The troopers' mechanized feet threw up plumes of the stuff as they hurried to the designated rally point with Alpha Company.

Chatter on the common band died as Yard and Colt took their places in front of the mixed companies. Only forty of them drove CASPers. They stood at the fore. The remaining forty wore powered armor affectionately known as RATs (Reactive Armor Teams when addressed individually), and carried hand weapons, mostly GenTok W80s, all-purpose rifles designed off-Earth, but meant for Humans. Like the armor, the gun had proven itself time and again in environments ranging from vacuum to the dankest jungles in the galaxy. Colt had no idea where FMT had gotten the RATs, but manufacturers everywhere were increasingly offering Human-compatible weapons as the demand from merc companies grew.

The planet they stood on was known by its colonists as Brigham, in a system they had named Zion. Brigham's atmosphere—mostly carbon dioxide with a little nitrogen mixed in—its rust-colored landscape, and its light gravity reminded Colt of Mars. But unlike Mars, Brigham's core was still spinning, which meant it possessed strong magnetic poles, giving the digital compass on Colt's Tri-V something to orient on. He looked eastward and could just make out the tallest spires of New Nauvoo, the planet's only city. Domed and exquisitely cared for by its inhabitants, the Galnet called it the "jewel of the system." Not that any jewel would have to shine particularly brightly to outclass Brigham's boring exterior.

Opposite the city, a long finger of black smoke trailing up from its rear thrusters, sat a copper-colored ship, its hull baking in the sun. It rested at an odd angle, the nose decidedly lower than the massive tail section, probably a result of its captain's hasty attempt at getting dirtside too fast.

Colt glanced at the status board on the right side of his cockpit. No malfunctions with any of their people's equipment. A good sign. He sent a signal to Yardley, and the cadet lieutenant colonel spoke on the company channel.

"Captains, take charge of your units. Let's get to work."

A general cry of approval echoed over the company band, and the platoons split into ten squads with four CASPers leading each. They dashed in orderly fashion toward the downed frigate, the larger suits careful to maintain a pace the RATs could match. Though the smaller suits were capable of flight, their removable fuel cells added weight which tended to slow them down. Colt and Yard had decided to forgo the fuel for more speed.

Chatter picked up as they neared the ship, squad leaders calling formation orders to their troops to clear their fire lanes and avoid blue-on-blue casualties. As he drew near, Colt noticed the frigate's front landing strut had sunk so deep into the dead planet's surface, the bottom hull was nearly touching sand. The smugglers likely wouldn't be leaving anytime soon, not without some digging.

"Attention crew of the downed vessel, *Ra'shrem Velq*. This is Lieutenant Colonel Stephen Yardley of Fulcrum Mercenary Training." Yardley read the words Colt sent him with power and authority. "You are in possession of stolen goods. We have been hired to return that property to its true owners. You will relinquish it now."

"Stolen goods?" The shrill voice that came over the comm, while translated into English by Colt's pinplants, still managed to sound outraged. Smugglers always did.

"You heard me right." Yardley sounded disappointed, as if he had expected this set of thieves to cooperate when no others ever had in any of their previous missions, not even the simulated ones aboard ship. "My deputy is sending a manifest detailing the items in question. Check it against your ship's stores but be quick about it. I'm giving you five minutes to start offloading, or we'll come take it."

Colt made a face inside his CASPer. He hated it when Yardley improvised. They weren't supposed to give smugglers and thieves time to think or plan. But it wasn't like he could countermand Yard, so he transmitted the manifest.

Twenty seconds passed. Then thirty. When the voice returned, it sounded even more frustrated than before. "This is ninety percent of my load! And it's not stolen! We bought these arms on Karma two weeks ago. How did you come by this inventory?"

Colt triggered his monitors to show him a crew roster and brought up an image of the frigate's captain. According to the database, its name was Germash, and it was an Aposo, a rodent-looking alien that despised bright light. It looked like a giant mole or, maybe, a bald rat. But despite its looks, Germash had a clean record and an exemplary reputation for on-time deliveries. Odd that he should throw all that away to smuggle weapons—or maybe not so odd. No doubt weapons smuggling paid better.

Colt dashed off a message to Yardley.

"Germash? That your name?" Yardley asked.

A long pause then, "Yes."

"Germash, our client has evidence those goods are stolen. Maybe you had nothing to do with the theft. I'm willing to believe that— these things happen—regardless, you now have less than a minute to start your offload."

"I don't need a minute. Your clients, whoever they might be, are either lying or mistaken. And as for your intimidation tactics, you've failed. You think you're the only mercenary crew in this system?"

A door opened high up on the frigate's port side and disgorged a swarm of armored figures, one hundred twenty-five of them, according to Colt's pinplants. Based on their IFF beacon, they belonged to a Zuul merc company called Resilient Marrow.

Colt stifled a laugh at the name. Maybe it sounded better in the original Zuul? Either way, he wasn't about to let their name lull him into underestimating them. The canine-like aliens had a reputation as smart tacticians.

"Eighty versus one twenty-five...think we can manage this?" Yardley sounded doubtful.

"Yeah, it's unfair," Colt said, his smile broadening. "Maybe they've got a few more aboard ship they can send out once we're done with these." With a mental kick to his implants, he sent Yardley a quick plan of action. "Try this."

"Onishi, move your CASPers twelve degrees to the east. Butler, hold position but stagger your suits. Both of you get your RATs filtered in close to the big guys." No hint of hesitation or doubt colored Yardley's voice over the common channel.

"Roger that!" Onishi got her people moving in less than three seconds.

Butler was a little slower, but quick nonetheless.

The Zuul mercs wore armor of their own, their mirrored helmets contoured to accommodate their muzzles and triangular ears. Colt could make no sense of the various markings they bore, but it appeared one of their number, a particularly short one, whose armor glistened with red, blue, and yellow designs like hieroglyphs, was their leader. Having watched Colt's forces split into a wedge formation, it made a series of hand gestures, and the Zuul warriors around it likewise spread apart.

Just as Colt had hoped they would. Sometimes, it astonished him how many alien races forgot CASPers could fly. He blasted a message to Yardley who relayed it with his basso voice.

"Go! Go! Go!"

All forty CASPers took to the air, the jumpjets on their backs screaming and churning up a cloud of red dust and small rocks. As one, they opened fire on the Zuul with lasers, rockets, and high velocity bullets fired from weapons mounted on their arms or on their shoulders. They could have fired guided missiles as well, but Colt had ordered them to refrain for fear of hitting the RATs, all of whom had charged the enemy's lines the instant their larger compatriots lifted off.

Colt fired his jumpjets to get a better view of the battle. He rose a little faster than he expected in the 0.75 G environment, but compensated quickly enough to avoid overshooting the combat zone. As he had predicted, the CASPers' dust cloud engulfed the Zuul. No doubt they had thermal imaging built into their helmets, which might have aided them against the average light infantry sort of armor, but RATs were a different story. Designed to match thermal conditions within a broad scope of environs, the powered suits became virtually indistinguishable from the dust cloud swirling about them.

They poured over the Zuul like ants. Most got off point-blank kills with their W80s within the first ten seconds of the go order, nearly evening the numbers on the two sides with their first salvo. Others let their rifles dangle from tac harnesses, preferring to take out targets with the blades set into the forearms of their suits. And, though most Zuul possessed superior dexterity compared to Humans, the mix of surprise, near blindness, and the RATs' enhanced speed, turned the dogs' attempts at fighting them almost laughable.

All that, combined with the unrelenting CASPer fire raining down from the red sky, made the enemy's casualty rates soar. It was enough to break any fighting unit. The Zuul were no exception.

"Humans!" a voice cried over the common channel. "Humans, cease fire. We will retreat."

"Do it," Colt said to Yard.

"Cease fire! Captains, call your people back into formation."

The Zuul with the many markings on its armor must have been barking orders to its troopers. They retreated quickly, drawing back into the lee of their employer's ship, leaving behind a field strewn with their dead.

Onishi and Butler got their people in hand; the CASPers landed and the RATs withdrew to their original formation points.

"What is this?" demanded the smuggler captain, Germash. "I paid you Zuul to protect my ship and stores!"

"About those stores," Yardley cut in. "We'll be taking the stolen portion now."

"This is theft!"

"No, this is justice." Yardley switched to the company's ship-to-shore channel. "*Uncanny Valley*, this is FMT Ground Actual. We've secured the smuggler ship. I'll inform you when we're ready for lift."

No answer came from *Uncanny Valley*, FMT's converted long-haul freighter which served as the battalion's home and university.

"*Uncanny Valley*?" Yard remained silent for a count of ten. "Colonel Belknap, do you hear me?"

Colonel Memphis Belknap, Fulcrum Mercenary Training's commandant and CEO, monitored all missions. Colt couldn't remember a time when he had failed to answer a comms request.

"What do we do?" Yard asked Colt over their private channel.

Colt started to answer, but Onishi's voice on the common channel cut him off.

"Sir, Sergeant Fielder says there are a couple of ships headed our way from orbit."

"Locals?" Yard asked.

"No, sir. These aren't Mormons."

Colt checked his Tri-V, but realized immediately he didn't need it. The ships in question were almost on top of them. He hadn't heard them in the planet's thin air and the heat of battle.

They landed in unison, a small sleek ship of a design Colt had never seen and a much larger frigate-sized vessel with gentle curves and gleaming metal. It didn't escape his notice that they boxed in his forces, landing on the long, smooth plains to the east and west.

A feminine-shaped figure climbed from the smaller of the two ships. She wore an armored power suit fitted with boosters that jutted from her back. The suit's engines flared, making little more than a soft whirr in Brigham's thin atmosphere, and she rose into the air. She passed over the former battlefield and landed in front of the nearest set of CASPers with impeccable grace.

Port doors opened on the larger ship, and a company of armed MinSha marched out on insectile legs. Colt's throat went dry watching the praying mantis-like aliens surge forward to take up guard positions behind the woman, some of them stepping on fallen Zuul as if they were nothing more than rocks.

"Attention, Fulcrum Mercenary Training cadets," a smooth female voice—it sounded Human, but there was no real way to tell over the comm—broadcast across the common channel. "My name is Casandra Brown. I am a duly appointed bounty hunter working under the authority of the Peacemaker Guild."

Colt's mind whirled. What would a bounty hunter be doing in the Zion system? And why would she involve herself with a smuggling operation? Didn't she have bigger worries? Most bounty hunters worked jobs for the Peacemakers, a guild that normally concerned itself with problems on a star system or bigger scale. Something didn't add up. Colt sent a quick message to Yardley.

"This is Cadet Lieutenant Colonel Stephen Yardley." Yard sounded surprisingly confident repeating Colt's words. Good. "We are acting on behalf of a client who hired us to return smuggled weapons. Why are you interfering in our contractual duties?"

Casandra Brown must have zeroed in on Yardley's broadcast. She lit her rockets and zoomed over to stand before him in a billowing cloud of red dust. Though her powered suit surely possessed a chameleon skin to match any environment, she had left its outer surface a gleaming black that seemed to swallow sunlight. She looked up at Yard, and it was like watching a mouse face off against an elephant, except Colt had a feeling this was one dangerous mouse.

"I'm interfering, Cadet, because the people you've been chasing aren't smugglers. You are."

* * * * *

Chapter Two

A contingent of armed flyers sent from New Nauvoo escorted Colt and Yardley, who had changed into their gray dress uniforms, to the city with Casandra Brown and a retinue of ten of her hired MinSha guards. The rest of the Human cadets returned to *Uncanny Valley* in orbit, to await further instructions. No doubt the rumor mill would be churning up some juicy gossip on what had happened dirtside. Would any of it rival the truth? Probably not.

They sat in an exquisitely appointed conference room with a roof tall enough to accommodate Brown's MinSha guards. Said guards carried rifles, which had been a point of contention when their group first entered the city. The Mormon guards protecting the main airlock had tried to confiscate the cannon-sized weapons, but at a word from Brown, they had backed off.

That told Colt something interesting. If New Nauvoo's officials recognized Brown's authority to bring weapons into the city against their local ordinances, it meant she was on official business, and what she had told him and Yardley out on the plain might well be true. It was a disquieting thought, and one he had, thus far, successfully avoided considering in-depth.

A genteel-looking man in a fine, blue uniform with copper oak leaves on his lapel sat at the head of the conference room's glossy table. He cleared his throat and turned his attention to Colt and Yardley. "My name is Bishop Major Jeffery Andersen. I'm the deputy commander of the New Nauvoo Defense Militia. You are Stephen

Fleerman Yardley and Colt Luan Maier, and I have a feeling you're wondering just what is happening here. Yes?"

Try as he might, Colt could not lift his eyes to meet the gazes focused on him. He stared at the table, and fought down his inclination to wilt under the attention.

"Yes, sir." Yardley's voice held firm. At a little over two meters tall, Yard looked older than his twenty-one years. With shoulders as broad across as a W80 rifle, arms like engineering pipes, and a beard he had to shave every day lest his face turn into a jungle, he could have passed for near thirty in Colt's estimation. "We believe there's been some sort of misunderstanding."

Colt breathed a silent sigh of relief. Thank goodness Yard had the sense to keep from saying, "lie." Who knew how the bounty hunter would have taken that sort of accusation?

As it was, Brown shook her head. The bounty hunter was a slim, older woman, probably in her thirties, maybe even forties, with a careworn face that spoke of hard labor. That face appeared grave. "No mistake, young man. I've been chasing you for seven months. You eluded me on Moorhouse, but barely. I think your commandant caught my scent and ran before I could catch up."

From the corner of his eye, Colt saw Yard stiffen, and he did the same. The bounty hunter was speaking the truth, at least part of it. They had been on Moorhouse two months earlier to capture a delivery of stolen laser rifles. They had managed to take the shipment, but Colonel Belknap had ordered them to stop loading the weapons with the job half done. He had given no concrete reason for the order, and Colt had wondered about it often ever since.

"I'm afraid your school's head master has been using you to commit crimes." Bishop Major Andersen looked pained at relaying this news. "According to evidence provided by Ms. Brown, he and his deputy, Lieutenant Colonel Rudd, have been duping the students of Fulcrum Mercenary Training for almost a decade."

"Even their ranks are a lie," Brown said. "Your *Colonel* Belknap was never anything more than a sergeant with a small mercenary concern called Fowler's Falcons."

"No. You're wrong." Yardley's tone had gone from serious to surly. "Belknap served with Tom's Triple Terrors and reached major. Even he admits calling himself a colonel is sort of a joke, but he's the CEO of Fulcrum, and the rank goes with the title."

Brown shook her head. "No, son. That man was never with Triple T. He might have subcontracted for them a time or two—Fowler's Falcons sometimes takes partial contracts the big boys don't want to waste resources on—but he was never part of their outfit. He's a con artist. Same goes for his supposed deputy. Rudd was never a merc. She's been running scams since she was eight years old. The two of them have been using you to rob legitimate merchants for months. Before that, they had you fulfilling unsanctioned contracts for wanted criminals."

Colt's insides felt like ice. He had spent the better part of four years training under the command of Colonel Belknap, Lieutenant Colonel Rudd, and their general staff of instructors. That couldn't all be a lie. He didn't want to believe it.

And yet...

There were oddities about FMT, like the fact it wasn't affiliated with any particular mercenary company. Most of the larger merc companies ran their own cadre training programs, which meant they didn't need outside schools like FMT. To stay in business, those outside schools paid big money to serve as feeder systems for the moderate and even small merc companies without training programs. Colt had studied dozens of merc training schools when he was first looking to join. All of them advertised their ties to merc companies.

All but FMT. It had none. Colonel Belknap had called that lack of sponsorship a strength—FMT wasn't beholden to anyone. But maybe they just weren't backed by anyone.

And then there was the matter of scholarships. Attending an academy, university, or even one of the fly-by-night diploma mills focused on merc training was expensive. Though Colt had scored high on his Voluntary Off-World assessments, called VOWs, his lack of a merc sponsor—no one in his family had ever desired such a common career—combined with his relative poverty and his dismal scores on the psych eval due to his Asperger's, had made attending one of the big universities impossible. And yet, Fulcrum had offered him a full ride with loans to be paid back after graduation.

Everyone knew mercs swam in galactic credits, so the idea of paying back a loan had seemed trivial at the time—not that he had understood much about money at twelve. But, if what Casandra Brown was saying held true, Belknap had pocketed all that loan money and had been paying for the school's upkeep through nefarious means.

Yardley sat up straight in his chair, his considerable chest straining the seams of his haptic suit as he drew breath to start yelling. He obviously didn't like Brown's insinuation that FMT had been working for, and as, criminals. But Colt kicked his ankle under the table, and Yard subsided.

Accessing his pinplants at the speed of thought, Colt broadcast a message to him.

Though Yardley's face blanched, he dutifully repeated Colt's words. "If what you say is true, what happens next? What are you planning to do with us?"

"Not my business," Brown said. "I'm here on behalf of the Merchant Guild. They wanted Belknap and his people arrested. I've done that. Far as I'm concerned, you all are free to go."

"Go?" Yardley looked around the table, his aquiline jaw set, his eyes pleading. "Go where?"

"Home," Bishop Major Andersen said. "Back to Earth or wherever you started from." He shrugged one shoulder. "Eventually, anyway. There is some question as to the legal ownership of Belknap's vessel. Our lawyers are pouring over the matter. In the meantime, you are welcome to stay aboard. Our port authority has docked the ship with Pratt Station."

Colt got the feeling when the Bishop Major said *Uncanny Valley* was now docked with their space station, it meant locked down tight. The cadets might get to stay aboard for a few days, but the ship wasn't going anywhere while the Bishop Major's lawyers worked out a plan to lay claim to it without legal hassles.

"If there's nothing more, I'd like to get back to my ship." Brown stood, and her MinSha guards prepared to exit with her.

Colt sent a hasty message to Yardley, his heart racing at a new, frightening thought.

"Wait!" Yardley stood, his expression worried. "Did you take all the staff? The pilots, engineers, armorers?"

Brown shook her head. "No. Not all. From what I understand, most of your instructors were duped, just like you. My people arrested only Belknap's command staff, the ones we're certain were in on the deception."

"And now, gentlemen, I'll thank you to speak with the cadets back on your ship. Explain the situation and assure them my people will do everything in our power to see to their comfort during your stay in the Zion system. But, please ask them to remain aboard your ship, at least until we clear up a few matters." Bishop Major Andersen stood to shake Yardley's, then Colt's hands as if they had just negotiated a deal on a used flyer.

Colt got the feeling he and Yard had gotten the raw end of the agreement.

* * *

"It's not good. In fact, it's worse than we thought." Colt sat in a large, leather-upholstered chair behind former Colonel Belknap's stateroom desk, his eyes dashing back and forth as he took in the reams of information provided by his pinplants. He didn't so much read the articles, news vids, school databases, and other corroborating evidence as absorb them. And what he was absorbing—had been absorbing for the better part of four hours—made him sick.

"How could it be worse?" Yardley sat across from Colt, his eyes flicking as he read a different slice of the data. "Is the colonel wanted on sexual harassment charges somewhere too?"

"No, but it looks like he cheated at least seven investors out of millions of credits just to get FMT up and running, and he's been tricking more and more people into sinking money into it ever since. No wonder we've been traveling farther and farther afield to find contracts. He's got people gunning for him everywhere."

"Where'd you find that?"

"His personal files. The idiot kept a portfolio of his best schemes."

"You broke into his personal stuff?"

"It wasn't that big of a deal. Belknap shared his files with Rudd, and she didn't keep her stuff encrypted, so I was able to backdoor into the colonel's private data."

"Not colonel." The surly tone had returned to Yardley's voice.

"And not sergeant, either." Colt flicked his gaze to a large flat display on the stateroom wall, and it came online, showing a twenty-seven-year-old service report and review from Fowler's Falcons. The rating gave one Specialist Memphis Wilson Belknap a *meets standards* rating across every category.

Yardley, who after four years of cadet training had seen his share of troop reviews, rolled his eyes. "He didn't get even one exceeds? What a turd."

Colt switched off his link to the ship's intranet and the planet's link to the Zion system's information network. He had seen enough. A bone-aching weariness made his entire body hurt. "We have to tell them."

Yardley nodded, his face glum. "How do you think they'll take the news?"

"Same as you and me. It'll suck. But they deserve to hear it from us."

Although Yardley had made a ship-wide announcement about the bounty hunter's accusations against FMT's command staff, he had also promised to launch his own investigation into their accuracy. Four hours earlier, he and Colt had still held a smidgen of hope that this entire fiasco was all a mistake. Four hours, and more research than they had done in four years as students at FMT, hadn't exonerated Belknap and his cronies.

Quite the opposite.

"What happens now?" Yardley sounded genuinely curious, as if he expected Colt to have an answer. And maybe he did. Colt always had an answer.

But not this time. At least, not the sort of answer Yardley wanted. Colt could tell his big counterpart wanted him to say everything would work out. They would continue as a team, graduate FMT, and go on to long and glorious careers as mercs.

Fat chance since FMT no longer existed. Who would sign their diplomas? Maybe they could sign each other's! The thought hit him so hard, Colt laughed out loud.

Yard looked at him quizzically. "What's funny about this?"

"Nothing. Everything. We got tricked into thinking we were becoming mercs by a guy who was barely ever one himself. You've got to admit there's something funny there."

"Funny like stupid, yeah. I think—"

"Colonel, uh, Steven, there's a call coming in for you," Captain Onishi said over the office's intercom.

Colt wondered why Onishi, who was Echo Company's executive officer, was answering comm calls on the bridge. Where were the comm techs? They must have abandoned their posts, since the school was no longer in business.

"Who is it?" Yardley gave Colt a look that said, *what now?*

"He says he represents Mountside Financial." Onishi paused for a moment, then said in a lower voice, "I don't know about you, Steve, but those are the guys I borrowed from to come here."

Yardley closed his eyes and swore. The ice that had formed in Colt's gut during their meeting with Brown threated to become a glacier.

"Can you route it to Belknap's office, please?" Yardley gestured at Colt for help before turning his chair to face the flat display on the wall. As if Colt would leave the commander to handle things on his own.

"Yes, sir—I mean, sure thing," Onishi said. Even without Colt and Yard's official word that the school had gone under, she seemed to have dispensed with company customs and courtesies.

Specialist Belknap's subpar review disappeared from the screen, replaced by the jowly visage of a sallow-faced man in a green button-up shirt with some sort of food stain on one collar. He smiled, but the expression lasted less than a second, just long enough to turn his finger-thick mustache into a wiry, upward curve before returning to its straight pipe look. "Hello. My name is Tory Howard. Am I speaking with Cadet Colonel Stephen Yardley?"

"Yes." Yardley sat forward in his seat. Though the big cadet might get nervous before commanding a fight, face-to-face meetings didn't faze him. In fact, he thrived on them.

Colt was glad he couldn't be seen in the vid pickup.

"Mr. Yardley, am I to understand that you are, or more precisely were, the cadet commander for Fulcrum Mercenary Training's student body?"

"I am." The word, former, must have rankled Yard. His eyes had widened when he heard it.

Howard seemed not to notice. "Good, good. As your secretary—"

"Executive officer," Yardley said, menace in his voice.

"Excuse me?" Howard's bushy eyebrows drew down.

"You said, 'secretary.' Cadet Captain Onishi isn't anyone's secretary."

"As you will. The captain told you I represent Mountside Financial?"

"She did."

"I doubt it will shock you that most..." Howard's words petered to a stop as his eyes flicked back and forth for a moment. Then that microsecond flash of grin cracked his lips a second time. "I take that back, all of your cadets, even you, Mr. Yardley, have outstanding loans with our company."

Colt knew the instant Yardley's thoughts froze at the overwhelming news. He hastily sent a message to Yard's pinplants, then cleared his throat to bring him back into the moment.

"FMT went out of business today," Yardley said, and Colt cringed at how much it sounded like he was reading someone else's words off a slate. Yard got that way, sometimes, when things confused or frightened him.

"Indeed. It did." The condescension in Howard's voice could have smothered a small goat.

"That's breach of contract. We don't have to pay for a product that was never delivered."

Howard tilted his head to one side as if he were inspecting some new species of mammal he would just as soon club as let live. "You a lawyer, Mr. Yardley?"

"No. But—"

"The breach of contract you're describing is with Fulcrum Mercenary Training, not Mountside Financial. We honored our terms of agreement. You and your fellow cadets, however, haven't."

Colt's eyes squeezed down to slits as he sent another furious message.

"How can we be in breach with you, when we've only just found out about the collapse of our school?"

"Ah!" Howard held up one finger like a professor whose student has finally made a salient point after hours of trying. "You see, you may not have been aware of it, but our loans, the very loans you used to attend FMT and buy enhancements like the nanites coursing through your blood and the pinplants in your skull, those loans require payment every month."

Yardley, his eyes as round as twenty millimeter bullets, made a face. He looked ready to eat glass. "But those loans were deferred until graduation!"

Howard shook his head sadly, yet there was mirth in his piggy eyes. "I'm afraid that's simply not true, Mr. Yardley. Your headmaster was making those payments in your stead until about three months ago. You, along with every former student ensconced in that ship with you, are in arrears with Mountside for three months of loan payments. And I'm here to collect."

Yardley looked at Colt, his face a mask of fear. They both knew what default on this sort of loan could mean. Mountside would essentially own them. No one in the Union would call the seizure of their persons slavery. Slavery wasn't allowed in the Union. But indentured servitude for debts unpaid? That was another tune altogether.

"Mr. Yardley?" Howard asked as the moment of silence stretched into uncomfortable waiting. "Mr. Yardley, I would like to come aboard the ship to discuss options. By my estimation, there are several ways we can come to terms over—"

While the debt collector spoke, Colt scoured the GalNet, both *Uncanny Valley's* copy, and the much more robust and up-to-date one offered by the planetary hub. There had to be something in Merchant or Trade Guild statutes that would protect them from being detained by a lender. But the deeper he delved into the many cases of this type, the more Colt's heart sank. Generally, anyone who defaulted on a loan was considered at fault and subject to the repayment terms outlined by the debt holder. Since Colt lacked the credits to pay even a drop of his debt back to Mountside, he figured his fellow cadets were probably in the same predicament. They had all gambled on becoming mercs before they had to pay back one red credit to the loan company.

"Uh." Yard glanced down, swallowed when he found no answers there, and looked up at Howard. "I guess we can—"

"Wait!" Colt shouted. He thought he had found what they needed, not in Merchant or Trade Guild law, but in Brigham's planetary edicts. He sent a message.

"Who was that, Mr. Yardley?" Howard asked.

A triumphant smile spread across Yard's face as Colt's words hit home. "Yes, that's a great idea!"

Howard raised an eyebrow. "What is a great idea?"

Colt rolled his eyes and gestured furiously at the screen.

"Oh, right!" Yardley rose from his chair, his massive hands planted on his desk, his face a mask of angry challenge. "We demand formal arbitration negotiated by local authorities! God help us, we're going to the Mormons!"

* * * * *

Chapter Three

The first time Colt dropped to the surface of Brigham, locked as he had been inside a CASPer, he hadn't been able to see the planet's red face glaring up at him like some baleful demon out of a nether hell. This time, sitting up front with the pilots in a comfy chair, he watched it all the way down, mesmerized by its simple beauty. If ever there had been a desert world, this was it, though signs of ancient waterways and volcanic activity marred its rocky surface, and puffs of white clouds, thinner than those of Earth, evidenced signs of its gradual change into a habitable planet.

"There's the city." Alice Onishi leaned forward in the seat next to Colt to get a better view of New Nauvoo and its three main domes. Her movement inadvertently gave Colt a better view of Onishi's ample breasts as they pushed against her coveralls. He quickly moved his gaze elsewhere.

Part of him had been more than pleased when she announced she'd be traveling with them planet-side. Colt had always liked Alice.

He bit the inside of his cheek.

No, that wasn't true. He'd had the worst crush on her since the day they met. That was the truth. Not that he had said one word about it to her. In fact, Colt got the impression Onishi hardly knew he existed. If she had romantic feelings for anyone, it was Yardley, given the way she sometimes looked at him. But mostly she focused on her job and her serious desire to become a legit merc within a couple of years.

Having her along distracted Colt. He kept focusing on not staring at her, which meant he wasn't focusing on the reason they were headed to New Nauvoo. Not that he blamed her in any way. The distraction was his problem. He needed to get over it, and he knew that. But knowing a thing and actually doing it weren't always compatible.

"It's something, isn't it?" Zorn, their K'kng pilot, filled his chair like four pounds of hairy rocks in a two-pound sack, but he made an effort to turn sideways, so his Human passengers could look past his broad shoulders.

"Of course, it is something, otherwise it would be nothing. And we would not have come here for nothing." Benwarst, Zorn's copilot and one of only two Jeha Colt had ever known, undulated his caterpillar-like body in a Jeha gesture that meant mild rebuke mixed with surprise.

Zorn looked balefully at his flying partner, which translated well to the Humans. His race looked like Terran gorillas with their dark fur, thickly ridged faces, and beady eyes. "Of course it's something. You think by saying it's something, I was saying it's nothing?"

"Logically."

Zorn slapped one of his beefy shoulders with an open palm in a show of frustration. He turned to the Humans. He cocked a thumb at Benwarst. "You think that's bad, you should see me trying to tell this one a joke."

"Looks like they've got crops growing inside the dome." Yardley had unfastened his safety harness despite the pilots' warnings. He slipped his bulk between their chairs for a better look. "Yeah, definitely crops. Looks like corn and maybe some kind of beans. And look, they've even got some trees growing in there. Big ones."

Colt barely caught a glimpse of what Yard was describing before the shuttle set down on a square pad outside New Nauvoo's largest dome, and a thick, blue concrete wall blocked their view.

The FMT pilots—former FMT pilots—shut down their craft while the ship's computer extended a docking tube to the city wall's exterior port. A bang and a series of trundling sounds like gears working sounded, then the shuttle's side hatch popped open with a hiss of equalizing atmospheres.

"Good luck." Zorn tipped a nonexistent hat, a Human gesture he had picked up at some point in his long life. "Call if you need us."

Benwarst reared up on his pilot's perch and spread thirty or so of his nimble arms/legs in a gesture of parting. "Yes. I wish you luck as well. I hope the loan masters let you keep your freedom."

"B'cha!" Zorn thumped his own head. "What a thing to say to young people. You'll frighten them."

"Should they not be frightened?"

"Come on. Let's get this over with." Yardley led the way through the blue docking tube, which felt like plastic but was really a nanite-derived polymer not too dissimilar from the kind found in a CAS-Per's armor. A two-meter-tall door loomed before them.

Though they had fought many simulated battles together, and even a couple of real ones—well, skirmishes at least—Colt felt a whisper of doubt pass through him when the port door boomed open in front of Yardley. Together, they had connived, planned, and generally thought their way through many challenges. But Colt worried this one might be the last.

Cool, clean air that smelled of good earth and plenty of moisture flowed into the tube. Colt hadn't been aware of the shuttle's staleness until he breathed a lungful of the fragrant stuff. Something about it made his mouth water.

Four armed guards dressed in powered armor, carrying rifles of a make Colt didn't recognize, flanked Bishop Major Andersen. The older man had traded his business suit for a set of armor, but where his troopers' suits, though immaculately clean, showed signs of use with the odd scratch or buff mark here or the not quite true color pixel emitter there, the bishop's armor showed no such defects. He had keyed it to an almost eye-watering white that flowed around his body like negative space. Across his shoulders, he wore a sash of purest, verdant green that could be unfolded to become a cape.

"Hello again, gentlemen. I assume the young lady is Cadet Captain Alice Onishi?"

"Yes, sir." Onishi braced to attention, but managed not to fire off a salute, though Colt noticed her hand twitch. Two years of indoctrination were hard to fight down.

"Welcome to New Nauvoo." Andersen gave them a nod that bordered on a bow and gestured toward the door opposite them. "Give us a moment, and we'll escort you inside."

The outer door Colt and the others had just come through slid shut on a curtain of air, a buzzer sounded, and the inside door leading into the city rolled open. Andersen smiled and led the group into the dome.

Colt, Yardley, and Onishi looked around like tourists visiting their first alien world. In some respects, that was true. Colt had heard rumors that the Mormons had leased an entire star system from the Union with the intent of terraforming one of its planets while mining the others, but he had never imagined the immensity of the project. New Nauvoo towered a hundred stories over their heads, its main dome so vast, Colt could barely see the other side from where he stood. Skyscrapers, brownstones, and cozy apartment buildings of no less than five stories defined the space without crowding the wide walkways where pedestrians meandered through every part of the city.

And the trees. The trees left Colt staring in awe. Sycamores, oaks, pines, and weeping willows graced every open area with hedges, and other greenery filled in between. Carefully pruned rosebushes in every hue Earth had ever produced, and probably more, ran along the city's main thoroughfare, one color slowly melting into another down the line.

"This way," Andersen said after he had given his visitors a moment to take it all in. They joined a throng of well-dressed people headed east, and Colt felt his anxiety rise. But the crowd paid him little attention, and no one tried to speak to him, for which he was grateful. He looked around without meeting anyone's gaze.

They went four blocks, then Andersen turned off the street to climb a set of stone stairs leading up to a twenty-story edifice at the center of the dome. A plaque on the wall proclaimed it the Heber C. Grant building. Inside, the place felt like a five-star hotel. Marble floors, their white surface broken in the most elegant manner by strips of natural blue and glints of red, covered the entrance.

Andersen nodded to a guard posted at the front desk and led his charges around to a freight elevator at the back of the building. They rode it to the top floor, which required both a keycode and voice command from Andersen. He ushered them through a security checkpoint where another set of guards scanned them for weapons before allowing them to progress toward a vault-like door at the end of the hall. It was white, made of steel, and no less than a meter thick.

Onishi whistled as the massive thing slid open before them, electric motors whining inside the wall under the strain. "All this for us?"

Andersen's ever-present grin stretched into a smile. "No, ma'am. All this for him."

The vault door had opened wide enough to reveal an old man dressed in a fine suit seated at a conference table. He stood and spread his arms. "Welcome, Mr. Yardley, Ms. Onishi, Mr. Maier. My name is V. Ronald Talmason. I am the president of the Church of Jesus Christ of Latter-day Saints and, likewise, the president of Zion."

Colt looked the man in the eye. It wasn't an easy feat for him, but he wanted the chance to match Talmason's image on the GalNet to the real life person standing before them. He swallowed when his pinlink confirmed the identity with a ninety-seven percent chance.

"Mister...President," Yardley stammered, and Colt understood his hesitancy. It wasn't every day you met the leader of an entire star system or a major religion.

"Ronald will be fine. Won't you three have a seat?" The president gestured to unoccupied chairs on either side of the conference table.

The cadets sat, each of them eyeing one another, then Talmason. Colt, who felt he had used up his full measure of eye contact for the day, stared out the expansive windows on the north side of the room overlooking a greenway filled with families playing soccer and flag football or spreading blankets for picnics. Beyond them a secondary dome, lower than the one Colt now occupied, was filled with row upon row of some crop he couldn't identify.

"Would you all care for something to eat or drink? We have lemonade, orange juice, even coffee, for our guests."

That last must have been some sort of private joke, because Talmason and Andersen chuckled, and their armed guards smiled, but Colt didn't get it. Either way, he couldn't have stomached anything at the moment, so he shook his head. Yardley and Onishi both had orange juice, which was delivered almost instantly by a young woman in a dress that looked at least a century out of fashion.

"The bishop has briefed me on your situation," Talmason said after they had their drinks. He had ordered a hot chocolate. The scent of it filled the room. It reminded Colt of Earth. "I'm sorry you were so ill-used by your former commandant."

"Thank you." Yardley, who had finished his orange juice in two gulps, pushed his glass aside and switched on his slate, a signal they had long ago established to show Colt he expected help should the meeting grow too intense.

"As I understand it, you've asked for legal arbitration between you, including the entire student body, and this loan company. What was it called?" Talmason darted his gaze to Bishop Andersen.

"Mountside Financial," Andersen supplied.

"Right." The president nodded his thanks to his aide.

"Yes, sir." Yardley said.

A chime sounded, and the conference room's vault door slid open, drawing everyone's attention. Tory Howard sauntered in with a retinue of mercenary guards at his back. Six of them wore body armor that bore the T³ symbol on the left shoulder to indicate they belonged to Tom's Total Terrors. Though they carried no weapons, the Human mercs held something far more formidable in Colt's estimation: pure menace. Howard's remaining three guards seemed less impressive in their basic gray uniforms with Mountside patches stitched over their hearts.

"Mr. President," Howard said with a formal bow as if he were meeting a king. "Thank you for overseeing this process. When the kids demanded it, I never imagined we'd be meeting the president of the church."

"I'm pleased to help." Talmason looked embarrassed by Howard's brown-nosing attitude. He quickly waved him to a seat across from Yardley, Onishi, and Colt. Howard's guards took up positions behind him.

"You've noticed their unit markings, have you?" Howard inclined his head toward Yardley who was indeed staring at the mercs' T^3 symbols. "I thought it only fitting I hire the company your former commandant claimed as his own to chase him down. Too bad that bounty hunter whisked him out of the system before we got our hands on him. I would have enjoyed the look on his face when a troop of real mercs showed up."

Despite the anger and betrayal Colt had been feeling toward Belknap for the better part of a day, he could have punched Howard in the face at that moment. Who was he, some fat loan shark who had surely never served in a military or merc unit, to question anyone, even Belknap?

And it was a battalion, or maybe a company, not a troop. The man's audacity mingled with his sheer ignorance was almost enough to make Colt glare at him. Almost. Accessing his implants, he sent a quick message to Yard.

"Perhaps we should get down to business." From his tone, Colt could tell Yard shared his estimation of Howard.

"Certainly." Howard consulted his slate, and the little smirk Colt had noticed when he first contacted them appeared on his lips. "According to our records, most of FMT's cadets are in debt to Mountside for at least seventy thousand credits. Those are the minimal figures. There are some, especially seniors and juniors, who owe considerably more. As per our contracts with each of you, if you fall behind with your repayments, you are required to immediately pay the full amount. If you can't, Mountside Financial is authorized to seize your person and your property until such time as the debt is cleared."

"In other words, slavery." Talmason sneered when he said the world.

"Indentured servitude, sir," Howard said. "A grand tradition on Earth, one that saw many families move into better circumstances than where they started out."

Colt gritted his teeth and broadcast a message to Yard.

"What are our options for arbitration, Mr. President?" Yardley avoided looking at Howard to focus on the church leader.

"It would seem there is a legal precedent—" Talmason began but was interrupted when the vault door, once again, chimed. He gave it an annoyed look as it rolled open.

A pair of armed Mormon guards ushered a woman dressed in a Mountside uniform into the conference room, each holding one of her wrists. Frank relief softened her expression when she caught sight of Tory Howard.

"I'm sorry to interrupt, sir," said one of the guards. He looked between Bishop Major Andersen and President Talmason as if he couldn't decide whom to address. At last he settled on the bishop major. "We caught this woman snooping about in the lower floors."

"I wasn't snooping, I swear." The woman turned pleading eyes toward her boss. "I was running a routine security scan when you all moved out. I got lost and was trying to find my way here."

The major considered her for a moment. "Did you check her for weapons?"

"Of course, sir," said the guard. "She has none."

Andersen turned to Howard. "Do you vouch for this woman, sir?"

"Yes. Vanessa is on my security team. I did order her to run a sweep—you can never be too careful—right before we came here. I'm afraid, in the hubbub of the street, I thought she was with us."

"Very well." One corner of Andersen's mouth turned up in a lopsided grin. "We have no laws against getting lost. Please, join us."

The guards released Vanessa, and she hurried around the desk to stand with her fellow Mountside employees. Something about the way she moved, her furtive air, brushed at Colt's attention, but he didn't have time to think about some wayward security drone. Not when Mountside was on the verge of foreclosing on his physical person and those of everyone at FMT. He sent another hectic message to Yard.

"Mr. President, we wish to ask for formal asylum." Yardley sat forward in his seat, his blue eyes earnest. "You said it yourself, Mountside is threatening us with slavery. Surely, peace-loving people such as you won't stand by while they commit this crime against us."

Colt was especially proud of the *peace-loving* part. But his attention was diverted when Vanessa bent to whisper in her boss's ear while Yard was still talking. At first, Howard looked annoyed by the interruption, but then his eyebrows drew down, and he pursed his waxen lips as if considering something weighty.

This byplay hadn't gone unnoticed by President Talmason, who watched Howard with shrewd gray eyes. Colt doubted the old man had heard what Vanessa said. Colt certainly hadn't, but the look on Talmason's face made him wonder. At length, the president raised one finger in the air and said, "Mr. Howard, I have a proposition for you and the cadets."

"I'm listening." Howard looked like a man who had just gotten away with cheating at cards, but Colt saw no reason for his smugness. He hadn't heard the president's proposal yet.

"I propose that the LDS church buy these cadets from you."

A swirl of emotions set Colt's head spinning. Though he had no desire to work off his debt as a servant, at least New Nauvoo looked like a nice place to do it. But he had heard some odd things about the Mormons and how they lived, and there was always the concern they would try to convert him to their religion, which was out of the question. Overall, Talmason's suggestion left him conflicted.

Yardley and Onishi must have felt much the same. She sat with her mouth open, both hands squeezing the arms of her chair. He flinched back like a guy avoiding the unexpected spray from a wave, or maybe a punch.

Howard, on the other hand, sat forward in his seat, his bushy eyebrows rising. "You're serious? You're going to pay off their debts?"

"Not the full amount, no. We haven't the resources to spare for that just now. How much did you say the cadets are in arrears with your company? How many months?"

"Three." Howard watched the old man warily, as if he suspected some trick.

"We will bring Fulcrum Mercenary Training up to current." Talmason turned to Yardley, Onishi, and Colt. "In exchange, we are buying six months of sentry work from you for no fewer than—" he paused to consider, "let's say, one hundred troops to supplement our city guard."

Relief washed over Colt, though it was short-lived. Yes, such a deal would clear their default payments, but what about the overall debt? He sent his concerns to Yard via his implants.

"That's certainly generous of you, sir." Yardley said. "But we still owe Mountside a huge amount we can't pay. A three-month reprieve doesn't really do much for us."

"I agree." Talmason steepled his fingers, his shrewd eyes focused for a moment on the table. Then he looked up as if an idea had struck him. "You've earned credits these past several years working mercenary contracts for FMT, have you not?"

"Yes, sir," Onishi broke in before Yardley could answer. "But from what we gather, a lot of that was illegal. Colonel—I mean Mister—Belknap had us guarding contraband for smugglers and smuggling in our own right. We simply didn't know it."

Talmason nodded, his expression sympathetic. "Yes, but the work you did, it was exactly what a merc company is expected to accomplish. And you did it with few casualties. From what I understand, no matter what else Mr. Belknap might have done, he forged you into a legitimate mercenary company."

"He had to," Yardley said bitterly. "It was that or lose his investment."

"Or do the work himself," Onishi added, matching his tone.

"Precisely. He spared almost no expense in training you, because he needed you to make his fortune. You are mercs, and nothing precludes you from working legitimate contracts to earn a living, or in this case, pay off a debt." Talmason turned to Howard, his eyebrows lifted inquisitively.

The Mountside rep rubbed one jowly cheek in thought. The sound of his hand rasping over two-day stubble sent waves of discomfort rippling up and down Colt's neck. "So you'll pay the arrears portion the cadets owe in exchange for a six-month contract for one hundred of their number. But those one hundred will not be paid during that time, am I understanding that correctly?"

"Correct. We clear what they owe, that is their payment."

"What about food and shelter?" Onishi asked before Colt could send the question to Yard.

"We'll provide for their physical needs." Talmason looked almost offended. "We tend to like well-fed guards in New Nauvoo."

"What about the rest of us?" Yardley asked, prompted by a message from Colt. "You say we can work contracts, but you've got our ship locked up on your station in orbit. Are you going to give it back to us?"

"I'm afraid that wouldn't be practical, Mr. Yardley." Talmason shrugged his narrow shoulders. "The Church is claiming *Uncanny Valley* under system salvage laws. As an abandoned derelict, it falls to our ownership."

"What if we claim it?" Onishi asked. "We were there first. We're living on the thing, for God's sake."

Talmason winced at Onishi's use of the G-word, and Colt had a sudden urge to kick her ankle under the table, though he would never do it. Still, these Mormons could be touchy about their religion, that much was obvious. Best not to offend them.

"I'm afraid, Ms. Onishi, you would be too late making such a claim. Our lawyers have already filed the paperwork in our courts."

"Your courts that will back whatever you decide?" Onishi's dark eyes bore into Talmason like twin drills.

Talmason's gentle smile never flickered. "Hear me out before you judge me too harshly. You and your crew are in default for some rather exorbitant debts. Should you gain ownership of *Uncanny Valley*, you would essentially be handing it over to Mountside Financial. Is that not so, Mr. Howard?"

Howard looked reluctant to speak. He squirmed under the combined gaze of nearly everyone in the room. "Yes. Our company would seize any assets the cadets own to help offset the debt."

"There you have it. Your ship is safer in Church hands." Talmason spread his hands as if to show how he could buoy the cadets upon them. "Unfortunately, we lack the trained personnel required to crew such a vessel, even if we wished to use it as a freight hauler."

"But you have us." Onishi's lips turned up in a slow smile. "You're going to let us crew the ship and work contracts to clear our debt?"

"For a small leasing fee, yes."

"How small?" Yardley needed no prompting from Colt this time. Big and plodding he might be, but when it came to money he knew how to count.

Talmason pursed his lips and drummed his fingers on the table for a moment as if in thought. "How about three credits per month?"

Onishi's eyes widened, and Yardley outright laughed.

Colt shot him a message.

"Oh, yeah! We'll take that deal! Thank you." Yardley turned to Colt and shook his shoulder gregariously.

"Why are you doing this?" Onishi asked. "I mean, I'm grateful and all, but you could sell the ship and make a tidy profit."

Howard nodded as if to echo Onishi's sentiments.

"Our church was once bankrupt. Did you know that? We lost everything in a series of financial blunders that shook the faith of many an otherwise loyal member." Talmason's lips curled into a smile. "That's why I'm a fan of second chances. We came together, plotted a new course, a new way of caring for one another, and we succeeded. I think you can do the same, given time."

Not to be dismissed, Howard cleared his throat. "I am in no position to protest this plan as long as Mountside receives its payments. But I have some stipulations, if you're going forward with it."

Talmason lifted one bushy, gray eyebrow at the loan shark. "Go on."

"Mountside will want observers aboard *Uncanny Valley*."

"You mean overseers." Onishi could have sharpened a Kabar with her words.

"Call them what you like, but my bosses will want someone keeping an eye on their investment."

"Who?" Yardley asked.

Smiling like an overstuffed weasel, Howard turned to regard the intimidating Triple T merc standing behind him. "Captain Torres, care to take on a new contract? I promise you'll find it pays well."

"What else?" Onishi asked.

"My people get full access to your operation. That means how you run your ship, every mission you take on, and all your financials.

If they ask to see anything concerning the business, you will show them without question."

Yard looked at Onishi who gave him a reluctant nod, then at Colt who did likewise, though not without a lump of anger forming in his throat. "Okay. You've got a deal."

Howard grinned like a cat. "Not yet we don't. We haven't talked terms yet."

* * * * *

Chapter Four

Colt sat behind Yardley in a folding chair while the cadet colonel addressed the bulk of Fulcrum Mercenary Training's former student body. Onishi sat beside Colt, her dark eyes bright with excitement. As far as he could see, she was the only one wearing that sort of expression.

While the Mormons' Pratt Station wasn't the largest space dock Colt had ever visited, it boasted a set of spin rings at opposite ends of its cylindrical body that approximated Earth gravity. They were outfitted with a host of offices, storefronts, and three independent hotels. President Talmason had been gracious enough to offer the largest conference room in the Hotel Deseret for this meeting. The place must have hosted plays in the past, because the front area sported a stage with curtained wings and a thirty-foot backdrop.

Despite its size, however, it could not accommodate the six hundred ninety-two students and nearly fifty staff members that made up FMT. Three hundred filled the seats of the large auditorium. The rest watched the broadcast from aboard *Uncanny Valley*.

It did not escape Colt's notice how many of the attendees had elected to wear civilian clothes to this meeting despite receiving no formal leave from the cadet command to do so. Yardley had wanted to discipline them for such laxness, but Colt had waved him off. They weren't FMT students anymore. There was no FMT.

Not that Yard saw it that way.

"Cadets," Yardley used his command voice which projected throughout the room without aid from the microphone set into the podium before him. "As you know, Memphis Belknap, our former commander and owner of FMT, was arrested this morning along with his entire command staff." A ripple of displeased groans and raised voices ran through the crowd, but Yardley overrode it. "Major Maier and I spent all afternoon trying to find evidence that might exonerate Belknap and the others. Unfortunately, I'm sorry to report, we found none. In fact, Belknap's own records only serve to further indict him and his accomplices."

The groans and complaints increased, until the auditorium was filled with outraged voices and demands for justice.

"Quiet!" Yardley's voice cut through the bedlam, silencing everyone in the room. He glanced at the prompter held in front of him by a small drone, but only for a second. Colt knew the instant Yard decided to abandon the words he had written for him, and he groaned inwardly, powerless to stop it. "Listen to me. Some of us have been training together for years. We've fought shoulder-to-shoulder in simulations and on real missions. We've faced every obstacle placed before us, and we've surmounted them. Someone said something to me earlier today, and it stuck in my head. Fake or not, the training Belknap and Rudd put us through forged our battalion into a true fighting force. They had to, otherwise we would have been a bad investment."

Some in the crowd chuckled.

Warming to his subject, Yard drove on. "Time and experience have made us a solid team. A team I still believe in, even if our would-be teachers were fake."

Nods and mutters of approval rose from the gathered cadets. Colt was shocked; Yardley was actually getting through to them.

"I called this meeting tonight to discuss where we go from here. As you read in the briefing notes Maier sent out a few hours ago, we are all in severe debt to Mountside Financial. It seems this was one more way Belknap double-crossed us. He made certain we all took heavy loans from those greedy bastards, so they would invest some of that money back into the school. Collectively, we owe them more than eighty million credits."

This pronouncement brought the loudest jeers so far, punctuated with plenty of swearing.

Yardley held up his hands. "I'll make this last part quick. If you check your slates or pinplants, you'll see we've cut a deal with the LDS Church on Brigham for one hundred of our people to provide them with sentry duty over the next six months. I've asked Cadet Captain Onishi to serve as XO for this mission. She'll lead Company Shortfall with an additional eight troopers to fulfill the duty. Her contract clears our current arrears debt with Mountside. Beyond that, we have leased *Uncanny Valley* and all of FMT's former material goods to use at our discretion. According to Mountside's lawyers, should we choose to do so, we may continue working merc contracts under the FMT moniker, even without Belknap at the helm. I propose we do so in order to clear our collective debts and avoid indentured servitude. We will take legitimate contracts and earn credits the same as any merc company, except our profit will go toward paying off our debt."

"How long will this take?" asked a young man in the front row. Colt recognized him as a sergeant from Alpha Company, though he didn't know the guy's name.

Yardley glanced at Colt. They had hoped to avoid this topic, but the question had been asked, and they would look weak if they didn't answer. Colt gestured for Yard to go ahead.

"Mountside wants the full amount paid within one year."

"That's not possible!" shouted Cadet Lieutenant Barbara Standridge, as the crowd erupted into cries of protest and veritable wails of doom.

"We might as well turn ourselves over to them now!" yelled a private in civilian clothes who rose from his seat at the announcement.

Yardley bent toward the microphone, his face set in grim determination and not a little anger. "We can do this! We will do this! There are nearly seven hundred of us. That's five companies, more than most merc enterprises. And we've been doing it for years. You think Belknap would have kept this sham going if he wasn't making money? We've looked at the books. We cleared more than sixty million for the last three years running. We're profitable, people. In fact, we wouldn't be in this situation if Belknap hadn't squandered it all."

"Better mention Mountside's other requirements," Colt said in a stage whisper while the audience considered Yardley's words.

"Right. Mountside has also stipulated we are to be overseen at all times by representatives from their company." Yardley gestured toward the front row of seats. "These are Captain Enrique Torres and Staff Sergeant Mona Flowers of Tom's Triple Terrors. They will travel with us for the next year, or until we clear our debts, and we are to give them access to every part of our operation."

The tall, dark-haired captain who had served as Tory Howard's main guard that afternoon and a shorter, yet no less intimidating, red-haired woman stood and nodded to the crowd. Both wore blue and black utility uniforms that would have been at home in a fire fight or at a formal dinner.

"Will we get paid?" asked a voice in the crowd once the captain and staff sergeant had sat down.

Colt's brows drew down as he flashed a message to Yardley. *They've got to be kidding, right?*

Yardley shook his head. "If we're paying you, we're not paying our debt. This is a collective effort."

Some in the crowd booed, but they were the minority. Most were nodding, which Colt took as a good sign, but not Captain Torres. He wore a perturbed expression though he said nothing.

"You don't have to join us in this ah..." Yardley glanced at Colt who shrugged. "...quest. You're free to settle what you owe to Mountside however you like. But if you leave, your debt is on you, and they'll withdraw their offer of a year to pay it back. You either pay the whole amount today, or they take custody of you. Personally, I'm staying."

More nods and grumbled assents.

"But we can walk if we like?" asked a specialist Colt recognized from the armory staff.

"Feel free. But know there are Triple T mercs hired by Mountside waiting inside Pratt Station for any cadet who elects to leave."

"So, it's slavery either way!"

"If you choose to look at it that way, sure. But I like to think of it as an opportunity. We get the chance to work our way out of this bind, on our own terms, doing what we love. Isn't that better than handing yourself over for God knows what sort of work?" Yardley stared at the crowd for a silent moment, gathering their attention, before he spoke again. "We came here to learn to be mercs. Now it's time to stop pretending and become what we wanted from the beginning."

Colt issued another message to get Yard back on track.

"Right. Some of you were asking how we can possibly pay back so many credits within a year. I've asked FMT's chief finance officer to address that issue. Most of you have dealt with her at some point, but in case you haven't met her before, I'd like to introduce Weep."

Floating out from stage left came a Flatar, an alien whose resemblance to a Terran chipmunk always gave Colt pause. She rode on a steel platform held aloft by drones, which she must have found backstage, because the plan was for Weep to walk out and let either Colt or Onishi help her up onto a large box they had positioned near the podium. Colt had to admit this was a more dashing entrance.

Yardley stepped aside, and Weep maneuvered her floating platform close enough to the podium for the mic to pick up her high-pitched voice. "Hello. My name is Weep and, yes, I know what it means in standard English. Don't go there. Anyway, as Cadet Colonel Yardley said, I'm here to address Fulcrum Mercenary's financial future. But let me start by talking about its past. I've been Memphis Belknap's personal secretary and financial planner for the better part of eight years—the entirety of FMT's existence. I brokered most of the contract negotiations that kept this school and the mercenary company attached to it afloat. I still have hundreds of contacts we can use to pick up jobs."

The sergeant from Alpha Company, whose name Colt couldn't remember, rose from his seat, his dark face growing darker with anger. "So, you're saying you abetted Belknap in tricking us and setting up illegal contracts, and you want to keep doing it now that he's gone?"

A chorus of voices rose to join his in denouncing Weep's words as an admission of guilt. She turned to Yardley, her nose twitching in agitation and anger.

Yard took the podium as Weep hovered back. "Shut-up and sit down!" His bellow shook the walls.

Embarrassment made Colt's stomach spasm, and his ears burn as he watched Captain Torres shake his head at the display. The sergeant next to him wore the same displeased expression. With a grimace, Colt sent Yard what he should say next.

"Weep isn't the one who did this. She's a loyal employee who did her job so well we never saw this day coming. We need Weep's expertise. She is an asset to FMT, and we're all going to treat her as such. Her contacts could mean the difference between success and slavery for us."

Yard's words got a nod from Captain Torres, which Yard must have noticed, because he nodded back.

"That's it for now," Yard said. "Everyone think hard about what you want your future to look like. Company commanders, take charge of your people. I want a full head count of those who elect to leave and those who are staying by 0600 ship time tomorrow. Dismissed!"

* * * * *

Chapter Five

*U*ncanny *Valley's* spin ring approximated Earth-normal gravity, so it contained the majority of the ship's crew quarters, storage areas, and conference rooms. The ship had started life as a bulk freight hauler, which meant it had more cargo area than your average gate ship, and its ring had made it attractive to many clients shipping gravity sensitive items like livestock or medical supplies. But space was still limited aboard the ship since the ring contained only two floors. Had its designers added more, the ring's narrowed circumference would have exposed crew members to an increased Coriolis Effect, the sense of dizziness most humans experience when spinning. Even so, most of the cadets had been forced to endure days of spin sickness when they first arrived. Colt had been no exception. In fact, he still got queasy sometimes on the ring's second floor, but that might have been psychosomatic.

Right now, he felt ill for an entirely different reason. He sat with Yardley in the ship's largest conference room. Fulcrum Mercenary Training's former staff, those Casandra Brown hadn't arrested with Belknap and his ilk, crowded the space. The thirty of them took up all the chairs at the meeting table as well as those Colt and Yardley had wheeled in from other offices to line the walls.

Captain Enrique Torres of Triple T, their now constant companion, leaned against a wall where he could observe the meeting. His placid face told Colt nothing of the big merc's mood or thoughts, but the set of his shoulders made it clear he didn't like what he was hearing.

"You have to understand, we can't afford to pay you for a while, probably this entire year. Every credit we get either goes back into FMT or to pay off Mountside." Yardley kept his voice mild, but Colt could tell he was fuming inside. They had already gone round and round on this point for thirty minutes, and nothing had changed.

"And you have to understand that we aren't your cadets." The speaker was a solid man dressed in FMT gray coveralls with an old-world style wrench embroidered over his heart. His name was Brandon Sloan, and he was the ship's main CASPer armorer, an indispensable asset if FMT had any hope of fulfilling contracts for pay. "I'm not working here for my health. I have a family back on Earth—a wife and children to feed. They rely on the credits I send back. You cut that, and you cut me."

"Look at it from the staff's perspective," said Weep, who sat across from Colt and Yardley on a raised chair designed for the diminutive Flatar. She waggled a small slate as if displaying key evidence in a court case. Colt knew it showed a crew manifest with annual, monthly, and weekly pay statistics. "We don't owe Mountside a single credit. So, when you ask us to work for free, you're essentially saying, 'Help us pay off the debt we made and you had nothing to do with.' No one's going to take that deal."

Colt keyed a message to Yardley, who voiced his words.

"Can we offer you contracts with payment promised at the end of one year? We could work everything in reverse, where the battalion takes no pay so we can reimburse you after everything's cleared up with Mountside."

Several of the permanent crew members laughed, and most shook their heads or commiserate appendages, depending on their race.

"No pay, no work." Sloan sat back in his chair and folded his arms.

Yardley turned to Weep, his brows drawn down. "Is it possible to keep everyone at their current rates and still pay off Mountside in a year?"

The Flatar twitched her head from side to side while she consulted her slate, numbers running across its screen like water, reflecting off her black eyes. "Yes. If we maintain a high enough average per contract payout and sheer off every corner we can, I think it's doable."

"I'll stay," Zorn said. The stocky K'kng overfilled a chair near the head of the table, his prehensile tail folded up to rest on one of his meaty shoulders. "I like my job. I like teaching new pilots."

"Agreed. We have discussed it, and we shall stay on as well." Benwarst and his mate, Rooysot, approximated human nods by folding their many legged bodies forward and back in their seats.

Colt could have hugged the three of them for their show of support and their willingness to teach their skills. Everyone in the room not only fulfilled crucial ship functions, they spent time teaching those jobs to the cadets. The sort of patience required to accomplish both had never really crossed Colt's mind, but finding people who possessed that combination now seemed as rare as a cold star.

Colt could probably replace the two pilots, Zorn and Benwarst, though not easily, but Rooysot was a brilliant engineer who could land a job on nearly any ship she chose. She was only here because of Benwarst.

"That's fine for you, but how about the rest of us? What's our incentive to stay, even if they do pay us?" Sloan looked around at the gathered staff. "Before now, these guys had Belknap commanding them. Yeah, he and Rudd might have been con artists, but you've got to admit, they hired legit mercs to run this place. I saw how they kept the cadets on their toes. Who's going to do that now?"

"We are." Yardley bristled at the man's blatant doubt. "We're in charge, and we'll see to running things."

Sloan rolled his eyes and made a rude noise.

Colt hated to admit it, even inwardly, but Sloan had a point. Belknap had hired a bevy of veteran officers and non-comms to run FMT. They had seen to things like scheduling, discipline, and overall training, while the cadets handled the school's five companies under their watch. Until yesterday, Colt hadn't realized how many of the school's everyday functions fell to them. He sent Yardley a new message.

Yard sat silent a moment, lips pressed together. He looked ready to argue, but finally shook his head. "Fine. We'll figure out how to pay you at your normal rate. I'll make it a priority. This ship doesn't run without you all doing your jobs, and we appreciate that, just like we appreciate your willingness to teach. We're going to rely on that in the coming days."

"I can help." Weep sent a broadcast message to their slates. It showed an advertisement for a weapons expo to be held on Cormsu'esh in three weeks. "This is an ad for the Fenres Weapons Bazaar. It's gigantic. Prospective merchants and buyers from all over the Jesc Arm and beyond will be there checking out the latest in everything from rifles to stellar defense systems. I know some of the organizers; we did garrison duty for them two years ago. Get me there in time, and I'll find us a contract."

"Not a bad idea," said one of the ship's engine techs. "Even if it's just guarding weapons displays, it's something."

"Who's in favor of checking this out?" Yardley asked before Colt could do anything to stop him. A commander didn't take votes.

Most of those gathered raised a hand, though Colt noticed Sloan didn't move. Captain Torres rolled his eyes.

"It's decided. We'll get underway as soon as possible, headed for Piquaw." Yardley shut off his slate. "Please, resume your duties and prepare the ship for departure."

The meeting broke up. People left in twos and threes, chatting as they went. Some grumbled about the changes, but most sounded excited about preparing their sections to move out. Zorn, Benwarst, and Rooysot remained behind.

"Can I help you with something?" Yard asked.

Zorn's ape-like face looked worried. "It's the ship's command structure. As you know, Captain Stallman was arrested with the rest of the command staff."

"Yes?" Yardley lifted his eyebrows impatiently. It was clear his mind was elsewhere.

Colt could have whacked the big officer's shoulder. As sometimes, but rarely, happened in mixed company, his urge to communicate overcame his fear of crowds. "You're worried there's no one to command the ship."

Zorn's heavy brow rose in surprise at hearing Colt's voice. "Exactly. We no longer have a captain."

"What did he do that you can't?" Yardley looked genuinely perplexed. "Didn't he just order you to do stuff you'd normally do anyway?"

Captain Torres' eyes widened. He shook his head in astonishment.

"Uh, no." Zorn turned pleading eyes to Colt, obviously looking for an ally.

Great. Colt shouldn't have opened his mouth. Now everyone was looking at him, even Captain Torres. The weight of their combined stares felt like a flyer coming in for a landing on his head. He swallowed and fished for his voice. "The ship's captain...they need the captain to get everything done in the right order. The captain is the boss, ya know? Otherwise...you get people tripping over each other."

Zorn nodded. "Pilots can't undock until engineering crews clear the airlocks. Engineers can't let us leave orbit until they've inspected the in-system engines and greenlit the flight path. There are thousands of little tasks that have to be overseen before we reach the gate and head for Piquaw."

"I thought all that was done by computer," Yardley said.

"It is." Benwarst spread a dozen arms in a conciliatory gesture. "But the tasks are overseen by sentient eyes. And their sequence must be precise. We may take space travel for granted with our sophisticated modern ships, but it is an exceptionally complex undertaking, even with the assistance of computers."

"So, you're saying we need to hire a ship's captain?" Yardley probably didn't mean to sound angry or frustrated, but his emotions showed in his voice.

"It would be a good investment," Zorn said.

Yard shook his head. "You just heard how broke we are. We can't afford it. Period."

"Nevertheless." Benwarst undulated his caterpillar-like body to convey the broad unfairness of the universe.

"How about this?" Yardley pointed at Zorn. "I hereby appoint you captain of the ship. I'll make that official however it needs to be done, but from here on, you're in charge when it comes to ship's operations. And Benwarst, you're first mate or whatever the next rank down might be. Just see to getting us to Piquaw."

Zorn jerk back as if Yard had slapped him. "Me? Captain?"

"Yes. You've been piloting a long time, right?"

"Almost twenty-five years."

"And you've been on *Uncanny* for how long?" Yardley made a broad gesture to take in Zorn and the whole of the ship.

"Seven years."

"So you know how things work, right? I mean, you've seen the former captain do his thing. You can fill that role, right?"

"I—yes. I think I can with Benwarst's and the crew's help."

"You will have it, old friend," said the Jeha.

"And I will see to engineering," Rooysot said. "I have a worthy staff there."

"You'll still need to pilot sometimes, of course." Yardley smiled at the flummoxed Zorn. "But maybe, if we get some especially lucrative contracts, we can take you off that duty. You can captain your heart out." He put a hand on the K'kng's back and guided him toward the door.

Too shocked to say anything more, Zorn let the Human gently push him out the door with Benwarst and Rooysot scrambling after him on their many feet.

"That went better than I expected," Yardley said once the door had shut.

"We should discuss that sort of appointment before you pull the trigger." Colt tried not to sound sour but failed.

"Hey, I was adlibbing. Those guys think they need a captain to do their jobs, and now they have one."

"But is Zorn the right one?" Colt started to resume his seat at the conference table. He and Yardley had a freighter full of things to discuss, but a voice over the office intercom stopped him in his tracks.

"Colonel Yardley? This is Cadet Sergeant Fisk. There's a fight going on in the mess. I think you should come down here."

Yard and Colt looked at each other. Captain Torres' eyebrows shot up.

"What do we do?" Yard whispered.

"We're on our way," Colt shouted to the air. Like Yardley, he had no idea what to do, but he knew they couldn't stand around dithering. "Come on!"

Running inside a spin ring increased gravity, making the going tougher than if they had merely walked. Colt felt like his feet weighed twenty pounds each as he hustled along the corridor. Luckily, the ship's mess was only six doors down from the conference room, so they reached it quickly. What they found sent Colt's stomach into his throat, first with shock, then with outrage.

Three noncom cadets stood in the middle of the mess hall, two tables and several chairs overturned around them, grappling with one another. Food stained their gray uniforms and the floor, and gobs of it hung from the low roof above. A crowd of onlookers encircled the combatants, jeering or cheering according to the tide of the battle.

No one stopped or took notice when Yardley, Colt, and Captain Torres entered the room. Staff Sergeant Mona Flowers, the enlisted Triple T overseer, stood among the crowd, arms folded. She did not cheer or jeer. Colt might not have a flare for reading expressions; in fact, that ability often escaped him, but he could spot the look of absolute disgust on her face.

Colt froze at the sight of so many people. He knew he should barrel into the fray. Everything he had ever read about effective leadership and the great heroes of military history said he should take charge of the situation, but his body refused to move, and his voice stuck fast in his throat.

Yardley, however, suffered no such impediment. Face enraged, he shoved his way through the gathered crowd and charged into the mix. As one of the school's top combatives participants, hand-to-hand combat held no fear for him. He casually blocked a punch thrown by one of the food-speckled combatants, trapped the man's arm, and twisted to slam him into his opponent. The two of them, assisted by copious amounts of the day's lunch special—tacos with fresh guac—crashed in a heap against one of the overturned tables.

The remaining brawler, a corporal according to the rank tab on his coveralls, his eyes wide at the sight of the cadet commander staring him down, held up both hands in surrender. "Hey man. We're cool. I'm done fighting. I was—"

Seizing the corporal's collar, Yardley drew back a fist roughly the size of a boulder, and his lips pulled back to show his teeth. The noncom cringed, preparing for the blow to come.

Colt wanted to shout at Yardley to stop, this wasn't the way to lead. But as usual, his traitorous voice had gone missing when he needed it most. He held up his hands like a man trying to stem a tide he had no hope of stopping, a particularly futile gesture since Yardley had his back to Colt.

"I really should smash your nose into your brainpan," Yardley hissed. Then he heaved a heavy sigh and turned the corporal loose. "All three of you are on report. Find your squad leaders and tell them that. Now!"

The former brawlers couldn't exit the room fast enough. Slipping and cursing, they disappeared through the door, all the fight seemingly burned out of them in the heat of Yardley's anger. Colt wasn't certain allowing them to leave together was such a good idea. Who knew if they'd resume fighting once they were safely out of the cadet colonel's view? And Yardley expected them to put themselves on report? Maybe they would, judging by the horrified looks they were wearing when they left.

"What happened?" Yardley spun on his heels, taking in the gaggle of bystanders.

"The two on the floor, Smith and Robinson, were saying we should kick you out and take over the ship," said a short female sergeant with raven black hair and the sort of pretty looks that made it nearly impossible for Colt to look her in the eye. He recognized her from the last promotion ceremony, a few months back, when she had picked up Cadet Sergeant First Class. Her name tag read Levin.

"They were talking mutiny?" Yardley's gaze flicked to the door where the three had just exited. He looked as though he might head after them.

SFC Levin shook her head. "Nah, they're just guys talking. Stirring up trouble. I don't think they were serious. Just seriously stupid." Colt was surprised to see blood trickling slowly from her nose.

Seemingly oblivious to it, she drove on. "According to them, we could sell *Uncanny* and pay off our debts. Beechly, that was the corporal you almost punched in the face, he was defending you. He told them to shut their mouths. That's when things got heated."

"What happened to your nose, Sergeant?" While Yardley didn't sound abashed, the seething anger had leaked out of his voice.

The sergeant wiped her upper lip. Her fingers came away bloodstained. "That idiot, Smith, decked me by accident when I tried to break them up."

"Go to the infirmary."

"Nah, it's not that big of a deal."

"Fine," Yardley said, "but don't complain later if you can't breathe right."

"Sorry to break up your powwow, but who's going to clean all this up?" The speaker wore the blue and white service uniform of all FMT cafeteria and sanitation employees. A small tab over his left breast pocket read *Supervisor.*

Yardley looked askance at the man. "Isn't that your job?"

The man folded his arms. "Hell no, kid. My job is serving food and taking out the garbage. I am not detailing my staff to clean up after your people, when you can't control them. This—" the guy gestured at the food on the floor, tables, and ceiling, "—is outside the scope of our contracts." He tossed a mostly clean rag from his shoulder to Yardley. "Your people made this mess. Your people can clean it up." With that, he turned on his heels and headed for the kitchen.

Yardley stood with the rag in his outstretched hand, looking dumbfounded. He might have remained that way for the next decade or so had Levin not intervened.

"Marshal, Lutz, Cramer," she snapped, pointing at people in the crowd, "get some cleaning supplies. I'm calling my squad leaders to get their people down here to help out. The rest of you don't go anywhere either. We're all on clean up detail until this place is fit for inspection."

It took the better part of an hour, and a ladder, to get the food cleaned up and the dining area set to rights. But with Levin running the show, the ad hoc crew had the mess cleaner than Colt had ever seen it. He and Yardley pitched in as well, working side-by-side with the cadet noncoms, taking Levin's directions as she organized the action.

By the time they were through, even the mess supervisor, who had come out of his kitchen to inspect their work, looked impressed.

"Everyone, thank you for your help," Yardley said as the detail broke up, and people headed back to their usual duties. "Good work, Sergeant Levin."

"Thanks, sir." Levin nodded and followed her people from the mess, each clutching an assortment of cleaning supplies from their duty area in their hands.

Colt and Yardley headed back to the command area with Captain Torres dogging their heels. The tacit captain had remained silent throughout the fight and subsequent cleanup, but his expression said he had something on his mind.

He let the doors to Belknap's office close behind him and leaned back against them, gazing at the ceiling.

"Something on your mind, Captain?" Yardley asked. He had already taken a seat behind the big desk but hadn't yet keyed on the holo-monitors.

Captain Torres let go a long sigh. "I promised myself I wouldn't do this. It's not my job. In fact, it runs exactly counter to everything written in my current contract."

Colt and Yardley exchanged looks. Colt shrugged.

"I'm not following, sir," Yardley said.

"Boys..." Torres paused, his expression suddenly calculating. "You're both over seventeen, right?" Although the age for recognized majority, otherwise called legal adulthood, varied according to race in the Union, for Humans it was seventeen.

"I'm twenty-one," Yardley said.

"Sixteen." Colt wanted to hold the big captain's gaze but couldn't. He stared at Belknap's desk instead.

"Colt turns seventeen in three months," Yardley said. "His parents gave him majority when he was twelve, so he could enter merc training early."

Torres lifted his eyebrows. "Impressive. Sixteen's close enough." He strode over to the desk to look down at the two cadet officers and shook his head the way a man does when the neighbor's dog has left him a surprise in the front yard. "Boys, you have got to get a handle on your people. I've only been aboard your ship one day, and I can tell you there's a serious discipline problem. You two think you're in charge, but nobody believes it. You're all cadets, and you know the textbook definition of cadet?"

Colt and Yardley shook their heads in unison.

"Fake." Torres sighed and sat in the chair next to Colt. "You're fake Lieutenant Colonel Colt, and you're fake Colonel Yardley. Your ship is filled with hundreds of fake sergeants, fake lieutenants, and fake whatevers."

"That's not fair." Yardley sat up straighter in his seat, his eyes challenging. "Our people are good at their jobs. They're serious about what they do."

"Didn't say they weren't." Torres met Yardley's stare without a flicker of fear or retreat in his eyes. "But that doesn't mean they don't feel fake. Or maybe counterfeit would be a better word. Your people know they aren't real mercs."

"But—"

"Let me finish, Cadet." Torres' acid tone bowled over Yardley's words like a ski boat running through a flock of ducklings. "They think they're fake because the world has told them that much—this school in particular. How many command staffers did you lose in yesterday's arrest?"

"Twenty-two." Yardley bit off the word with a growl.

"Mostly noncoms who ran the show, am I right?"

"Yes," Colt said, surprising himself. "They...kept us running."

Torres nodded, his expression tight. "I'm not here to help you. I'm working for Mountside, so you could probably say I have a vested interest in watching you fail at this little experiment. So I'm going to give you this one piece of advice, and you won't get anymore, got it?"

"Got it." Yardley sounded happy, as if he had just solicited a promise of silence from the Triple T captain.

"Yes, sir," Colt said. No matter how brusque Yardley acted, he knew they could use the voice of experience.

"First, drop the cadet nonsense. No matter what this place was yesterday morning, it's a merc company now. And mercs need a disciplined, strict rank structure the way they need air. You got a sergeant in your battalion, she's a sergeant. Period."

Colt nodded. He could see the sense in that. If they were really planning to execute legitimate mercenary contracts, their clients would expect real mercs working for them, not students.

"Second, you cannot co-command. One of you has to take control, or this enterprise will fall apart. Those are your only choices. Colt, I see you passing messages to Yardley all day."

"You hacked our channel?" Yardley's brows drew down in sudden anger.

"Didn't have to, kid. It doesn't take a Peacemaker detective to see your expression losing focus every minute while Mr. Deep Space over there twitches his eyes. It's obvious Colt has the ideas. Let him take command."

Colt shook his head, his stomach a sudden a knot of snakes. "I can't. I—I get in front of people, and I freeze up. My head explodes."

"Well, which is it? Freeze or explode? You can't have both."

"You haven't...seen me lead a brief. Or even command a couple of underclassmen. It's always a disaster."

"Okay then, decision made." Torres turned to Yardley. "You're the brevet colonel and CEO of Fulcrum Mercenary Training. You take charge. And no more of this power behind the throne crap. You lead. Colt is your XO, which means he executes the commands you initiate. He's your fixer, not your invisible brain. Got it?"

"Yes, sir," Colt said. It only occurred to him much later that he had witnessed a captain promoting a colonel.

Yardley looked at Colt, then back at Torres, his expression an odd mix of reluctance and interest. "Okay. Yeah."

"As for the name of this outfit, I don't think training works. How about tactics? Fulcrum Mercenary Tactics. That has a ring to it, and your clients won't be turned off thinking you're a bunch of school kids."

Yardley nodded. "I like it."

"And one other thing." Torres threw his hands up. "Get yourselves a Top. That won't end fights in the mess, but they won't reach your level, except in a report about what happened and how your Top handled it. A battalion commander and his XO shouldn't be cleaning taco cheese off the mess floor. It just ain't done. Got it?"

"Yes, sir," Colt said again. Though part of him felt embarrassed that the Triple T captain had been forced to dress them down, gratefulness mostly overrode that reaction.

"Okay then." Torres stood to resume his usual spot near the bulkhead. He leaned back and crossed his arms. "That's it from me. From this point on, I'm once again your silent observer."

* * * * *

Chapter Six

It took three days for the crew to get underway to the stargate, and another week for them to cross the Zion system to reach its L3 Lagrange point. While such speed would have astonished early astronauts more than a century earlier, the wretched slowness of it left Colt wanting to bang his head against one of *Uncanny's* steel bulkheads.

"We'll be transitioning in about twenty minutes." Captain Zorn, his new rank insignia gleaming on his barrel chest, swiveled in his chair to address Colonel Yardley on his Tri-V. "It took some work getting everything organized, but all looks good on our end. Fusion plants are functioning at ninety-eight percent efficiency, and we have plenty of F11 for the trip."

Despite Colt's initial reservations about Zorn's spur-of-the-moment promotion, most of the crew agreed he made a great captain. By all accounts—well, most accounts—the crew had Zorn's attention to detail to thank for their leaving Zion in only ten days. He had overseen the readiness plan to get their stores in order, taken on provisions bought at excellent prices from the Mormons, and tended to a thousand other little necessities required before they could clear the dock at Pratt Station.

Of course, there were those who groused about the K'kng getting a promotion over a Human. But as Yardley pointed out, the only other pilots interested in the captain's position were cadets, and he wasn't about to make one of them the ship's commander when he had experienced crewmembers aboard. On the off chance there might be some hurt feelings, Colt had taken the liberty of sending Kelly Lauren, a drop pilot who preferred the nickname Kit, a message, asking if she felt overlooked with Zorn's appointment. Her terse and rather comical answer had been a simple, "No, thank God he didn't choose me." And that was that.

"Good work. Keep us posted." Yardley keyed the holo off and turned to his gathered company commanders. "We've got one-hundred seventy hours of transit time ahead of us, and we're going to spend that drilling. With Onishi and her hundred gone, I figure we can get our people in the simulators much more often. We might not be dropping into hot zones anytime soon, but I want us training like we will. That includes physical and combatives. Yeah, we've got armor, but a merc never knows when it will fail. I want you four to work out a schedule so all your squads get equal training time."

Heads nodded around the desk as the captains made notes on their slates or blinked commands to their pinplants. Though Colt had never seen any of them display any sort of doubt or reluctance, they seemed more serious and confident than they ever had in Yardley's command and their own abilities. Colt chalked that up to losing the cadet moniker. Ever since Yardley had advised the crew to stop using that term, the entire battalion had seemed more legitimate and more real, even though nothing had really changed. That feeling ran through the entire ship, from these company commanders down to the privates and corporals who made up the bulk of the unit.

Colt had to admit, Captain Torres had been right.

"Colt, you're in charge of making sure they get the new training schedule to me by 2200 tonight," Yardley said.

"Yes, sir." Colt nodded, and made a note with his pinplants, marveling at how he felt the weight of true legitimacy after dropping cadet from his title, and he had been there when Torres suggested it.

Psychology was weird.

"One other thing." Yardley, who had been about to stand, likely to dismiss everyone before transition, sat back down. "Save some saddle time for me and Colt. We're going to rotate in on the simulations and physical conditioning at least three times per week, more if we can afford the time."

Colt fought back the urge to widen his eyes at Yardley. The commander hadn't mentioned anything about this to him. Not that Colt feared training in any capacity. He loved it. He could always find his voice inside a CASPer when talking to Yardley, and he didn't need it on the hand-to-hand floor. But since he had stopped sending Yardley orders, Colt had assumed they wouldn't be taking the field.

"If there's nothing else, you're dismissed." Yardley rose and ushered the company leaders from the conference room. Once they were gone, he returned to his seat. "You looked surprised when I said we would be training with the squads."

"I thought—"

"You thought I'd be too scared to command without your help." Yardley's blue eyes flicked to Torres who remained perfectly silent and still near the wall. While Yard's tone held no menace, it did carry some challenge.

Colt nodded. He saw no reason to lie, even to protect Yardley's feelings. "If I'm honest, yes."

An instant of anger burned through Yardley's expression, but then he seemed to get hold of himself, and he grinned. "You're right. I am afraid of screwing up. In fact, that's why I'm not going to command in the simulations. You are."

"I—what?" Colt sat up in his seat, bug-eyed.

"You've done it since we were freshmen, and you're the best at it. You and I both know I wouldn't be the commander if it wasn't for you."

"Fine. I've helped. But I was only talking to you. If I'm supposed to command the entire company, I'll have to talk to other people— the company commanders, squad leaders, everyone. I can't do that." Colt's throat tightened just thinking about it.

"What's the difference?" Yardley asked. "You get in a CASPer, and you can talk. It works with me, you can make it work with them. Just pretend you're talking to me the whole time."

Colt squeezed each joint in his hands, methodically, one after the other, a nervous habit he hadn't been able to break since he was seven. "Maybe."

Yardley glanced at Torres as if to say, *a little help here?*

The big merc said nothing, his face impassive. He wasn't in a giving mood apparently.

"Anyway, you're going to do it because that's my order," Yardley said, turning his head to eye Colt. "If you don't like it, blame yourself, *Lieutenant Colonel* Maier. You put me in command. And don't worry. I'll take my turns. I need to practice without your help. If I can do it, so can you."

"Okay, I'll try."

"This is going to work."

* * *

"This isn't working, sir!" Sergeant Victor Young from Charlie Company's second platoon scrambled across Colt's Tri-V display, his CASPer taking heavy fire from an enemy emplacement his squad had failed to clear in two attempts.

Colt keyed second platoon's secure channel. "Young...uh, get, uh." A sudden alarm blared inside Colt's CASPer, wrestling his attention away from the debacle playing out on his screens. He had been so preoccupied with managing the battle, he had lost control of his suit. Stumbling backward, the CASPer kicked up plumes of white sand as Colt tried in vain to regain his balance, but the angle of the dune he was standing on was too steep and his reactions too slow to save it. With a muted series of thumps and bangs, he toppled over backward in the sand, turning a half somersault that almost sent him back into the sea from where the simulated assault had begun. Though the CASPer's driving harness kept him mostly secure, it didn't save Colt from banging his head against the cockpit roof or jarring his crotch painfully where the suit's legs met.

Simulated or not, that hurt.

As if to mock his incompetence, his CASPer's Tri-V screens never so much as flickered but went right on showing him a real time display of his company getting chewed up by an entrenched enemy. In this case, the ship's computer had randomly chosen a nighttime beach assault on some planet with three moons floating in a star-strewn, black sky. Their enemy, a company of MinSha, had so far rebuffed every advance on the perimeter of their beachhead, allowing their human enemies not one meter of ground.

Even as Colt watched, four more of his precious CASPer pilots faded from green to gray on his status board, their screams over the channel anything but simulated. While the computer couldn't do lasting physical harm to the mercs, the pain it simulated through their pinplants felt real enough until they were designated full casualties. At that point, they were out of the game.

Colt tried to rise, but his CASPer had ended up on its back with its armored legs stretching half way up the weed-infested dune. Try as he might, he couldn't do more than slide and flail against the sand.

"Lt. Colonel Maier," 1SG Levin called over the channel, her voice cool but insistent. "Sir, we're getting steamrolled at the assault point. Permission to fall back to the staging area."

"No." Colt managed to gasp the word as he continued to flail like a seasick turtle on its back. He wanted to add that she should lead squad one south to join two and three. Their combined firepower would surely overtax the MinSha laser pillbox in that area, making it possible for the Human forces to not only find some cover, but leapfrog from there to the next hard point along the enemy line.

But none of these thoughts reached Colt's lips no matter how hard he tried to issue them as orders. Speaking to an entire company wasn't the same as addressing one person. And no matter how hard Colt tried, he couldn't imagine himself talking to Yardley when he had to constantly rotate from one unit member to another to keep his troopers in check. He couldn't trick himself.

"But sir, I—" A nearby explosion shook the ground hard enough for Colt to feel it through the CASPer's armored back.

"Levin?" Colt gasped.

A series of lesser explosions followed the first big boom as Colt's Tri-V registered multiple heat plumes radiating from two of the MinSha's established firing points. Each blast coincided with two, three, then five troopers disappearing from his display.

The bugs must have gotten their crew-served weapons online. Colt had seen the enemy gunners assembling them at the beginning of the simulation. He had ordered his forces to attack immediately, hoping to take them before they could get the big guns up and running.

He had failed.

Colt was still struggling to get his CASPer back on its feet when the simulation froze, and Yardley's voice came over the comm.

"I think that will do for now, Charlie Company. Better luck next time."

The lights came up in Colt's simulator, and the plastic hood popped open with a hiss. A disgruntled Colt jerked the shunt leads from his pinplants and shook his head, trying to reorient himself to the real world and its microgravity environment. The pinplant-based simulations mimicked every aspect of real life. Sometimes they were tough to leave behind.

Other simulator cockpits hissed open all around Colt. He tried not to look anyone in the eye. Still, he couldn't help hearing a few whispered grumbles about his inept command. Crammed as the simulators were into the training room, each of the one-hundred fifty egg-shaped devices afforded its occupants just enough space to exit by floating up to the ceiling and pulling their way via handholds toward the exit. In such close confines, even whispers carried.

"Thank God we don't have to follow him in a real battle," said Specialist Proctor, who obviously thought she was out of earshot. "Yardley makes him look like a two year old driving a flyer."

Yardley hovered, upside down from Colt's perspective, near the exit. He patted the sweaty troopers on their backs as they passed, sharing a few words of encouragement, likely because he knew their sergeants and lieutenants were about to eviscerate them in the coming debrief.

Captain Torres floated next to Yardley, a calculating expression on his face. No doubt he was totaling up how many people Colt had just gotten killed.

Colt made certain he was the last person to reach the door. He hung his head, unable to meet Yardley's eyes. "Told you how that would go. I can't do this."

Yardley shrugged good-naturedly. "It was your first try. I'm not upset about it."

"It was a disaster. I couldn't even run my own suit, let alone direct the company."

"We're not the only ones who can command. Maybe we should focus on running the battalion and let our execs handle tactical. Commanders aren't supposed to put themselves in harm's way anyhow. Right?"

That made Captain Torres' head snap around though he dutifully kept his mouth shut.

Colt glanced briefly at Yardley's face to see if the colonel was joking. He looked serious. "Never thought I'd hear you say something like that."

"I figure I'm pretty good at overall strategy, and with your help, we're basically unbeatable. So what if I'm crap at real time strategy and you can't talk to give orders? That won't matter if we're not in the thick of things."

Colt nodded reluctantly. He knew Yardley was trying to make him feel better after the debacle in the simulators. Neither of them wanted to miss a chance to join field operations, even if they could find other leaders. Sure, most commanders remained out of the action and controlled their forces in battle from relative safety. But those officers had already survived relatively long merc careers and attained high enough rank to accommodate that sort of luxury.

Four years earlier, Colt had been a twelve-year-old high school senior who was homeschooled his entire life. That certainly hadn't prepared him for *life on the metal edge* as FMT's advertisements had described merc training. And his experience since then had mostly entailed long stints of standing around on guard duty with a few minor standoffs in between. He yearned to see more action, like the fight they had back on Brigham, though he would never say that in front of a veteran like Captain Torres.

"I hate that the NCOs are probably dressing down all the troopers who just died because of me." Colt glanced up the long hallway where they floated. They were near the main elevators that led down to the spin ring. If he listened closely, he could hear the ring's steady drone reverberating through the bulkheads.

"We could drop in, let them scream at you a bit if it'd make you feel better." Yardley grinned at him devilishly.

"I'll pass, thanks," Colt said, as the two of them pulled their weightless frames toward one of the three elevator tubes.

The air in the zero-g part of the ship always felt colder and tasted staler than in the spin ring. It could be his imagination, but Colt figured the spin ring air got more spread around due to the fake gravity produced by centrifugal force. Still, it would be nice to get out of the float and plant his feet on the deck.

"Colonel Yardley!" A voice echoed down the steel corridor plastered with much-used crash pads. A corporal Colt didn't know scrabbled toward them, moving from handhold to handhold faster than Colt could have managed.

Yard spun around, his back to a starboard window that showed the unblemished white of hyperspace. "Yes, Corporal—" he squinted at the newcomer's name tag, "—Neilson. What can I do for you?"

"Well, uh, sir, I'm sorry to bother you. I wouldn't bring this up, but I'm sort of in a bind. You see, Captain Sampson—I'm in Bravo Company by the way—she told me to organize a garbage detail for the hydroculture bay, but I was already under orders from Staff Sergeant Benson to help run new chip sets and relays in the water purifiers for that section, and he wanted them done by 0800 yesterday. I tried to tell the captain, but she wouldn't listen, so I focused on the detail, because, you know, she's an officer. But now Sergeant Benson's put me on report, even though I told him what happened with the captain."

Colt blinked at the corporal's rapid fire barrage of words, but Yardley seemed to take it in stride.

"And what did Judy, I mean, Captain Sampson have to say when you told her you're on report with the sergeant?" Yardley asked. "I assume you told her about the mix up."

The corporal shrugged. "I tried, sir. She really didn't care. The job she ordered me to do was done. She told me to get my extra duties finished and quit complaining. But it's not fair. Why should I be on report for getting overtasked?"

"You shouldn't, and you're not," Yardley said. "I'll see to the captain and the sergeant."

"Thank you, sir." The corporal looked suddenly worried. "I'm not getting either of them in trouble, right? I'd rather just stay on report if so."

"No." Yardley's utter lack of expression sent a shiver down Colt's spine. "No trouble at all."

* * * * *

Chapter Seven

For some reason Colt could never figure out, dropping out of hyperspace always made him nauseous. Entering the gates never fazed him, but exiting felt like stepping off the galaxy's longest looping rollercoaster.

"Keep it together." Yardley slapped Colt's uniformed shoulder. "The captains will be here in two minutes. You don't want to be green when they show."

Colt nodded and swallowed against the sick feeling in his belly. The two of them stood in Belknap's former office in *Uncanny's* spin ring. No, Colt had to quit thinking of it that way. Yardley, as FMT's commander, had claimed the space. The office belonged to him now.

"Transition to real space complete. Welcome to the Tolo Arm." Zorn sounded pleased with himself even over the comm.

"Good work, Captain," Yardley said.

"Thank you, Colonel. And I have some more good news. The gate spit us out just twenty degrees off our desired trajectory for Vilo Beresk. We only have to shave off about ten percent of our current speed to get oriented on the proper trajectory, and then we'll be underway. I project we'll reach orbit within eighteen hours barring any slowdowns."

"Excellent, thank you."

Colt, feeling better though still queasy, poured himself a near-freezing glass of ice water from Belknap's—Yardley's—minibar. "Are we kidding ourselves?"

Yardley looked up from his report-filled slate, brows furrowed. "About?"

Colt rotated his glass in a smooth circle to take in the office, the ship, the universe at large. "Everything. It's been two weeks, and I keep thinking all of this happened so fast; we really haven't discussed what we're doing. One morning we were cadets and that afternoon we were running our own merc company. It's—"

"Insane?" Yardley sat back in his chair, a crooked smile turning up one corner of his mouth. Though he usually looked older than his twenty-one years, that expression brought out his youth. He could have been a kid driving his dad's flyer for the first time. "Yeah, Colt, all of this is insane. That's why I'm not stopping to look around. Better to keep moving, to keep driving toward our goals, and to avoid thinking too deeply about this house of cards. Breathe too hard on it, and the thing's liable to collapse."

The door chimed.

"Just keep doing what you're doing," Yardley said. Lifting his chin he called, "Come!"

The office door slid open, and FMT's four company commanders walked in. They took their accustomed seats in front of their commander's desk, and Colt sat off to the side. Yardley had, at first, loathed holding company staff meetings every two days. Why meet face-to-face when they all had pinplants and holo displays? He could host impromptu meetings anytime.

Against his natural inclinations, Colt had insisted they were necessary, not only to keep abreast of what was happening within FMT from top to bottom, but as a morale booster. This way, the captains knew they had ready access to their commander and his executive officer.

Now, if Yardley could keep them from devolving into bitch sessions.

"Good morning, all." Yardley favored the company officers with a genuine smile. "Welcome to the Cormsu'esh system if you haven't been here before. I visited once when my dad took me on a business trip, but that was ten years ago. Still, I remember Vilo Beresk as a beautiful planet. A lot like Earth. I figure while we're here we can give the crew some shore leave—let them soak up some UVs since we've all been cooped up for two weeks. But business first. Weep says she won't have any problems finding us some garrison-style duty, but if any of you or your people have ideas for earning some contract credits here, don't be afraid to speak up."

The officers looked around at each other for a moment before Sirena Catlett of Delta Company cleared her throat. "We are headed to a weapons expo. Maybe we should revisit the idea of selling some of our equipment." She held up a hand at the instant murmurs of disagreement from her fellow officers. "I'm not talking about liquidating our armament. I'm just saying we could make a bundle if we sold off a few of our newer Mk 8 CASPers and some of the extra RATs."

"What happens when we need them for later contracts?" Captain Terrell Butler of Alpha Company turned his gaze from Catlett to Yardley. "I know we don't have much in the way of liquid assets, but I'd rather we keep an eye out for deals on new equipment. We've got more CASPer pilots than we do suits right now, and they're our main selling point if we're competing with non-Human merc companies to get contracts. We should be buying, not selling."

Colt automatically started a message to Yardley via his pinplants, then cleared it. He had vowed to quit doing that. He wanted to tell the colonel both ideas should be on the table. Assuming FMT won a lucrative contract, they could buy more—possibly better—equipment. If, on the other hand, they found no contracts in the coming week, they might be forced to sell off some weapons just to keep FMT afloat.

He drew a breath to say all of this, but managed only an embarrassing gurgle, which he turned into a cough when the company commanders turned to look at him.

"I'm not selling anything." Yardley held Catlett's gaze, his look intense. "Butler's right, we should be looking for ways to expand our capabilities, not stifle our growth."

"Typical." Captain Sampson of Bravo folded her arms, her eyes rolled to the ceiling, and Colt groaned inwardly.

"Got something to add, Captain?" Yardley asked.

"No, sir. Not a thing you'll hear, I'm sure."

After their chance meeting with Corporal Neilson from Bravo Company—a meeting Colt doubted had anything to do with chance now that he thought about it—Yardley had called Captain Sampson and Staff Sergeant Philip Benson into his office for a thirty minute dressing down about how they were running their company. If a corporal was on report for not knowing whose orders to obey, the fault lay with the originators of those orders. Yardley had subsequently put the two of them on report and sentenced them to thirty days extra duty, which meant helping out in the mess for the noncom and working as the command team's executive secretary for the officer.

Sampson made no bones about her resentment at having to serve as her fellow captains' lackey. Butler, in particular, took advantage, using her to execute the more menial tasks of running Alpha Company. She had tried to talk to Colt, since he was the battalion XO and second in rank only to Yardley. But he had turned her away. He couldn't very well countermand his boss's orders, and he knew Yardley well enough to realize pleading for a reduction in punishment would go nowhere.

Colt disagreed with Yard's choice to punish anyone. In his estimation, the entire matter should have been company business. Corporal Neilson should never have jumped the chain of command to speak with the CEO of the company. That just wasn't done. Unfortunately, he had, and to make matters worse, it had worked. Colt worried about the sort of precedent that set.

Though a hint of displeasure crossed Yardley's expression like the shadow of a cloud, he kept control of his emotions. Ignoring Sampson's inflammatory words, he addressed the group again. "Any other suggestions?"

Feliks Petrov of Charlie raised a hand. "I've been thinking. We don't necessarily have to take on merc contracts to earn money. With CASPers and powered armor, we could earn some credits working as stevedores. I know a lot of races have robots for that kind of thing, but there are always those who don't—especially races who hate robots. More than one world has fought off a robot uprising in their history. Maybe some of them could use help loading and unloading equipment."

"I like that," Yardley said. "Look into it and see what you can find for us."

"There're always less than savory ways of making credits if we're willing to go that route. It worked for Colonel Belknap for years," Butler said, his tone leading.

Yardley was already shaking his head before the captain of Alpha Company had finished speaking. "No way. We're not pirates. And I have no intention of ending up like Belknap who, by the way, was no colonel."

"You said all suggestions. I'm just pointing out that we have over a hundred and twenty CASPers at our disposal."

"Noted and closed. Don't bring that up again. FMT isn't going there."

"Yes, sir."

"Anyone else?" Yardley looked at his officers. When no one spoke, he rose from his chair. "Very good then. Put together a shore leave schedule, but remind your people we may have a contract to fulfill in the coming days, so they need to remain flexible. Dismissed."

With that, the meeting broke up, and the captains exited the office. Colt sipped his water and regarded his polished shoes for a moment. "Sampson's still pretty pissed at you."

"Oh? I hadn't noticed." Sarcasm rang in Yardley's voice as he scrolled through a list of reports on the Tri-V projected above his desk. "You think I need to address the situation?"

Colt shook his head. He couldn't imagine Yardley getting through a meeting with Captain Sampson without losing his temper, and that would only make things worse. "Honestly, I have no idea what to do about it. Let her serve out her punishment, I guess— maybe we could tell Butler to lay off giving her crap tasks though. He's taking advantage."

"That's the punishment part." Yardley turned his attention from his reports to Colt, his expression challenging.

Colt considered his drink to keep from having to meet Yardley's gaze. "It's overkill, and he knows it."

Yardley looked as if he might say something hot. Instead, he sighed and turned back to the projection. "Fine. You handle it. But I don't want you to let her off. I can't dish out a punishment, then take it back. That sort of thing makes me look weak in front of the entire battalion."

"Me handle it?" Colt's stomach muscles tightened.

"Yeah. You're so concerned about me overdoing it, you fix it."

"I'm just saying Butler should back off a little."

"So tell him that."

Colt shook his head, his mind racing. "It's not like Sampson will be on report much longer though."

"Seriously, you have got to get over your phobia of talking to people. It worked when we had Belknap and the others running everything for us. All you and I had to do was score well in the simulators and outfox a few lackluster guards when they tried to stop us from repossessing stuff."

"You mean stealing stuff."

Yardley rolled his muscled shoulder. "Hey, we didn't know. Point is, your phobia, or whatever it is, didn't matter much then. We might have held senior ranks, but we didn't have senior responsibilities in FMT. Now we do. And if you can't cope with them, it's going to weaken our effectiveness as a management team."

Colt stood still for a long moment as he fought down the sudden flare of anger trying to rush up his spine and into his head. He had to view Yardley's argument logically. Yes, Colt could run rings around Yard on the battlefield. But that, by no means, made him a better commander. In fact, this situation proved that. Colt might not agree with the punishment Yardley had doled out to Captain Sampson, but Yard, at least, had the courage to address the problem. What would Colt have done in his place, cower in his office, hoping the subject never came up? Probably so. And now that Colt felt Butler was taking advantage of Sampson's punishment detail, what did he propose to do about it? Have Yardley address it, of course.

All of this made sense. And it surely meant Colt should handle the situation. Yardley was right about that. But that didn't make Colt any less the coward he had always been when it came to confronting people.

"I'll try to do better—try to talk more," he said.

"I hope you do. I need your help to make this plan work. Does that mean you're going to speak with Butler?"

Colt shook his head. "Not this time. You're right. I don't want it to look like I'm countermanding your orders. Sampson can serve out her extra duty and maybe Butler's picking on her will drive the point home."

"Good. I like it when we agree."

* * *

"You were right," Colt said, staring at the Tri-V display on *Uncanny Valley's* bridge. "It really does look like Earth."

Vilo Beresk, a blue planet mottled with continents bearded in white, swirling clouds, hovered in the ship's display. Three immense space stations orbited the inviting sphere, each sporting a set of spin rings.

Yardley, holding himself in place with a handle built into the bridge's ceiling, grinned. "The Lask might not look Human, but we like the same sort of climates. Oh, and atmosphere too. The air down there is pure oxygen-nitrogen mix in just the right amounts. Mostly. It's why so many Humans like to vacation here."

"We've just received permission to dock at Lask station Comer'eal Shaeru. I'll take us in." Benwarst flexed in his co-pilot's chair, stretching to reach the control panel before him. The odd—to a Human anyway—belt arrangement he wore kept his millipede-like body from floating away in the zero-g environment, but afforded him enough leeway to perform his duties. The belts, hoops really, that linked under four sets of his insectile arms were attached to his narrow seat by cross straps and metal anchors. The contraption looked uncomfortable to Colt, but didn't seem to bother the Jeha.

Uncanny Valley's in-system engines rumbled many hundreds of meters away from the cockpit. The vibrations hummed through the strap Colt held to steady himself. The view ahead shifted and the stations grew closer as the converted freighter slowed to shorten its orbit. At first, he feared Benwarst might have overshot his target. Slowing from a higher orbit to dock took precise changes in speed and approach angle. One mistake, and *Uncanny* could go bouncing off Vilo Beresk's thick atmosphere. It would likely crack apart from the sheering forces or bounce into one of the many thousands of satellites, space craft, or meteors orbiting the planet. But within a minute, he could see Benwarst had timed his retro burn perfectly. Comer'eal Shaeru, the largest of the three space stations, seemed to roll sideways like a mother whale, offering up an array of docking ports that could reconfigure in real time to fit thousands of different ship configurations. Most already had one type of ship or another attached, but a free one glowed green on the Tri-V, and Benwarst guided them toward it.

According to the GalNet, the Lask, the sentient species native to Vilo Beresk, were only provisional members of the Galactic Union, but had dedicated themselves to earning full membership status. Part of that campaign included trying to entice other species, especially oxygen breathers like Humans, to consider Vilo Beresk the meeting place of meeting places in the Tolo Arm. Their government, in conjunction with a dozen of the planet's top advertising firms, had embarked on a campaign to push this message hard over a decade earlier. According to all sources, it was working. Landing the Fenres Weapons Bazaar was a big win for them, and judging by the space traffic around the stations and dropping to the planet, it had attracted incredible interest.

Colt hoped some of that interest would translate to lucrative contracts for FMT.

A massive boom like tectonic plates moving deep under the sea followed by a slight reverberation through the bridge, and the ship was docked.

"Zorn, have you got ears on Weep?" Yardley asked.

"Line's already open." Zorn tapped a button on the holographic Tri-V display floating in front of him.

"This is Weep." The Flatar's high-pitched voice sounded slightly distorted, likely because of all the radio traffic in and around the station. She had gone ahead to Comer'eal Shaeru aboard a courtesy shuttle while *Uncanny* waited for permission to dock. "I already met with my contact. We've worked out a deal, though our potential client would like to meet you in person before he commits to anything, Colonel Yardley. Should I bring him aboard?"

Yardley looked at Colt, a familiar look of self-doubt crossing his face. Both of them had hoped to make this deal through Weep without the client ever seeing their faces. Their youth could be a detriment.

Colt shrugged, then nodded. The client would see them eventually.

"Yes. What's his name and how many are in his retinue? We're not opening our doors to a potential invasion team."

"I wouldn't let that happen, sir." Weep sounded amused. "Our client is a Blevin. His name's Renvis. He and three bodyguards will be coming aboard. He wants to see if we can actually field CASPers and what our force looks like."

"Roger that. Bring him aboard. We'll be at the airlock."

"On our way."

Yardley lifted his eyebrows at Colt. "Ever met a Blevin?"

"Never even heard of one."

"I have." Captain Torres twisted so he could look at both of them at once. "Usually brown-skinned, look like lizards. If this one's hiring you, it's probably because your Flatar gave him a good rate. The ones I've met know how to hire plenty of mercs. It's like they were born to it. I'd be wary about how good a deal you're getting."

"Thought you weren't helping us anymore." Yardley tilted his head at the big merc.

"I'm not. Consider it friendly advice, one merc to another."

"Alright then. Let's go meet our employer."

* * * * *

Chapter Eight

"I'll admit, this is impressive." Renvis rolled one yellow-green eye back to gaze at the double row of CASPers mounted in steel cages along the armory wall. This was the only part of *Uncanny's* spin ring without a second floor, an accommodation made to store the oversized battle suits. "How many of them do you have?"

"One hundred and twenty-three." Yardley punched a large red button next to one of the suits, and a hydraulic arm as big around as Colt's waist lowered it to the floor with a whine of gears and a hiss of compressed air.

Colt suppressed the urge to clap a hand over his commander's mouth, and even managed to keep his face calm, at Yard's blithe rundown of their CASPer complement. Technically, they didn't have one-hundred and twenty-three, only ninety-eight. Onishi had taken twenty-five of them with her for the Mormon job on Brigham. Still, telling someone outside the company how many CASPers they owned seemed like a bad idea on several levels. Captain Torres, who had come along to observe FMT's first contract negotiation, must have agreed because he made no effort to hide his look of incredulity.

Renvis's tongue flashed out and in of his lipless mouth almost faster than Colt could track as the gnarled Blevin ran a hand along the accelerator cannon mounted on the CASPer's right arm. "I've heard how Humans make themselves quite formidable in such armor, but I have never seen one up close."

Weep, astride the floating drone platform she had appropriated on Brigham, gestured toward the seven-foot-tall battle suit. "You've heard right. These suits are made for mercenary duty. You won't find a better class of guards in this system. Not for the price."

"Ah, the price, yes." Renvis rubbed the scales beneath what was probably an ear hole on the side of his head. The skreetch-skreetch-skreetch sound sent uncomfortable shivers racing up and down Colt's spine. "I don't know much about Humans—you're the first I've seen outside of holo plays and news vids—but I think most of your crew are quite young, aren't they? Even immature?"

"Some, yes." Yardley squared his shoulders, a ploy to draw the Blevin's attention. And it worked. Though Yard stood only an inch or two taller than Renvis, his girth made him hard to ignore. "We are a young crew, but experienced. We've spent years training in mercenary techniques."

"I sent you references for garrison work FMT has performed in the past," Weep said.

Renvis made a sound that was half hiss, half musing hum. "Yes, I saw. But the work I'm offering will require delicacy. I need smart guards who are ready to follow my orders without hesitation."

"My people can do that." Yard's face never wavered.

"And we will be moving some...items. Your company has no problem with that?"

"Not if you can pay our fee."

"With an initial investment of twenty percent up front," Weep added, guiding her platform a bit closer to Yardley. Its six fans blew a cool stream of air across Colt's face.

"Very well, but I'm taking five percent off the top due to your young crew." Renvis stared at the Humans and the Flatar, his vertical pupils daring them to counter him.

"That wasn't the deal." Weep buzzed a little closer but stayed out of arm's reach as if she didn't quite trust the lizard man.

Colt waved at Yardley to grab his attention and shrugged when the colonel looked his way. Did it really matter if they lost a little cash up front? They were about to get a paying job. If nothing else, even if they only came out even after expenses, they were getting some practice fulfilling a contract.

Yardley pursed his lips and looked at the cement floor for a long moment. "Weep, how much are we talking about? In all the hustling to get here and find a client, I don't think you ever told us what we're getting paid for this job."

"Eight hundred thousand."

Colt's mouth dropped open. "Eight hundred thousand credits?"

Everyone looked at him in surprise—it was the first thing he had said in an hour. He fought the urge to flinch or hide behind one of the CASPers.

"Yes." Weep gave him a Human-style nod. "Eight hundred thousand credits for two weeks of guard duty and moving freight for Mr. Renvis...minus five percent now, I suppose."

Yardley's eyes were as wide as Colt's, and he looked just as gob smacked. "We'll do it."

"Definitely," Colt said without having to search for his voice.

"Very good." Renvis nodded at each of them before turning to Weep. "Draw up the contracts. We have a deal."

"Already done, sir." Weep pulled the small slate she carried with her from a pocket affixed to her hovering platform. "Press a digit here, please. Good. Now, Colonel Yardley, press here and we're set."

Yard pressed his thumb to the slate after which Weep did the same as witness.

"Done and done," Weep said, grinning without showing her teeth. She turned to FMT's first official client. "Come on, Ren, you old skin shedder, I'll buy you a drink on Comer'eal Shaeru to celebrate!"

As Weep and Renvis started for the armory's exit, Colt noticed the look on Captain Torres' face. The big merc looked like someone had spit in his salad. He stood next to the CASPer cradle shaking his head, a look of utter disbelief on his scarred visage.

"What?" Yardley asked.

"You two are—" Torres literally bit his lip. Colt had heard of people doing that before, but he had always thought it was just an expression. Torres glanced at the retreating aliens, waited for the armory door to seal behind them, then tried again. "Do you not recognize a criminal when you see one?"

"Criminal?" Yardley looked perplexed. "He wants us to guard some equipment at a weapons expo. That hardly makes him a criminal."

"Did you miss the part where he said you'd be moving some 'stuff?'"

"Of course not. So what? That doesn't mean—"

Torres opened his hands and stared at the bay's high ceiling like a man being electrocuted. "That's exactly what that means. He's going to have you move stolen merchandise."

"No way."

"Bet me." Torres raised an eyebrow at Yardley. "I win, you've got to—" he looked around the spacious room, "give me one of your CASPers."

Yardley laughed. "Are you insane?"

"But you seemed so sure a second ago, Colonel." Never in the history of the galaxy had any sentient being made the word colonel sound so much like twerp.

Yardley's face flushed. "I'll bet one suit of powered armor."

"Uh-uh. CASPer."

"Okay, fine! But what do I get if we win?"

"Yard, don't do this," Colt said with about as much hope as a man trapped on a magnetic track with an oncoming train barreling straight at him. "This is stupid."

"You win, and you get three full days of my advice. I'll help you with every aspect of running your company from top to bottom. It'll be like you hired an expert consultant for free."

"That's not worth a whole CASPer." Yardley folded his arms, his jaw firmly set, but it was all for show. He knew just as well as Colt that the big merc's decades of experience were worth a CASPer made of gold.

Torres didn't bother defending his resume or its unquestionable worth, he simply raised an eyebrow.

"Fine! You're on. But I'm telling you, Captain, you're going to regret this because Colt and I are going to have you sliding around here like an Oogar on ice." Yardley stuck out a hand, and Torres, grinning, shook it.

Colt had a feeling FMT had just lost a CASPer.

* * *

True to the climate reports, Vilo Beresk looked and felt much like Earth. Though Colt had been born in Stanford, California—his parents were both professors there—much of his extended family lived in the broad steppe regions of South Africa. This part of Vilo Beresk reminded him of that land with its long swaths of grassland hemmed in by distant peaks that kissed the horizon. Blue skies and pure white clouds completed the picture. According to the local net, much of the flora and fauna mimicked Earth's, though the colors varied more, and many of the animals were a sort of mix between Terran mammals and amphibians. The same went for the planet's native sentient species, the Lask.

Colt guided his CASPer along a broad street in the city of Sreelav, a combination space port and merchant's paradise. As far as he could tell, two-thirds of the place had been constructed in the last several months to host the weapons expo. Massive steel and plastic warehouses, encompassing millions of square meters of floor space, rose on either side of the thoroughfare, their silver facades shining in Vilo Beresk's golden sunlight. Aliens of all types crowded the road, buying food from vendors or stopping to inspect small-time merchants selling the latest in merc tech.

"Jackson, stay in formation," said Staff Sergeant Parker, who was riding herd on this part of the detail.

"Yes, Sergeant." Jackson, who had stopped his CASPer to peek inside a warehouse full of aliens milling around tanks and dropships, hurried to rejoin the rest of the squad. "Sorry about that, but those are the new Lorphor Eights. Jeha-designed, but made for easy retrofit. You can resize them for hundreds of different races in minutes. They're amazing."

"There's a lot of amazing stuff around here." Parker sounded both sympathetic and stern. "You'll have time to look at everything when you hit the shore leave lottery. Until then, we're here to do a job."

"Yes, Sergeant."

"Squad, watch out for the group of MinSha up ahead. Give them plenty of room. We don't want any trouble."

Most of the towering MinSha, aliens that looked much like Earth's praying mantises, except for their horrifying size, loomed as large as Colt's CASPer. One or two of the fifteen standing in the middle of the street were even taller. With their iridescent blue armored bodies and multi-faceted ruby red eyes, they looked like something out of a nightmare. Smaller aliens gave them a wide berth, as did Parker's squad.

Colt, who was observing the squad, followed as they left the busy main road and entered another warehouse filled with weapons and vehicles that bristled with weapons. With so many races milling about, it was hard to keep from stepping on anyone, especially those the size of a Flatar or even smaller. Colt nearly squashed something that looked like an oversized mouse wearing a skin suit, and the little thing gabbled at him vociferously, hopping up and down on its long, curved legs.

"Sorry. Very sorry." Colt hoped his translator covered the little thing's language.

"Don't sweat it, sir." Parker said over the comm. "Everyone here should know better than to get under our feet. Those who don't probably deserve a little squeeze."

The squad trooped to the far end of the warehouse where the crowds and vendors petered out, and into a wide open space with lines painted on the cement floor where more stalls and building-sized displays could be erected.

"What's back here, Sergeant?" Colt asked over a private channel.

"This is where Renvis has us working. He's got a ton of stock back here." Parker led the way to a loading dock entrance that could have accommodated three CASPers standing abreast with three more standing on their shoulders. A semi-circle of MinSha armed with rifles guarded the exit. They stared at the approaching humans but made no move to stop them.

"Who were they?" Colt asked as the squad stepped outside again, back into the sunlight.

"Don't know their company name," Parker said, "but they're mercs Renvis hired to guard his merchandise."

Colt keyed his Tri-V to show him a rear display of the receding MinSha mercs. Why would Renvis hire another company? Didn't FMT offer him enough protection? Colt would have been happy to send a dozen more CASPers down to guard whatever their client needed guarding, especially if it meant they could recoup the five percent they had lost.

A swatch of grass, much trampled by CASPers and dozens of armored treads, led from the warehouse's wide exit to a fat lander that reminded Colt of a beetle. Three squads of ten CASPers were busily trucking metal pallets and boxes from an adjoining building into the waiting ship. Via the translator displayed on the holographic Tri-V, Colt could see the maker marks and serial numbers imprinted on the equipment they were moving included at least seven different languages and warehousing guides. While that didn't necessarily mean the goods were stolen, it reminded him of Captain Torres' earlier comment.

He brought his CASPer to a halt in the freshly turned mud while Parker put his squad to work hauling crates of weapons from a stockpile just inside the next building. Colt zoomed in on the open doorway. Eight MinSha mercs stood guard while a mixed group of aliens bustled about with forklifts and light-duty cranes, hauling equipment into view from deep inside the building.

Against his better judgement, Colt tapped into the city's net and cross-referenced several of the serial numbers on the crates. The blood drained from his cheeks as he scanned the results. Not only were the goods listed for sale, supposedly in several different sectors of the expo, all but a scant few belonged to veritable titans in the weapons industry—the sorts of corporations with the credits and clout to hire mercs of their own. Real mercs. Some of the stuff was even registered to the Merchants Guild. Nobody in their right mind wanted to tangle with them.

Colt hesitated, uncertain what to do. The right thing would be to withdraw his people immediately. Breaking the contract with Renvis would cost them money, but it was better than getting caught stealing merchandise at the galaxy's biggest weapons expo in history.

Then again, there were the MinSha mercs to consider. Did they know they were helping Renvis steal equipment? Colt tried not to take a Human-centric view of the Union. Humans had been hunting wooly mammoths with spears when some of the ancestors of the aliens at this expo were already charting the stars. But he had read too much about the MinSha to believe them innocent.

Innocent? Is that what he and Yardley were? Try stupid. Colt shook his head. Captain Torres had warned them, but they hadn't listened. Even Colt, despite his doubts, had convinced himself over the past week that Renvis could be trusted. Foolish. And now thirty of his troopers were complicit in a major theft while under guard by armed MinSha warriors.

"Sergeant Parker." Colt's voice wavered despite his best efforts to keep it strong.

"Yes, sir?" The sergeant, who had just delivered a crate of what looked like accelerator cannons made for Oogar, guided his CASPer Colt's way.

Stupid words. Stupid voice! Colt sneered at himself. Why wouldn't they come when he needed them? He was talking to Sergeant Parker over a private comm. No one else could hear them.

"Sir?"

Colt bit his tongue so hard, he almost drew blood. "Sergeant, I think we're breaking the...the law. I need you to form the squads up."

"Okay...where, sir?"

Hands shaking, which caused his CASPer's arms to shudder, Colt pointed toward the open area just beyond Renvis's ship. The passage between the ship and the two nearest buildings was tight, but Colt figured if his people moved fast enough, they could use the narrow gap to their advantage. Should the MinSha follow them, they would be forced to pass through single-file, which would make them easy targets for the CASPers.

"Hold!" The sudden voice over the supposedly private channel made him jerk in surprise. It took several seconds before he realized it was Renvis. "You're not about to back out on our contract are you, Mr. Colt?"

Colt froze. A voice inside his head screamed for Parker to follow his last order and send the squads through the gap with all haste. But his mouth refused to move. His heart, pounding a fearsome tattoo against his breastbone, threatened to explode, and all the blood in his body seemed to have fled into his face and ears. He had to move, yet he couldn't.

Renvis barked an order over the comm. From the sound of it, he was no longer speaking directly to Colt.

In the next instant, the MinSha in both buildings started forward, their nightmarishly long weapons held before them. In seconds, they had taken up firing positions against the humans.

Only then did Colt's people seem to take notice of the situation. They stopped loading, their voices an incoherent gabble over the main channel as thirty confused Humans bellowed inquiries, yelps, and angry challenges.

"Mr. Colt." Renvis's voice sliced through the squad chatter like a knife sliding into Colt's ear. "You are young. I do not wish to kill you. Tell your people to march their armors into my ship, and I will gladly set you all free without harm. Cross me, however, and my mercs will end you."

* * * * *

Chapter Nine

"Sir?" Parker called over their private channel. "You heard that, I assume?"

"Yes." Colt squeezed the single affirmative through clenched teeth.

"What should we do?" Parker turned his CASPer to more fully face Colt. No doubt he was marking the seven MinSha advancing on their position. Like all the FMT troopers, his suit was only lightly armed with a high velocity machine gun on his right arm and a rocket array bolted to the opposite shoulder, since their mission requirements had emphasized hauling over fighting. Compared to a single Human merc, even one dressed in powered armor, such an arrangement would be a formidable allotment of weapons. For a CASPer however, Parker and all the Humans were painfully under equipped.

Colt considered taking Renvis's offer. He knew enough about the MinSha's reputation for coordinated fighting to realize that despite their superior numbers—FMT's twenty CASPers to Renvis's fifteen MinSha mercs—the MinSha could probably rip his people apart. Sure, his troopers had plenty of hours in the simulators, and that probably prepared them for a fight like this, but in those digitized battles, Colt had been able to lead them through Yardley. Now they didn't have Yardley, and they really didn't have Colt.

Yet giving up would be stupid. FMT needed these CASPers. They were the crew's best means of earning enough credits to pay off their debt. On top of that, Colt didn't trust Renvis. The ugly lizard had been way too interested in the number of CASPers FMT could field. If he could get Colt and the others out of their suits, he could easily try to ransom them for more equipment. Or maybe force his way aboard *Uncanny* and take it from Yardley by using Colt and the others as bargaining chips.

"Parker to Dugout." Sergeant Parker's voice sounded nervous, but he managed to keep it remarkably steady as he reached out to the crew on *Uncanny*.

"Sergeant Parker, this is Dugout actual." The sound of Yardley's voice made Colt look up as if he could somehow see *Uncanny* through the roof of his CASPer.

"Actual, we've got a situation down here. It seems our employer has had us loading stolen equipment from the warehouses onto his ship, and he is now threatening to take our CASPers from us. Lt. Colonel Maier—" a short pause. "I'd say Colonel Maier is suffering an anxiety attack. He's out of comms with the unit."

Inside his CASPer, Colt screamed at his body to move, his mouth to work. Sweat leaked down his temples and the back of his neck as he moved his jaw to no avail. In desperation, he accessed his pinplants. They didn't require his voice or his hands. It took less than a second to send a message, though doing so was probably useless.

Yardley cursed. "Are you in danger, Parker? What's the tactical—"

The channel cut off with a squeal, and Colt's Tri-V flashed red as jamming icons appeared over the squad's comms channels, including their satellite uplink to *Uncanny*.

"Get in the ship." Renvis's voice broke over the squad channel like a whip crack. "I will give you no further warnings."

Later, as he repeatedly watched an edited playback from the twenty FMT CASPers, Colt would realize that comms call had sparked the short, horrible battle that followed. Whether one of the MinSha mistook Renvis's words or his tone as an order to attack didn't matter. One of them shouldered his cannon-sized rifle and fired on Parker.

Even inside his CASPer, the booming crack of the magnetically accelerated round hurt Colt's ears. It scored a direct hit on the main body of Parker's suit. Yellow flames and bits of armor exploded in every direction, and the big mecha teetered in place, shuffled a step, then fell over.

Colt felt like someone had smacked him in the head with a mallet. He spun around to see which of the MinSha had fired and found four of the naturally armored killers bearing down on him, weapons trained on his CASPer. The one in the lead fired at point-blank range. The sound was deafening, and the concussive force slammed Colt backward into the mud. Even with the suit's harness system snug about his torso, he banged his head against the back of the cockpit. It was like the beach simulation all over again, except no one could switch it off.

Stars flashed before his eyes for a moment as pain drilled through his head. He groaned but managed to stay conscious.

Warning alarms blared through the cockpit and stacks of malfunction errors showed up on his Tri-V. The smell of burning plastic and ozone filled the cockpit. Part of the suit's holographic display had gone dark, and most of the functions on the left side of the suit were inoperable. Colt tried to roll over to his feet, but his CASPer only rocked in place a bit before falling still.

The MinSha who had blasted Colt came into view. It stared down at him with pitiless eyes as it placed the business end of its rifle against the suit's armored cockpit.

Colt squeezed his eyes shut, certain he was about to die. If only he had gotten control of himself and the situation, they could have beaten these stupid bugs. His troopers deserved better, but he had failed them. Swearing on the last beats of his heart, he prayed his would be the only death in this debacle because the fault lay fully at his feet.

A chorus of explosions, sonic booms, and crackling laser fire made Colt open his eyes. The MinSha mercenary standing over him was suddenly flung from view by a barrage of flame, eye-piercing laser fire, and anti-personnel missiles. The ground rumbled with their force.

Colt reoriented his Tri-V on Renvis's ship, and a flush of cool relief washed over him. His gamble had paid off. Two dozen Mk 8 CASPers, most of them bearing the winged spear emblem of Wayward Javelin, a merc company Colt had seen listed on the invoices of the stolen equipment, were descending into the square on jumpjets. With them came several others bearing different company logos and scores of alien mercs dressed in varying types of armor or wearing no armor at all.

Their combined fire, though poorly orchestrated, made short work of the outnumbered and outgunned MinSha. In less than a minute, they covered the churned-up field in bloody and burned carapaces.

A deep bass rumbling caused Colt to refocus his display on Renvis's lander. While he had been watching the mercs, Colt hadn't noticed the ship's cargo door seal shut. The four boosters tucked into its beetle-shaped exterior had begun to belch smoke and blue-white jet flames that scorched the ground beneath them. Renvis was trying to take off, and Colt had a feeling the Blevin wasn't concerned with safety protocols that would have him ease his craft clear of the city before trying to attain escape velocity. He was about to melt everything within a thousand feet of his ship.

And Colt couldn't move.

Voices once again crackled over the comm as the jamming signal dropped. Colt could hear a dozen commands vying for attention. Some called for a hasty retreat, while others demanded their combined forces attack the fleeing lander. Incensed at their disorganization and fearing for his life, Colt did the only logical thing.

He keyed the FMT common channel and gambled on his fear to see him through. For once, it worked.

"All units! Fire on that lander—take out those engines. Now!"

Several of his squads' CASPers lay in the mud, smoking, or in one case smoldering, but most appeared functional. They focused their weapons on the unprotected engines of the rising ship and fired. Though the anti-personnel missiles they had armed for this mission didn't pack the sort of punch expected from armor piercing weapons, they still delivered enough explosive force to damage the lander's fragile booster rockets. And because the missiles were small, FMT's armorers had managed to pack far more aboard each unit than they would have had they been higher-yield weapons. Even better, seven of Colt's troopers stood close enough to Renvis's ship to fire their missiles directly into the engines' downward facing nozzles. Hundreds of explosions echoed between the buildings, accompanied by the distinct sounds of intricate machinery breaking apart in horrible ways.

Seeing the fun their counterparts were having, and not wishing to be left out, the other mercs opened fire on the ship, though they were careful to avoid hitting the cargo bay. Three armored Tortantulas, each bearing a Flatar armed with an XT-12 on its back, raced to the fore, their tiny riders peppering the already damaged engines with hellfire. The Wayward Javelin mercs joined them, opening up with much heavier missile salvos than the FMT crew had, punctuating that with dual high-velocity machine gun fire that perforated the ship's underside.

Listing to port, the huge ship rolled unevenly, belching smoke and flames.

"Everyone back up! It's coming down!" shouted someone over the comm.

Mercs of all shapes and sizes scattered toward the warehouses, the Humans zooming ahead using their jumpjets, as Renvis's ship began to tear apart. It collided with the nearest warehouse, its port side crushing part of the steel and plastic building as its landing struts hit the ground. The forward strut buckled under the stress, and the ship's nose slammed down, sending sprays of mud and dust into the air. Some of the mud sloshed over Colt's dead CASPer, and he sighed in relief. It could have been the ship slamming down on him, and he didn't think his armor would have held under that sort of weight. He was lucky to be alive, and he knew it.

* * * * *

Chapter Ten

Despite FMT's light casualties—Private Ivansky from Charlie Company suffered a concussion and Corporal Desoto from Bravo required medical attention for smoke inhalation—Colt couldn't put the disastrous op out of his mind. He spent the next three days cooped up in his private room aboard *Uncanny*, pouring over the playback of the fight from every possible angle. He had even prevailed upon the mercs from Wayward Javelin to share their CASPer footage from the moment they first launched the counter offensive that saved Colt's and his squads' lives.

Colt leaned back on the small couch and focused on the digital feed playing in his mind through his pinplants. No matter how he looked at it, the entire fiasco was his fault. His troopers, especially Sergeant Parker, had acted honorably, despite their utter surprise and their lack of preparation. They had been caught off-guard, which had given the MinSha a decided advantage. Colt's failure to lead had nearly cost them their lives—likely would have had the other mercs ignored his desperate message about the stolen equipment. Colt couldn't imagine a scenario where Renvis would have let the FMT troopers go had they exited their CASPers. The Blevin had been on the verge of making a clean getaway with the stolen weapons. Why leave evidence behind?

Renvis would have killed Colt and his people. Or maybe taken them hostage. He had seemed quite interested in how many CASPers

107

FMT had aboard *Uncanny*. Would a criminal like him risk using Colt and the others to gain entry to the ship? Why not? He had the MinSha mercs on payroll. Using them as shock troops would have been all too easy.

A new series of images that had nothing to do with his pinplants flashed through Colt's mind. Unbidden, he imagined the MinSha infiltrating *Uncanny*, marching from room to room, bringing death and carnage wherever they went. FMT had never practiced defending against boarders; it hadn't been part of the curriculum. In his mind's eye, Colt saw his people unarmored and cowering before the invaders, powerless to stop the slaughter.

The doorbell chimed, and the door slid open before Colt had time to react.

Colt expected Yardley to come barging in, but was surprised to see Captain Torres duck inside. Dressed in black pants and a military-style shirt with the T^3 insignia embroidered over the breast pocket, he looked freshly polished, like a man on his way to an important meeting. Torres stood at the center of the small room, hands behind him in the parade rest position. He stood there so long without speaking, Colt grew tired of looking at his combat boots and shifted his gaze to the man's face.

Torres wore an expression Colt didn't recognize, not that he was all that good at recognizing expressions. It might have been curiosity, but Colt thought he also read some disapproval in the cast of Torres' eyes and the set of his jaw.

"I wondered how long it would take you to look up." Torres didn't move to sit or to adjust his feet. He stood as still as Colt's discarded clothes decorating the floor.

"Do you need something, Captain?" That wasn't what Colt wanted to say, but his father had taken great pains to teach him manners when he was a kid. Telling the captain to get out of his room would have been rude.

"How are you, Colt?"

"Fine."

"How long have you known you're on the spectrum?"

Colt started, then shrugged. "Got the diagnosis when I was about eight. Probably knew before that. I remember the other kids not making much sense to me back in first grade. I knew I was different from them. I don't talk about it, though."

Torres nodded. "May I sit?"

Colt fought the urge to say no. He didn't want Torres to sit. He didn't want to discuss his condition, especially not with a virtual stranger. But he could hear his dad's voice in his head. He had to take other people's feelings into account. He had to listen and think about what might hurt someone else. He had to show his manners.

He gestured at the stool which served as the only chair in the cramped quarters. Not even the deputy commander of FMT rated luxury accommodations aboard *Uncanny Valley*.

Torres sat, but not too close, which Colt appreciated. "I told Yardley he should demote you."

Instant anger boiled up in Colt's throat, only to die the moment it reached his tongue. He hung his head. He had no right to be angry. In a real merc company, he wouldn't be facing demotion, he would be looking for a new job. "I understand."

"He wouldn't hear of it. He defended you."

Colt frowned. "He shouldn't have. I nearly got my people killed."

"No, he was right. You belong where you are." Torres drew a long breath, watching Colt. "He showed me vids of you two training in the simulators. Got to admit, I was skeptical at first, but then I saw you in action. You're a gifted battlefield commander, Colt."

"I'm an anxiety attack waiting to happen."

"Not when you're paired with Yardley."

Colt shook his head. "I guess."

Torres was quiet for a long moment. He shifted on the stool. "What is it about him that allows you to speak under pressure? Are you—I mean, do you have feelings for him?"

"No. Nothing like that." Colt's ears burned. This wasn't the first time someone had wondered, either aloud or in whispers, if he and Yardley were an item. Some of their fellow cadets had even taunted Colt with the idea to get a reaction.

"It's perfectly fine if you are."

"It's not like that." Colt cracked his knuckles one after another, then began methodically rubbing his hands. "We started out together freshman year. I had a hard time—socially. I don't always know how to get along with people. I say the wrong things."

"In the vids, you knew just what to say, just how to move your units," Torres said.

"I was terrible in the beginning. I got into FMT's officers' track because of my VOWs scores. At least, that's what the review board told me. Knowing what I do now, I think I was just a warm body with a big enough loan from Mountside to cover tuition. I said I wanted to be an officer, and they took me. My scores were good, excellent even, in every category except leadership."

"You were saying you were terrible on the field?" Torres prompted.

"Yeah. I could take commands well enough, and I'm not half bad piloting a CASPer, but giving commands was something else. It was just like on Vilo Beresk. Worse even. I routinely got my troopers killed. Thank God it was just simulations in those early days."

"How'd you discover you could command through Yardley?"

Colt realized he had been rubbing his hands for an inordinately long time. He placed them in his lap. "It wasn't an accident. We were running combat drills as teams the first time I sent Yardley a message. He had command, and he was making a mess of it. I could see his mistake. He was sending his troopers in at too high an angle on their jumpjets. That made them easy pickings for enemy fire. I sent him a better strategy. We won."

"Yes you did. Yardley showed me that op. You didn't just win. You took no more casualties, and you quickly had your people swarming over the enemy position."

"After that it got easier and easier to talk to Yard. No one knew I was helping him, at least not for a while. Then Belknap promoted him quickly through the ranks; so quickly, Yard left me behind. I was still a lowly cadet first lieutenant when he made captain."

"Let me guess, the new Cadet Captain Yardley suddenly lost his mojo when he was no longer working with you?"

Colt tapped his nose. "Yard told Belknap how he had won so many battles in the simulators. I thought he might get in trouble, but Belknap didn't seem to care. He was more than happy to promote me and put us back together."

"Every scam artist knows a good thing when he sees it." Torres scratched his chin, his gaze cast toward the ceiling as if in thought. "But things have changed. The school died when Belknap and the others were arrested. Now you and Yard are running a serious merc company, and that means a lot more administrative work than when you were students."

"Yard's good at that kind of stuff."

Torres shook his head. "Nah. He's learning, but both of you are kids. You didn't earn the ranks you've got."

Again, Colt started to bristle but thought better of it. "Yeah. I guess not."

"You earned cadet ranks. The real thing usually takes years to obtain. I've seen people try to jump into the mercenary trade with both feet. They start up a company with almost no experience, promote themselves and their friends to ridiculous ranks, then die horrible deaths the first time they take a contract, assuming they ever get one. Most clients see through them."

"I guess that about sums up FMT," Colt said with a glum nod.

Torres tilted his head to one side. "Yes and no. From what I've seen, Belknap and his ilk *did* train you and the rest of the cadets in real merc techniques. I'm not one for simulators. They can't give you the feel of real combat because you always know, deep down, your mistakes don't mean death for you and your people. But I'll admit, the ones Belknap installed here are as close as I've ever seen to the real thing. Your people acquit themselves well, top to bottom, in battle."

A flush of pride warmed Colt. "Yes, they do."

"FMT's problem isn't training, at least not battlefield training. A few missions to give you a little real world experience, and you'll be solid. No, the problem I see in FMT is mainly administrative. All of you, from the lowliest private to your vaunted Colonel Yardley, are accustomed to having other people run the school for you while you go about learning to be mercs. Now there is no school, and you're finding out the hard way that merc companies aren't only about killing aliens and getting paid. You've got hundreds of people to organize, equipment to maintain, a ship the size of a small city to keep running, and about a billion other little things that require constant attention."

Colt nodded and sat up straighter. "I'll admit, I never knew all that stuff was going on around me. I never thought about it."

"You said, a moment ago, you thought Yardley was good at that stuff."

"Better than me, that's for sure." Colt couldn't keep the defensive tone out of his voice.

Torres watched Colt closely. "You're jealous of the way he gets along with people, aren't you?"

"Not jealous," Colt said, with complete certainty, then faltered. "Maybe a little. He's good with people. They like him. He knows what to say and when to say it."

"Does that make him a good leader?"

"Yes."

"No." Torres bent forward, hands on his knees, and stared at Colt, who squirmed under his gaze. "That makes Yardley popular and well-liked. It doesn't make him a good leader. Charisma is a handy tool when it comes to leadership, but it's not the thing, itself. That's like saying salt is the container it comes in. It's not true. You can learn to deal with people."

Colt was already shaking his head before Torres finished. "I can't."

"Yes, you can. You see, you've got something Yardley hasn't yet developed. He's on his way to finding it, which is encouraging from my point of view, but he's not there yet."

"What's that?"

"An eye for efficiency. You know how things should work from both a broad perspective and at the smallest levels."

"Yardley—"

"Doesn't have a clue when it comes to organization. That's why things ran better when you were sending him hints through your pinplants. It's also why one of your troopers is in the brig right now."

Colt looked up, and his eyes met Torres' for the briefest second. "What?"

"I thought you knew. One of your armorers, that Sloan fellow, tried to sneak planet-side in a lander. Seems he had some equipment he had slowly written off the books, mostly CASper parts, rifles, a couple of RAT suits, those sorts of things. He was going to fence them for a profit. One of your drop pilots, Kit, caught him. Yardley hit the roof. He's sentenced Sloan to thirty lashes tomorrow morning to be carried out by him."

Colt stared agog at the captain.

"Thought that would get your attention." Torres nodded sagely for a moment like a man sizing up a used flyer he might buy. "You're both young, Colt. Too young for the responsibility you've taken on. But you've got it. Yardley's learning, but he acts on impulse. You're the measured one. You're the one who should be in charge."

"Captain, like you said, I'm on the spectrum. I don't—"

"Those are just words head shrinks came up with to label people. Tell me something—what made you want to become a merc in the first place? Deep down."

Colt shrugged. "I always excelled in school. It was easy for me. My parents—they're tenured professors—taught me at home. I reached high school equivalency when I was ten. After my first day as a freshman, my mom took me aside and told me I would have to take a test to graduate, one to determine my fitness for off-world service."

"Your VOWs."

"Yep. Mom didn't give me many details. She said I shouldn't worry about them, that they didn't matter to the sort of academic I would become. My mom's warning about the VOWs made me curious. I read up on the tests. Even as a kid, I knew about the Four Horsemen and other famous mercs. I'd have to have been living in a bunker not to. Studying them taught me about military history all the way back to the Romans and the Greeks. It fascinated me. I couldn't get enough of it. And I knew, contrary to what my parents' desired, I wanted the best VOWs scores I could get." Colt stared at the chintzy carpet. "I guess that sounds pretty stupid—a kid wanting to play soldier."

Torres shook his head. "It's not stupid at all. Do you think Jim Cartwright was born a merc commander? The kid's just getting started. How about Sansar Enkh? Every soldier, every merc, every warrior in history started out the same way. They were all greenies with no idea what they were doing. You're in good company."

"But they didn't have my handicap."

"How do you know?" Torres lifted his eyebrows. "You don't. Colt, I've known mercs just like you—well, somewhat like you. Plenty of people in our business are a little..." Torres scrunched up his nose, searching for the right word.

"Awkward?"

"Yeah, awkward. But that doesn't stop them from being some of the best troopers I've had the pleasure to fight with. And, in some ways, it helps. They see things others miss."

"Yeah, because we're missing things others don't."

"Maybe," Torres said with a shrug. "But there's a difference between missing something and lacking it. Colt, you're a good commander on the field, and believe it or not, in the office. I've watched you lead through Yard. You need to learn how to lead without him."

"How am I supposed to do that when I can't talk in front of people?"

Torres grinned. "Now you're asking the right question, and I might just have an answer. Have you ever heard of the OODA loop?"

* * * * *

Chapter Eleven

Yardley paced across his office aboard *Uncanny*, turned, and paced back. It was a short walk, but he was quickly turning it into a five mile trek. "I didn't know what to do, okay? We had just gotten you and the rest of the troopers back from the surface, and I had Vilo Beresk authorities calling me every minute asking who was going to pay for their damaged property, then this whole Sloan thing hit me in the face."

"I get that." Colt kept his voice level. That had been one of the first things his dad had taught him as a kid. Control your tone unless you want to make an upset person unreasonable. It was a constant battle inside Colt's head, since his immediate reaction to any social situation amounted to fight or flight. "But I don't think a public whipping is the right answer. Do you?"

Yardley ground his teeth for a moment, still pacing, his long strides cut short to make the walk last longer. "Part of me says no, but a bigger part of me wants to rip Sloan's back to shreds. He stole our equipment, Colt. Equipment we need to pay our debts, or Mountside's going to make us perpetual servants."

"I know that, but more importantly, so does Sloan."

Yardley came to an abrupt stop. "You spoke to him?"

Colt nodded. "I was just in the brig. He's scared to death."

"Good, he should be!" Yardley slammed an open palm down on his desk with a resounding SMACK. "He put us all in danger."

"So did we, Yard." Colt forced himself to look the colonel in the face. Even with someone he knew well, it took great effort, but he managed it.

"That's different. We made a mistake contracting with Renvis. Sloan intentionally tried to steal money from the company."

"Do you know how many kids Sloan has back in Chicago?"

Yardley looked taken aback by the seemingly off track question. "No."

"Seven. His wife works, but they depend on the credits he sends home. He's staff, but he was a student with FMT three years ago. He's carrying about as much debt as any of us, and he's got a big family to feed."

"And we cut off his pay." Yard looked thoughtful.

Colt nodded.

The vehemence had left Yardley's eyes, but something made of steel remained. "That's no excuse for what he did."

"Yes, it is." Colt rose from the visitor's chair and, keeping his eyes fixed on the point where Yardley's nose met his brow, he moved in front of the much taller colonel. "That's the thing you and I can't really comprehend. We don't know what it's like to have other people to take care of, not like that. I'm not saying Sloan had the right to steal from the company, and he certainly deserves punishment, but whipping him like a dog isn't the answer. It will weaken your command. Who wants to work for a maniac who whips his employees?"

"He's not just an employee. He's a merc. He's a trooper." Yardley looked as if he might say more, but he lost steam.

"Yep, but he's not property. Isn't that what you and I are trying to avoid, letting any of our people become property?"

Yardley let out a heavy sigh. He seemed to deflate as the air rushed out of him. He pulled out his office chair and flopped into it. "So, what do we do? You say I'll look weak if I go through with it, but won't I look just as weak if I rescind my order?"

"No. You'll look like a leader who corrected a rash decision."

Yardley tilted his head to one side. "What's gotten into you? You're gone for three days, then you come back all...I don't know, assertive. I thought Captain Torres advised you to stop telling me how to run the company."

Colt detected no animosity in Yardley's words or tone. In the past, he had made mistakes reading people, but he had spent a lot of time in the colonel's company, and he felt he knew Yard's genuine curiosity when he heard it. Otherwise, he might have clammed up. It was what his traitorous brain wanted him to do. He fought the urge. He had never had trouble talking to Yard, and he wasn't about to start now. "Torres told me I should intervene."

"Didn't he say he was done helping us?" Yard folded his arms across his big chest. "I'm not sure I trust the guy. He already tricked me out of a CASper."

"If by tricked you mean won fair and square when you and I made a stupid decision, you're absolutely right. The man knows more than us, Yard, and that proves it."

"He works for Mountside."

"His company has a contract with Mountside. That doesn't make him their employee."

"Mountside wants us to fail, so it's in his interest to see that happen." Yardley sat forward as if to punctuate his point. "His advice is suspect in my book."

"You think stopping us from publicly beating our best armorer is bad advice?" Colt once again met Yard's eyes. Now, it was the colonel's turn to look away.

"No. But that doesn't mean Torres isn't scheming to get something from us. Maybe he has his sights set on taking FMT for himself. You ever think of that?"

"If so, I can't see how giving good advice would be the right course of action." Colt held up a hand to forestall whatever Yard was about to say and consulted his pinplants. "If we want to know what Torres wants, let's ask him. I invited him to join us, and he's here."

Colt opened the office door just as Torres was about to ring the doorbell.

"That's not ominous," the tall captain said as he sauntered into the room with his NCO counterpart, Staff Sergeant Mona Flowers, trailing behind. "You track me all the time?"

"It's our ship." Yardley sat up straighter in his chair and pointedly did not stand to greet the newcomers.

"I only track people when I'm expecting them," Colt said, ignoring Yardley's challenge. "Won't you sit down?" He gestured toward the room's small couch, a twin to the one in his quarters.

"Colt, what is this about?" Yardley didn't try to hide the suspicion in his voice as the captain and sergeant sat.

"To paraphrase an old military adage, it's about getting our asses out of a crack." Colt kept his eyes on Yard to avoid looking at Sergeant Flowers. Although she was far too old for him, she was pretty on a level he had rarely seen outside vid movies. She made his voice want to flee. "The captain and I had a long discussion this morning about a lot of things."

"I'm beginning to see that." Yardley looked decidedly uncomfortable as his gaze flicked from Colt to their visitors and back. There was some mistrust, but also some wonder in Yardley's eyes, probably because he couldn't believe he was hearing Colt speak out loud in mixed company.

"We need to make some changes around here, Yard." Colt's throat threatened to tighten up. Thinking about losing his voice was making it happen. He swallowed hard and stammered, "I brought Torres and Flowers here to help."

At this, Flowers turned a steely gaze on her captain. "Sir, I'm with Yardley. What's all this about?"

"I'm sure you've noticed, Sergeant, this outfit isn't functioning at its highest efficiency. I've decided to give Colonel Yardley and Lieutenant Colonel Maier a little advice."

Flowers's eyes went from steely to round in a picosecond. "Permission to speak freely, sir?"

"Yes, Sergeant."

"Are you sure that's a good idea, sir?"

Colt noted Flower's subtle inflection on the word sir. She punctuated it with just enough poison to make it sting, but not nearly enough for her captain to call her out on it for anything approaching insubordination.

"As a matter of fact, Mona, I think it's a terrible idea. Our clients wouldn't appreciate it, and if Major Zuckerman catches wind of it, I'll probably be out of Triple T on my ear."

"So we're doing this because…?"

"Because I can't not help." Torres looked disgusted with himself. "Watching these guys flail around in the dark is eating the core right out of my heart. You've got to be feeling the same way, watching the noncoms. I know you. You're dying to help as much as I am."

Flowers stared at her commanding officer for the better part of ten seconds, her lips pursed, before she sighed. "Yes, but that doesn't mean we should."

"Nope, it doesn't. And if you want to recuse yourself from this right now, maybe even put me on report for doing it, go ahead. I won't hold it against you."

Flowers looked at Colt, who managed to hold her gaze for a moment before he had to look at the floor. So much for his new-found bravery. She turned to Yardley and sighed again. "No, sir. You're right. Watching what's happening here is rough. People are going to die if someone doesn't step up. I'll stay. But I don't like it."

"Duly noted, Sergeant."

"What are we doing that's so terrible?" Yardley's expression had darkened as the two spoke.

"Not terrible," Torres said. "But you're missing some of the fundamentals—basic things that make the difference between a successful merc company and a disjointed bunch of jackoffs who get themselves killed the first time they face real battle."

Yardley sat forward and placed his arms on the desk like a man leaning over a precipice, his face set in a near snarl. "Like what?"

"To begin with, you still haven't chosen a top." Captain Torres looked wholly unimpressed by the young colonel's bluster. "You wouldn't have this problem with Sloan if you had taken my advice. You need a top non-commissioned officer to oversee your noncom troopers. Same goes for your officer corps. You've got great people, folks who are committed to FMT and its mission to clear your collective debt, but even the most enthusiastic people need someone to point the way forward—someone to check their azimuth every once in a while. Otherwise, you end up with a ship full of self-starters running in different directions and accomplishing nothing."

"We got here, didn't we?" Yardley spread his arms.

"Sure, but it took your crew ten days to break orbit and reach the stargate at Zion. An efficient merc company would have done it in two, three tops. And you only made it because you happened to install a competent ship's captain, but he had to spend all his time managing every detail of the lift."

Yardley started to retort, but Colt cut him off. "Do you have suggestions about who to appoint?"

A ghost of a smile touched Captain Torres' lips. They both knew he had suggestions. "On your org chart, Colt is the executive officer or chief of staff. That's fine for his rank, but I don't think it makes the best use of his skill set, not at the moment anyway. I suggest you move him to your personal staff, Colonel. Most commanders have two or three officers on their personal staff that help make decisions, pick up threads that have been dropped, and generally work as second sets of eyes and hands when it comes to day-to-day operations."

To Colt's surprise, Yardley didn't immediately balk at the idea. He furrowed his brow. "So, pretty much the job Colt's already doing?"

"Right. Just make it official."

"I guess you've got someone you think would make a good XO in his place?" Yardley asked.

"Feliks Petrov," Torres said without hesitation. "I've watched your company commanders at work; Petrov is the best. He's always got his people in order, at least as well as he can at his level, though he could use some noncom help. But the guy's organized, and he knows how to deal with people. In meetings with his fellow commanders, he tends to take the lead, and the others let him, even if they don't realize they're doing it."

Colt couldn't disagree with Torres' assessment. Petrov had been a good officer for the three years Colt had known him, and from everything Colt had seen, Petrov's troopers not only respected him, they truly enjoyed working for him.

Yardley was nodding. "Okay. I agree. Petrov's a good choice."

"As for your top, which I think is an even bigger necessity right now, I'll defer to Sergeant Flowers. She's been in the ranks."

Flowers tapped her chin. She still looked reluctant, but also thoughtful. "The captain's right, you've got some great enlisted working for you. Some should have come in as officers, though that would have been a horrible waste of technical expertise." She grinned at Captain Torres who nodded slightly. "Your highest ranked noncom is Master Sergeant Richard Finnegan, but if you want my honest opinion, the guy's sort of a dope—a real plodder. Your best choice for top is Nichol Levin. She's a sergeant first class working in life support, and she's the reason we're breathing right now. She's got that place running at peak efficiency, because she's great at managing her people—and I mean all her people, those under her *and* the LT who thinks he's in charge."

A hint of a smile curled one side of Torres' mouth. "I had someone else in mind, but forget it. She's your top, boys. Send someone to grab her and see to it that she's first sergeant before tomorrow. And while you're at it, bump Petrov to major. That will go a long way toward clearing up the confusion you're seeing in your ranks."

"Who's going to train them?" Yardley asked. "Belknap never gave those positions to students. Cadre members held them."

"You train them. You and Colt." Torres eyed Flowers for a fraction of a second. "And maybe the sergeant and I will lend a hand once in a while. Maybe. But really, it's up to you to set the standards for what you expect from your staff. They'll get it, or you counsel them until they do. They take too long, you replace them. Good news is, your people generally know their business. Give them responsibility for their own little slice of the enterprise and see if they don't perform some magic for you. You'll be amazed."

"But if we field promote them, increase their rank outside the normal promotion cycle, won't other people get jealous?" Colt asked.

"How did you obtain rank before?" Flowers asked.

"The cadre members, I guess you'd call them Belknap's military instructors, made us stand before review boards every semester," Yardley said. "They based promotions on our performance in the field—a lot of that was simulator time, but some was real-life mission time—and on peer reviews by senior students. If the cadre thought we were performing exceptionally well, they'd promote us a little faster."

"And now?" Flowers lifted her eyebrows.

Colt and Yardley looked at each other.

"We haven't discussed it." Colt's face turned red with shame when he realized neither of them had considered promotions in the ranks. They hadn't had time with all the other details they had been handling.

"The system Belknap implemented is solid." Torres nodded as he spoke. "Sounds a lot like the one we use in Triple T. I say keep it in place. Maybe Flowers and I can review it for you, see where you might want to tweak it. As for people getting jealous over field promotions, that's always going to happen. The key is not to sell the changes that way. They're not promotions. They're part of a top down reorg. And based on some of the talk Flowers has heard from your troopers, now is the best time for that."

Sergeant Flowers looked at her captain in surprise. "Sir, are you sure we should share that?"

"I'm not ordering you to do anything that makes you uncomfortable, Mona," Torres said. "But I promised Colt a day's help, and I'd be remiss if I didn't share what you told me."

Flowers stared at Torres for a long moment, reluctance returning to her expression. Finally, she sighed and turned toward Colt and Yardley. "Maybe you already know this. Maybe you don't. But, there are those in the ranks questioning your positions as commander and exec. People are asking why you got to take over the company. They're questioning the chain of command, because it was instituted by Belknap and his people. Is it legitimate? And Colt, you're one of the youngest mercs here. Some of your subordinates are in their thirties. They came to FMT after leaving the civilian workforce, and now they're taking orders from a sixteen year old. After what happened on Vilo Beresk..."

"I look like I'm incompetent," Colt finished for her, his heart a lump of crystal in his chest.

Flowers nodded.

"That's why you need new contracts." Torres caught Colt's gaze. His expression seemed to say, *hold fast, don't let memories bog you down, keep moving forward.*

"We're doing our best," Yardley said. "Weep is already combing through her contacts for new ones."

Sergeant Flowers wrinkled her nose. "You trust the Flatar after what happened with Renvis?"

"Weep's assured us she didn't know Renvis would turn like that, and I believe her," Yardley looked surly, his cheeks growing red. "If she had been in on it, she could have frozen our assets—she has full access to all our financial data. It wasn't her fault, and it certainly wasn't Colt's."

"I never said—"

Torres held up a hand to stop Flowers. "None of that matters. I'm not talking about those kinds of contracts, though you need those too. I'm talking about new company-employee contracts."

"I've heard rumbles from people, including some of your higher-ranked troopers, about taking a vote to see who should run FMT. They say they don't work for you, because their contracts were with Fulcrum Mercenary Training. They never signed on with Fulcrum Mercenary Tactics."

Yardley shot to his feet, his face flushed red, his brows drawn down almost into a V. "That's ridiculous! You don't run a merc company on votes."

"Technically, they're right. We don't own the crews' contracts," Colt said. He felt like someone who just realized his true insignificance in the universe.

"These people act like we owe them something," Yardley said. "But we're the ones who kept them free when Mountside came calling. They'd all be slaves if it wasn't for us."

"Yes, they would. And it won't hurt to remind them of that when you draw up new contracts for them," Torres said.

"Will they go for that?" Colt asked. "What if they don't?" A swell of fear washed over his face, making it burn. "What if they fight?"

Torres reclined on the couch, smiling confidently. "Some may try to fight, but not enough to matter. In the end, you're going to give them a better chance to, how did you put it, get their collective asses out of a crack. Show them you have a plan and the means to implement it. And pay them. You were stupid to take their pay away."

Yardley shook his head. "We can't afford it."

"You can't not," Torres said. "This is a merc company, not some state-based military on the dole. Mercs can be loyal, they'll kill and die for a cause, but they don't work for free. It's not in their nature. You can tout paying off debt as reimbursement for their work, but that sort of agreement doesn't last. They need to see some income. Sloan proved that."

"And you can afford it," Flowers put in. "You've got everything you need to run a successful company."

"Everything but experience," Colt said.

"Everything but paying clients," Yardley added.

Torres pursed his lips and stared at the floor for a moment. "Mona, you're going to have my scalp for this."

"Sir?" The NCO looked wary.

When Torres lifted his gaze, Colt could have sworn the temperature in the room dropped three degrees. "We're going to Karma-IV."

* * * * *

Chapter Twelve

"How'd we do?" Yardley eyed the gathered company commanders and non-merc department directors led by the newly promoted Major Feliks Petrov.

"To be honest, sir, better than I expected," Petrov said, glancing down at the slate in his hands. "We only had nine major dissenters, and all but three eventually signed their new contracts. The three were Corporal Echols and Corporal Beatty from Bravo Company, second and third platoons respectively, and Lieutenant Vosk from Charlie Company."

"We've stripped them of their ranks and required they sign passenger agreements that restrict them from sensitive parts of the ship." First Sergeant Nichol Levin maintained a strict level of professionalism that didn't fool Colt. He knew she was turning cartwheels inside her head over her new rank and responsibility. And her enthusiasm was catching.

All over the ship, troopers were abuzz with details of the reorg and the new compensation plan. To pay the crew, Colt had proposed spreading shares of the newly reformed FMT among the entire battalion. It wasn't exactly a novel idea, most merc companies worked that way, but Colt proposed a limited existence for FMT's current incarnation. While the Mormons still owned the ship and all its material goods, the crew owned the enterprise, but that would last only until the end of their Mountside contract, and much of what they made would go toward that debt.

The idea harkened back to ancient whaler days. Crewmembers would earn a salary based on their rank and time in FMT, but seventy percent of it would go toward paying off their collective debt. Compared to what most merc companies paid competent mercs, the remaining income wasn't much, but everyone agreed it was far better than nothing.

Yardley nodded, a look of relief on his face. "I worried we might lose half our strength."

"I think opening the books to the battalion went a long way toward avoiding that situation." Petrov glanced around at the company commanders, who all nodded.

"Definitely," Levin said. "Our noncoms aren't stupid. They know we have a better chance of paying off Mountside working together. I'm hoping the three holdouts will come around before we reach Karma-IV. I hate to think of them trying to earn enough on their own."

"Or trying to make a run for it." Yardley looked pained. "I wouldn't want to live life on the run. Hopefully they'll see reason."

"I'll work on them, sir."

Captain Torres, leaning unobtrusively against the far wall, grinned ever so slightly. Colt could guess what the big merc was thinking. Levin was already earning her promotion. Colt agreed.

"On to other business." Yardley's eyes unfocused momentarily as he checked the notes on his pinplants. "Right. That mess I got us into on Vilo Beresk. We earned back a few credits after we proved the fight wasn't our fault and local authorities liquidated Renvis's ship. But it wasn't enough for us to break even. Weep, how bad was it?"

The Flatar turned her drone platform to face the gathered leaders. She wore a red dress with a small gold brooch shaped like a star with many rays flaring from it. She looked quite fetching despite the grim set of her jaw. Colt had a hard time judging human expressions, let alone those of aliens, though his implants helped. But even he recognized the look of doom worn by the diminutive accountant.

"It's dismal," she said. "We've depleted what little cash reserves we had to make the trip to Karma-IV. So we're flat broke. And with the decision to pay the crew, our timetable is in the crapper. I have serious doubts as to whether we can pay off Mountside within a year. We need contracts, preferably more than one at a time, and we need them now."

"I don't see any problem breaking out platoons to work short-term contracts, but we'll have a transportation issue." Yardley spread his hands on the table. "We've only got four dropships; we're not going to be able to work more than a couple of contracts at a time."

"We could negotiate transport with potential clients." With her previous work detail complete and the advent of the new pay scale, Captain Sampson seemed much happier, though her tone was still cool when she addressed Yard.

"That's not how it usually works," Weep said. "But it's not a bad idea. Someone wants mercs badly enough, maybe they'll be willing to pay for lift."

"But that cuts into our profits," Catlett said.

"Better than having people sitting idle on the ship." Yardley lifted his chin and looked at Weep. "Let's look into it when we reach Karma."

"Will do."

"Anyone else have any ideas how we can maximize profits?" Yard looked around the table. "Anyone got a rich aunt or uncle who needs a little double expense garrison duty?"

"I've got a cousin back in Detroit who runs a used flyer lot," said Captain Terrell Butler with a flash of his dazzling, white smile. "I'll bet he'd love to have a CASper in one of his adverts."

Yardley chuckled with the group. "If we get back to Earth, we'll give your cousin a call. Anyone else?"

Weep looked around the table several times then raised her platform a little higher. "If none of the captains is going to suggest it, I feel I must. Why don't we go back to the sort of work FMT performed under Belknap?"

Yardley's smile melted away in an instant. "You mean working for crooks to protect stolen goods?"

"We made credits doing it. A lot of credits."

Several of the captains nodded, though Colt was glad to see Major Petrov and 1SG Levin didn't join them.

Yardley shook his head but, to everyone's surprise, it was Colt who spoke.

"How'd that work out for Belknap?" He looked around at the company commanders and department directors. "And how'd it work out for us with Renvis? No. We've already addressed this. We're taking Mercenary Guild approved contracts only from now on."

"Very well," Weep said, nodding at Colt.

Torres smiled.

"Here's an idea," Yardley said, "let's ask the crew. Someone's bound to think of something we haven't."

"I'll handle that, sir," Levin said.

Not for the first time, Colt felt a warm sensation trickle up his neck when he looked at Levin. She wasn't as classically beautiful as Alice Onishi, nor did she possess the galactic good looks of Staff Sergeant Flowers, but her midnight black hair and olive skin coupled with her no-nonsense attitude made her far more attractive than either of the other two. He had first noticed it the day she took charge in the mess. She intrigued him as much intellectually as physically. But he had to remember his rank and position. Crushing on one of his subordinates was highly frowned upon in the leadership books Captain Torres had Colt reading every night.

On the other hand, none of the people who wrote those tomes were sixteen.

"In the meantime, Lieutenant Colonel Maier is going to brief you on our weapons stores and this cycle's training plan." Yardley turned an impassive gaze on Colt, though there was no mistaking the hint of anxiety in the colonel's eyes.

The two of them had rehearsed this part of the brief for an hour before anyone showed up, and Colt had felt ready. Of course, that had been before a dozen sets of eyes had zeroed in on him, two of those belonging to Levin. His heart rate increased, and his palms instantly began sweating.

Colt drew a deep breath, and let it out slowly. He remembered Captain Torres patiently explaining the centuries old method for breaking down problems into manageable components, the OODA loop, which stood for Observe, Orient, Decide, and Act. The big merc thought it an excellent way for Colt to combat his anxiety, since it would allow him to focus on solving his problems rather than worrying about what those listening to him thought. Concentrating, he sought to understand the goal at hand—he needed to brief his people—and saw almost instantly how anxiety had nothing to do with that. Once he dissected the problem, the solution appeared obvious. He lifted his gaze to his audience.

"Mercs, here's how we're going to proceed..."

* * *

Colt tried not to stare at the crowds of aliens milling past him on the broad thoroughfare. He, Weep, and Yardley had been following Captain Torres through the pedestrian walkways of the Karma-IV orbital transfer station for more than an hour, and he was still seeing new species at every turn. The station's spin ring seemed to go on forever. If he concentrated, he could see the far distant street curving upward, the slope appearing gentler than that of any ring he had ever ventured onto before.

"Captain, why aren't we headed to Peepo's?" Yardley asked as their group skirted around six Tortantulas conversing in the middle of the street.

"Couple of reasons. First of all, I'm not exactly famous, but there's a chance I'll run into someone I know there. I don't want to be spotted in some place like Peepo's if I'm going to help you guys out. And then there's your rep."

"What rep?" Yardley asked.

"I figure, with Belknap's tendency to take unregistered contracts, FMT is either known for underhanded dealings or not known at all." Torres turned right, leaving the main road and the bulk of the foot traffic behind. "Either way, we're better off cutting deals at a smaller venue. Make a name for yourself, a good name, then take your chances in Peepo's. Right now, you'd get eaten alive in there with or without my help."

"Just as well," Weep said from her floating platform. "There are definitely some unsavory characters who frequent Peepo's that I'd rather not run into."

Fewer people walked along the narrower path Torres had led them onto. The buildings, while just as tall as those on the main road, looked seedier than the ones they had left behind. Same went for the crowd. Colt purposefully did not finger the C-Tech XT-70 holstered at his side despite the feeling of unease that had him looking around for danger. Yardley must have felt it too. He reached for his weapon when an orange, bipedal alien that looked like a walking mound of cotton candy skirted past them.

"Careful, Yard." Torres spoke quietly. "Not everyone here is a merc, but according to the numbers, there are a lot of us. You draw that death stick—even make a move to—on the wrong creature, and we're all dead."

"Sorry. I'm feeling jumpy."

The streetlights had dimmed appreciably in the last couple of blocks. Several looked like they had been shot out and never replaced.

"Are we supposed to be here?" Colt asked, trying to keep the fear out of his voice.

"'Supposed to be' is a relative term. Follow me." Torres climbed a set of stairs and pushed through a heavy, old-fashioned door. "Welcome to The Merc's Delight."

Rows of heavy tables, no two quite alike, lined the room, and sets of comfortably padded benches filled the corners. A long bar opposite the door ran the length of the room. Despite the relative quiet of the street outside, The Merc's Delight was filled nearly to capacity with aliens, most of them from merc races. The smell of exotic spices made Colt's mouth water and nearly overpowered the stench of so many bodies stuffed into such a tight space.

An electronic sign, written in what Colt's pinplants told him was Oogar, stood just inside the door. It advised patrons to seat themselves, and a waiter would attend them shortly.

"Should we just do this on the local net?" Colt could feel eyes of every description flitting over him like bugs. His stomach felt queasy.

"We could, but not if we want a good deal." Torres scanned the room, looking for an open table. He spotted one and started in that direction, the others following. "You want a high-paying contract with a reputable client? You go through a pit. It's all about meeting someone face to face."

"If they've got a face." Yardley looked askance at a being two tables over that was roughly human-shaped except in place of its head rose what looked like a lobster on a flagpole covered in red and black mottled skin.

"Don't piss anyone off by staring, kid." Torres ushered them into a booth with a Tri-V mounted in the center. Pages of text scrolled languidly across the screen—advertisements for merc contracts.

A particularly large Oogar stood behind the bar polishing a crystal mug. The bear-like alien's purple fur had faded over the years. The hairs on the back of his neck and poking out from his sleeves shone a ghostly white. He wore an old-fashioned eyepatch made of brown leather and a camouflage suit.

"Welcome," he rumbled, his voice as deep as an ocean. He put down his mug and eyed the newcomers. "We don't get Humans in here too often. Are you mercs or food?"

The Oogar's comment must have been funny, because it elicited bouts of laughter from everyone within earshot.

Torres smiled, showing his teeth. "Some people mistake Humans for food, it's true. But they don't usually live to rate the meal."

All fell quiet in the bar as heads turned to watch. A lump of ice seemed to drop into Colt's stomach. He wished he hadn't already taken a seat. It was easier to draw his handgun standing, but this way he could hide the fact that he had it halfway out of its holster under the table.

The silence seemed to stretch out forever as everyone in the bar prepared for bedlam, but then the Oogar began to laugh. He opened his wide chops like a braying donkey, spittle clinging in filmy ropes to his long teeth, and bellowed until the walls shook.

"I always heard Humans were tough for shrimps!" The Oogar slapped the bar with one clawed hand. "Welcome, mercenaries. I am

Be'klat, owner of The Merc's Delight. You will have a round of Flatar ale on me."

"Thank you!" Weep bounced on her platform. "It's been a while since I had a brew from home."

"I've always said you little rodents were good for two things—you can shoot, and you sure as the nine hells make some fine spirits." Be'klat made short work of delivering the promised drinks. He moved with a grace that belied his size and his generous gut. The Flatar ale tasted like pecans, sweet figs, and smoke. Colt loved it, though he made himself sip the stuff. The only time he'd drunk alcohol was when he broke into his dad's liquor cabinet to impress a friend. They had gotten so drunk, Colt had vomited all over his mother's hand-woven Indian rug. Not a good day.

"I take it you are in the market for a contract, yes?" Be'klat slapped Torres on the back in a friendly gesture that almost snapped the human's back, though the captain didn't flinch.

"Yes we are. Got any leads for us?"

"How big is your company?"

Torres glanced around the room. "We can field over five hundred mercs if needed, but that's mostly in powered armor. We have fewer CASPers."

Be'Klat scratched his furry chin. "I might have just the client you're looking for. He's been in here several days in a row, but hasn't had any luck. Most of my clientele run small merc outfits. He's looking for more numbers than they can front. Maybe you've got what he wants."

The Oogar snapped his claws several times. "Hey, Pendal. Yes, you. Get your wiry ass over here. I might have something for you."

Colt's eyes widened as a short, four-armed alien from a race he had never seen before approached them from the other side of the bar. The thin being wore a dark gray military-style uniform that bore no badges or insignia. A cape made of fine cloth like silk dangled from his shoulders, and a hood of the same material covered his head, which it threw back with its top set of hands.

"Yes?" it asked, its voice a whisper. "What are these?"

"Humans." Be'Klat gestured at them. "They're small like you, but savage. Their leader says they can fulfill your contract."

Yardley looked mildly insulted when Be'Klat tagged Torres as their leader, but at a gesture from Colt, he wisely kept his mouth shut.

"Hmm." The Pendal, whose eyes were set on either side of its head, with a third one above its mouth turned its neck to better view its prospective employees. "Savage you say? Can you fight?"

Torres pushed a chair out for the Pendal. "Yes. We can fight. The question is, can you pay?"

* * * * *

Chapter Thirteen

Colt was in the simulator with two squads from Delta Company when Captain Zorn informed him they were entering the orbit of their destination planet.

"I'll be right there." Colt switched to the simulator's squad channel. "Sorry folks, duty calls. Lieutenant Gibson, take command."

"Roger that, sir."

"Sure you've got to leave right this second, sir?" Sergeant Daniel Billings from second squad charged ahead of Colt to take on a Tortantula-mounted Flatar. He took one laser blast for his effort, which did negligible damage according to Colt's Tri-V. In return, Billings wasted both the rider and its mount in less than two seconds with his right arm minigun. "We haven't cleared this side of the mountain."

"Gibby will get you there," Colt said. "I've got to arrange for us to earn some credits."

A chorus of cheers went up across the comm from the combined squads.

"Yeah, get us paid, sir. I've got this," Gibson said.

"Signing off." Colt powered down his sim pod, unhooked the links to his pinplants and his restraining harnesses, and opened the cockpit.

The sound of active sim pods—whirring gears and pneumatic actuators extending and retracting—made him grin. His units were taking their training seriously, and their stats showed it. Colt took every opportunity he got to train with the various FMT companies. Relying on what Captain Torres had shown him about proper decision making and how to break every facet of life down into manageable steps, Colt had increased his combat efficiency by twenty percent, though Torres was always quick to point out those numbers came from a simulator. No matter how well the sims mimicked real life, and FMT's sim-pods were perfect as far as Colt was concerned, they couldn't provide a real-world experience. They weren't life and death. Colt saw the captain's point, but that didn't dull his sense of accomplishment. A month earlier, he couldn't speak over a common broadcast channel.

Colt launched himself toward the ceiling, then, moving from handhold to handhold, pulled his weightless body across the simulator bay to the exit. After four years of training aboard *Uncanny Valley*, zero-g felt as natural to Colt as standing dirtside. He exulted in the freedom of flying, and often made a game of timing his travel from one destination in the ship to another. The trip from the sim bay to the main airlock normally took him seven minutes, mostly because he was forced to scamper up—or was it down?—two floors in addition to several long corridors to reach it. Today he set a new record according to his pinplants: six minutes forty-two seconds.

Yardley and Captain Torres looked up when Colt shot through the bay door like a space marine.

Torres' hand flew to the GP-90 at his hip, but Yardley just grinned.

"New record?" The colonel, who floated languidly next to the sealed airlock doors, lifted an eyebrow toward Colt.

"Better by fifteen seconds."

Torres rolled his eyes but said nothing.

"Good, our employers are waiting on us." Yard keyed a code into the panel next to the door, and it slipped open with a hiss. The three of them floated inside, waited for the interior to normalize pressure, then went through the next door into *Osmosis*, the smallest of FMT's four dropships.

Malfren Kaz, the Pendal who had hired FMT on Karma, sat in one of the spare strap-down seats near the command console, behind the pilot. The hooded alien waggled his head at the newcomers—his race's version of a friendly nod—then turned, so he could look at them with one of his side-mounted eyes.

"Sorry for keeping you waiting." Yard pulled himself into a rear seat, leaving room for Torres and Colt to join him.

"No wait. We've only been here a short time."

Next to him, also strapped down in the microgravity environment, sat his business partner, a Zuparti named Vernox. The Zuparti looked somewhat like ermines or weasels to Humans, with downy fur covering their bodies and large dark eyes affixed to bullet-shaped heads. The Zuparti were known for being nervous, and Vernox was no exception. In fact, Colt thought him a prime example.

"It's fine. It's perfectly fine!" Vernox squeaked, nodding his non-existent chin in what he probably thought was a Human gesture, though his bout of nerves made it look spastic.

"We ready for drop, sir?" Kelly Anderson turned the pilot's seat around to face her passengers.

"Let's get this over with, Kit." Yardley fastened the five-point harness across his chest as did Colt and Torres.

Kit called in her departure to *Uncanny,* then blew the seal on the airlock. A blast of the ship's precious and highly pressurized air kicked *Osmosis* clear of her mother, and Kit fired up the engines to alter their trajectory. In moments, the sound of atmosphere rushing around the ship was accompanied by the familiar shaking of reentry turbulence.

The distant curvature of a green and brown planet fringed with the orange light created as the ship sliced into the atmosphere was displayed on the dropship's main viewer. According to the briefing put together by FMT's intelligence division, supplemented by data from Malfren and Vernox, the planet bore the unfortunate name of Spimu. To Colt, it sounded like something you did in the toilet after catching an alien virus. Though the world boasted no intelligent aboriginal species, it had been settled for almost a millennia by dozens of different races who, surprisingly, got along well enough to form a loosely organized global government. Loosely, because most of the power lay in regional sectors where local municipalities ran things as they saw fit.

Despite its thousand-year history of space-borne settlement, large sections of Spimu remained unspoiled. Most of its population centered around three major spaceports and a smattering of cities focused on intra- and extra-system trade. This made the place perfect for entrepreneurs like Malfren and Vernox, who had spent the last thirty years building a sizeable trading co-op that now serviced three star systems.

Unfortunately, that same ecosystem attracted unsavory characters who thrived on bilking honest businesses, especially those run by peaceful races who didn't have the stomach for battle.

Not that Mal and Vern were idiots. They had hired what they thought were competent mercenary crews to safeguard their fleet of trading vessels, and they had kept them well-paid for years.

Then came the Ten Whispers.

According to the intel Colt's people could dig up, they were old-Earth mafia, a merc company, and a cult of personality rolled into one. They were led by a Besquith. The Besquith were a werewolf-looking mercenary species known throughout the galaxy for their ferocity. Covered in hair and roughly seven feet tall—though some grew even larger—the race reminded Colt of the nastier class of Hindu demons, the sort rumored to frequent battlefields in search of flesh to devour. With multiple rows of overly large teeth and piercing black eyes like ball bearings, they were everything nature had taught humans to fear.

Not all Besquith became mercenaries. Many became traders or business moguls. Regardless of their chosen profession, they tended toward aggressive, which meant they produced their share of tyrants, and Lyret T'erimez certainly fit that category. Suave, intelligent, and by all accounts a particularly adroit strategist when it came to building his personal fiefdom, Lyret was something of a pirate prince—an unexpected departure from the usual Besquith leadership. He insulated himself with loyal, highly paid mercenaries trained in boarding operations and interdiction, but he was always careful to keep his criminal activities reasonably small lest he run afoul of one of the guilds or the Wathayat Trading Consortium.

That made Malfren and Vernox's trading co-op a prime target for the Ten Whispers. Rather than take several of their ships by force, Lyret had insinuated his people into the merc companies guarding them. Over the course of three years, those forces had been replaced one by one, until Lyret owned them outright. At that point, they simply seized five of the fleet's ten bulk freighters, executed their crews, and brought their shipments to Spimu.

Mal and Vern had hired a private investigator to track their stolen goods and, once they had located them, decided to take their chances on hiring an independent merc company to help get them back. Colt prayed FMT could do the job. If not, and they lost this contract, FMT would fail.

The rumble of reentry settled into the smooth roar of the air rushing across the lander's hull as the turbulence abated. Kit rolled the ship west toward a sprawling spaceport called Unity City in the mixed patois of Spimu's many races. Not as big as Houston, the industrialized planetary capitol was nonetheless impressive with its thousand story, self-contained megaliths and rushing flyer traffic. Kit eased their ship into the flow and headed for the largest of the city's steel and plastic buildings, the Unity City government offices. She landed on the pad and opened the ship's main hatch.

"We've got this spot for about two hours." Kit preceded the group outside into the city's humid afternoon. "Any longer than that, and I'll have to lift and come back for you later. This place is busy as hell."

"I'm impressed you got a spot at all." Yardley stepped down from the ship and gazed around at the thick flyer traffic buzzing past them. They stood on the two hundred twenty-first floor of the government building. Even this high up, ships filled the air.

"I didn't," Kit said, as she guided weasel-faced Vernox down the ship's steps. The little alien looked around as though he expected an assassin to dive at him from behind one of the seven ships parked around them. "It was First Sergeant Levin who bullied the authorities into getting us on the docket. That girl's a phenom. Kudos on hiring a competent top."

"Thanks." Yardley flashed a reluctant grin at Torres who acted as if he hadn't heard the compliment.

"Thank you for the flight down," Malfren said, spinning all four of his hands in an elegant gesture of appreciation toward Kit, who nodded. He turned to the others. "We should be near the Mercenary Operations Oversight Court. Follow me."

The Human mercs shared worried looks as they followed their alien employers through a beautifully crafted steel and glass door into the planetary government building. The air inside was cool, but smelled of many races perspiring as they hurried about their business. A horse-like Equiri nearly barreled into them as they entered.

"Sorry! I'm late," it bellowed, as it clopped off down the hall.

"Drop me in a hot LZ with a thousand enemies screaming for my blood, and I won't feel half as uncomfortable as I do right now," Torres said as they progressed through the rushing crowd of aliens. "Nothing makes me jumpier than government. Except maybe big government."

"Look at them." Colt stared around in wonder. "They look, I don't know, frightened."

"Most probably are." Torres turned a corner and nearly ran into a Tortantula dressed in a black suit made of silk.

Colt had never seen one of the ten-legged creatures wearing anything other than body armor. He tried not to stare.

"You get this sort of government, and suddenly private citizens are jumping around to appease a bunch of faceless bureaucrats. They have to pay their property taxes on this date or plead with that court to build something on their own land. And it's all made-up nonsense."

"I don't know," Yardley said. "At least with government, you've got laws to protect you."

Torres lifted an eyebrow at him as if trying to judge whether he was joking. "What law keeps anyone from doing anything whenever they like?"

"The laws people set for themselves as a society."

"But do those laws stop pain? What's a law except an agreement? I've never seen an agreement that could stop bullets or nuclear strikes or even petty theft. Laws come into play after the bad guys are caught, when people have to decide how to treat them. Before that, they're as useless as a fart."

"We're in this building right now because of laws, so we're jumping through government hoops just like everyone else," Colt pointed out as they followed Malfren and Vernox through a door made of wood. An ornate plaque hanging on it proclaimed it the Spimu Mercenary Operations Oversight Court.

"Yeah, because we're playing nice." Torres gave him a meaningful look. "And I'm not really here, I'm just observing."

Colt agreed with the captain. He was eager to begin fulfilling the contract, but Spimu planetary law required all mercenary companies planning to conduct business of any kind on their soil to submit a full plan of operations, including estimated armaments, possible damage to planetary infrastructure, and statistical analysis of the likelihood of causing non-combatant injuries or death. The requirements were exhaustive. Not only that, the planet's Mercenary Operations Oversight Court required representatives to defend the plan in person before a judge. It was enough to make Colt consider backing out, but Yardley was there to do the talking, and FMT needed the credits.

They entered a short gallery with a smattering of chairs arranged in uniform rows facing a judicial bench that stood no less than two meters off the floor. A grossly overweight Gtandan dressed in a purple velvet robe sat behind it, listening to a MinSha plead its case for running a garrison operation to aid a local land baron.

"You are the...F-M-T group?" A lavender-skinned alien dressed in purple livery with a government badge over the breast pocket eyed Colt and the others.

"Yes." Yardley handed the court official his Universal Account Access Card (UAAC), pronounced Yack, and pressed a thumb to the thing's proffered slate.

"Very good. The judge is almost done with the current case."

As if on cue, the decidedly porcine judge snorted once at the MinSha and rang a bell, signaling that its request was approved. The enormous insectile mercenary nodded its thanks to the judge and lumbered from the room, opening up space for Colt and his group.

"I've read your plan of operations," the judge said without preamble once they had gathered beneath his bench. He cast a sour look at them, the corners of his jowly mouth turned down. "This is more than safeguarding equipment and facilities. You're planning a full scale assault on a private residence. This court exists to limit incursions by mercenary forces on our sovereign land and to protect our people from extralegal harm."

Vernox cowered under the judge's baleful glare, but Malfren straightened his shoulders and lifted his upper arms in a gesture that Colt's pinplants interpreted as pleading and a declaration of rightness.

"Honorable judge, our co-op was crippled when the Ten Whispers pirates made off with three-quarters of this year's shipments.

The loss forced us to lay off nearly half of our employees. We sought remedy for this theft through the government's Home Defense League, but they have done nothing but bury us in court orders and demands for redress. These pirates live in a veritable fortress. The defense forces want nothing to do with them, so they leave us to our own devices, the cowards."

Colt held his breath, and he felt Torres and Yardley stiffen next to him. The moment dragged on until he thought his chest might explode, then the judge threw his fat head back and laughed.

"A Pendal with a spine! Good for you. I like to see honest merchants standing up for their businesses. It means our economy is strong." The judge favored the Humans with a second, more calculating look. "You think you can unseat the Ten Whispers pirates? The Pendal is right. They have been a yarsin seed in the teeth of our defense forces for years. Too big to dislodge and too small for the Merchant Guild to worry about."

"We can, sir," Yardley said.

"Good enough. If anyone asks, I told you to be careful of the natural flora and fauna on that gods-cursed continent of Salva. Go. Have your fun." The judge rang the bell.

* * * * *

Chapter Fourteen

"Y ou ready?" Yardley asked over a private channel from his CASPer locked in its cradle across the dropship's bay. They had considered using a high altitude drop to deploy companies Alpha, Bravo, and part of Charlie to the surface, but eventually nixed the idea. None of their troopers, including Colt and Yard, had ever attempted that sort of thing outside a simulator. Doing it for the first time on an actual mission seemed overly risky.

"Yes." Colt scanned his Tri-V. All systems checked out. His CASPer was fueled, armed, and ready for combat.

"I want to say something, but I don't want it to be weird."

Colt's brows drew down. "Um, okay. Go ahead."

"You've been doing great lately."

"Uh...thanks, Yard."

"No, I mean it." Yardley sounded sincere, though strained. Neither of them ever complimented the other. It just wasn't done, or hadn't been until now. "I think whatever Torres has been teaching you is paying off. You're talking more, taking charge. It's good to see."

"You know the really strange thing about it?" Colt's cheeks were burning, but he ignored them. This was just Yardley. "It's leadership stuff, like how to make decisions in high pressure situations, and most of it's old—stuff military leaders have been preaching for centuries. But it's not just helping me understand how to lead people, it's giving me tools to cope with my problems."

"Like talking."

"Yeah. It's showing me how everything we experience, from how to run a tac team to what you should eat for breakfast, can be broken down into decision cycles. Applying that principle when dealing with people removes the pressure from social interaction. I don't think about failure or embarrassment, I focus on meeting end goals, and that allows me to speak freely."

"That sounds sort of cold, don't you think? Like, right now, you're trying to win some sort of game by speaking to me?"

Colt shrugged inside his CASPer though he knew Yardley couldn't see it. "In a way, yeah. I want you to understand what I'm doing. Even though I seem to be interacting with others the way normal people do, I'm going about it differently, though I doubt my expectations are really any different than anyone else's. Isn't everyone trying to get something out of every social interaction, even if it's just strengthening their bonds to other people?"

"I guess so, when you look at it that way. But it's not intentional."

"My way requires intention. I have to have a goal, or I fizzle out. I don't consider that calculating. I just...I don't know, work differently than most people. I want meaningful and fruitful relationships with the people around me. I simply have to remain aware of that goal to make it happen."

"Huh."

A warning claxon blared through the ship, and Colt's Tri-V switched to a radar feed from the tactical suite. Red icons sliced through the atmosphere on a collision course with FMT's three dropships. The smart missiles were boosting for orbit even as the ships hurtled toward land, making the real time display look as though it was sped up. Colt couldn't imagine trying to blast those deadly harpoons before they reached the ships. Fortunately, he didn't have to. He and his team had planned and prepared for this contingency.

"You called it; they didn't bother to check if we were friend or foe," Yardley said over their private channel.

"You'd think they would ask why mercs are dropping on them," Colt said.

As he watched, all three ships' forward-mounted lasers engaged the targets, slicing through their metallic hulls or detonating them on the fly. A series of spectacular explosions flashed in Spimu's upper atmosphere as the projectiles died.

Cheers erupted over the common channel. Cooped up in the transport bays, the mercs could do little but fret over air assaults. If one of the missiles got through they'd be powerless against it.

"Don't celebrate too soon," Yardley said dryly. "We're not on the ground yet."

"And there's a second volley headed our way." Kit sounded stressed.

A new contingent of red icons filled the screen, this one much broader than the last. Though FMT's dropships had basic energy shields, they would do little good in such an onslaught. Once again, they were forced to rely on point defense lasers and a smattering of interceptor missiles to stave off the attack. His heart raced.

Though his people's intelligence reports insisted the Ten Whispers pirates possessed considerable weapons systems, they had failed to anticipate this volume of missile fire. Colt's Tri-V glowed red.

This was the sort of defense an assaulting force expected to see from a military operation or a fellow merc company. Not ragtag pirates.

The cheers died as the troopers took stock of the oncoming hail of death. Colt knew they must be thinking along the same lines as he. If the missile estimates in the intelligence report were off by this much, what else had it gotten wrong? Maybe, if they managed to survive the assault, they'd find out.

Colt's dropship, *Hermes*, juked and rolled as Kit maneuvered and the lasers blasted the deadly cloud heading their way. All Colt could do—all any of the troopers could do—was hang in his harness and will himself to remain conscious whenever the sudden reversals of g-forces threatened to make him gray out.

The ships' crews and the targeting computers assisting them did a masterful job cutting their way through the enemy's fire. A surge of pride made Colt grin as he watched the red icons disappear from the scope at a phenomenal rate.

Unfortunately, even the best missile defense system couldn't cope with that many targets at once.

Kit cursed over the comm, something Colt would have to chat with her about later, should they live through this drop, and atmosphere screamed across *Hermes'* hull as the ship flailed to avoid an incoming missile, one of the last in the salvo.

"Prepare for impact." Kit's voice, though stressed, remained calm. Colt knew she must be struggling mightily against *Hermes'* controls.

Less than a second later, two cataclysmic BOOMS rocked the ship, followed by a banshee wail that caused Colt's CASPer to automatically dampen the outside noise lest it damage his ears. *Hermes* shuddered and went into a spin that flipped the up and down g-forces the troopers had been experiencing. Suddenly, a massive hand pressed Colt against the back of his cockpit, the force making it hard to catch his breath.

Several people screamed, but most of Colt's troopers kept their cool. They had faced similar scenarios in the sims and knew expressing their fear wouldn't help. In fact, it would only add to the confusion and possibly cause the loss of unit cohesion.

Five seconds went by, then ten, and then *Hermes* broke from its tailspin, evened out, and flew. Though it wobbled, jittered, and roared like an injured beast, Kit coaxed the craft back onto its assigned trajectory.

"We're dropping faster than we should, but we're tracking again," Kit said. "Looks like I'll have to put you about three clicks from our assigned LZ."

"Petrov, you copy that?" Yardley asked.

"Yes, sir. Are we scrapping the mission?" Petrov, who had command of the combined Alpha and Bravo companies, sounded a bit disappointed but kept his voice professional.

"Negative. Proceed as planned. We'll just be a little late to the party."

"Roger that, sir. We'll save you a dance."

"Kit, will you be able to get *Hermes* back to orbit?" Colt asked.

"No. The aft engine is only cranking out about fifteen percent of normal thrust. Looks like we're grounded until the mission's over. I'd rather not lift unless things are dire."

"Think we should leave a couple of troopers to guard *Hermes*?" Yardley asked over their command channel.

Colt analyzed the situation using his pinplants. Between the three dropships, they had brought fifty CASPers and twenty-five RATs.

Though they were landing within easy reach of the Ten Whispers' fortress, the surrounding wilderness boasted no modern infrastructure—no towns, no forward enemy outposts, and best of all, as far as FMT's reconnaissance could tell, no patrol stations or movement detection devices. As the pirates had already demonstrated, they expected attacks from above, both air breathing and spaceborne, not from ground forces. That could bode well for Kit's lame duck, especially if the CASPers kept the pirates busy enough, or the Ten Whispers could rifle *Hermes* from the air and be done with it.

"Let's leave behind four RATs," Colt said. Though they were nowhere near as tough or loaded with firepower as a CASPer, the armored RATs were still lethal.

"Two," Yardley said. "It's mortal math, and I hate it, but we run the risk of losing fewer people if the pirates decide to punch *Hermes* from the air. I want all the armor we've got pounding that fortress."

"Makes sense." Though he agreed with Yardley's assessment, Colt couldn't fight a strange feeling of discomfort. Never before, in a sim or during real fighting, had Yardley second-guessed his advice. But that was a good thing, right? It meant Yardley was coming into his own, learning to manage the battlespace according to his experience, his analysis. And Colt couldn't fault the colonel's logic. Two RATs should suffice to safeguard *Hermes* crew with the threat of ground attack this low.

So, why did Colt feel like a man whose dog had just growled at him?

"Hitting improvised landing zone in twenty seconds," Kit said. "Sister crews will be kicking dirt about thirty seconds after that. We've got enemy targets in the jungle, two clicks out from our target position, and it looks like the fortress scrambled flyers."

"Lieutenant Brindle, Captain Graves, *Hermes* is out of the fight. I need you both for close air support the instant you've dropped your teams." Yardley's voice sounded calm over the battalion channel as he addressed the other pilots. "Captain Zorn, you and Benwarst take Kit's place. It looks like we're facing more air defense than we anticipated."

"Roger," Zorn said from orbit. They both knew precious minutes would pass before he and his crew could drop.

"We should task the Sky Raiders with surface-to-air support while we wait," Colt said. Five of Bravo Company's third squad were outfitted with missiles designed for destroying airborne targets. The shaped-charge warheads packed enough punch to blast through most air breather ships' shields and usually destabilized flight even when they didn't.

Yardley passed the order as *Hermes* touched down and the ship's main door folded open. Colt keyed the sequence to uncouple his CASPer from its shipping cradle and hit the ground with a satisfying thump, his heart racing with exhilaration.

He turned to survey the damage the missiles had done to *Hermes* and almost swore. A man-sized rent in the gray hull, blackened and burnt, still smoked at the impact point. One of the ship's wings looked nearly chewed through where it joined the fuselage.

"Wilson and Sternwheeler, stay behind and guard *Hermes'* crew," Yardley said as he turned his CASPer to face the distant enemy fortress.

"Yes, sir," said Sternwheeler over the comm.

"First Sergeant," Yardley said. "Get these people heading for the target. We've got ground to make up."

"FMT!" Levin shouted. "Death before default!"

The company repeated her words with gusto, filling the channel with their raised voices.

"How long you been holding onto that one, Sergeant?" Yardley asked on the command circuit.

"At least three days, sir. Been chomping at the bit to use it, but never found the right time 'til now."

"It's perfect." Colt keyed his pinplants to save the snippet so he would remember it. "That's our new company motto."

"Definitely!" Yard said.

Levin chivvied the mix of assembled CASPers and RATs into an arrowhead formation and got them pushing through the jungle with Corporal Christine Abramowitz on point. Colt and Yardley took up the rear. The RATs moved at a loping run and the CASPers at a moderate walk. The pace suited Colt, it gave him time to think about their strategy going forward.

Their plan had been delayed due to the missile strikes, but the command platoon, as Colt had designated their group, was never meant to reach the Ten Whispers' fortress ahead of the others. Rather, they were to lend support as the mission-designated companies, Alpha and Bravo, attacked from the east and north respectively. That part of the operation was, so far, proceeding as planned. Colt hoped their lead platoons only met the expected resistance. But those numbers had been formulated from the same intel brief that had underestimated the pirates' missile defenses.

Despite the noonday sun, dusk held sway under Spimu's heavy jungle canopies. According to his CASPer's environmental gauges, the humidity was seventy-six percent and the temperature a balmy forty degrees Celsius. Nearly centered on Spimu's equator, this area boasted the planet's richest variety of plant and animal life. Though the animals posed no threat to his troopers, the tree cover and heat were playing havoc with Colt's CASPer's sensors. Using his pinplants, he switched to an overhead view provided by the network of drones the dropships had deployed on their way dirtside.

The tactical picture didn't look good. The network identified one hundred and thirty-six targets moving out from the Ten Whispers' fortress to meet FMT's advancing companies: sixty-eight heading west and the same number heading east. The pirates weren't supposed to have this many boots on the ground, but Colt supposed that paired well with their air power. A bevy of flyers rocketed up from the north to meet FMT's two dropships which, while formidable in their own way, hadn't been built with air-to-air combat in mind.

From the chatter across the battalion net, Colt knew his air combat team was tracking the enemy flyers. Less than five seconds later, a salvo of missiles screamed toward the enemy ships, taking out four of them in the first round of strikes.

Colt had only a moment to exult in their victory before an ominous warning sounded over the comm.

"Sir, we've got drone contact," Sergeant Eastman of Alpha company said, the rattling of machine gun fire punctuating his words.

"Microwaves," Yardley said.

Careful to keep his CASPer moving forward while monitoring the burgeoning battle on his pinplants, Colt zoomed in on Alpha Company's position. A cloud of dark fog resolved into thousands of quadcopters no bigger than Colt's palm surging toward his troopers like a wave. He gritted his teeth. The intel report had included information on this part of the Ten Whispers' defense, but that did little to assuage Colt's fear.

As he watched, the drone wave's leading edge collided with Alpha Company and exploded. First dozens, then hundreds, of yellow bursts erupted, visible from overhead now and again through the heavy tree cover, but the sound rode the airwaves via the battalion comm as troopers yelled and fired their high velocity machine guns at the assailing host.

Though no single drone could damage a CASPer or the RATs interspersed among them, combined strikes posed a real problem. Repeated strikes could damage a suit, but more importantly they could make the troopers lose focus on the real threat heading their way.

Colt used his pinplants to single out a channel to the Alpha Company commander. "Captain Butler, tell your people to use their microwave emitters. Now!"

"Yes, sir. On it, sir."

It would have been nice to follow up on that portion of the battle, but Colt's attention, along with that of everyone in the command platoon, was drawn away by Levin's voice on the comm.

"Sir, we've got drones too. Coming in hot, dead ahead!"

At first, Colt's brain told him the black things zooming out of the bush must be bats or some other natural creatures. In the next second, their unnatural speed, coupled with the way they moved in perfect synchronicity, told him otherwise.

A series of small, quick explosions bowled Corporal Abramowitz's CASPer over onto its back and sent the rest of the party into a frenzy of desperate swatting and undisciplined gun fire. The RATs took most of the damage, and though they managed to bring their rifles to bear, the few targets they hit didn't make any difference to the maelstrom of tiny vehicles.

"Engage with microwave bursts, you idiots!" Yardley screamed into the comm as he followed his own orders, firing into the tide with the high-powered microwave emitter, or HPME—pronounced hip-me—affixed to his CASPer's left arm. Drones fried, some of them bursting into flame, others detonating when their explosive payloads ignited. Those that didn't go down in a blaze did go down, crashing into tree boles and disappearing into the bush.

Colt fired his HPME, taking out scads of the little nuisances in a coordinated attack with the rest of the command platoon. Dozens more pummeled his CASPer, flashing on his Tri-V display like over-sized fireworks. The unrelenting explosions made his head ache. The hits did negligible damage, but several systems flipped from green to yellow under the barrage.

Though they risked damaging a friendly by employing the HPMEs, Colt was glad they had decided to mount them. They had to forego the grenade launchers they often carried, and Colt had worried his people might miss the firepower. But he couldn't be more pleased as the curtain of drones lightened. They still had a side-mounted laser on their left arms, which came in handy when the drones' coordinating computer grew wise to their microwave attacks and tried to evade. While the HPME took about a second and a half to burn out one of the drone's main processors, the lasers scored instant kills.

Colt cheered as the drone attack lessened then fell off, but his joy withered when he realized he had fallen for the feint he had warned Alpha Company about. While he and his troopers had been engaged in slaughtering mostly inconsequential targets, the Ten Whispers' host had surged to meet them. According to the plots on his Tri-V, Alpha and Bravo companies were under heavy fire from teams of combatants armed with lasers, machine guns, missiles, and grenades. And a third force numbering nearly thirty was on its way to confront the command platoon.

Colt switched to his private channel with Yardley. "Have the platoon reform into a box. We can lure the enemy into crossfire."

"No, they're too close for that." Yardley spun his CASPer to face forward. Black strike marks mottled its armor, but the suit looked intact. "Command, this is FMT actual. We've got incoming. Fall back into a skirmish line. We're taking these jerks out!"

"Yard, pulling back is not the answer. That will take too much time."

"I don't have time for arguments. Execute my orders."

Colt ground his teeth but did as Yardley commanded. At least the jungle kept their enemies from deploying tanks or armored personnel carriers. The pirate mercs had to run to meet them, and they were fast.

The trees and vines ahead shook, telegraphing the appearance of two dozen MinSha, Tortantula, and Oogar defenders armed with rifles, handguns, and grenade launchers. Most wore armor, though the MinSha trusted their natural chitin to protect them.

The enemy attacked the instant they saw the FMT troopers, opening up with every weapon at their disposal. Corporal Abramowitz, still trying to pull back into the single line formation, took a missile strike to the back of her CASPer. Though the ensuing explosion didn't penetrate the suit's thick armor, the energy it imparted sent her staggering into a tree which, in the eyes of her enemies, made her a wounded target. Two rocket propelled grenades and a laser strike followed closely on the heels of the original attack, and Corporal Abramowitz's CASPer exploded.

She didn't have time to scream, and she wasn't the last.

* * * * *

Chapter Fifteen

"Those aren't pirates, they're mercs!" Yardley shouted over the command channel.

"They're both." Colt brought his shoulder-mounted rail gun to bear on a MinSha as he took out an oncoming Tortantula with the high velocity machine gun on his CASPer's right arm.

The tactical display looked like a weather report from Jupiter. Enemy icons swarmed forward, only slowing a little as the command platoon laid down an uncoordinated wall of fire.

"Colonel! We're getting mauled. Orders?" 1SG Levin fired a series of missiles from one shoulder while lancing their enemies with her magnetic accelerator cannon from the other. She took out a Zuul carrying a laser rifle, and another immediately took its place.

"I...I don't know," Yardley stammered, and Colt mentally cursed. The last thing their troopers needed was to hear indecision in their commander's voice. While keeping up his defense, he turned part of his attention back to the Tri-V, searching for a way to tackle the problem.

Unfortunately, Yard had put their troopers into the unenviable position of facing their enemies like beads on a string—all lined up for the slaughter. Arranged east to west, the CASPers reminded Colt of an ancient Roman cohort, except Roman soldiers carried shields and always had buddies to back them up. Colt had trees.

Whoever had organized the enemy's drone attack had been inspired. What little damage it had caused supplemented its primary purpose, to utterly distract its targets, giving the heavy infantry time to move into position.

Colt froze, and it almost cost him an arm when a Zuul took a pot shot at him. The beam singed his CASPer's left shoulder, and he was forced to fall back behind a tree. A warning alarm sounded, and the servo icon for that arm turned orange on his display. But it was still working, which made Colt think the damage was almost worth it since it had given him an idea.

Moving at the speed of thought, Colt accessed the fleet of drones FMT had stationed over the battlefield to ease command and control (C2) within the space. This time, instead of monitoring their live feeds, he seized control of them.

"FMT dropships. Deploy all drones at this time. Command group, heads up." Colt spoke calmly, but with steel in his voice, cutting through the increasingly frantic chatter over the platoon channel. He didn't do it because he had magically overcome his anxiety. He still felt anxious as hell. He did it because his people were in danger, and they needed leadership. "Assume the following formation and concentrate your fire on the targets I designate."

Sending commands through his pinplants, he drew a U shape with designated positions for his fourteen remaining CASPers and nine RATs.

Though the RATs couldn't weather enemy fire like their bigger cousins, the powered armor's size and strength made it highly maneuverable, even in the dense jungle underbrush. While the CASPers lumbered into position, hindered not just by trees but by the disorganized fire of their enemies, the RATs shot through the thickets like panthers, keeping low to avoid drawing fire.

Yardley, who had taken up a position behind a massive tree, made no move to join the formation. Colt considered trying to raise him on the comm, but there was no time. Instead, he stepped from behind his cover and started laying down fire using the laser on his left arm and the high velocity machine gun on his right. Thank God his pinplants made this sort of multitasking possible.

At the same instant, he painted one of the enemy targets purple on the command platoon's shared display and embossed it with the word KILL in bold, red letters. The Besquith howled in fury and pain as bullets ripped into its side and the superheated, chemical-driven laser set its fur aflame. An instant later, four, then five, blue-white laser blasts fired by RATs who had reached their designated positions incinerated the wolf-like creature.

Colt was suddenly glad CASPers were airtight. He had no desire to smell roasting wolfman.

Though he had made himself a target as the only CASPer standing still at the bottom of the U formation, he drew little enemy fire. The pirates were too busy trying to fend off the horde of FMT drones homing in on them like killer bees. FMT's drones lacked explosive warheads, but they moved fast enough to annoy anyone, even a naturally armored creature like a MinSha, when fifteen of them hit at one hundred and twenty kilometers per hour. The sounds of the impact carried over that of the gunfire from the CASPers who had reached their firing positions and were executing targets as fast as Colt could mark them.

The pirate mercs had shown little fire discipline before, and they now fell to complete disorganization as members of their force began to drop one after the other. In seconds, the rout was complete, and what remained of the Ten Whispers' mercs beat a hasty retreat, no two in the same direction. Some dropped their weapons in their haste to escape the whirring drones above and the flashing death at ground level.

"Good work, people." Colt considered his next set of problems and began breaking them down into their component parts as fast as his thoughts would allow. With a flick of his eyes, he ordered the remaining drones to take up a recon posture above the jungle stronghold, then flashed an order for the command platoon to move out for their secondary waypoint. He switched to his private channel with Yardley. "You coming?"

"I got her killed, Colt. Abramowitz. That was my fault. I thought she'd get back to us in time."

Pushing through the dense overgrowth to keep position with the rapidly deploying command platoon, Colt considered the situation. FMT needed Yardley, especially now. Though he chaffed at the idea of wasting time coaxing the colonel into doing his job, the need was clear. He had to try.

"Yard, this isn't the time to fall into a funk. You got me? I did that before, and it was stupid. I don't care what it takes, you've got to get that CASPer moving to waypoint two. People are counting on you. Living people. If you don't move, you're going to get them killed too."

Seconds passed while Colt held his breath, glancing now and again at the blue icon that represented Yardley's CASPer. For a long moment it didn't move and then, almost reluctantly, it started Colt's way.

Good enough.

"Zorn, Brindle, Graves, how'd the air battle play out?" Colt's tac display indicated all three ships were still airborne, though Lieutenant Brindle's craft had suffered minor damage to the aft engine. Its power output display showed only eighty percent efficiency.

"Touch and go for a few moments there, sir." Zorn's voice sounded deep and reassuring over the comm. "Having the ground teams aiding us certainly helped. We managed to down four of their craft, and the rest scampered. None of them was space worthy, so they can't have gone far, but I doubt we'll find them if they make it to one of the planet's spaceports. Should we pursue while they're still over the continent?"

"No. I'm not concerned about the flyers. Our focus is to unseat the pirates dirtside. Stay close, we might require more air support. I have no idea what they'll throw at us next."

"Roger that, sir."

Alpha and Bravo companies had beaten the forces the pirates had thrown at them, though it looked like they had suffered heavy losses. Colt's pinplants informed him he now had thirty-seven of his original fifty CASPers still mobile, though he wasn't sure if Yardley was fit to fight. Best to count him as a casualty until he proved otherwise. That left thirty-six CASPers and fourteen RATs. Those figures weren't heartwarming.

If the Ten Whispers had spent only a fraction of their full complement on that first ground defense, FMT was toast. No question. But Colt didn't see any more red icons pouring from the fortress walls, only a trickle of enemy combatants skulking about, most of them running for the jungle to escape the invading mercs.

The Ten Whispers had cleared the jungle down to the dirt for about thirty meters around their stronghold. Colt scanned it from his position at the edge of the jungle. He noted dozens of abandoned outbuildings surrounded by ground cars, loaders, and other service vehicles. Beyond them, lit by the blazing noonday sun, stood what Colt could only think of as a castle. Four pure white towers, each at least a dozen stories high, loomed over a curtain wall made of the same material. It looked like ivory, but must have been synthetic to withstand the weather.

Unlike the towers, the wall showed signs of battle damage. Blackened scorch marks indicated that small missiles and lasers had scored its otherwise unblemished face. Colt grinned.

"First Sergeant, what's the defense situation?" Colt asked. Intel showed the fortress's designers had planned it with ground attacks in mind. Missile and laser batteries lined the wall at even intervals. But from the looks of things, those were the scorch marks Colt had noticed.

"Neutralized as far as we can tell, sir," Levin said. "Bravo got the party started, and Alpha joined once they cut through their share of defenders."

"So, they left nothing for us?" Colt asked, and several voices laughed over the battalion comm. "What about armored defense? I don't see any more ground pounders coming to say hi, but my sensors aren't showing anything beyond that wall. I guess that's to be expected."

"Yes, sir." Levin managed to keep her voice perfectly neutral though Colt imagined her eyes rolling at his stupid question. Like any modern, armed stronghold, the Ten Whispers' fortress was mostly impervious to electronic snooping or attack. The same sort of shielding that protected an armed frigate in space could scatter EM transmissions. Though the building wasn't shielded to stop a missile or laser, it nonetheless looked like a black hole on the electromagnetic spectrum.

Colt eyed the pock-marked walls for several more seconds while his people waited. Perhaps their enemy was in a more talkative mood now. He keyed his comm link to broadcast across a wide spectrum focused on the massive building. "Attention, Ten Whispers base personnel, this is Lieutenant Colonel Colt Maier of Fulcrum Mercenary Tactics. Your ground and air defenses have been neutralized. Any attempt to escape will be considered an act of aggression. Lay down your arms and exit the building in an orderly fashion."

Colt hoped he sounded official enough. He had never demanded the surrender of an entrenched force before. He had dropped his voice an octave or two in an attempt to sound older, though he worried he sounded pretentious instead. Fortunately, none of his troopers laughed.

"You'll get no surrender today, vermin." The voice over Colt's comm sounded like a garbage disposal chewing on a fork.

The castle's massive gates swung open, and forty armed Besquith stormed out. Their otherworldly war cries sent a shiver down Colt's spine. It wasn't the giant, upright-walking wolves that commanded his attention however, it was the four tanks rolling out behind them. Now the patch of cleared land ringing the fortress made sense.

Someone swore over the battalion channel, and Colt couldn't fault them. The Ten Whispers' tanks weren't the sort of light armor pieces a CASPer could take out with a few missiles or rail gun rounds. They were large enough to sport fusion engines, which meant they had shields. Each carried two turrets. One looked like it fired multiple munitions fed from an internally housed magazine. The other was a much longer particle accelerator. And that didn't take into account the anti-personnel lasers, machine guns, and missile launchers bristling along their turrets.

Flicking his gaze back and forth across the Tri-V, Colt sent a series of position assignments to the battalion. He had no time to dither about what should be done. He looked at the situation and made a decision. He had to get his people fighting before shock and awe could root them in place.

"Petrov, you have orders," Colt said over the battalion channel. "Execute!"

"Yes, sir." Petrov sounded like a man waking from a dream, or maybe a nightmare, but true to his nature, he immediately got his people moving.

While Colt's command platoon held steady, Alpha and Bravo companies burst from the jungle, using their jumpjets in a series of short hops to close with the Besquith ground forces. The companies' RATs followed on the ground, cutting through the jungle with all haste. Following Colt's orders, the combined units concentrated fire on the Besquith, zeroing in on targets designated by Major Petrov.

They reached the first of the outbuildings in under a minute and the battle morphed from open field skirmishing to an urban assault. Both sides used the buildings for cover, though FMT's forces had the upper hand. They could fly.

"Command platoon, with me." Colt had given the tanks enough time to exit the fortress and begin engaging Petrov's people before launching his own attack. He activated his jumpjets and bounded forward, approaching the enemy flank, careful to keep his CASPer upright and absorb the shock of landing with bent knees.

While most of Alpha and Bravo traded fire with the Besquith infantry around the outbuildings, a handful strafed the tanks when they came in range. As Colt had feared, the tanks' shields blocked all the laser fire and most of the high velocity rounds his people threw at them. And while their missiles made a dazzling light show, they caused no real damage. The few bullets that got through slid off the rolling death machines' armored hides like sleet. Without concentrated fire, and there was little possibility of that with the bulk of his troopers engaged against freaking Besquith, the tanks were virtually impenetrable.

But that invulnerability applied to energetic attacks on the shields. It couldn't stop a CASPer from getting close. And that, Colt hoped, would be the tanks' downfall.

Broadcasting simple commands over the platoon channel, he quickly outlined what he needed done. His troopers, aside from Yardley, spread out behind him, angling their trajectories to land where Colt commanded.

Worry gnawed at Colt as he made his second jump. His plan would bring the command group within close proximity of the tanks, whose operators probably knew their business. He was putting his people in extreme danger for a plan he had come up with less than a minute ago.

Scowling, Colt abandoned that line of thought. As Captain Torres had taught him, making no decision was the same as making a bad one. He had to trust himself and his troopers, otherwise they might as well give up now.

The first two tanks concentrated their fire on Alpha and Bravo companies in support of the Besquith infantry. The remaining two altered course to take on Colt's command group. The lead tank took out Alpha Company's Nathan Spearman with a shot from its particle gun, while the rearmost did the same to Sergeant Shannon Peterson from Colt's unit. Their CASPers split apart in eye-searing, blue-white balls of fire that sent molten pieces of metal in every direction.

Colt ground his teeth at the loss, but kept moving. Death was the price of doing business on the battlefield. He would have time to mourn later.

As he closed on the nearest tank Colt marveled at its size. At over twelve meters long and nearly four wide, it looked more like a space ship than a ground-based piece of rolling armor. He blasted it with railgun rounds, most of which pinged harmlessly off its gray hull. But that didn't matter. All Colt wanted was the tank crew's attention, and he was getting that in spades.

The turret spun to meet the oncoming command group, machine guns blazing. Apparently, the particle beam had to recharge before it could fire again, otherwise it likely would have fried Colt with a second shot by now. The same didn't apply to its secondary cannon however. The big gun boomed, the noise deafening even inside the CASPer, and Sergeant Michael Brand, who had been keeping pace with Colt a couple of meters to his right, screamed in anguish as his suit exploded.

Another good trooper gone—another face Colt would surely see in his nightmares, assuming he survived. He ignored the pain and fear threatening to overwhelm his senses, same as he ignored the hypervelocity tracers whizzing past his cockpit. He focused instead on sticking a landing within arm's reach of his target. This close on, the tank's crew couldn't bring their main guns to bear on Colt and those who landed with him. That left the tank's laser and machine guns which the crew attempted to train on the attacking CASPers, but the angle proved too steep. Bullets pinged off the FMT troopers, and beams of coherent light scored their suits, but to little effect.

The tank hadn't stopped moving, but slowed as its driver performed a sharp turn in an effort to bring the CASPers within range of its anti-personnel weapons.

"Dig in," Colt ordered. "Don't let it turn. Get your hands in position and prepare to fire jumpjets! And be careful of the treads. I don't want anyone getting their arms ripped off!"

Colt and his troopers dug their mechanized feet into the ground and slid their hands under the armored skirting meant to protect the tank's treads. Heaving together, they managed to slow the vehicle though they couldn't bring it to a stop. Its engines roared as it continued to spin in a circle. The treads opposite them spun an arching plume of dirt into the air as the tank's driver sought to dislodge them. And it was working. Warning bells sounded in Colt's suit. He was overstressing its servos. Their CASPers couldn't maintain this sort of effort for long, but if things went according to plan, they wouldn't need to.

"Fire jumpjets!" Colt took his own order, and activated the powerful thrusters built into his suit. While a single CASPer could never topple a tank this size, four working in tandem might have a chance.

The suits' rockets roared, sending up sprays of dirt and sand. The tank's treads lifted, slowly at first, but with increasing speed as the CASPer's rose. In a panic, the tank driver poured on more speed. The ploy almost worked this time as the single tread still in contact with the ground chewed up the dirt and spun Colt and the others in a circle.

Thank God for all those hours spent in the simulator practicing flight maneuvers. By reflex, Colt angled his jets to match the tank's speed and retain his grip. He grinned as his troopers did likewise. In the next instant the tank flipped onto its turret, the one tread churning along for several seconds before grinding to a stop.

Colt changed direction to land opposite the tank's underbelly. Levin landed next to him.

"Shall we find out if this thing's shields cover the bottom?" Levin asked.

Before Colt could answer, an armored hatch opened and three then four Zuul tumbled out onto the dirt. They wore pale blue uniforms and light body armor, but must have left their personal weapons aboard the tank. Prudent. Colt would have dispatched them otherwise. They placed their hands atop their heads and stood looking at the ground like bad dogs caught in some mischief.

"What should we do with them?" Levin asked.

"We don't have time for prisoners." Colt made sure to send his voice through his CASPer's exterior speakers.

The Zuul tankers perked up at his words.

"If you let us go, you won't see us again," said the one in the middle. A set of vertical slashes on his uniform sleeve set him apart from the others. Colt figured him for the tank commander.

"If you come back here, you'll regret it." Colt waved the aliens away. They ran for the jungle without looking back.

"You sure that was a good idea?" Levin had turned to regard the fleeing Zuul.

"There's no more fight left in them, and I'm not going to kill anyone who surrenders."

"Agreed, sir. But maybe we should have captured them? They could come back with friends."

"In this jungle? I doubt it. Besides, we don't have the resources to handle detainees and fight."

In the distance, two of the other tanks were already flipped. Apparently, their crews hadn't given up, because FMT troopers were busy hammering at their undersides with lasers, missiles, and railgun rounds. Though the vehicles' shields were formidable, they couldn't cope with that level of concentrated fire. In seconds, they failed, and the tanks went up like fireworks.

The final tank, however, had managed to throw off its assailants. It performed a lightning speed turn, got its main guns to bear, and destroyed Corporal Briana Skeens with its particle accelerator.

Colt cursed. Without thinking, he activated his jumpjets and leapt into the air. He landed atop the tank and was immediately joined by two other troopers. They took up precarious stances on the hull and turret. Sergeant Andrew King extended a blade from his CASPer's right arm and began hacking at the common munitions cannon. It took three swings, but he successfully sheered it off in the middle while Colt focused on taking out the tank's gun and laser defenses with high-velocity rounds.

The other trooper, Corporal Amy Vattershin, seized the particle accelerator cannon with both hands and lifted. A sound of groaning metal rent the air as she bent the precision weapon into a useless piece of alloy metal, leaving its business end facing up at about twenty degrees.

The tank's main hatch flew open, and a torrent of black smoke issued out followed by a Besquith's snarling head. Moving fast for a creature so large, it brought a laser rifle to bear on Sergeant King. The high intensity beam turned King's shoulder into instant slag. Sparks flew, and the sergeant grunted over the comm, no doubt enduring haptic damage feedback through his pinplants.

Colt shot the offending Besquith in the back of the head with his railgun. The alien's cranium exploded in a cloud of gore, and its body dropped out of sight. Unwilling to wait around for one of the creature's fellows to emerge, Colt dropped two K bombs through the open hatch, slammed it shut, and placed an armored foot on top. Shouts and scrabbling sounds erupted inside the tank and someone tried, unsuccessfully, to reopen the hatch.

A muffled boom and all fell still.

Petrov's Alpha and Bravo Companies had met similar success against the Besquith infantry. They had suffered some losses, Colt noted, but the humans had managed to turn the tide. Their former savagery forgotten, the Besquith fighters attempted to flee back to the fortress, but Colt ordered his troopers to cut them off. As fast as they could run, the enemy couldn't match a CASPer's jumpjets. The combined FMT units made short work of the pirates who tried to mount an attack to reach the entrance. A few dropped their weapons and raced for the jungle. Colt let them go, his attention focused on his next problem. The walls.

"Levin, we got enough charges left to breach the gates?"

"Yes, sir. Darnel and Wimberley are still with us."

"Do it. Let's finish this."

Levin passed orders to the demolitions fire team. The four CAS-Pers and two RATs approached the wall with care. When no one shot at them and no mines exploded under their feet, they placed the specially designed charges they carried.

While the CASPers could have flown over the fortress walls, Colt had elected to field the RATs without fuel to save space for munitions. He wasn't about to split his force, especially since the RATs would likely prove more maneuverable inside the fortress. He dreaded the idea of dropping the CASPers into an unknown situation without full support. So they waited.

Colt used the downtime to examine the tactical picture. The sudden silence of what had only moments earlier been a battlefield felt disquieting. He switched to the command channel. "Why aren't the Ten Whispers shooting?"

Major Petrov moved to stand next to Colt. "My guess? They spent the bulk of their forces on the initial attack. This place isn't all that big, and our intel showed most of their raiders are out hunting prizes in space. I think they sent everything they had at us. Sure felt that way to me. I don't know about the command group, but it got a little dicey for a while in Alpha and Bravo."

"Why aren't any ships taking off?" Yardley asked. It was good to hear his voice, though he sounded somehow diminished, like a man who had just been rescued from drowning.

"Maybe they sent their pilots to fight?" Colt asked.

"I doubt that very much, sir," Levin said from her position near the explosive ordinance detail. "I think they got a taste of our missiles and gave up. Royston shot down three ships, and our pilots took out at least five more. Anything that's left, they're keeping grounded for safety's sake."

"Ordnance set," Sergeant Wimberley said. "Permission to breach?"

"Granted," said Levin.

"Fire in the hole!"

A single, thrumming BOOM cracked the right gate, sending up a billowing plume of smoke and chunks of steel alloy. Colt stared, muscles taut as the smoke floated lazily away on the hot air to reveal an oblong hole half again as wide as a CASPer.

When it was obvious no one was coming out to greet them, 1SG Levin strode forward. "Fire teams Alpha Two and Bravo Three, with me on initial entry. The rest of you file in by team assignment."

* * * * *

Chapter Sixteen

The shooting began as soon as Levin was through the gap. Bullets and tepid laser fire scored her CASPer but did no significant damage. She ushered in her designated fire teams, spreading them out in a defensive formation that grew as more of the combined companies surged through to join her.

Colt chafed at waiting. But as Captain Torres had warned him before the drop, he and Yardley were in command, and that made them indispensable to the team. No matter how harsh it sounded, the loss of a field commander would hurt their unit more than the loss of a regular trooper. Losing troopers weakened the company's fighting force. Losing commanders would cripple it.

The Ten Whispers' fortress was laid out in a long rectangle with three towers at the north end and a paved landing pad opposite. Several large, white buildings that lined the walls were laid out like barracks or apartments, which made sense to Colt. According to FMT's intelligence estimates, the main pirate force consisted of a continuously rotating six thousand individuals drawn from hundreds of races. Right now, most of those were off-world plundering innocent traders like Malfren and Vernox. Or, so Colt hoped. So far, it looked like the intel pukes had gotten that part right.

No Tortantulas or Besquith came pouring out of the barracks, only a handful of inexperienced Zuul. The dog-like aliens, while armed with laser rifles, lacked the fighting prowess of the Besquith and Tortantulas. They blundered into one another, and in at least one case, managed to shoot members of their own side in their zeal to attack the invaders.

"Watch for snipers on the buildings," Colt said as he fired on a particularly ambitious Zuul who had dashed from cover to try his laser rifle at pointblank range. Unfortunately for him, the gun didn't have the juice to do more than mar the CASPer's exterior. Colt took him out with a three bullet blast, the least his arm gun could manage.

"I haven't seen any, sir." Levin bounded right to pick off an enemy taking cover behind a small private flyer at the edge of the landing pad.

"Humans!" A guttural voice broke over the mostly silent battalion channel. "We surrender. We will lay down our arms and give ourselves over to you."

"Cease fire." Colt drew up short from taking out a Zuul cowering next to stairs leading up to one of the barracks halls.

A smattering of bullets pinged off his troopers as the remaining pirates fired a few parting shots. Colt fought the urge to resume the battle. It wasn't like this ragtag group was organized. Likely as not, most of them hadn't gotten the word their side had given up. Besides, their underpowered weapons posed little threat, even to the RATs.

After a few seconds, the shooting stopped, and a group of five armed Zuul exited the nearest building, pushing the fattest Besquith Colt had ever seen before them.

"Is that Lyret?" Colt stared in wide-eyed amazement.

"That's the pirate prince?" Despite the derision in his voice, Major Petrov waved for squads three and five to close ranks in front of Colt and Yardley.

"Humans," said the lead Zuul, a particularly tall, skinny specimen with blue-gray fur and a scar that split his black nose in a thick pink line. "Yes, this is Lyret, leader of the Ten Whispers."

The portly Lyret snarled, showing three rows of yellowed teeth, but he made no move to escape or attack his Zuul captors. From what little Colt knew about the two races, being taken this way must have been particularly insulting to the Besquith. But the fat, wolf-like creature appeared to be in no position to fight. He looked old. Patches of gray decorated the otherwise black pelt along his thick neck, and threads of silver stuck out form his scalp. And though rings of fat hung from his neck, belly, and the undersides of his arms like balloons full of jelly, there was a frailness about him like a desiccated tree branch.

"Who are you?" Lyret demanded in a querulous voice.

Colt squared his suit with the creature. "We're Fulcrum Mercenary Tactics. We were hired by the Sandonian merchant co-op to retrieve the goods you stole from them, and to see that your criminal operation is retired."

Lyret growled deep in his chest, and for a moment, Colt thought his troopers might have to intervene should the aged Besquith attempt a foolhardy attack. But the growl faded, and the pirate dropped his muzzle, a long string of drool dripping from his lips. "I knew this day would come, but I never imagined my own would turn against me."

"You've grown weak, Lyret," said the lead Zuul. "Weak and indulgent."

Lyret swiveled a baleful eye toward his former minion, his lips drawing back from his teeth as his growl returned, far more menacing than before.

Quick on her feet, 1SG Levin trained her weapons on not just Lyret but all the alien pirates. "Enough. Drop your weapons, and we'll accept your formal surrender. Alpha Two and Three, take charge of the prisoners. The rest of you break into squads. I want this facility cleared within the hour. We need a full inventory, but we can't do that until we've made sure there aren't any holdouts." She turned to Colt. "With your permission, sir."

"See to it, Sergeant."

* * *

Three hours later, Colt and his commanders sat around a large table with Malfren and Vernox in an abandoned bar, drinking spirits that tasted like strawberry wine or maybe kiwi. It wasn't a strong drink according to Captain Torres, but Colt had had little alcohol in his sixteen years, and the stuff was giving him a pleasant, sleepy buzz.

Lyret's private residence, the centermost fortress tower, was reflective of the pirate prince's luxurious lifestyle, with its holographic gaming suite, two fully staffed restaurants, and this bar. Not to mention dozens of bedrooms, bathing rooms, and cryo-vaults and saunas.

"We've recovered most of what we lost." Malfren took a long sip from his drink. The red liquid painted his lips burgundy. "And I think we'll make back far more than we lost from selling the salvage. All in all, your company was a fine investment for me and my partners."

After the Ten Whispers fell and 1SG Levin had pronounced the fortress safe, Weep had swooped in to itemize every piece of equipment and every square inch of real estate in the place which, as far as

Colt could tell, was the Flatar's version of heaven. Afterward, she negotiated a fair salvage deal with Malfren's co-op. More than fair. Colt was no accountant, but having looked over the contract, he thought FMT's purser had gotten the better end of the deal. She had claimed a seventy percent share in all goods, property, and cash reserves seized from the operation that hadn't previously belonged to Malfren and his company—after Spimu planetary taxes stole their share—then hired the Sandonian Cooperative to act as FMT's agents in liquidating their portion. That would take some time, but according to Malfren's estimates, FMT would likely receive the better part of twenty million credits over the next few months from the sell-off. And that was on top of the nine million the co-op had already paid them for the contract.

"Good to hear." Colt forced himself to put his drink down and ignore it. His pleasant buzz was threatening to grow if he kept nursing it. He wasn't keen on getting drunk in front of a client or his officers, though he knew why the inclination to drown his feelings had taken such a hold on him. Whereas Weep's only concern was for the physical costs of doing business as a merc enterprise, Colt found himself grappling with the emotional and spiritual ramifications.

He had lost four troopers that day. Eight more had been wounded beyond the abilities of their personal nanites and those contained in medical sprayers to heal quickly. Though FMT had no doctors, a problem Colt decided he should remedy as soon as possible, each company contained a squad of dedicated infantry medics trained in field expedient triage and treatment. According to their lead sergeant, the eight wounded would survive, but they'd need time to recoup.

The bar's doors split open, wresting Colt from his grim thoughts, and Levin entered. Still dressed in the haptic suit meant for better interfacing with a CASPer, Colt couldn't help but notice the sergeant's pleasing curves. It occurred to him that although he thought of Top as far older than he, she was just seventeen according to her personnel file, a mere year and three months older than Colt.

She smirked when she saw him staring, and he immediately dropped his gaze to his drink.

"Is this the o-club, or can a chevron jockey join in?" Levin pulled out a chair but waited to sit.

"No rank in here right now, Nichol." Petrov fished a crystal tumbler from the rack next to their table and poured Levin a generous measure of the alien liquor.

She collapsed into the seat next to Colt and breathed a long, exhausted sigh. "Good, because I'm making this last report, then I'm off duty. Somebody else can wrangle grunts for a while."

"What's the report?" Petrov asked when neither Colt nor Yardley spoke up.

"Kit managed to get *Hermes* onto the landing pad—that lady's a hell of a pilot—but the damage is bad. Larson and Abbot, our best mechanics, looked at it. Both agree they don't have the equipment or spare parts to get the thing back to *Uncanny*. I checked, and there's a repair facility in Turskar; that's a spaceport about an hour's flight from here. They're willing to haul *Hermes* out for a fee, but the bill is going to hurt."

Colt wanted to ask if Levin had checked for alternatives, but he couldn't seem to get his stupid tongue in gear. He could feel Captain Torres, who leaned against the bar feigning nonchalance, willing him to take charge, but no matter how Colt tried to dissect the problem, he couldn't seem to wrap his head around it. Either the booze had stolen his edge, or he had suddenly lost his ability to focus around Levin.

Probably both.

Colt again found himself staring at Levin, her dark hair cascading past her shoulders and her striking green eyes focused on Petrov. Only they weren't focused on Petrov. They were staring back at Colt.

"I'm sorry, what did you say, Sergeant—Nichol?" Colt stammered out the words like a duck waddling through a tire run. He could only hope the other officers hadn't noticed, or if they had, they would be gracious enough to ignore his awkwardness.

Levin grinned, and Colt thought his heart would catch fire. What was in that strawberry concoction?

"I said, you look tired. Maybe now isn't the best time to brief you on *Hermes*."

"No, it's fine. What about *Hermes*?"

Petrov did nothing to hide his grin. Neither did Torres. Only Yardley didn't smile; his face remained completely neutral as if he hadn't heard a word said around him.

Levin's indulgent smile told Colt she was either laughing at him or with him. He wasn't sure which, but in his fuzzy state of mind he sort of liked both.

"The way I see it," Levin said, "our best bet is to pay for the repairs. It will mean an extra two weeks on Spimu, but that beats abandoning *Hermes* altogether. Repairs won't cost half as much as buying a new ship, and we can't do without one. Also, we might dredge up some more jobs while we wait, just to keep our hand in."

"Not a bad idea." Petrov took a fast swig and put down his glass. "Maybe we should stay on Spimu so long as we can keep drumming up business. That way we're not wasting time in hyperspace."

"I don't know." Weep, who had kept quiet while celebrating her deal with Malfren and Vernox, swirled her drink for a moment, her eyes downcast as she ran numbers in her head. "We've already burned up almost two months of our twelve, and until today, we were earning at a deficit. We need high grossing contracts if we're going to clear our ledger with Mountside, and I don't see us getting those on Spimu. Yes, we stand to make a tidy profit after Malfren sells our share of the loot, but that money isn't in our accounts. It might take longer than we've got. With what we were paid today, we're barely breaking even after fuel costs, trooper and staff pay, repairs, and all the other expenses that make an operation like this possible."

"I thought we cleared nine million credits?" Colt squinted at the Flatar, trying to make his eyes focus.

Weep shook her head. "Not even close. We got paid nine million. And that was after our combat bonus and the cooperative's initial fuel purchase to get us here."

Colt rubbed his temples with a sigh. Just when things were looking up it seemed like a great phantom hand came in and swept away FMT's gains.

"I may be able to help you." Malfren twisted his head this way and that to give his sidewall eyes a view of everyone at the table.

"Oh?" Weep perked up, sensing a chance to negotiate—her favorite sport.

"We will need to safeguard this facility until we secure a buyer, not to mention all of the ships, equipment, and foodstuffs stored here. I had already planned to hire a garrison team for that purpose, but I hadn't thought to make you the offer since you planned to leave so quickly."

"I don't know if we can accept," Colt said. He found that as long as he didn't glance Levin's way, his voice worked passably well. "Weep's right, we need high paying jobs, and unless you're willing to pay far more than the going rate for garrison work, we'll have to decline."

"Yet you must remain here until your ship is repaired. Perhaps you can fulfill our garrison needs for several weeks until we hire replacements?" Malfren persisted, spreading his lower hands palm up in a conciliatory gesture while his upper ones supported his head.

"I don't—" Colt began.

"We'll do it." Yardley's voice cut through Colt's like a bullet. "And not for a few weeks. We'll cover your garrison needs until this fortress is sold."

For a moment, Colt couldn't speak, not due to anxiety, but sudden rage. Yard hadn't said a word in hours, he had completely disengaged on the battlefield in the middle of a firefight, and he chose now to speak up?

"I'm not sure that's the best use of our time and resources," Weep said, far more diplomatically than Colt could have managed at that moment.

"It's simple," Yardley said. "We break off an expeditionary unit like we did for Onishi on Brigham. They remain here, serve out the garrison duty for full pay, and the rest of FMT continues to seek out more work. We talked about doing this weeks ago."

"How many troopers and CASPers are we talking about?" Colt asked. "If we reduce our main force by too many, we won't be able to pursue the more lucrative contracts. No one will hire us."

"A platoon of twenty—ten CASPers, five RATs, and five tech support." Yardley folded his arms across his chest as if daring anyone to counter him. "And I'll lead them."

"I'm not sure that's a good idea, Colonel." Levin used her talking-to-officers-voice, the one she whipped out whenever she thought one of her superiors was being a moron, but couldn't say it outright. "You're the CO. The company needs you at the helm."

"I agree." Colt purposefully did not look Levin's way.

Yard opened his mouth as if to say something, shut it, then leveled his gaze at Colt. "Can we talk? In private, I mean." He motioned over his shoulder toward the bar's exit.

Colt wanted to say no. Yard might as well air whatever was going on with him in front of their officers, they were bound to find out sooner or later. But the sound of his father's and Torres' voices gave him pause. Something was eating at Yard, something big enough to rob him of his normally gregarious personality. Colt understood that sort of loss. He nodded.

Yard led Colt out the residence's main doors to a stone porch overlooking the landing pad. Days on Spimu lasted eighteen hours and a few spare minutes. The evening sun lay low on the southwest horizon. Its dying rays painted the clouds pink and purple and orange.

A group of former pirates was offloading materials from one of the larger ships under the watchful eyes of six RATs troopers. Most of it looked like sealed food containers and other comestibles.

Yard stood quiet for a long time, watching the work, before he turned to Colt, his face awash with worry, though Colt didn't understand why.

"I need this." He said the words simply, earnestly. "I got people killed today, Colt. I thought I could run things the way you do in a fight. I thought because I was doing well at running the company, I could do the same in the fur ball." He dropped his gaze to the floor. "I was stupid."

Colt wanted to argue, to tell Yard he couldn't afford to shirk his duty, not when their people were relying on him. But the words wouldn't come, not because Colt felt anxious or afraid, but because they rang hollow. For better or worse, they both knew Colt had been leading FMT for years. Yard wasn't asking to shirk his duty, only his façade.

Perhaps Colt had been the one shirking all along.

Slightly drunk or not, Colt could feel Yardley's shame, disappointment, and heartache. He knew, in that moment, he could manipulate the big colonel. Hadn't he been doing that for years? It wouldn't take much to steer Yard back into his role as the face of FMT—a convenient spot for Colt. But doing so would obviously bring Yard pain.

"Okay." Colt nodded at the colonel, despite his own inner turmoil. "You stay here on garrison duty while Kit and a squad remain behind to get *Hermes* repaired. I'll take the rest of FMT back to Karma to search for a new contract."

"I expected a fight." Yardley ran a hand through his short blond hair. "You'll have to take over. You'll be running everything."

"I know."

"Can you handle that?" Yard searched Colt's face, and it was all Colt could do not to look away, but he managed it.

"We have a good command team. They'll get me through."

Yardley nodded, his eyes distant. "We're trading ranks."

"What?" Colt found himself staring at Yard without having to force himself. "No."

"Yes. I'm stepping down as CEO and colonel. I'll take light colonel. That means someone has to step up."

"This is temporary," Colt protested. "Just until the garrison duty is over."

Yard shook his head and put a hand on Colt's shoulder. "No. This is for keeps. You've been the colonel since I've known you. I was just your mouthpiece. Maybe one day I'll run a company again, but I'm not ready yet. Once this whole thing's through, and we've paid off Mountside, I'm going to find a small merc outfit that will take me on as a lieutenant, maybe even a sergeant, and learn all the stuff I should have learned in the first place. Until then, I'm your staff officer, not the other way around. You're in charge."

Colt was still reeling from Yardley's words when the bar doors whooshed open, and Levin poked her head out. "Sirs, sorry to interrupt, but I thought you would want to know, a ship just transited into the system with the latest GalNet updates. There's a message from Onishi."

* * * * *

Chapter Seventeen

"What's your read on this?" Colt tapped the slate bearing Alice Onishi's message from Brigham. He had read it three times during the flight back to *Uncanny*, and he still wasn't sure what to make of it.

"She sounds well, but also sort of paranoid." Major Petrov had followed Colt back to his room aboard ship at Colt's behest. They had spent the last hour discussing the details of the next day's change of command ceremony. Colt found the idea completely unnecessary—why make a fuss?—but the command staff found it indispensable. The staff, at Captain Torres' urging, had won that argument.

"I agree with you on the paranoid bit," Colt said.

Onishi's message, encrypted for FMT eyes only, made it clear she felt odd around her Mormon employers. Colt would have chocked that up to cultural differences—everyone knew Mormons could be strange—but the captain had addressed that idea. She said it was something more. According to her, the Mormons were hiding something. They seemed particularly interested in guarding the entrances to a series of underground bunkers beneath their city, but whenever Onishi inquired about the contents, the Mormon authorities politely demurred. She had even tried sneaking around in their computer networks using her pinplants, something Colt would not have approved of had she bothered to ask, and had run into the most aggressive firewalls she had ever encountered. That was saying something. Onishi had a reputation for hacking. She was the best in the battalion.

"I don't get the feeling Captain Onishi's in any sort of danger." Petrov spread his hands. "Should I send her a message to stop snooping around where she isn't wanted?"

Colt considered for a moment. He had had a crush on Alice Onishi since the day she arrived at FMT as a freshman. Separating that crush from his duty as a commander didn't come easily. He wanted to tell Petrov to forget it. Her suspicions were innocent and not likely to cause problems. But if she was caught trying to break into their client's computer, even for a supposedly good reason, she could cost the company a payday.

"Yes. Do that, Feliks. She needs to stick to her mission. I'm betting she's bored. You and I both know sentry duty on a dead planet can suck the life out of you. She's probably seeing conspiracies that aren't there. And even if she's right, and the Mormons are hiding something, so what? It's their planet. They can hide whatever they like as far as we're concerned. Tell her that."

"Yes, sir." Petrov looked around the room. "Would you like me to send up some orderlies to move your personal effects to the command suite?"

Colt frowned at his XO, though he knew Petrov was right. He couldn't go on living in the cramped accommodations while running FMT. It wouldn't look right. As Torres had quipped when Colt had balked at the idea of moving, "You don't want to look like a reluctant commander. Fear breeds fear."

"Sure. And have them alter my uniforms while you're at it. I can't walk around with Lieutenant Colonel insignia after tomorrow morning."

"Will do." Petrov flashed his commander a winning smile. "Don't worry, sir. You'll do great, and you've got a first-rate staff to make certain of it."

"Thanks. Seriously, that really does help."

"Anytime, sir. I'll go make the arrangements." Petrov headed for the door.

Colt started pulling clothes from his dresser to make things easier for the orderlies when they came to pack his stuff, but a memory struck him, and he turned back to the XO. "Feliks, one more thing."

"Sir?" Petrov stood half in and half out of Colt's door.

"Tomorrow, after the ceremony, have the guard bring Sloan by my office. I should be settled by then, and it's time I decided what to do with him."

"Can do, sir." Petrov tilted his head, his expression curious. "Have you?"

"Have I what?"

"Decided what to do with Sloan."

"Maybe, but ultimately it's up to him."

* * *

Colt wondered if the big desk in the commander's office would ever feel anything but foreign to him. Humans had nanites for most common diseases, but a cure for impostor syndrome had yet to be invented. Despite his gray dress uniform with its embroidered colonel's insignia, the crew complement of over five hundred who called him 'sir,' and the power to call down merry hell on anyone who stood against him, the desk made Colt feel like a kid playing merc. He only hoped it didn't show on his face.

Seated before him, his face pale, the former Sergeant, now Private First Class Brandon Sloan watched him with worried eyes. The private had spent the entirety of their one-hundred-and-seventy-hour trip to Spimu as well as the battle with the Ten Whispers in *Uncanny Valley's* eight-by-eight brig. His guards had let him out once each day for physical training and a shower. That sort of treatment usually resulted in one of two outcomes. Either the prisoner saw the error of his ways, or he became angry enough to rage. Fortunately, Colt saw no rage in Sloan's face. On the contrary, he looked repentant.

"Do you feel you can return to duty without another incident?" Colt saw no need to mention the crime. They both knew what he was talking about.

Sloan cleared his throat and nodded. "Yes, sir. I'm ready to go back to work."

"Good. That's what I wanted to hear. I'll have the first sergeant place you back on the duty roster."

"May I ask a question?" Sloan glanced at the guard standing behind him, "in private, sir?"

"You're dismissed, Sergeant Richards. Private Sloan is no longer a prisoner."

"Yes, sir." Richards headed for the door.

Colt waited until she left then nodded at Sloan.

"I heard it was you who kept Colonel Yardley from giving me lashes."

"Yes." Colt wanted to add how stupid an idea that had been, but refrained. No need to bad-mouth a fellow officer in front of a junior enlisted man.

"Thank you for that. I can't say I loved living in that cell for so long. I sort of thought you had forgotten about me after a while, but every time I wanted to curse your name, I reminded myself how much worse things could have been."

It didn't take much insight, or much analysis, to see how Colt could best help Sloan, whom he certainly *hadn't* forgotten about while he was dealing with pirates and promotions and all the other insanity that went with running a merc enterprise. On reflection, breaking this problem down with the OODA loop had been easy compared to everything else.

"I know you worry about your wife and children back home," Colt said, willing his voice to remain stable. Emotion always made the task of keeping his anxiety at bay much harder.

"Yes, sir." Sloan looked as if he might say more, but clamped his jaw shut.

"You can speak freely."

"It's the reduction in rank, sir. I'd like to ask that you reinstate me as a Sergeant. Not for me, but for them. My pay's so low, I don't know if they can feed themselves."

"I can't do that, Private."

Instant anger raced across Sloan's face. It was there and gone in a blink, replaced by bitter disappointment, then a sort of doleful acceptance. "I understand."

"But on the subject of your family, I want you to know they were never out of my mind while you were incarcerated. I knew your demotion would hurt them, so I ordered Weep to send my pay to your family in addition to yours."

For a moment, Sloan sat perfectly still, his eyes tracking back and forth uncomfortably across Colt's face. He looked like a man trying to comprehend a foreign language. "You did what?"

"I don't need my pay right now." Colt shrugged his shoulders at the stunned private. "All my needs are provided for by the company, and I don't have time for shore leave. What am I going to do with credits? I had asked Weep to add my pay to the monthly Mountside payments so we could get out of debt quicker, but I figured your family needed that money more."

"Sir, I—" Sloan rose and reached a hand across the desk for Colt to shake.

Colt stood and shook. For one disconcerting instant, he worried Sloan might come around the desk to hug him, but the moment passed, and the private released his hand.

"I don't know how to say thank you." Sloan's eyes were glassy, though he managed to hold back his tears. "I want to decline. I should decline. But—"

"Don't be stupid. And don't think about it. Earn back your stripes. I'll stop the stipend once you're a sergeant again. But tell your wife not to grow too accustomed to double paychecks. I am going to need mine eventually."

"Yes, sir." Sloan snapped off a sharp salute, and Colt returned it.

"Now get out of here. We've both got work to do."

Colt allowed himself a small smile once the door shut behind Private Sloan. Sometimes it felt good to be a colonel.

* * *

And then there were other times.

"So, after all expenses, including this month's regular payment, we can afford to pay back only one one-hundredth of what we owe Mountside?" Colt stared at the slate in his hand in disbelief. The figures Weep had sent him made his head ache.

"It would have paid more, but they're charging usurious interest as you can see in column twenty-four C.

Colt was in a foul mood before the general staff meeting. That morning he had sent four messages informing loved ones their children, spouses or significant others had been killed while serving FMT. The pain of sending those letters had been augmented because Colt knew the recipients had sent their students to a school, one that had rarely suffered any sort of casualties, only to learn that they had become full-time mercenaries—that the school had transformed into a merc company, not just a training cadre.

Looking at Weep's numbers worsened Colt's mood. Had he spent good people's lives for so little gain? At this rate, the entire student body would end up in bondage, perhaps for a fraction fewer years than they would have otherwise, for what? Colt would have rather worked as a Mountside slave forever than tell Corporal Dionte Lassiter's mother her son was killed by a Tortantula on a remote planet she had likely never heard of while assaulting some minor pirates' stronghold.

Weep swept her floating platform around Major Petrov's chair and approached Colt. "I understand you feel like we earned almost nothing for the Ten Whispers' job, but you're wrong, sir. In reality, we profited more on this contract than nearly any Belknap worked. And the figures you're looking at don't contain our projected pay from liquidating the pirates' former holdings. Yes, that might take too long to make a difference, but I think we have a friend in Malfren. He knows we're on a strict timeline."

"And on the topic of the Sandonian Cooperative," Petrov said, "Malfren has been advertising for us. He sent word an hour ago that he might have found us a new client."

"Details?" Colt managed to flick his gaze up to his new XO before looking back at his slate.

"Preliminary ones, yes. Looks like Malfren has a contact inside the personal security detail for Grennis Bredge. She's a Veshan, an underrepresented minority on Spimu." Petrov tapped his slate, and an image appeared on the office's central Tri-V display. The creature reminded Colt of the mythical Sasquatch from Earth, except she wore a plum-colored dress and golden earrings. Her hair, which covered most of her body, was brown and silky, and expensively well groomed.

"What does she need mercs for?" Levin asked.

An image of the sergeant in her haptic suit after the battle of the Ten Whispers flashed through Colt's mind, but he dashed it quickly. That kind of thinking would incite his anxiety like nothing else. He had to focus.

"She's from the spaceport city of Domarstall." Petrov waved a hand and an image of a sprawling metropolis replaced the alien. "Like I said, the Veshan are a small minority on this planet. Bredge recently won Union Envoy in a hotly contested election. A lot of people, some of them in the Spimu government, have questioned whether her win was legitimate."

Colt consulted his pinplants, calling up Petrov's preliminary report on Spimu politics, which he had filed the night before. Colt had read it, but he had read a lot of things in the last eighteen hours. Scanning the highlights brought back the particulars.

Eight races controlled the bulk of Spimu's business and government concerns. While hundreds of different groups of aliens had settled on the planet over the last millennia, their influence paled in comparison to what had become known as the Major Eight. Like most multi-cultural, multi-species planets, Spimu's government made an effort to encourage inclusiveness among the various races, which was all well and good, except Spimu's bureaucrats took it to the point of social engineering. They attempted through various means, including targeted taxing and zoning laws, to force mixed species communities to intermingle. They used social programs to build high-rise apartments with living spaces for Tortantulas next to those for Oogar next to those for something completely different all over the planet. The result? A lot of empty high rises that entrepreneurs bought on the cheap for refurbishment into single-species living spaces.

As with communities throughout the Union, species of one type tended to buy real estate together. That didn't mean they hated aliens from other worlds. In fact, social integration on Spimu far exceeded that on any other planet in the known galaxy. Unfortunately, that wasn't enough for some activists. During the last thirty years, a movement had sprung up calling for more minority representation in Spimu's government. Colt agreed with that idea wholeheartedly. Unfortunately, in several cases over the last five years, minority candidates were found to have cheated their way to the top using various corrupt means. In one case, a Zuul labor representative had hired a disreputable merc company to kidnap her opponent's daughter to win her seat in a lower chamber of the Spimu government.

Which brought Colt to Grennis Bredge. As Petrov had said, Bredge belonged to a small minority race, the Veshan, yet she had won the coveted position of Planetary Envoy to the Union. No non-Major Eight race had ever taken that seat.

"Was it?" Weep looked around at the Humans. "Legitimate, I mean."

Petrov rolled one shoulder in a half shrug. "The Spimu government thinks so. Their prime minister convened a special court to investigate the results, and they found no proof of corruption. Unfortunately for Bredge, people are now saying she somehow bought off the prime minister."

"And the court?" Colt couldn't hide the doubt in his tone.

"And the special investigators appointed by the court," Petrov said, nodding. "It's all lunacy. Worse, some of Bredge's loudest detractors come from her own community. They say she's not representative of the Veshan as a species."

"What?" Levin looked askance at Petrov, then realization dawned in her eyes. "Oh, let me guess, because she's female? Is this some sort of patriarchy we're dealing with?"

"Almost." Petrov rolled his eyes. "It's not because she's female, it's because she refuses to wear the traditional headdress known as a toomloc. It's a cross between a turban and a cape, from what I can tell. Veshan tribal leaders wore them for thousands of years to show status, and that tradition survived into modern times. But Bredge has said she finds the thing uncomfortable and unfashionable. No one else in the Spimu government or the Union wears such a thing, so she doesn't see why she must."

"I like her already," Levin said with a wicked smile that made Colt swallow and look away.

"Does Bredge want something in particular or general sentry duty?" asked Captain Sampson. Colt could see her forming squads for a guard detail in her mind.

"Short term sentry duty, though I think if we prove ourselves, we might win follow-on contracts." Petrov tapped his slate again, and the table's Tri-V zoomed in on a street level map of the spaceport. "Representative Bredge has been on Capital Planet for the last four Spimu months. She's due back a week from now, and the city has organized a parade in her honor as she's the first minority to act as envoy."

"That doesn't sound like a good idea given the political climate." Captain Butler looked wary. "I take it she wants our protection?"

"The head of her security detail does, and she has the backing of the city government that really wants this thing to go off without a hitch. It will look good for the spaceport."

"How much does it pay?" Weep floated her platform back to its place between Petrov and Levin, her dark eyes taking on the shrewd cast they got whenever she talked credits.

"We're leaving the negotiating up to you," Petrov said with a chuckle. "But I contacted the head of Bredge's security team last night, and she guaranteed ten million."

Weep dropped her Flatar-sized slate on the table, her small mouth falling open in shock. "For guard duty?"

"Obviously, they expect trouble." Levin pointed at the holographic image before them, and a red line appeared along the planned travel route. "The parade route leads right through the heart of the city. We're talking about an urban canyon nearly two miles deep in some places. I notice Bredge's flight takes her pretty low too, so that means her flyer will be susceptible to snipers on all the major walkways as well as fire from the street and the surrounding buildings."

"We're the largest merc company in the sector, and Bredge's people haven't been able to entice any others to take the contract," Petrov said.

"Really? I can't imagine why." Captain Sampson shook her head in faux amazement. "It sounds so easy."

"My point," Petrov said, lifting a warning eyebrow toward Sampson, "is that the offer is high because Bredge's people are growing desperate. She insists on attending, and the city wants it to happen. Whether we take the job or not, Bredge is going to be in the line of fire."

"We're taking the job." Colt put down his slate and briefly looked around the room at his gathered command staff. "We have to. Weep, I want you to squeeze every credit you can out of this one. Sounds like the city's paying, so that means there's plenty more than what they're offering. And make sure you negotiate a combat bonus. A hefty one. If we have to fight in an urban environment, I expect it to be worth our while."

"You know I will, sir." Weep's lips curled up in a feral smile that reminded Colt why the diminutive Flatar were one of the Union's thirty-seven merc races. "They'll beg for mercy."

* * * * *

Chapter Eighteen

L ike most starports Colt had seen, Domarstall was an industrialized metropolis that sprawled across the land in every direction. Silver towers and pyramids, sports domes, and green spaces described its skyline and interior, providing homes, work, and entertainment for the people who lived there. Most of the mega scrapers housed populations larger than entire cities on less industrialized planets, and they were self-contained in that they produced or shipped in everything a resident could need. Anyone with the credits could move in and never leave.

Colt imagined that sort of life as he watched the cityscape pass below his flyer. The thought gave him a chill. What must it be like to work the same job in the same place on the same planet forever? Sure, life aboard *Uncanny* sometimes got stale, but sooner or later, the crew turned up at a new place with a new set of problems to solve. City living felt too much like prison in comparison.

"I've tentatively placed RATs in these key areas." Levin sent a command to the flyer's floorboard display via her implants. It showed the streets below crisscrossed with hundreds of enclosed walkways linking the starport's stately buildings, zoomed out to show the entire parade route, and a series of red dots appeared along its six-kilometer length.

"I feel safer already." Grennis Bredge flashed Colt a smile, her pearl-white, uniformly square teeth gleaming, even in the enclosed flyer's semi-darkness.

The Spimu dignitary had insisted FMT's officers outline their plan to safeguard her and her staff during the parade. Colt had taken that as a bad sign at first. He had envisioned her trying to make changes according to her whims rather than the necessities of the operating environment, and he had come ready to argue. But so far, the genteel alien had done no such thing. On the contrary, she appeared fascinated with the whole enterprise.

Bredge's chief of security, a massive Jivool named Onteb Nashun, grunted his agreement in a deep rumble. "Good layout. You've hit all the weak areas. I'll arrange my forces at line-of-sight counter points in alignment with yours. That should help them work together."

"Thank you, sir," Levin said with a nod.

"I never thought six clicks could feel so long." Colt swiped at the image with his hand and used his implants to zoom in on a group of flashing icons. The motion, and his interest in the plan, kept his anxiety at bay, even in the mixed company. "Are those the CASPer positions in orange?"

"Yes, sir," said Major Petrov, who sat opposite Levin. The two of them had collaborated with FMT's company commanders for the past several days to formulate the plan. "The CASPer teams will escort Representative Bredge's flyer directly, while the RATs cover the front and rear."

That made good sense. Although the armored suits could make short-duration flights, they did so using kerosene-based rocket fuel. The RATs could sustain flight for about ten minutes—plenty of time to cover the parade route once, but not nearly enough should an attack occur. In that case, Colt would want his RATs as full of fuel as possible, not wasting it on trailing after their charge.

The afternoon sun, hot outside their air-conditioned vehicle, glinted off the many fan-driven machines passing below. Colt knew city officials would divert the traffic for tomorrow's parade, but seeing it triggered a concern. "How are we set for overhead defense?"

"*Hermes* is still down for repairs, but we've got our other two dropships." Major Petrov squeezed one eye shut like a man expecting a slap. "I know they can't compare to computer driven jets, but they did well against the Ten Whispers. Also, our overhead coverage is somewhat redundant. Domarstall will be handling air support, and they've got a huge number of drones set to guard the route."

"Are they calling in their military?" Colt asked.

"No sir." Petrov sounded apologetic. "That's why I grimaced. They're using security volunteers. Sort of a citizens' flying patrol thing."

Captain Torres, who sat squashed between the flyer's rear door and Bredge's enormous security chief, sighed but displayed no other outward signs of his disgust at trusting a government to handle security matters.

Colt grinned at him. He couldn't agree more.

"See to it we have our drones flying and get Zorn to aid the dropships with our lander. Hopefully, we won't need any of them, but you never know."

* * *

Having read the reports put together by his intel squads, Colt had thought Grennis Bredge a polarizing, unpopular character in Spimu politics. But those reports had focused, and rightly so, on all the possible threats looming over the envoy's head. Judging from the tens of thousands of cheering citizens who turned up to line the streets, the pedestrian bridges, and the roofs and balconies of some of the lower buildings, Bredge certainly had her share of fans. Many of them carried holographic signs with messages of support or noisemakers they shook or slung or keyed to produce resounding blats as the representative's flyer passed by.

Colt's stomach twisted in knots. There were too many people down there, too many possible angles of attack. He was a bundle of nerves as he watched the envoy's procession pass the halfway mark of the parade route.

"The midway point has come and gone," Major Petrov said, sounding relieved. Wearing his CASPer, he stood next to Colt aboard the dropship, *Doubleday*, watching the parade through the ship's open bay door and his Tri-V.

"And half to go." Colt used his implants to focus in on Bredge's open air flyer. The Veshan diplomat, dressed in a flowing green outfit devoid of any headdress, smiled and waved at the passing crowds. She looked genuinely comfortable under the sort of scrutiny that would have sent Colt scrambling for something to hide behind. No amount of focusing on breaking down problems would have gotten him through that sort of stage fright.

"How are things on the ground, Levin?" Petrov moved his CASPer to the edge of the bay for a better look at the distant streets.

Though swarms of citizens milled about below, Colt could pick out his troopers at a glance, since the crowds gave his CASPers a wide berth. Higher up, set at intervals along the route, reinforced platforms affixed to the encroaching buildings gave the CASPers places to land and stand guard. As Bredge's flyer passed, the CAS-

Pers joined the procession, moving from one position to the next so her coterie of guards grew as the flyer progressed.

Captain Torres, who also wore a CASPer, his possession since winning his bet with Yardley, pointed toward one of the aerial bridges that spanned between two buildings. "Colt, you should run a chemical spectral analysis on that walkway. It's giving off some strange readings."

Without hesitation, Colt switched his Tri-V to scan the area in question. Though it was now over a century old, the technique of examining light emissions to judge chemical content remained one of the best methods for ferreting out bomb creation and bomb emplacement.

The results made Colt jerk against his harness. According to his suit's computer, the air immediately around that footbridge was rife with nitroamine, a key ingredient in several types of explosives, including K2. "Petrov!"

"Already on it, sir."

Three RATs boosted from a lower roof to the covered bridge. One landed on top, while the other two scrambled along the bottom, searching for the emissions source.

"You think it's a bomb?" Colt turned to Captain Torres who had more experience with explosives than anyone in FMT. Though he knew the captain disliked giving him advice in front of anyone, lives were at stake, and Colt wasn't about to let a breach of protocol take one of his people.

Torres must have agreed. He didn't hesitate in answering. "Yes."

"Petrov, tell your RATs to clear that bridge, then get out of there," Colt ordered.

"Yes, sir."

Unaware of the possible bomb threat, Captain Zorn had continued to slowly edge the *Doubleday* around to follow Bredge's progress, thereby obscuring the bridge.

"Zorn, I need you to swing us back about fifteen degrees in the opposite direction. Petrov and I need to see something."

"Will do," came the K'kng captain's reply.

The *Doubleday* came to a stop and its engines pulsed a bit louder for a second. The ship rotated back to where it had been just in time for them to see the pedestrian bridge explode in a brilliant gout of flame and chest-thumping noise. People screamed in fear, pain, and confusion as the steel alloy structure disintegrated, the bulk of it toppling toward the ground in a superheated fireball. The three RATs who had been attached to the bridge went flying with the rest of the detritus and dropped forty stories to the ground. Only one of them, PFC Sinclair, managed to regain consciousness before hitting the road. He fired his jets with a few meters to spare, cushioning rather than avoiding the collision. He broke his left leg despite the armor, but thankfully didn't lose his life.

Petrov cursed. So did Torres.

Colt stared in shock for a moment, his brain seemingly frozen. Fear and anxiety threatened to smother his rational mind, but he fought them down. He didn't have time to lose himself. There were people relying on him for their lives.

Harkening back to hours spent with Torres learning the technique, Colt analyzed the situation, looking for the set of problems so he could address the most urgent first. His fear and worry sloughed away as his mind worked with frenzied haste.

Though a bomb had gone off, it had missed Bredge's flyer. While Colt had lost two of his people, the bulk of his force remained. Levin was already on the battalion channel coordinating efforts to secure their charge's vehicle. She sent the forward CASPers to surround it in the air. She also wisely refrained from ordering the flyer's pilot to scramble, as that might have been just what the unknown assailant wanted.

FMT troopers had swept the parade route three times that morning, most recently within forty minutes of Bredge's arrival. Since Colt knew those sweeps included the same sort of environmental check Captain Torres had used to detect the bridge bomb, it meant that whoever had planted it had done so in the last half hour. While that didn't guarantee the perpetrator was still in the area, it certainly raised the possibility.

Calmly, Colt keyed the battalion channel. "Good work, Top. I want everyone performing constant spectral scans for nitroamine. It looks like that was the key accelerant used on the bridge. RATs, I need you watching the crowd. It's likely the attacker is still nearby. FMT pilots, remain vigilant for incoming. Whoever did this might have been trying to flush the envoy away from the parade route."

Colt scanned every building and walkway in sight for the telltale chemical signature. Every centimeter he found lacking the stuff sent relief coursing through him.

Local law enforcement and rescue craft flew out of a cross street, sirens wailing, heading for the downed bridge. Colt fought the urge to send troopers after his fallen people. He didn't like the idea of anyone else recovering their remains, but he knew better than to send his people in close to the local authorities. Why risk having a uninformed cop mistake a CASPer for a terrorist?

Despite a slew of lightly armored police on the street and a growing number of their vehicles crowding the fly space between buildings, chaos ruled below. Citizens of all types, mostly Veshans like Grennis Bredge, hustled along the streets and across the dozens of walkways that hadn't been hit. Luckily, most people had the sense to abandon the walkways as quickly as possible. That was why fewer people died when the next bridge along the parade route exploded.

"How?" Colt demanded. "I just scanned that one less than a minute ago. It—"

"—wasn't a bomb! Look!" Torres shouted, pointing an armored finger back along the parade route.

Colt's blood ran cold. In disbelief, he zoomed in on the writhing mass of bodies scrambling at ground level, not trusting his eyes. He was looking at well over a dozen MinSha leading a veritable army of Tortantulas and Zuul. Armed with laser rifles and a few rocket-propelled grenade launchers, the warriors mowed down civilians and blasted out the facades of businesses, in a play to start fires and cause general havoc.

"What are they doing?" Petrov asked.

Before Colt or Torres could answer, something explosive struck the *Doubleday's* fuselage on the right side. Colt lost his footing and crashed to the bay floor. Torres weathered the shaking and remained on his feet, but Petrov's CASPer tumbled out the bay door. He screamed profanities as he plummeted toward the ground. Fortunately, he had the presence of mind to fire his jumpjets and arrest his fall.

Alarm claxons blared inside the *Doubleday* as the dropship shuddered in the air and started to list. The bay door shut with a clang, and the ship's emergency lighting snapped on. Colt, his head still smarting from where he had banged it against the cockpit bulkhead, started to get up, but Torres held up a warning hand.

"Don't bother yet. This bird doesn't feel too stable. I might be down there with you any second."

"Good advice." Colt gave the captain a thumbs up, then switched to the FMT pilots' channel. "Zorn, what happened?"

"I'm a little busy here, Colonel!" Zorn sounded as if he was trying to push a boulder up an ice cliff. "Missile to the fuselage. Debris in the starboard engine fouled the thing up. We're spinning, if you couldn't tell."

Colt stretched his arms and legs as far as they would go, bracing his metal hands against one bulkhead and his feet against a set of stanchions meant for anchoring heavy equipment racks. The heavy suit shifted a bit, but he managed to keep it from bouncing around the dropship's bay like a wayward ping-pong ball. Feeling at least partially secure, Colt tried focusing on his Tri-V in an effort to track developments outside, but even with his pinplants, he found the task impossible with the ship spinning so fast.

A rending, screeching sound told Colt some part of the *Doubleday* had collided with a building, though without any windows to look out he had no idea what part or which direction the collision had sent them. Heart hammering, he clenched his teeth and held on, cursing his inability to do anything useful.

As he had predicted, and despite gripping a stanchion, Torres' CASPer finally toppled over. Fortunately, he managed to guide it away from Colt so he ended up on the floor at the opposite end of the bay, gripping the bulkhead.

Colt's body grew light inside his suit as the ship's downward spiral increased. Reverse g-forces tried to pry his hands from their positions. He locked the CASPers arms, denting the steel to keep from hurtling to the roof.

"This is going to hurt!" Zorn shouted. "Prepare for impact!"

Colt knew he was going to die. The feeling washed over him with utter certainty and, to his surprise, a grim sort of acceptance. He had tried to accomplish something with his sixteen years, and if this was the end, he could accept it since, in his limited way, he had found success in trying. What he couldn't accept—wouldn't—was the knowledge that his death might mean the deaths of his troopers. Petrov and Levin were both capable leaders, but Colt knew, in his heart, he could protect the battalion better than anyone. Maybe that was arrogant, but he figured if ever there was a time you could let yourself indulge your ego, it was the instant before you died.

The impact slammed Colt back against the Mk 8's headrest, then forward so his restraints bit into his shoulders and chest. A sound like God ripping apart the inside of a star hammered through the fuselage and Colt's bones. He tried to fling his arms out to arrest his movement, but only managed to wrench his shoulder. A bolt of searing pain shot up into his neck.

Then they stopped. Colt hung on the edge of consciousness for several seconds. He squeezed his eyes shut, opened them, and squeezed them shut again. His ears rang. The throbbing pain that ran from the top of his head and down both arms, especially the right, kept time with the beating of his heart

He had to rise. He had to fight. The forces he had seen from the air had been arrayed on the ground. And now, so was he.

Fear caused Colt to open his eyes. He drew a shuddering breath and scanned his Tri-V for damage. The holographic display's left side looked dim, but remained functional. Several systems, none of them key, bore yellow outlines indicating they required maintenance, but to Colt's utter astonishment, the CASPer had fared better than its pilot. Upon reflection, that made sense. Colt was made of meat.

Moving as quickly as he dared, he got his feet beneath him and stood. Torres did the same.

"Are you okay?" Colt asked.

"Honestly? I think I might have a cracked rib, but that's a lot better than I expected."

Voices rang over the battalion net, many of them distressed, but Colt ignored them for the moment. He turned toward the crew compartment, his heart in his throat. "Zorn? Are you hurt?"

The bulkhead door separating the ship's cockpit from the bay popped open with a hiss, and the barrel-chested K'kng limped out, brushing gray desiccated flakes from his fur. "I'm alright, Colonel. The ship's crash foam saved me. But I'm afraid all three of us are in a world of hurt." He pointed behind them.

Colt's feeling of dread doubled as he turned his CASPer to face the bay door. The crash had jammed it mostly open, its frame bent at an awkward angle. Sunlight streamed into the bay. With it came smoke, the sound of gun and laser fire, and the sight of armed MinSha scrambling toward them with all haste.

* * * * *

Chapter Nineteen

Cloistered inside the ruined dropship, Colt couldn't tell how many enemy combatants were heading his way. But he, like Torres and Zorn, knew the answer without their sensors.

Too many.

"Colonel Maier!" Levin's voice cut in on the command channel. She sounded distressed. "I read your vitals as healthy, but the tac says the *Doubleday* went down. What's your condition?"

"We're alive but about to be overrun." Battling his fear, Colt zeroed in on the factors arrayed against him. Though he had assets—his CASPer and Torres'—things looked grim.

"Roger that, sir. We're under enemy attack as well, but they're more heavily grouped on the ground near you. I've dispatched three squads of RATs and one squad of four CASPers to aid you." Levin paused, the command channel silent for a moment. "I'm sorry, Colt, it's all I can spare. They're after the envoy."

"Understood. Do your duty, Sergeant." Colt's shoulder burned like fire, but he ignored it. He turned to Zorn. "Any way to exit out the front?"

The K'kng shook his silver-furred head, his brown eyes focused through the wrecked bay door on the approaching enemy. "No. This bucket doesn't have an emergency exit from the cockpit. Even if it did, you wouldn't be able to get through in your armor."

"Our best bet now is shock." Torres negotiated the row of bent and twisted equipment stanchions and approached the rear door, his dual hyper velocity machine guns trained on daylight. "We go out laying down fire like our ammo's endless, and we might just buy enough time for Levin's reinforcements to arrive."

Seeing no better alternative, Colt switched his CASPer into full combat mode. "Zorn, get in the cockpit and seal the hatch. We'll come back for you once we clear the threat."

"Good luck, Colonel." Zorn hurried back through the cockpit door as ordered. A second later its pneumatic seals hissed, and the indicator light next to it turned red.

"Ready?" Torres took the lead, one armored foot on the gnarled ramp leading to the street.

"No. But I'm going anyway."

Torres laughed as he placed his armored hands against the bay door's roof and shoved upward. His suit's servos groaned at the strain but the gap widened, letting in more sunlight, and making space for the two of them to escape the ruined ship. Lasers flashed past Torres' CASPer. He growled and dropped to the street to return fire.

Colt trailed after the captain through the ruined door and into bedlam. His Tri-V lit up with enemy icons, but he hardly needed its input. Though the *Doubleday* had crash landed almost a kilometer from the original rally point, the attackers had already covered that distance. The MinSha rushed forward on their four legs faster than any human could run, almost as fast as a CASPer pushed to its limits. Though that sort of exertion might hamper them in the long run, it appeared to have no ill effects in the moment. And this moment was all that mattered.

"On me!" Torres shouted, guns blazing at the enemy's front line as he deftly ran sideways to keep his aim true. The twin muzzle flares made it look like his CASPer's hands were aflame. Three MinSha dropped under the captain's initial attack.

Colt mimicked him, firing his accelerator cannon with his right arm. He had opted for a laser on the left arm to save on weight, so the armorers could mount a missile rack on that shoulder. He painted four enemy targets in his display and fired a salvo that closed the distance in less than a second. True to their design, the projectiles homed in on their specified targets, made nearly supersonic contact, and exploded in flashes of fire and thundering booms that shook the street. Even with his armor absorbing most of the concussion and all of the back blast, firing the missiles sent javelins of pain through Colt's injured shoulder.

But it was worth it.

Colt's MinSha targets shattered like porcelain dolls, chunks of chitin and charred meat flying in every direction. Like a human inside a CASPer, the MinSha became as vulnerable as any other living creature once you got past their ultra-tough exterior.

"Good!" Torres shouted as he led Colt in a backward march and continued to chew up the enemy lines with his guns. Despite their numbers—according to Colt's computer there were more than seventy enemy combatants heading their way—Torres' fire caused their remaining opponents to slow, many of them obliged to take cover behind parked flyers.

Together, he and Colt hurried behind the *Doubleday*. Zorn stared out at them from the cockpit windows, his eyes wide.

"You cover right," Torres called over the comm as he retrained his guns on the horde and stepped out from behind the ship to deliver more blazing death.

Colt, his heart in his stomach, scuttled right in a sort of grapevine step and activated his laser at max output. Though a few laser beams ricocheted off his armor, he managed to avoid any direct hits.

Luckily, the majority of the oncoming host consisted of Zuul and other human-sized or smaller merc races. Though the MinSha among them led the way, their numbers were few. Better yet, Torres and Colt had focused their fire on the chitinous monsters by unspoken agreement. As he watched, Colt saw four more missiles stab into the enemy lines, pinpointing MinSha warriors.

Unfortunately, their limited fire couldn't stem the flow. As more of the enemy caught up with their faster compatriots, their massed fire rose in volume. Warning alarms sounded as systems began to fail under the onslaught.

Colt swore and withdrew behind the *Doubleday*. Torres joined him twenty seconds later. One of his CASPer's knees looked partially melted and would hardly bend.

They could have escaped, and they both knew it.

"You fly, I'll wait here for reinforcements so we can get Zorn out." Torres leaned around the dropship to spray bullets. Colt doubted the big man had time to aim, but with the enemy clustered so thickly, how could he miss?

Colt considered Torres' suggestion for about a tenth of a second before dismissing it. If his objective was to safeguard his pilot, having two CASPers do the job beat having one. Abandoning Torres to protect Zorn seemed like a good way to get them both killed. "No, Captain. I'm staying."

"Colt, be reasonable." Again, Torres stepped out from behind cover and fired at the enemy with both guns only to scramble back a second later as laser fire filled the air. "There's no reason for both of us to die here. You have a company to run."

"And you have a job to get back to." Colt selected four more targets within half a block of the ship and fired missiles at them. That done, he turned a critical eye toward his display. Though it felt like Levin had dispatched her support squads to his position hours ago, only a few minutes had passed, and said units appeared to have run into pockets of resistance between here and there. A battle icon encompassed the group as they engaged targets about half a mile from where Colt and Torres fought.

"Those missiles of yours are the only reason we haven't been overwhelmed yet," Torres said. "But you're almost out, and these guys know that. How many have you got left?"

Colt ground his teeth. He was hardly listening to his merc observer, his mind racing over possible solutions to his problem.

"Three," he said absently.

"Fire those and fly. It's the only way you're going to survive this. Go!"

"No. I have a better plan. Give me covering fire. Now!"

Torres hesitated as if he might argue, but something in Colt's voice must have overridden his natural inclination. Firing his jumpjets, Torres darted right this time, bounding over Colt at a steep angle, his guns beating the air like supersonic drum synths set to max tempo.

"Zorn, go into the bay until I tell you otherwise."

"Sir, I don't know what you're planning, but forget it. Go. You can find a new ship's captain." Zorn made a face through the *Double-*

day's cockpit window, a toothless grin full of mirth and bravado. "Just don't expect them to work so cheaply!"

"Into the bay, Zorn. That's a direct order!" Colt used his implants to override three key safety protocols in his left arm laser cannon. "If you're not out of there in three seconds I'm putting you on command report."

Zorn argued no further. He hurried through the bombproof cockpit door and slammed it shut behind him.

More alarms sounded inside Colt's suit, letting him know what he was about to do was extremely foolhardy. Though his CASPer's laser could potentially fire a sustained one megawatt beam, preset dampeners blocked that kind of power due to the potential for causing a critical failure and blowing the unit. Unfortunately, with said dampeners in place, the laser's max intensity would take hours to burn through the *Doubleday's* steel alloy and nanotube reinforced hull.

Colt didn't have hours.

The last of the software safeguards eliminated, he turned the full brunt of his maximum intensity laser on the ship. It emitted a blue-white finger of light that caused his CASPer's cockpit monitors to immediately darken and the heat warning lights to blaze red on the Tri-V.

Colt expected some resistance from the *Doubleday's* armored hull, but the nearly impervious material split like a potato peel under a hot knife. In fact, the laser melted through the top section of the ship and shot into the atmosphere. Colt brought it down quickly drawing as straight a line as he could manage. The hyperintensity light left behind a line of glowing red metal in its wake.

"Zorn, you okay?" From what Colt could see, the laser had chewed through the cockpit and the sealed door behind it. He held his breath when the K'kng captain didn't answer right away.

"Yes!" Zorn finally called. "You could give a lowly pilot a little warning before you saw his ship in half though. You nearly set me on fire."

"Sorry about that. I had no idea my laser would go through the entire ship." Colt slid his metal hands through the still glowing gap and started to widen it only to have a spear of pain stab through his injured shoulder. He gasped, but didn't back off. According to his display, though Torres had momentarily slowed their enemies, they were almost upon them.

Colt screamed as he willed his body and his CASPer to work as one. The servos in his left arm whined, and a double plume of smoke rose from his right elbow, but the cockpit's armor slowly gave way under the insistent pressure. Sparks flew as the control panel split apart with a mighty crash and the sound of rending steel.

Zorn opened the bay door, and knuckled through the opening to stand next to the CASPer. "Now what?" He peered farther down the street to where 1SG Levin's relief force fought a pitched battle between buildings with MinSha and other aliens.

"Now we fly." Colt cinched one arm around Zorn's torso, careful to use just enough pressure to hold him without crushing his ribs, and switched to his private channel with Torres. "Captain! We're evacuating! Follow me!"

"Sir!" Zorn shouted. "This is not what I signed up for. I'm supposed to be the pilot. You're supposed to be the passenger. I do not like role reversal."

"Too bad, Captain. Hold on." Colt fired his jumpjets at full power, and his CASPer roared into the air. Torres followed immediately after, narrowly escaping a line of enemies converging on his position.

Careful to turn his back toward the mass of aliens overrunning the *Doubleday*, Colt headed for a fifty-story building. Several lines of laser fire managed to score hits on his armor, but most missed, and he was already passing out of their effective targeting range by the time he reached the roof.

He released Zorn, who rubbed the hairy arm that had been pinched beneath the CASPer's hand.

"Thank you, sir." The K'kng gazed around the high rise rooftop. "Looks like there's an exit over there."

"Get to it and stay inside until this is over. I don't know how many of these guys there are. They could have people inside any of these buildings."

"Will do." Zorn shook his head.

"What is it?" Colt asked.

"Imagine if all this might be over a stupid hat."

* * * * *

Chapter Twenty

From his vantage point atop the building, it looked to Colt as if an army had dropped on the spaceport, though how they could have managed it he had no idea. Fortunately, from what his Tri-V showed, the enemy's numbers were no longer growing. They must have all attacked at once. Unless they held some of their forces in reserve. A frightening thought.

Whoever they were, they hadn't brought many flyers. A handful sped along the unnatural canyon of skyscrapers, but most of the fighting was taking place at street level. Tapping into the battalion's network of drones, hovering well above the city, he saw three pockets of fighting: Levin's at the end of the parade route where she battled to keep their charge safe, one almost directly below Colt where his reinforcements had gotten bogged down, and the one he had just left. That last force seemed bent on causing as much destruction and mayhem as possible. As he watched, local cops converged on their position, and several dozen lightly armored and armed troopers attacked from the air and ground. Where were they two minutes ago?

"Captain Torres," Colt turned to face his watchdog. "I'm dropping to reinforce my reinforcements. I know you're not supposed to get involved—"

"Don't be stupid, kid. I'm with you. These bastards, whoever they are, attacked me too. I take that kind of thing personally."

Though Colt couldn't see the grizzled veteran inside his CASPer, the suit's pockmarked and scarred exterior served perfectly as a stand in. He could almost see Torres' furious expression. Torres strode purposefully to the edge of the building where he could peer down at the melee through his exterior cameras.

Colt followed, but took a further step and dropped off the building like a meteor. Warning alarms sounded as his falling CASPer picked up speed. The street rushed up to swat him, but Colt fired his jumpjets just in time to cushion his fall, the exhaust blowing up dust and detritus in swirling plumes. He landed in the center of a raging battle between a gaggle of his troopers and ten enemy combatants. A MinSha armed with a laser looked at him, its otherwise expressionless face emoting the only way it could. Its mouth hung open in shock.

Using his uninjured arm, Colt punched the alien in the face. The force of the CASPer's blow sent the MinSha reeling backward across the street into the reinforced plastic façade of a clothing boutique. Rather than shatter, the resilient plastic bounced the hapless alien back the way it had come. Struggling for balance and trying to bring its weapon to bear, it barreled toward Colt who punched it again. This time the MinSha collapsed, unconscious, on the street.

"Yes!" Corporal Wendy O'Malley pumped an armored fist in the air.

But Colt had no time to celebrate. Though his sudden appearance had momentarily stunned the enemy, they were already reorienting on the new threat in their midst. Unfortunately for them, Colt wasn't the only reinforcement dropping in on the party.

While the enemy focused their fire on Colt, Captain Torres hit the street like an extinction-level impact. Shards of cement flew into the air when Torres' steel alloy feet cracked the surface. He landed in the center of the massed force, both arm guns firing in unison, bent on annihilating every armed alien in range.

With the enemy force in sudden disarray, Colt's troopers surged into the fight. The four CASPers Levin had dispatched ran headlong into the fray while the lighter RATs took up oblique positions on the flanks. All fired and fought with admirable determination and the precision of many hours of practice. Tracers and laser beams lit up the street. The sounds of battle shook the surrounding buildings and echoed through the city.

In seconds, the enemy force was cut by a third as they tried to pull back and return fire. Their unit cohesion sucked. They fought more like individual warriors than trained soldiers—no fire discipline, no sense of purpose other than destruction and death and saving their own skins.

Routed, and watching their comrades fall in droves, the remaining force fell apart. Those at the rear tried to hold strong, but the front line disintegrated into a free-for-all retreat and bowled over anyone in their way.

Colt's troopers started after them, the rage of battle driving them to take revenge on the monsters who had tried to kill them, but he called them off. "Leave them. We've got to reinforce Levin. Looks like things are heating up for her."

Colt's Tri-V showed a pitched battle raging from air to ground at the end of the parade route. A storm of red icons engulfed Levin's blue. Explosions and the clatter of machine gun fire echoed from that direction.

Colt glanced at the names of the troopers surrounding him on his Tri-V. "Corporal O'Malley, you the ranking member here?"

"Yes, sir," said a voice that sounded almost as young as Colt's. "They took out Sergeant Bossley." The Corporal pointed to a burned out, mangled wreck Colt hardly recognized as a CASPer.

The sight threatened to overwhelm Colt. He had to look away quickly and focus on his immediate problems to avoid losing himself to anger and grief. "Take charge of your people and report to Top."

"Yes, sir."

Colt didn't wait to see if the corporal followed his orders. Instead, he sent a brief message to Torres outlining his intentions, then fired his jumpjets. Though his CASPer left the ground slowly, in seconds it was screaming along the roadbed, two and a half meters above the surface. The few civilians who hadn't taken shelter despite the raging battle screamed and huddled for safety as he blasted past them. One or two armed warriors, stragglers from Levin's fight, took some potshots at him, but nothing came close.

As he roared through the city, Colt established a direct comm link with Levin through her pinplants. "How are you holding up?"

"We're giving as good as we're getting, but we could use a hand."

"Any idea who these guys are?" Colt had almost reached Levin's position.

"Not sure, but they want Grennis Bredge dead. Political rivals I guess."

"When Bredge said she wanted a guard detail, I figured she was worried about a lone gunman or a bomb threat, not an armed death force." Colt raced around a bend and found himself staring at the backs of an army of aliens massed behind half a dozen overturned and burning ground cars and flyers. More heavily armed and armored than those Colt had faced before, these must have been the group's elite. There were no fewer than fifteen Besquith, a dozen

MinSha, and an eclectic mix of other merc races all bent on destroying the Humans arrayed before them.

Two blocks away, using another slew of wreckage as cover, FMT
troopers returned fire in quick, precise bursts and salvos of armor-
piercing missiles. Despite their discipline and bravery, several of the
CASPers lay in heaps, their hulls scored by laser fire. To Colt's horror, his displays showed that several contained the corpses of dead
troopers. Others held pilots with light injuries, but they weren't going
anywhere unless they had death wishes.

Some of the enemy combatants noticed Colt's arrival, alerted by
the sound of his jumpjets. A handful of Zuul and Tortantula spun
around to fire at him, but he deftly swerved right, avoiding the bulk
of the attack.

But that wouldn't do. For the first time he could remember, Colt
wanted attention. Everyone's attention. And he wanted it now.

Flipping over, Colt fired his engines, slowed his backward momentum until he stalled, then flipped again to spin his CASPer upright so that he landed with his suit's knees bent, one armored hand
on the ground. Without a moment's hesitation or remorse, he cycled
his overclocked arm laser to full power, pointed it toward the right
side of the enemy's front line, and fired. Moving from right to left
like a samurai slicing through rice stalks, Colt cut a swath through his
enemies.

Aliens screamed. Some lost limbs. Others lost heads or torsos.
The piled wreckage couldn't protect them. The laser sliced through
the plastic and steel alloy frames as easily as it burned through flesh.
All the while, it emitted a high-pitched scream that overwhelmed the
chatter of machine guns and the explosions triggered by bombs and

missile fire. A warning icon popped up on Colt's Tri-V, his left arm outlined in red, but he ignored it.

Torres arrived on Colt's heels, leading the reinforcements in a high arc to avoid the street-level laser fire. They landed behind Colt and opened up with an array of weapons. With the overpowered laser sweeping their lines, the attackers were obliged to keep their heads down, for all the good it did them.

Emboldened by the arrival of their commander and the reinforcements, Levin's people emerged from cover to join them.

With nowhere to run, the would-be assassins tried to rally. More than a dozen of them rushed forward in an ill-conceived attempt to come to grips with the CASPers. FMT's combined fire cut them down like a machete slicing through bamboo shoots, but still they came, the fear of impending death having whipped them into a frenzy.

Colt took out two Tortantulas and a Besquith with his rail gun before switching back to his laser. He aimed at a Besquith headed his way, already scanning for his next target, but something inside the CASPer's arm went POP. Instead of producing a coherent beam of laser fire, a curtain of smoke rose from it.

The Besquith, its lips peeled back to reveal row upon row of glistening teeth, howled in triumph as it plowed into Colt, claws ripping at his upraised arm. Haptic feedback gave way to actual pain when the alien's claws found Colt's flesh. He screamed at the sudden jolt of agony in his forearm.

As they fell together, the Besquith attempted to flip Colt and thereby use him as a shield against FMT's combined fire.

"Hell no!" Colt kicked a leg out to one side, arresting their spin so that the Besquith landed atop his CASPer, but it was a near thing.

The beast was strong and insane with rage. Servos and gears whined inside Colt's suit as he struggled to keep the Besquith from sinking its claws into something more vital than his arm.

Colt tried to punch the Besquith with his uninjured hand, but the alien trapped that arm in a powerful wrestling lock. Try as he might, Colt couldn't free it. Pressing its advantage, the Besquith again sank its claws through the CASPer and into Colt's injured arm, higher up this time, near his armpit, eliciting another scream from him.

"Colt!" Levin sounded distraught. "We can't shoot it. We might hit you. Try to kick it away so we can get a clear shot."

"What do you think I'm doing?" Colt howled. "It's using some sort of martial art on me. I can't get away from it."

"Fire your rail gun," Torres said.

"What? I'll blow my own leg off."

"It's not aimed at your leg. It's pointed at the Besquith's boot. Fire now before it moves."

Colt squeezed his eyes shut against what he figured would be the worst pain of his life, and fired the rail gun. To his surprise, his leg remained intact. The Besquith's, however, did not. The high-velocity round made the bottom third of the alien's leg one with the street.

The Besquith screamed and jerked back, releasing its hold on Colt, who slid the railgun under its chin and fired a second time.

Colt pushed the now-decapitated body away and stood, his arm throbbing. He surveyed the battlefield through a smear of gore on his forward cameras and a pall of smoke that filled the area. Most of the enemy had died fighting, though a handful cowered in the rubble, their weapons at their feet.

"Is it over?" Ignoring the pain in his arm, Colt scanned his Tri-V for enemy icons. He expected another wave of attack any second.

"Yes. You won," Torres said.

"Did we?" Colt's gaze fell upon a burned out and partially melted CASPer. "Then why doesn't it feel that way?"

"Because you've got a heart. Don't lose that. It'll help you keep perspective when you suffer losses. And no matter which side of a battle you come out on—victory or defeat—you'll always have losses."

* * * * *

Chapter Twenty-One

"How long will this take?" Colt sat in a sterile doctor's office about ten blocks from the parade route. A flexible cast ran the length of his arm from shoulder to wrist. It contained a viscous orange suspension filled with nanites furiously working to repair Colt's injuries. A readout built into the cast displayed their progress as they knit the gouge marks on his lower biceps and mid forearm back together.

"About thirty hours," said a Pendal who had introduced itself as Dr. Nihnt.

"Is there any way to speed this up?" Colt hopped off the doctor's examination table and tried to pull on his shirt, pleased that Major Petrov had thought to send a change of clothes from *Uncanny*. Dr. Nihnt had cut Colt out of his wrecked haptic suit when he arrived for emergency surgery.

The Pendal deftly slipped Colt's cast into the sleeve using two of its hands. "Ah, youth. You repair an adolescent's mangled arm, and they want it hurried up!"

"I have a merc company to run." Colt stood still while the doctor buttoned his shirt for him. "Thank you."

"It was a pleasure healing you. I had never worked on a human before. Your people have a fascinating bone structure."

"Uh, thanks. I'll have my purser contact your office for payment." Colt started to scratch his cast, but he caught himself and relaxed.

231

"The Flatar? She already paid." Dr. Nihnt opened the door and ushered Colt into a short corridor leading to the waiting room. Even on an alien planet filled with a thousand different races, some things never changed.

Torres, Petrov, and Levin stood when they saw Colt. Though Torres remained stoic, the other two grinned like sloths, and Levin moved to give Colt a hug but checked herself at the last second. She settled for sticking out a hand to shake, though her cheeks flushed crimson.

Despite his promise to himself to keep things professional between them, Colt would have preferred the hug.

"What's the verdict?" Petrov did a good job pretending he hadn't noticed Levin's near breach of company etiquette, but not that good.

"I had torn ligaments in my right shoulder and a cracked rib that I never noticed and my other arm was sliced down to the bone." Colt lifted the black cast. "Doctor said it will be fine in three days. Wish we didn't have to spend the money on it though."

"Don't," Levin said, warning in her tone. She, along with the other two, had fought vehemently with a still-dazed Colt after the battle. He had insisted they find someone to patch him up as cheaply as possible. They couldn't afford the cost, especially with several of their CASPers, including Colt's, sidelined or destroyed. And that didn't take into account the loss of two dropships. Kit's *Hermes* was still under repair, hopefully soon to return, but Colt couldn't imagine the *Doubleday* ever leaving Spimu. Repairing or replacing the ships and equipment were more important than his arm.

Levin had called her commander an idiot, and Petrov had told Colt to shut his stupid mouth. Gazing at his rapidly healing arm, Colt decided to forgive the insubordination. His officers had been right.

They held off talking shop until they reached the small lander parked outside Dr. Nihnt's office building. Though the city around them seemed at peace with its bustling traffic and the sounds of orbital lifters taking off and landing, dark columns of smoke still rose in the west, marking the spot where Grennis Bredge's parade had met its end.

Colt checked his pinplants' chrono and whistled. "Hard to believe less than an hour ago we were fighting for our lives."

"Not for me it isn't," Levin said as she took a seat in the rear and fastened her harness. "I'm still replaying it in my head every second."

"Same." Colt took the seat directly across from her, not realizing it until Petrov wedged himself into the seat beside him. Now he would have to spend the entire flight to orbit making eye contact with her so he wouldn't appear rude.

The pilot sealed the lander's doors and cycled the engines. Within seconds they had left the ground and were boosting for space.

"What have you found out about the group who attacked us?" Colt turned his gaze to Petrov's jaw, then back to a point on Levin's forehead above her brows. Torres might have taught him how to deal with his anxiety in social situations, but it didn't alleviate his awkwardness. He had a feeling he would always struggle with looking other people in the eyes.

"Not much." Petrov shook his head, his dark hair pressed down by the added g-forces of liftoff. "Local authorities are refusing to share any information with us. But our intel group has managed to piece together some info. Unfortunately, what they've turned up doesn't make a lot of sense. Some of the guys we were fighting are affiliated with an alt-political group here on Spimu, called Social

Foundation. They're opposed to Grennis Bredge, so maybe they were behind the assassination attempt."

"But only some?" Colt cinched his harness tighter with his good hand as the ship passed out of Spimu's full gravity, into low orbit. His stomach dropped in a familiar way that had become comforting to him.

"The bulk weren't Social Foundation members," Levin said. "And what's more peculiar is that they don't seem to be affiliated with any organizations on Spimu. Most hold citizenship on other planets and came here by untraceable means."

"They're not mercs?" Colt looked from his ranking officer to his ranking noncom. "They all looked like they were from merc races."

"If so, they're not part of any company registered with the Mercenary Guild." Petrov's hair now rose in spikes in the microgravity. Colt would have to remind him to get it cut soon.

"Then you were right," Colt nodded at Levin. "They were pirates."

"Could be." Levin sounded dubious. "Problem is, we know they're not the two pirate companies Lyret dispatched. Turns out those guys got intercepted while attacking a convoy near Chimsa. They were all killed or taken into custody. Someone else organized this group, and our people are at a loss as to who."

"I'd wager ten credits the Spimu authorities don't know either," Petrov said. "That's why they're stonewalling us every time we ask for information. They haven't got a clue, but they're not willing to admit it."

"Agreed." Colt shifted in his seat as the lander's engines fired to adjust their orbit. "What about our people? What was our final casualty count?"

Petrov looked uncomfortable, but Levin spoke up, though her expression was somber. "We lost twenty-six."

Colt swore. He wasn't given to profanity, but sometimes it was all you had. "So many."

Torres looked at him sympathetically.

Levin nodded, her lips pursed. "We also had fifty-seven injured, but not so severely their nanites or sprays couldn't fix them. Sloan and his people are still finalizing the estimates for how many CAS-Pers he can salvage, but we do know that we have forty-three that are totally inoperable and another fifteen that will need substantial repairs before they're fit for service. I detailed his crew to make them the top priority. We've got twenty-three RATs in various states of disrepair as well, along with too many damaged rifles, cannons, and other weapons to count."

Colt was stunned. His brain began to pound. "All this is going to tank our profits."

"This is why a healthy company is a working company," Torres said, momentarily dropping his guise as silent observer. "If you're not actively working contracts, you're not earning credits to pay for repairs from previous ones."

"At this rate, we won't be able to take on new contracts." Colt wanted to slam his healthy fist on his arm rest but resisted the urge. No need to let his people, even Petrov and Levin, see his rage. He needed to maintain his cool exterior if he expected to win other people's confidence. He drew a deep breath, held it a moment, and let it out slowly. "I'll start writing up the death notices as soon as we get back. We'll give our people the merc funerals they deserve."

His three listeners nodded solemnly.

"I know this wasn't part of the plan going in," Petrov said, "but it might be time to start recruiting. We're not hurting for people right now, Levin and I can make adjustments to the company duty rosters, but with Yardley's people working the garrison job and the losses we took today, we're going to be understaffed if we take many more hits. I'd rather fill our ranks than wait around hoping we don't come up short in a fight, especially since we lost some of our key CASPer and RAT operators."

"You're probably right," Colt said as a telltale rumble ran the length of the ship's hull, signaling the lander had docked. He unfastened his harness and lifted out of his seat. "I don't know how much we can afford to pay new recruits. It's not like they're going to work for table scraps like the rest of us. They aren't in debt to Mountside."

"You might be surprised." Torres, who was in the rear, pulled himself even with Colt. "There are always young mercs looking to sign up, and a new company, recruiting for the first time, might entice them. Even some veterans like the idea of getting in early with a company if they think it has a chance of succeeding. But you've got to be careful who you choose."

Colt glanced at the others, painfully aware that this was the second time their observer had broken his silence—the third if you counted his heroics on Spimu.

Torres followed his gaze and shrugged.

Levin and Petrov looked curious, but not overly surprised by Torres' advice.

"Are you offering to help us vet new recruits?" Colt asked.

"This once, yes. You'll need help picking the right people, and I might be able to pull some strings."

The group passed through the main airlock into *Uncanny's* largest starboard bay, pulling themselves along using handholds set into the bulkheads. Holding on with one functional arm was a challenge, but Colt managed it after some fumbling around.

The place buzzed with activity as troopers used compressed air packs to zoom about the oversized bay, trundling CASPer and RAT parts toward the armory. To Colt's surprise and relief, most of the CASPers and RATs looked intact if a bit scratched or scorched from the enemy fire they had endured. Others, however, were little more than flame-blackened and melted parts.

Hearing Levin state their losses in cold numbers hadn't sufficiently driven home just how mangled some of their assets had become during the fight. Looking at the losses reminded Colt again of the lives they had spent trying to fulfill their duty.

"I don't suppose you've already talked to Weep about your hiring idea?" Colt opened the bay door with his pinplants and pulled himself through. He had planned to go straight to his room for a shower, but turned toward the ship's combined bridge and CIC instead.

"I did have an hour while you were napping in surgery, sir." Petrov favored Colt with a grin.

Colt chuckled despite himself. "And?"

"According to her, since we earned a combat bonus protecting Bredge, we can handle taking on some new hires, but it will slow our fundraising. We're going to need at least seven big jobs before the end of the year if we hope to avoid defaulting."

Colt's eyes widened. "That would be asking a lot, even from a veteran crew."

"Yes, sir," Levin said, "but if we stay on Spimu, we might be able to swing it. Cutting out travel time will save on fuel costs as well."

"And we now have the local Union Envoy as a reference," Petrov added. "Grennis couldn't say enough good things about FMT after the firefight was over. She's vowed to help us find more jobs on her home world. In fact, according to Weep, she's already got something lined up for us—sentry duty at a refinery."

"Okay, I'm definitely open to the idea of staying in one place as long as we find big enough jobs. But right now, we need to make at least one transit before we settle anywhere."

They had reached the ship's bridge. Colt tried to key the door open, but couldn't manage it with his single hand. He fumbled for a few seconds before Levin caught his wrist to stop him—he had been pushing himself slowly away from the door with his clumsy fumbling. Her touch sent a shiver up his good arm as she grinned and pressed a hand to the door's activation square.

"After you, sir," she said.

"Thanks." Colt hauled himself inside, trying not to notice the lingering cool spot where Nichol's fingers had clasped his arm.

Zorn, looking no worse for wear after his unsanctioned CASPer flight, gave his commander a quizzical look. "Colonel? Shouldn't you be resting?"

"No time for that," Colt said as he brought himself to a stop a meter from Zorn's command chair. "How soon can we get underway for Karma IV, Captain?"

"We just picked up the last of our equipment from the surface." Zorn pursed his lips in thought. "Give the crew at least four hours. We've got to secure everything. And they're going to grumble, sir. They'll be wanting to rest after the fight dirtside."

"We can rest in transit, Captain. Right now, we need more people, but I don't want to be away any longer than we have to." Colt turned to Levin, Petrov, and Torres. "I want to get back as soon as possible. We're going to find out who attacked us and why, and we're going to get some of our own back."

* * * * *

Chapter Twenty-Two

Something about the pure white void of hyperspace depressed Colt, and yet he had a hard time looking away from it. He stared at it through his office window aboard *Uncanny Valley*, contemplating the nothingness, and wondering idly if he might be the first person to spot anything in its unfathomable depths.

The losses on Spimu weighed on him. Perhaps if he knew who had organized the attack, he would feel less angry, but probably not. Still, tracing their identities occupied much of his downtime. Like his intelligence officers, he found no significant connections in the ship's current copy of the GalNet between the enemy company and anything else. DNA traces, forensic evidence—what little the Spimu authorities would release—and good, old-fashioned searches of the aliens' pockets had turned up nothing. Their gear had been standard merc weapons and body armor from manufacturers in this arm of the galaxy. Following the trail of purchases that eventually led to what Colt mentally referred to as the Phantom Mercs resulted in dead ends. That didn't stop Colt's intel people from tracing every weapon and armor product number they could glean off pinplants, CASPer, and RAT recordings. Though their eagerness made him proud, their efforts came to nothing. Every trace eventually doubled back on itself or disappeared in a mire of transaction records.

Colt's doorbell chimed. He opened it with his pinplants, thankful for the interruption.

Captain Torres stepped inside. Colt hadn't seen much of the Triple T merc for several days. Supposedly, he had been observing Major Petrov and the various company commanders performing their duties. And while Colt had no doubt Torres did so—the captain was a man of his word—Colt suspected Torres had also decided to give Colt some space after the battle on Spimu.

"How are you, Colonel?" Torres sat in one of the empty seats in front of Colt's desk.

"I've been better." Colt glanced over his shoulder at Torres before turning back to the endless white of the transit field. "How are you?"

"Same. I saw you got the troops back to simulator training today."

"It was time. I plan to give them liberal leave when we reach the station. They deserve it." *Uncanny Valley's* crew had spent the first four days of the transit to Karma IV performing necessary shipboard duties only. Colt had wanted to give them downtime to recuperate after losing so many of their comrades in battle, but not so much that they grew rusty or lost their willingness to fight.

"Couldn't agree more. I watched Bravo Company training today. They looked good. Petrov and Levin have them easing back into heavy loss scenarios. It's the best way."

"Were you able to send your message before transit?" A little voice that sounded like his father's reminded Colt that holding a conversation with his back turned to the other person was quite rude, something he sometimes forgot. He turned his command chair around and tried to look Torres in the eyes, but had to settle for the man's forehead.

"Luckily enough, yes. There was a tramp freighter headed out in the cycle before ours. The message should have enough time to circulate to the right people."

"Let's hope it works."

"I think it will," Torres said. "I know several large companies that only subcontract mercs when they need them for special jobs. That sort of work is okay, but it gets old after a while. I should know, I did it for the first five years of my career. You work six months, hunt for that next job for three, then work three or four more before you're again out of a job. You never feel safe, because you're burning up all the pay you earned from your last gig traveling around trying to find the next one. Offer a merc that's been doing that for a while the chance to join a company full-time, and they'll jump on board. And they'll be some of your most loyal employees, because they know what it's like on the fringes."

"Honestly, that doesn't sound like fun." Colt imagined himself trying to live that sort of life. He was young, but he quailed at the prospect of going months without a source of income.

"It has its charms. Traveling is good for the soul. And nothing teaches work ethic like struggling to survive."

"When I signed up for FMT, I thought I'd graduate and move right into an officer's slot in one of the big companies." Colt spun the slate on his desk around in a circle. "That was an insane plan. Even with a graduation certificate from this school or any other, I would have been just another supplicant begging to join. Worse, I'm only sixteen, and I look twelve. Those guys wouldn't have given me a chance."

"I dunno. I think Jim Cartwright would have. He's pretty young. Once you showed him and his command group what you could do on the battlefield, they would have taken you."

"I want to be a good commander, but sometimes I wonder why I want that, you know?" Colt spun the slate again, his gaze fixed on it. "I chose to become a merc because I thought it sounded cool, and I didn't want to end up like my parents. They lead these little bubble lives, where they're protected from all the craziness out here in the galaxy, and they carp at the people who make those lives possible. They seem so petty to me now. I can't understand what they want out of life. But then, I'm struggling to figure out the same thing."

Torres' expression softened in a way Colt had never seen before. He leaned forward, his hands on his knees. "You know what most sentient creatures in this galaxy want? It isn't conquest or power or fabulous wealth. What most of them want is to watch their children grow up in peace. It's about happiness, fulfillment—seeing the next generation make a way for themselves. And no matter how simple you and I might find that sort of life, there's treasure in it.

"As for what people like us want out of life, the good among us want justice. It sounds simple, I know, but that's what it boils down to. Mercs take jobs for those who can't find justice some other way. Whether that's guarding their hard-earned possessions from thieves or going to battle to right some wrong, the end result is the same."

"Justice." Colt said the word out loud. Hearing it in his own voice made it more than an abstract concept floating around in his head. "Is that one of the ultimate outcomes of good leadership and decision making?"

Torres shook his head, his face grim. "No way."

The captain's answer surprised Colt, and he looked up to meet Torres' gaze for a second before returning to his slate. "Why not? Didn't you just say that's what mercs do? They find justice for their clients?"

"Good ones do. But leadership isn't about doing the right thing. It's about doing the effective thing. Those two don't always coincide."

"So how do you know if you're doing right as a leader?"

The ghost of a bitter smile touched Torres' lips. "That's the problem, Colonel. You can't ever know for sure. You have to make it up as you go along like everybody else."

* * *

They returned to the Merc's Delight. Colt had wanted to visit Peepo's Pit on the other side of the station to conduct their recruiting interviews. It had a reputation as the mercenary pit of pits. But Torres had argued that Peepo's was too busy. The staff wouldn't appreciate FMT's command group taking up a booth for hours to conduct business that wasn't about new contracts. Be'klat from the Merc's Delight, however, was more than happy to host what Levin called FMT's job fair once Weep greased his paw with a hefty rental fee for one of his larger tables.

Be'klat met Colt's team at the entrance with a jovial growl that made Colt reach for his gun, until Be'klat slipped a furry arm over his shoulders. "I heard about your exploits on Spimu! Made me proud that I recommended your team to that puny Pendal."

"You've already heard about that?" Colt blanched. Part of him worried potential hires might not be interested in signing on with a merc company fresh off taking casualties in the field, though Captain Torres had assured him the opposite would likely hold true.

"Of course I have. The GalNet's like a weed. The more you try to suppress it, the more it spreads."

"Let's hope that's good news for us," Levin said.

Be'klat stopped near a large booth, his massive arm still resting companionably on Colt's shoulders, and stared around his pit-bar with an expression Colt couldn't read. "Humans. I've never seen so many Humans in one place."

"At least most of them are buying drinks." Colt looked up at the Oogar pit master.

"I'm not complaining. Just observing. All mercs are welcome here. This is the most business we've seen in a centicycle. Anyway, this is your booth. Let me know if you need anything." Be'klat ushered his guests onto a curved, cushioned bench with a rectangular table made of real wood in front of it.

The Merc's Delight wasn't a large place, and it felt like every spare meter of it was filled with people of all merc races, though Be'klat was right, they were mostly Human. Not all of them were applicants, as proved by the confused reactions from the place's regulars, but more had turned out than Colt expected.

"How many companies did you contact?" Colt whispered to Torres who had taken a seat next to him.

"Five. I mostly hit up their recruitment officers, asking if they had any worthwhile applicants they'd had to turn away but would recommend."

"Looks to me like they sent them all."

"Recruiters tend to know other recruiters. My job offer probably got passed around to places I hadn't intended." Torres winced. "I sure hope it didn't get back to anyone at Triple T, or I might be looking for a new position myself."

"I'm sure you'll be fine," said Major Petrov who sat on Torres' right. "It's a big galaxy."

Raucous laughter caught Colt's attention. A group of FMT troopers were carousing at two tables near the entrance. He smiled. It felt good to see them laughing, drinking a bit, and generally enjoying their downtime. Private First Class Sloan sat at one of the tables telling some tale that had everyone on the edge of their seats and periodically hooting in delight. Reduced rank or not, he still had plenty of friends in the crew.

He caught Colt looking his way and lifted his beer in salute. Colt nodded and turned back to the business at hand, his heart gladdened.

"We'd better get started with the interviews if we want to finish sometime this year." Levin consulted her slate. "Our first contestant on who wants to marry a CASPer is Lawrence Finnegan. Shall I?"

Colt nodded and Levin called out the applicant's name.

A lanky, dark-haired fellow dressed in denim pants and a button-up shirt, the best one he owned, Colt would wager, approached the table. He looked about twenty-five, maybe a little younger, though he bore worry lines at the corners of his eyes and mouth.

"Have a seat, Mr. Finnegan." Levin gave the prospective merc a cursory look before turning back to his application. "It says here you've been serving aboard the Typhoon for the last four months. Which merc company is that?"

"Tom's Triple Terrors, Sergeant."

Torres stiffened in his seat, and Colt almost laughed but managed to stifle it.

"You were subcontracting, I take it?" Levin asked. Either she didn't realize Captain Torres was trying to hide his face from Finnigan, or she was a supremely good actor. Knowing her, Colt figured it could go either way.

"Yes. My hitch with Triple T lasted nine months. Before that I was with Conrad Usta's group for three months, and I did a stint with Bert's Bees before that. Bert's Bees wasn't combat duty, just garrison work." Finnegan looked from face to face as he spoke, and though he paid no particular attention to Captain Torres, he did stare a long time at Colt.

Colt studied his slate to avoid the man's intense stare, but he could feel his insides wanting to clamp down.

"And your CASPer experience?" Levin lifted an eyebrow at Finnigan until she had regained his attention.

"Six years, all in Mk 7s and Mk 8s." Finnigan squinted at Levin. "Can I ask a question?"

Levin nodded, though she looked wary.

"How old are all of you? The captain looks older than me, but..." Finnigan trailed off, his gaze back on Colt. "He looks fourteen, and he's wearing a colonel's insignia."

"This is Colonel Colt Maier," said Petrov, his voice stern. "He is our top commanding officer."

"That's insane. This is some kind of joke, right?" Finnigan directed his question to Torres.

The captain didn't flinch. "No."

Everyone in the bar was staring at him now, or so it felt. Steeling himself against the scrutiny, Colt stiffened his spine and sat as tall as he could. He couldn't fight the feeling that doing so made him look like a kid trying to appear older than his years, but it bolstered his confidence. Who was this part-timer to question his experience? "I've led FMT through three battles in the last two months."

"Oh? How'd that go?" A sonorous voice boomed from across the pit. An overlarge Besquith dressed in a blood red uniform with black accents stood to address Colt directly. Compared to others of its species, the wolf-like creature was massive. Its head almost grazed the ceiling.

"Who are you?" Torres asked.

The Besquith placed a fur-backed hand the size of a catcher's mitt on Finnigan's shoulder, and the human's eyes widened. Showing his teeth, the Besquith placed a tankard of something diabolically alcoholic from the smell of it on the table. "Name's Styver. I'm here for a job."

"You'll have to wait your turn," Levin said, meeting the huge creature's gaze without balking.

"I believe it is my turn." Styver looked down at Finnigan. "What about you? You think your interview's over?"

Finnigan spun out of his chair like a top. Even fully erect, his head only reached the Besquith's elbow. "Yes. Absolutely. I'm done. Completely done."

Mercs about the pit chuckled, some mirthfully, some nervously.

"You aren't next." Petrov tried using the same tone he had with Finnigan, but his nervousness showed when his voice cracked.

"Check again," Styver said. He leered at Petrov as if the Human was his next meal and sat down. The chair groaned under his weight.

Levin glanced at Colt. Beyond placing his hand surreptitiously on his GP-90, he had no clue how to proceed. They could use some real muscle down in the ranks, and the Besquith were known for their ferocity, if not their discipline. Assuming Styver could follow orders, he might be an asset to the company, even if Colt disliked him.

Colt nodded at Levin, signaling she should continue.

"Which job are you applying for?" Levin's eyes had unfocused as she used her pinplants to run through the applicants on her slate. "I don't see your name in our database."

"That's because you neglected to list my position."

Levin tilted her head to one side. "And what position is that?"

Styver flashed three rows of teeth and stabbed a clawed finger at Colt. "Commander."

Colt's insides seized up. His hands shook under the table, from fear, anger, and insulted pride. He tried to think of a retort, but nothing came to him. It felt like all the blood in his body had rushed to his head and drowned all his thoughts.

Petrov stammered his indignation though he couldn't seem to get a word out. Torres sat up straight, his jaw set in grim anger.

Cool as ever, Levin smiled sweetly. "Make no mistake, sir. That job is already filled. If you'd like to hire on as a trooper or support staff, we can talk. Otherwise, this interview is over."

Colt cheered mentally. Levin's aplomb under the Besquith's glare acted like a balm for Colt's anxiety. While it wasn't gone, she soothed away enough of it for him to piece two thoughts together.

"We have business to conduct." Colt managed to keep his tone measured, his voice even, despite his fear. Though he couldn't look Styver in the eye, he lifted his gaze to the Besquith's shaggy ears and showed his teeth. "We don't have time for jokes."

Styver's heavy brow lowered, and the fur on the back of his tree-width neck rose. He growled low in his chest, a rumble that made Colt want to cower under the table. "I never joke, pup. You are no commander. I've heard how your security was so lax on Spimu you let some unknowns nearly annihilate your company on the ground."

"That isn't true." Levin looked as though she might dive across the table at Styver, even though she was only a quarter of his size.

"Same goes for the pirates you took on." Styver cut a furrow in the table with one of his black claws. "I heard you barely took their compound even though more than half of them were off looting elsewhere."

"What's any of this to you?" Torres asked. He too, Colt noticed, had one hand on his gun.

"Your company is new, or so I've heard. You worked some safe contracts before the bottom fell out and your school's command staff got arrested, but you've done nothing except flounder since then. And it's all because you have this child leading you. It's time FMT hired a true commander."

"And you're that person?" Torres cocked his head to one side.

"I am."

Faster than Colt could comprehend, Torres had drawn his GP-90 from under the table and leveled it at Styver's snout. The red, triangular laser sight hardly wavered on the Besquith's nose. "You have five seconds to vacate that chair before I spread your putrid brain all over this pit."

Styver growled again, low and deep in his chest, as he bared his fangs. "You're making a deadly mistake. I don't let anyone point a gun at me and live."

"Makes two of us." Torres' finger tightened noticeably on the trigger. "Three seconds."

With a final snarl, Styver rose, nearly toppling the table in his haste. "Have it your way. Follow a fangless child to your deaths. I'll laugh when I hear you've all been eaten by Tortantulas." He spun on his heel and strode out the front door, the other patrons and applicants making way for him.

Colt let out a breath he hadn't realized he had been holding and loosened his grip on his gun. Torres slid his back into its holster.

"That could have gone better," Petrov said as he wiped sweat from his brow.

"You think he was serious?" Colt asked.

"Could be," Torres said. He lowered his voice. "But Besquith are generally jerks. He might have heard about our interviews and decided to intimidate you for no reason. Who knows how those mongrels think?"

"Hey, I know you." Finnigan, who hadn't gone far after Styver interrupted his interview, pointed a finger at Torres, his expression bemused. "Aren't you with Triple—"

"Next!" Cried Levin, Colt, Petrov, and Torres in one voice.

* * * * *

Chapter Twenty-Three

Colt stood inside his newly assigned CASPer in *Uncanny's* armory. Technically, the massive suit was still locked down in its transport frame, but Colt had initialized the main release so he could access the cockpit. The shipboard day had passed, and the bay's overhead lights were dimly lit to approximate nighttime operations mode. None of the armorers were working at this hour, and the only sound in the usually raucous space was the deep, abiding thrum of the ship's fusion engines.

The close confines of his suit and the quiet usually helped Colt think. Unfortunately, though three days had passed since the disastrous recruiting event at the Merc's Delight, he kept thinking about what Styver had said. Again and again he tried to dismiss the jibes. Obviously, Styver had been trying to bait Colt into doing or saying something foolish, but it hadn't worked. However, his descriptions of FMT's latest battles had rung true to Colt on some level.

Maybe if he had reacted differently here or made another choice there, fewer of his people would have died. He had been caught unaware by the phantom company while guarding Grennis Bredge; the traceless mercenaries had come out of nowhere. Surely, Colt could have planned better or more precisely observed his environment and detected them.

But Colt couldn't see how. And that, more than anything, frightened him. Was it possible he had missed something right in front of him, some clue a better commander would have caught?

A door across the bay slid open, interrupting his train of thought. Using his pinplants, Colt zoomed the CASPer's display in on it. A woman strode into the bay.

"Is something wrong, Top?" Colt asked through his external speakers.

"No." Levin wore civilian clothes, a pair of burgundy pants, a loose-fitting cream top, and boots that clicked as she approached him. She stared up, her black hair—free from its customary bun—cascading beyond her shoulders in delicate waves. "I thought I would find you here."

"How'd you know?" Colt had no problem looking into Levin's eyes through the Tri-V. His CASPer shielded him from that fear, though his throat had gone suddenly dry.

"I noticed this is where you go when you can't sleep."

Colt's eyes widened. She had seen him come here before? "You never said anything."

Levin shrugged one shoulder, then turned her attention to the suit next to his. She unlocked the main release. With a whine of hydraulics, the suit trundled forward on its platform and dropped to the floor. Levin agilely climbed the CASPer's side and opened the cockpit so she could pull herself inside. The suit's main running light illuminated as she powered up the basic systems without firing up the motor.

"There," Levin said over a discreet channel, "now we can talk face-to-face."

"We're standing next to each other," Colt said.

"Exactly!"

Colt laughed.

"Do you mind if we drop rank for now, Colonel?" Levin asked with the same stiff formality she used on the job.

"No rank in these CASPers," Colt said, and his heart fluttered. So what if she wanted to talk openly? She probably wanted an out for dressing him down over his performance since becoming commander. No doubt, Styver's attack had made her realize she was following a fool.

Levin remained quiet for a tense moment during which Colt's mind ran a thousand scenarios that all ended in her telling him he should find a new line of work. When she finally did speak, he almost missed her words.

"Do you think it's completely inappropriate for an officer to date one of his noncoms?" Levin asked.

Had she tossed a flash grenade into his CASPer, Colt didn't think he could have been more floored. He swallowed, cleared his throat, and swallowed again. Only then did he feel capable of speech. "Uh, why do you ask?"

"Colt."

"Yes?"

"Seriously?"

He bit his lip. "Nichol, are you asking me out?"

"Nope."

Colt felt like the ground had just broken apart beneath his feet. "You're not?"

"Not if I don't like the answer to the first question I asked you."

"Oh? Oh!" Colt stammered for a moment, his thoughts battling each other as he remembered all the things he had read about not getting involved in company relationships, especially those between officers and noncoms. Supposedly, they were bad news. But the other half of Colt's brain, maybe a bit more than half, was thinking about Levin in her haptic suit after the battle of the Ten Whispers.

"Is that all you've got to say?" she asked after a few seconds.

"No."

"No, you don't think officer-noncom relationships are a good idea?"

"Yes. Uh, no." Colt drew a breath and closed his eyes. He imagined a diagram of the OODA loop, breaking down his current problem into its smallest parts. A cool tingle washed over him when he saw Levin standing at the end of the cycle. "I've heard that kind of thing can be hard to manage, but I don't have any problem with it."

"Good, because I've had this thing for Feliks for months, but I didn't think I should say anything."

For the second time in less than a minute, Colt's stomach dropped. "Oh. I—okay."

Levin's peal of laughter made Colt jump. "I'm kidding. I like Feliks just fine, but I do not want to date him. I want to date you, Colt."

Having had only one girlfriend, back when he was twelve, Colt had to wonder if this sense of psychic whiplash was an ongoing thing or if it would eventually lessen over time. "Really?"

"You sound surprised."

"I am, a little." Colt listened to his voice and was relieved to find it solid, not quavering or cracking, despite the giddy feeling in his chest. "You never said anything."

"I gave you looks." Levin's voice had risen an octave. Did that mean something? Colt wracked his brain for any articles he had read about girls and their vocal nuances. He really needed to study up on the subject—girls, not voices.

"I'm not all that good at looks." Yes! He still sounded cool, at least in his own head. For one thing, he was speaking. Thank you CASPer! For another, he hadn't said anything outrageously stupid.

Yet.

"I've noticed. You don't like to look people in the eyes. That's okay. But you've been getting better at it. I've noticed that too."

"I'm trying."

"You came down here because of what Styver said, didn't you?" Levin's voice dropped, and Colt was pretty sure she was worried he might not like her asking about that. He didn't, but then, he liked Levin, so that made it all right. Besides, she was correct.

"Yeah. I keep telling myself he was just trying to get under my skin, to make me say or do something to weaken my position. Stupid as that was, I think he really did want my job."

"If he could get the crew to lose confidence in you, maybe. Problem is, you've already proven yourself to us ten times over, Colt. We all knew you were helping Yardley out when FMT was just a school. Well, most people knew. There might have been a few who refused to believe it, but they believe now."

"I got people killed on Spimu."

"No, you got people through. Do you know how many Human mercs die, on average, during a regular contract? It's something like thirty percent. Granted, things have gotten better with improvements to our CASPers and other weapons, but we still have a high death rate compared to other races. Before first contact, armies would break if their losses approached ten percent. You haven't come close to that."

"I know, but I can't shake the feeling I could have done better." Colt pulled his hands out of his CASPer's arm controls to rub his knuckles.

"I feel that way sometimes. I'm working with these people; they're my responsibility. Some of them are years older than me. I know I make mistakes—"

"You don't."

"Yes, I do. We make mistakes, Colt. Not just because we're people, but because we're teenagers. I'm seventeen years old. Yes, I wanted to become a merc, but this was *not* the way I envisioned doing it. I wanted to get my degree and learn to run a CASPer. Now I'm Top, and I feel like a total imposter a lot of the time. Seriously, I'm making this stuff up as I go along."

Colt angled his cameras to the side so he could see Levin's CASPer in his display. He stared at it for a long moment, unsure what to say. "You're kidding, right? I've never gotten that feeling from you. You're always confident. You always know what to do."

Levin snorted. "No way. That's you. I see you thinking about things, turning them over in ways I can't imagine, then coming up with some plan in a meeting or on the field. And you make it real, because you've looked at it from every angle."

"I try to do that. But that's not the truth." A sense of melancholy tried to wash over Colt again. He fought it without much success.

"You're a teenager too, Colt. We didn't come here to run a merc company. We came to learn how. And suddenly everything's riding on our learning on the job. Yeah, we make mistakes, but we've got each other and Feliks and the whole crew to back us up and help us through. Leading people isn't monolithic, at least it shouldn't be. It takes teamwork."

"Who said that?" Colt asked, unable to place the quote.

"I did."

Colt laughed, his mood lightened by Levin's sentiment as much as her words. "I'll add that one to my daily quotes calendar right next to the company motto you created. Death before default. I love it."

"Thanks."

"Are we dating now?" Colt blurted, unable to contain himself.

"Yes. Definitely."

A goofy smile split Colt's lips. "Okay."

"But we're taking things slowly," Levin said in a voice that brooked no argument. "And that means everything. I haven't dated much."

"You haven't? But you're...you're beautiful."

"Thank you."

"So why didn't you date?"

"I was focused on school before I came here. I graduated early. I didn't have time for boys. So dating's a little new for me."

"Me too," Colt admitted. "I wish we could go places, like a holoball game or a Tri-V but..."

"But you're the colonel, and I'm the Top. If people see us going out, it could cause problems."

"I could promote you." Colt knew he had said the wrong thing the instant the words left his mouth.

"Are you crazy? We'd have a mutiny on our hands. People are already pissed they're not getting paid as full mercs. You promote me to officer, and they'll riot in the halls."

"So, we keep it a secret. We're dating, but we're not really because we can never see each other."

"We're seeing each other now." The teasing tone of Levin's voice made Colt grin. "But I think we can do better." She opened her cockpit and climbed down from her CASPer, nimble as a doe, and beckoned to him from the bay floor.

Heart racing, Colt opened his suit and clambered down. His hands felt as dexterous as a couple of pancakes, but he managed to reach the floor without falling on his head.

"First things first." Levin slipped her arms around him. She was a smidge taller than Colt, but that didn't matter. Not one bit.

She kissed him, and Colt thought his head might explode. He slid his arms around her waist so that he held her as she held him and leaned into the kiss. For one exquisite moment, he knew nothing but the electric feel of her lips on his. All the pain and worry and stress of running FMT fled in the face of her attention.

When she broke the kiss—too soon!—she looked into Colt's eyes, and he didn't flinch. For the first time he could remember, he not only met another person's gaze, he consumed it like a starving man. He didn't want to look away. He wanted to stare into her green eyes forever.

"Okay." Levin sounded slightly out of breath. She looked as shocked and hungry as Colt. "Okay," she said again as if she couldn't focus. Colt totally understood. "We're dating, but secretly, right?"

"Right." Colt didn't trust his voice, so he whispered.

"This isn't a bad time, is it?"

"I'm having a great time."

Levin swatted his shoulder. "I meant this time of night, or morning, I guess. It's a good time to meet and talk and—"

"Kiss?"

"Some, yes," she said, grinning. "This way, we don't have to worry about anyone seeing us, right?"

Colt nodded.

"During the day, we keep it professional." Levin looked at him questioningly.

"Totally. Professional." This time, Colt kissed her. He felt it in his toes. He suspected he wasn't going to miss the sleep he'd be losing to get up early with Levin.

* * *

"You seem chipper." Captain Torres, leaning against the conference room wall, raised an eyebrow at Colt. "Don't think I've ever seen you smiling before a pre-mission brief, especially an early morning one. You usually hate these things."

Colt tried to bury his smile, but couldn't. He and Levin had spent the past two hours talking in one of the ship's abandoned maintenance bays. They had kissed a bit, but their conversation had been almost as exciting. He had never known another person so like him. She loved everything merc, she obsessively studied military history, and she had an ingrained sense of right and wrong that matched his so perfectly, they might have lived the same life growing up. She wanted to help people. She lived for it. And her enthusiasm inspired him to do the same.

"Just feeling good." Colt took his seat at the head of the table and busied himself with his slate and pinplants. Nothing he scanned went further than his eyes, though he did check *Uncanny's* position. They were about four hours from entering orbit around Spimu.

Torres grunted noncommittally, his gaze boring into Colt, who refused to look up, though he could feel his stare.

The conference room's door slid open, and Levin entered. Colt remembered wondering once if she was a good actress. She was the best. The two of them had agreed to leave their secluded meeting spot separately. He had gone first since he always arrived early for meetings, and she had waited five minutes so no one would see them together. She glanced at Colt and nodded, her face perfectly neutral. "Good morning, Colonel."

"Morning, Top." Colt thought his attitude and voice were fairly normal, though he couldn't seem to wipe the stupid grin off his face. Unfortunately, he made the mistake of glancing at Torres.

The big merc grinned knowingly as his dark eyes flicked from Colt to Levin and back. He knew. Somehow, the grizzled veteran of a hundred firefights who Colt would have never guessed had a romantic bone in his body, knew the commander and first sergeant were dating. His grin broadened into an all-out smile when he saw the expression on Colt's face.

Colt resolutely turned back to his slate and tried to work on something that required his utmost attention, but his ears were burning.

That feeling cooled, thankfully, as the rest of the command staff filtered into the room. Once the company commanders, Weep, and Major Petrov had taken their seats, Colt called the meeting to order, and they got to work. He couldn't help surreptitiously glancing at Levin now and again, but she seemed not to notice. She looked at him with nothing more than her usual, professional courtesy.

"Colt? Sir?" Petrov leaned forward in his seat to catch Colt's attention.

"What?"

"You seemed to drift off for a second. Weep was asking if you'd like a rundown of our current financials."

"Of course. Yes. We need that. Yes." Colt clamped his mouth shut before anymore stupidity could dribble out. Everyone was staring at him, and he knew his ears were red again.

Weep looked around the table as if trying to read her Human colleagues' expressions and failing. Finally, she wobbled her head in a Flatar expression of mild agitation and launched into a breakdown of FMT's expenses for the last month.

Colt heard every syllable, though little of it reached his brain. Not until something she said struck home.

"Taking on the new crewmen set us back, as expected, but replacement parts and ammo resupply for our CASPers and RATs is what really hurt us this pay cycle. You can't buy that sort of equipment from any old vendor. I had to make deals with several merc outfits while we were in orbit, and believe me, they know how precious those parts are. And shuttling between here and Karma IV ain't cheap either. We had enough fuel for this trip, but we'll need to get more within the next two transits."

Colt looked briefly at Weep. "How bad is it?"

Weep shook her hands in the Flatar equivalent of a Human shrug. "Pretty bad, to be honest. We made our regular Mountside payment this cycle, and I'll be able to cover the crew and staff pay, but that's it. FMT is otherwise broke. Somehow we're going to have to pay for *Hermes'* repairs in the next couple of days. I spoke with Kit this morning. She says the ship's flight worthy, but the repair yard is holding it until we clear the bill, which we really can't afford right now."

Colt's head swam with possibilities as he broke down the problem, thankful for the distraction. "We haven't finalized the refinery contract yet. We could ask for a sign-on bonus, just enough to get *Hermes* out of hock."

Weep nodded sagely. "That could work. I'll contact their finance department as soon as we're done."

"In the meantime, see what paying jobs you can drum up. At this point, moving freight or guarding rich, fat cats sound fine to me. We need some working capital and a way to enlarge it. Maybe local investments with a quick payoff?"

Weep made a face like she had stepped in something foul. "I'd advise you to avoid investing in the stock market with that fast of a turnaround. We'd need to make a profit within four or five months. Better just to work for it."

Colt nodded. "Okay. But in the meantime, the old door is still open. If anyone here, or any of your people, have good ideas for bringing in some credits—legal ones—don't hesitate to suggest them. Is there any other business we need to attend to before the contract signing this afternoon?"

"One thing, sir." Major Petrov lifted a hand. "Captain Onishi sent a message while we were out of the system. She says there's been an influx of traffic coming through the Zion gate. It's all legitimate, as far as anyone can tell, but several frigates have claimed to need repairs and have parked near a heavy meteor cloud between Brigham and its sister gas giant, Hyrum. That's got the Mormons worried. Eleven days ago, they weren't overly concerned, since they have a space navy composed of three heavy cruisers and plenty of ground forces that can fend off anything a couple of frigates might drop. But if more arrive, they and therefore Onishi, might have a problem on their hands."

"She got any clue who these ships belong to?" Captain Butler's heavy brows furrowed into a knot whenever he faced a problem he didn't like. "They even related?"

"That's the worrisome part." Petrov glanced at Captain Torres, but continued on. "You know how Onishi is, never one to leave a mystery un-tweaked. It took some digging through the GalNet, but she managed to trace both ships' registries back to shell corporations that suffered foreclosure bankruptcies. Two guesses as to the lein holder."

Colt lifted an eyebrow. "Mountside Financial?"

"Got it in one," Petrov said, his face serious.

"That is odd." Colt tapped his fingers on the table as he turned the new information over in his head. "It could be a coincidence. Mountside loans a lot of money, and we know they're more than happy to call in a debt first chance they get."

"Doesn't feel like a coincidence." Captain Catlett glanced around the table, looking suspicious and confused. "What could they want from the Mormons? Their planet isn't exactly hospitable. I mean, they're pulling some resources out of the system, but nothing to write home about. Spimu has more to offer than Brigham."

"Was Onishi asking for assistance?" Colt asked. "I know it's about time to pick her up or renew our contract with the Mormons. Maybe, this time, we can finagle some credits out of them."

Petrov shook his head. "The opposite really. She's not shy about wanting this tour to be over, but she said we shouldn't bother going back to Brigham until the contract's done. She doesn't want us wasting the time we could be using to make credits. I have to agree."

"Same here," Colt said. "If this upcoming refinery job works out, we'll be done just in time for transit back to Brigham to pick up Shortfall. In the meantime, send Captain Onishi a message. Ask her to speak with whomever she deems fit about follow-on contracts. Maybe we can turn the pickup trip into a paid job."

* * * * *

Chapter Twenty-Four

"So, you and Levin, eh?" Captain Torres, floating next to Colt as they pulled themselves along *Uncanny Valley's* main corridor, lifted an eyebrow.

Colt missed his next handgrip, fumbled on the one after that, and caromed off the bulkhead. He managed to get a finger hold in a seam, otherwise he would have bounced into the opposite wall.

"I'll take that as a yes." Torres looked supremely proud of himself.

"How did you know?" Colt couldn't help the hot flush running up his neck, but he managed not to stammer.

"I've got eyes." Torres had brought himself to a standstill. "She's pretty good at hiding it. You, on the other hand..."

Colt hung his head though there was no gravity to pull it down. That was an odd thing about microgravity. While floating, Human gestures felt strange, sort of forced. No one told you about it before you experienced it.

"You think anyone else has noticed?" he asked.

"Nah." Torres pawed at the air in front of him as if shooing away a worthless notion. "Leastways, I don't think so. Petrov might have, he's pretty close to both of you, but he's loyal. I doubt he'd say anything."

"Okay. I'll try not to show it when I'm around her."

Torres nodded, but Colt could tell he had more to say.

"I know what you're holding back," Colt said.

"Do ya, now?" Torres raised his brow again.

"You're going to say it's a bad idea to date within the company, and the difference in our ranks makes it worse."

"More or less. But I was also going to say I remember what it's like to be sixteen. If you had told me to stay away from a girl who liked me, I would have said, 'Yes, sir!' to your face, then gone straight to her the second I was free. Company romances aren't uncommon. You press a bunch of people together, especially young people, and it's inevitable."

Colt glanced up in shock. "We're not the only ones, are we?"

"I've seen your VOWs scores. You're a smart man, Colt. But sometimes you can be rather slow on the uptake. People are pairing off throughout the entire ship. It's been going on since I came aboard, and I'm sure it was happening before that."

Colt could have slapped his forehead at his naivety. Plenty of people had been dating before Belknap's arrest. Did he think they had stopped just because the school's charter changed? No. He had never paid much attention to who was dating whom before the proverbial wheels came off, and even less so after he became commander. But just because he hadn't thought about it didn't mean it wasn't happening. Like so many things in his life, Colt only paid attention when something directly affected him. He hadn't given a thought to shipboard romances until he had one.

"I sense the gears turning in that head of yours," Torres said. "You told me what I was thinking. Now it's my turn."

"Okay."

"You're wondering how much this will disrupt your troopers' combat effectiveness. What happens when there's a firefight and one half of a couple comes under fire while the other is ordered to stand down? That can lead to chaos and death. And what about breakups? I haven't done a study, but I'd say the average age of your company is about twenty-three. Old guy like me breaks it off with an equally aged lady, and we're probably going to end up friends, or at least cordial. Young people don't act that way."

"They fight." Colt shook his head. He couldn't imagine fighting with Levin, but he had seen too many couples go for each other's throats after a break up to think it couldn't happen to them.

"And worse, they get jealous."

"What am I supposed to do? Tell the crew they can't date? I'd be breaking my own rule."

"I notice breaking up with Levin wasn't on the table in your last statement."

Colt knew Torres was tweaking his nose, or at least he assumed so, yet he couldn't fight the twinge of anger that darted through his chest at the mention of ending his relationship. "No. It was not."

Torres held up a placating hand. "No need to get pissed. I'm not suggesting you break it off. I know a lost cause when I see one. I just think you should consider setting some ground rules for dating at FMT. First rule should be, 'No dating at FMT.' Second should be, 'If you must, no dating within your unit.' And that one should be hard and fast. That way, you're at least limiting the chances a couple will end up on the same assignment."

"Seems fair to me." Colt didn't mention that Levin was on his command staff, and therefore part of his company unit, and he got the feeling Torres was being diplomatic by doing the same.

"I wonder—"

A deep boom resonated through the passageway before Torres could finish his thought, and the strap in Colt's hand shook like an earthquake.

"Colt!" Levin shouted through the comm pickup attached to his uniform collar.

"What was that?" he asked, uncomfortably aware of Torres' eyes on him.

"I don't—okay, we're getting a report that it was an explosion near engineering. Environment doors have sealed around that section. Looks like no breach, but we've got—" Levin's voice died away in a squeal of feedback that made Colt cringe and cover the pickup with his fingers until it fell silent.

"Nichol. Nichol!"

Nothing. A frisson of fear coursed through Colt's veins as his mind supplied a dozen horrific reasons for the break in comms, each of them more frightening than the last.

The ship shuddered, and a cacophony of screeching metal being wrenched apart ran its length. The corridor shook so hard Colt went spinning toward the floor. Torres did the same, and they rebounded off each other toward opposite ends of the hall.

"What's happening?" Torres had managed to catch a strap to arrest his flight. He looked more alarmed than Colt had ever seen him.

Colt's comm screeched again, and Levin's voice returned.

"Can you hear me?"

"Finally, yes!" Simple relief didn't begin to describe what Colt felt at hearing Levin's voice. "What's happened?"

"You'd better get to the bridge. We think it was a bomb."

* * * * *

Chapter Twenty-Five

C olt was out of breath by the time he floated into the bridge, Torres fast on his heels. The place was abuzz with crewmembers passing reports to Zorn and the rest of the command staff. The big K'kng twisted this way and that as he spoke with his people in a never-ending torrent of updates and commands.

Levin had gathered three of the four company commanders along with Major Petrov into one out-of-the-way corner of the bridge. Since *Uncanny's* captain was too engaged to answer any questions, Colt pulled himself over to them.

"Where's Bethann?" he asked after a quick headcount. Bethann Granger, the new Charlie Company commander, who had replaced Petrov after his promotion, was nowhere to be seen.

Levin looked at him in anguish. "She was on the ring when the bomb went off. We haven't been able to contact her."

Colt hooked a boot into a loop on the floor, took a moment to focus his mind and tamp down his drive to run and hide, and got a mental grip on himself. Was it wrong that his first concern had been for Levin? Without a doubt, yes. Could he help it? Probably not. But now that he could see her, and she was unharmed, he had to focus on the rest of his people. Analyzing his feelings would have to come later.

"Tell me what we know," he said.

"We're certain it was a bomb," Petrov said. "Engineering had no system warnings before the explosion. Everything was nominal. Pressure readings show a monumental concussive force at 0923 hours. Chemical sensors, the ones that weren't destroyed, report K2 and other explosive byproducts in the air. The computer immediately sealed off that section of the ship, which contained the fire that followed. That's been put out."

"Was anyone in that section when the bomb went off?" Colt readied himself for the answer.

"Three we know of."

"Conditions?"

"All dead, sir." Petrov's pain showed in his face. He swallowed hard and continued. "We gave the computer the go ahead to bleed off the air in engineering, which stopped the fire. It's re-pressurizing now."

Someone could have passed a hand through the hole in Colt's stomach, he felt so hollow. It was one thing to lose troopers in combat, but seeing them killed this way and knowing he could do nothing about it made him want to scream. "What about damage to the ship? Is our orbit threatened?"

"Orbit's stable, but we don't know much about the overall damage." Levin's normally unflappable demeanor had broken. She looked to be on the verge of tears, but she held it together, cleared her throat, and continued. "Zorn and his people got backup power running, but it looks like the ship's power systems were the prime target. That and the maneuvering thrusters. The bomb took out the hydrazine pumps we use for fine orbital adjustments. That could have been a mistake, maybe they hit them without realizing it, but it seems fishy to me. I think our bomber wanted to leave the ship intact but unresponsive. We'll know more once we get a crew in to recover the bodies and look at the target site."

Colt nodded. "You said Lieutenant Granger was on the spin ring when the bomb went off. Is there some reason why she can't get here?"

Petrov ran a hand through his dark hair as if that would flatten it in zero-g. "The bomb damaged the spin ring's main drive. Again, we can't tell if that was the intended target, but it did its share of damage."

"Did the ring stop spinning?" The mere thought of *Uncanny's* spin ring stopping sent a shiver of panic through Colt's chest. He couldn't begin to imagine the problems that would cause, mostly for the large part of the crew who were on it. They could be looking at hundreds of casualties or fatalities.

"No, sir. It didn't stop," Petrov said and Colt breathed a heavy sigh of relief. "But it did slow significantly, and the change was sudden. We don't know the extent of the damage, but we've got at least fifty people hurt, and everything that wasn't tied down went flying. At its current speed, the ring's making about a third of an Earth normal gravity."

"And that's complicating the rescue effort, because anyone who goes down there is getting sick from the Coriolis Effect," Colt finished for him.

Petrov looked grim. "Yes, sir. We've got five teams evacuating those stranded, but it's slow going."

"It's tough to help someone else when you feel like puking your guts out." Colt clenched his jaw in anger and disgust. What had the last few moments of his dead crewmembers' lives been like? Fire and fury, pain and suffocation for some; instantaneous oblivion for others.

Colt looked at his command group, unafraid to meet anyone's gaze. To their credit none of them looked away either. "Can any of you guess my next question?"

The captains looked perplexed, but Levin nodded, her lovely face a mask of fury. "You want to know who did this."

"Every moment we're not saving the survivors, accounting for the damage, or making repairs, we're going to spend searching for this murderous piece of shit. No one leaves this ship until we've caught whoever did this."

"We have shift rotations coming up to relieve the sentries at the refinery, sir." Petrov looked pained at voicing this reminder in the face of Colt's wrath.

Colt squeezed his jaw tight and swallowed. Every fiber of his being wanted to light into Petrov like a rabid dog off its leash. But one glance at Captain Torres reminded him of his place as commander. Petrov wasn't trying to countermand Colt or hinder the investigation. He was doing his job as deputy by reminding his boss that they had other obligations to consider. Colt's company commanders were watching. They would always remember whatever he chose to do next.

Colt took a breath, and let it out slowly. "You're right. The ground troops are expecting relief, and they deserve it. But no one with access to engineering is leaving. And I want to know where every trooper was for the last twenty-four hours. Do we have any idea when the bomb might have been planted?"

Levin shook her head. "Not really. We might get some indication once we inspect the blast area, but none of us are trained for that sort of investigatory work. We might consider hiring someone. I'm sure Spimu has arson experts."

"This is one expense I can't argue. Find Weep and see what you can arrange."

"Will do, sir. In the meantime, I've already started compiling personnel whereabouts from everyone's pinplants. I hate doing it. Feels like I'm digging into their private lives, but I think it's the best way to proceed."

"We all signed waivers." Colt's face was stern, though he mentally kicked himself for forgetting the crews' implants. As part of each crewmember's contract, they agreed to random and specific surveillance. The agreement stipulated that FMT leadership could track members' whereabouts aboard ship via their implants whenever they deemed it necessary. The data collected would only show their physical position, not their activities. Such an invasive clause had felt excessive to Colt when Yardley had suggested it, but it seemed more than sensible now.

"Yes, sir, we did." Levin met his gaze, her jaw set. "We'd know everyone's whereabouts already, except for the number of crewmembers who were hurt or knocked unconscious when the spin ring was hit. I've got a couple of sergeants I trust pouring over the shift schedules for all four companies. If nothing else, that should give us a place to start."

"Good. I want the rest of you focused on rescuing our people. See what you can do to speed things up. Maybe we've got some troopers who aren't affected by dizziness who can help pull casualties from the ring. Feliks?"

"Yes, sir."

"You're in charge of vetting the next sentry crew we send dirt-side. Get with Levin and her sergeants. I don't want us accidentally sending our bomber to Spimu in a multimillion credit suit of armor. Got that?"

"Got it, sir."

"Pardon me, Colonel." Zorn spun his command chair to face Colt. His ears were twitching, a sign that K'kng was agitated.

"What is it, Captain?"

"We're being hailed by a large frigate. It detached from a station in low orbit about ten minutes after the bombing and has been speeding up to intercept us ever since. I thought nothing of it earlier. This is a busy planet. Ships are docking and undocking around here constantly. But now they're calling, and they're asking for you direct-ly, sir."

Colt's stomach tightened. While it was possible some neighborly frigate captain had detected *Uncanny's* distress and was coming to assist, something told Colt the oncoming ship had something else in store. "Any idea who they are?"

"Ship's registered on Karma IV, but they're flying a Spimu bea-con which means they've got trade rights here. The captain calls him-self Styver."

* * * * *

Chapter Twenty-Six

Colt floated to the center of the bridge, and Captain Zorn keyed the Tri-V to show the incoming call. Styver, his tooth-filled maw open in a Besquith approximation of a smile, appeared full-size before Colt. The wolf-like alien's eyes gleamed.

"Colonel Colt Maier, the pup merc." Styver leaned forward in his command chair as if he might take a bite out of Colt. "You don't know how pleased I am to see you again."

Though he felt miniscule compared to the all-too-real image of the Besquith, Colt did his best to straighten his spine and look the beast in the face. Seething anger made that task much easier. "You sabotaged our ship."

"Me?" Styver somehow sounded innocent while grinning like the big bad wolf that ate grandma. Humans and Besquith shared at least one thing, they showed their teeth when pleased. "I've never set a boot on your ship."

"You somehow got a saboteur on board when we took on hires." Colt forced his hands to relax. He had been squeezing them so hard, he feared his nails had drawn blood.

Styver twitched an ear in delight, though he wasn't going to cop to such allegations. "I'm a merc, young pup. That means I'm an opportunist. I see a salvageable ship, obviously mismanaged and allowed to fall into disrepair, and I think to myself, maybe this fine vessel could benefit from new ownership. How can you fault me for that?"

A small rectangle on the Tri-V displayed Styver's frigate rising in orbit to intercept *Uncanny Valley*. It bristled with missile launchers and laser cannons, and its particle accelerator swiveled to bear on Colt's ship. A triple line of ridges along its sleek hull marked its shield generator platform. From everything Colt could see, Styver's ship outclassed *Uncanny* five to one. Colt's converted freighter carried no missiles and only had a laser-based point defense system more suited to blasting orbital trash than enemy attackers. Its shields were laughably inadequate and unlikely to survive a hit from the frigate's outsized laser cannons, let alone a particle accelerator or a missile.

"I'm not going to let you board my ship," Colt said, surprised at the iron in his voice.

Styver laughed. "Before we start trading threats, I think I should make something clear to you, pup. We Besquith aren't a sentimental lot. But brood mates are something we take seriously. You made a fatal error when you unseated my brother, Lyret."

The smattering of conversation on the bridge died, and the room fell silent as Colt's heart skipped three beats. Brood mates. That was why Styver had sought Colt out on Karma station. FMT had devastated his brother's pirate enterprise, and the wolf had come for revenge. The confrontation Colt had agonized over for almost two weeks had been nothing but a ploy. Styver's allegations of mismanagement and poor leadership had soured FMT's recruitment efforts. Only a handful of mercs had signed on after that, and at least one of those—maybe more—belonged to Styver.

Everyone was staring at Colt. For a moment, he couldn't breathe. He wanted to run and hide, to pretend none of this had ever happened. For the first time since leaving, he wanted to go home. In some ways, Styver was right. Colt was just a pup. A pretender. A young man drowning in problems too complex for his experience.

Styver's horrific grin widened and revealed several rows of shark-like teeth. "You let my brother live. Therefore, I will show you the same courtesy. You and your command staff will shuttle over here as my honored guests. I will then allow your crew to debark without interference. Once you've all evacuated, I will drop you at Syphrum station."

Colt would remember the next few moments for the rest of his life. In later years, he would think about them, and how they changed his view of himself and his close friends.

To his shame, he briefly considered taking Styver up on the offer. *Uncanny* was no match for Styver's frigate which had now taken up a position slightly under and behind the larger ship. His crew couldn't weather an attack from the war machine.

The same went for boarding actions. No doubt Styver had brought an experienced infiltration team with him. Though Levin and Petrov sometimes drilled the FMT crew to repel boarders in the simulators, that sort of training wasn't their primary focus, especially in the last three months. Even fit and hale, the crew had little experience fighting onboard ship. And with an untold number of his people incapacitated from the bomb and subsequent spin ring slowdown, Colt doubted they were in any state to fend off a well-armed, organized attack.

Giving up might be the best way to save lives.

That thought died a screeching death when Colt glanced at Levin. Her steely gaze, so full of trust, put fire in his belly. He would not—could not—yield the ship and the company to some dishonorable thief who had used pawns to cripple FMT rather than take them on in a straight fight. Who was this mongrel to challenge them? They had defeated his brother because his brother was bad news. And they would defeat Styver for the same reason.

But how? He needed time to think.

Deliberately grimacing as if anguished by indecision, Colt turned back to the alien hologram. "I'll take your offer. It's not like we're in any position to argue. But we have casualties. I need at least an hour to evacuate the spin ring. It's damaged."

"You have thirty of your minutes. If you and your command staff aren't enroute to me in thirty-one minutes, I'll send a company of shock troops to finish up your evac. I doubt you'll like the techniques they'll use to finish the job."

Styver's image disappeared.

"Sir?" Petrov, whose face had gone pasty, stared at Colt in disbelief. "You're going to give him the ship?"

Most of the bridge crew and the company commanders wore the same looks of shocked disappointment.

Not Levin. Her expression had never wavered during the entire conversation. "What's the real plan, sir?"

Colt could have kissed her in that moment. Stressed as he felt, he almost gave in to that desire, but he checked himself at the last second. Instead, he favored her with an iron shod grin.

"Where's Weep?" he asked. "Was she injured in the explosion?"

"No. She checked in a few minutes before you arrived. I told her to remain in her quarters for safety."

"Get her up here as quickly as possible. We need her negotiation skills." Using an overhead handgrip, Colt spun to Zorn. "Captain, can we tight beam a message to the surface without Styver's people detecting it?" Messages sent via tight beam, essentially an infrared laser, required direct line-of-sight, meaning a straight line that could be drawn between the sender and receiver, no easy feat when dealing with ships in orbit communicating with the surface. But under the right conditions, they provided a much more secure means of sending messages than basic radio broadcasts.

Zorn rubbed his cheek with one fat palm, his whiskers sounding like sandpaper. "Possibly. Depends on where you're trying to send the message. If it's any spot directly below us or to our rear, they'll intercept it."

"Where are we in relation to the salvage yard that repaired *Hermes*?" Colt asked.

"Oh!" A closed-mouth grin split Zorn's face, and he pounded a fist against his barrel chest. "That, we can do, Colonel." He spun to the comms tech on his right. "You heard the commander, get the Beltar repair yard on tight beam. And I have a feeling you'd better call Kit while you're at it. Am I right, sir?"

Colt bared his teeth in what could only euphemistically be called a smile. "Definitely."

* * *

Twenty-seven standard minutes later, after a heated negotiation between Weep and the repair yard, and a hasty strategy meeting between Colt and his command team, Captain Zorn opened a conference channel to Styver's ship. No one, including Captain Torres, seemed particularly enthusiastic when they heard what Colt planned to do. Torres had argued against the idea. But with no other suggestions, and time running out, Colt had cut the meeting short and signaled Zorn.

Styver reclined in his command chair, his fine, red and black-accented uniform tight across his huge shoulders and thick neck. He tilted his head, waiting for Colt to speak.

"We're almost done with the rescue operation." Colt let his anger and nervousness show in his face and voice. If Styver knew anything about Humans he would expect such a display. Colt had no problem giving it to him.

In truth, Colt's rescue teams had pulled only about half of those stranded on the spin ring to safety. They had tried ordering an emergency stop, but the ring's control system had suffered fatal damage during the explosion. No matter what order his engineers sent, it continued its slow, vomit-inducing spin. Most of the crewmembers still stranded there were too sick to crawl out on their own, and the rescue crews dispatched to save them could only work for a few minutes at a time before they succumbed to the nausea and headache caused by the lazy wheel.

Colt had finally been forced to order them to stop their efforts and strap in while he dealt with Styver. He hated the image of the sick and injured troopers that flashed through his mind as he faced down the Besquith.

So, anger and fear were easy enough to conjure.

"By my count, you have less than three minutes to board a shuttle. I'd advise you to move with alacrity, pup."

"We're moving as fast as possible," Colt ground out through his clenched jaw. "You might not realize it, but your bomb blew out some of the ship's vital functions. We've had to work around those to save people's lives."

Styver sat forward and showed his impressive teeth. "I don't care. Get moving in two minutes, or my tac teams will make your rescue efforts a moot point."

A sudden rumble shuddered through *Uncanny Valley* like the hand of God giving the vessel a good shake.

Colt swore and looked at Zorn. "Now what?"

"We're losing attitude control, sir. I'm trying to compensate, but our hydrazine bottle was compromised in the attack. Our thrusters don't have much pressure. They can't right us. I need to bring the orbital engines online to maneuver, or we're going to lose our orbit."

Shaking his head, Colt turned back to Styver. "You heard that?"

"Yes." The Besquith did not look pleased.

"Can you not fire on us if we heat up the in-system maneuvering thrusters? If you do, you're going to lose this ship."

"Fine. Your captain may adjust orbit, but I want you and yours off that bridge, now!"

Colt signaled Zorn, and the big K'kng, who had taken control of the helm for this operation, fired a precisely calculated burst that bled off some of *Uncanny's* orbital velocity. Though distances in orbit could be vast, Styver had positioned his attack frigate less than a kilometer below *Uncanny* on a slow approach vector. Zorn had just sped up that approach. Significantly.

An unseen speaker shouted something on Styver's ship, and the Besquith growled. "What are you doing? You're closing on us too quickly."

"Sorry!" Zorn, playing the big, dumb, incompetent pilot, rapidly tapped at the slate attached to the command chair. "Looks like attitude control was more damaged than reported. Thrust vectors are way off their predicted coordinates. I'm trying to compensate."

More cries of alarm from the other vessel made Colt's heart sing, though he managed to look concerned. "Zorn?"

"Got it, sir." Zorn played his deft fingers across a series of keys displayed on his Tri-V, and the engines fired again. At first, he opened his mouth in a K'kng gesture of triumph, only to shut it with an audible click. "Uh oh."

Again *Uncanny* bled speed, which in turn hurried it toward the frigate. Discordant collision warnings sounded, and Colt wanted to plug his ears. A crimson reticle appeared around the frigate in the forward display accompanied by a set of figures, rapidly counting down the number of meters between the two ships.

Of all the unknowns critical to this plan, Colt had worried most over this one. He had gambled that Styver, who obviously prized *Uncanny* enough to try taking it rather than turning it into orbital detritus, wouldn't decide to cut his losses and fire on them. Hopefully, someone on his crew would point out that scuttling *Uncanny* this close to his own ship would likely destroy them both.

Of course, Styver could simply maneuver to safety and fire on them once he was in a good position, but that would mean giving Colt a chance to run, and he doubted the Besquith had enough patience for a long chase, even if it would undoubtedly end with *Uncanny* taken or destroyed.

Time to entice the big alien to do what Colt wanted.

"Back off your speed. Give us some room. My crew will get our ship in check in a few seconds. Right, Captain Zorn?" Colt's tone was admonishing when he said Zorn's name, though he lifted his eyebrows when he turned to face the ship's captain.

"Yes, sir!" Zorn snapped. In Colt's mind, the K'kng was overplaying his role, but all races and people acted differently under stress. Like Styver.

The Besquith howled in frustration, then turned to someone on his bridge and barked out several orders.

"We're going to taste atmosphere if we back off much, sir," said a disembodied voice from somewhere to Styver's right.

"We have shields, don't we?" The Besquith's tone could have eaten through the deck at his feet, it dripped so much acid.

"Yes, sir. Of course, sir."

"Then back off before that bloated freighter rams us!"

To Colt's relief, the frigate reversed engines with a mere ten meters of space between it and the underside of *Uncanny's* hull to spare. Bigger or not, FMT's converted freighter wasn't armored like the smaller ship. Mass was one thing, and *Uncanny Valley* would certainly damage the other ship if it bounced the frigate off its underbelly, but it would also rip *Uncanny's* hull to shreds. With most of his crew taking refuge in the ship's main fuselage, such a breach would have cost many lives.

Colt breathed a sigh of relief and gave Zorn a slight nod.

"We're still having trouble with these thrusters," Zorn said as *Uncanny* rumbled a third time, slowing even further, and again closing in on the frigate.

"What are you playing at?" Styver, his body shaking against his restraints, peered into the Tri-V display, a low growl rumbling in his throat. "You're lying to me!" He turned to one of his crewmembers. "Ty'von, get us out from underneath these scum. I want a missile firing solution, now!"

Its underside beginning to glow orange from friction with Spimu's upper atmosphere, Styver's ship was obliged to again reverse fire its engines in an attempt to outpace *Uncanny's* rapid slowing. Speeding up would have lifted their orbit and slammed them into the encroaching vessel.

Colt could well imagine his opponent's helm controller grinning as the planet's atmosphere aided in slowing the ship. Designed for landing planet-side, the frigate had no problem adjusting its delta V to slip behind *Uncanny,* then raising its orbit once the way was clear. *Uncanny* enjoyed no such advantage. It wouldn't take much atmospheric turbulence to damage the old freighter. Not that Zorn would let that happen.

"I don't know what you were planning," Styver said, glowering through the Tri-V at Colt. "But it's failed. When I'm done with you, that sorry excuse for a ship will be nothing but a greasy smear in Spimu's skies."

"My thoughts exactly," said a new voice on the comm, one that made Colt grin like a feral cat.

For at least a century before first contact, Humans had dreamed of spaceships with energy shields. Once aliens had finally deigned to say hello, they brought with them technology that made those fantastic dreams a reality. But unlike the shields Humans had imagined, actual force fields, while highly effective against energy attacks from particle beams and even nuclear strikes, were far less trustworthy when it came to lasers and ballistic projectiles. Especially when they were compromised by attempts to disperse superheated atmosphere during reentry. In fact, as far as Colt knew, shields were always most vulnerable upon reentry.

Like now.

Hermes screamed out of Spimu's gravitational embrace at the cusp of escape velocity. It bore down on Styver's frigate like a silver fish knifing through water to catch an unsuspecting insect bobbing on the surface.

A salvo of missiles, their protective nose cones glowing red as they shot across the gap between *Hermes* and the frigate, hit the underside of the bigger ship. Flashes of laser fire preceded them as if to soften the target before the missiles struck, though Colt doubted it could get much softer.

The small image of Styver's ship belched a plume of fire. The bigger image of Styver, himself, shook and rumbled, as the Besquith roared in frustration. Then the comm link failed, and the Besquith disappeared.

Kit bellowed a triumphant, "Whooo!" over the comm, and *Uncanny's* bridge crew broke into cheers.

As if in slow motion, the frigate broke apart, with chunks of its main fuselage spinning off in all directions. Some struck *Uncanny*, no doubt doing some damage, but it was nothing compared to what could have happened if Styver had fired on it.

Colt turned to Levin and, again, almost kissed her. She smiled, but shook her head slightly as she turned to look at everyone now focused on Colt. The crew and his command staff slapped his shoulders, succeeding mostly in sending him and themselves flailing around the bridge in the microgravity environment.

Captain Torres, hanging steady from a hand hold, caught Colt and set him upright. "Good work."

"Thanks."

The older merc's slight grin faded. "Now, it's time to pick up the pieces. You've got people stuck on the spin ring, and whoever planted the bomb is still aboard."

Colt nodded, some of his elation evaporating at the pointed reminder. He sighed. "It never ends, does it?"

"No, son. It never does."

* * * * *

Chapter Twenty-Seven

"We heard you had some unpleasantness up there." Sandiset Belorrogg, Deputy Director of Nexvar Refining, lowered his muzzle and eyed Colt critically via his Tri-V. A member of the Jivool race, the massive alien reminded most Humans of a walking, talking, hunchbacked bear. Though the Jivool originated from a planet known as Ja-Wool, Sandiset's ancestors had long ago migrated to Spimu, becoming one of the great eight races who controlled just about everything on the planet.

"Everything is fine." Colt disliked lying. It made him feel dirty. But the bombing and subsequent attack had no bearing on FMT's ability to field sentries for Sandiset's refinery. Very little, anyway. He pulled his chair closer to the Tri-V on the ward room table. "We did have an altercation with a misguided Besquith, but that drama is behind us."

Sandiset rolled his shoulders in reluctant acceptance. "I'll admit, your officers have performed exemplary service for us thus far."

"And they'll continue to do so. You have my guarantee." Colt very deliberately did not sigh in exasperation or slam his fist on the table. He felt as though he had been on the comm non-stop with one planetary agency or another for the past forty-eight hours. And now FMT's clients were calling to check up on them. If it wasn't the Spimu Environmental Protection Agency, or the planet's mercenary field office, it was one type of lawyer or another calling about a string of different lawsuits from wrongful death to the firing of missile salvos without a permit.

Colt had patiently explained his reasons for defending himself and his people at least a hundred times since Styver's attack. Not that anyone in power really seemed to care. They just wanted their piece of whatever fine FMT was likely to be charged by the Spimu government. Each telling of the story wore at his patience a little more until he wanted to scream.

"Very well then," Sandiset said in his resonant voice. "But be warned, if we detect even a slight reduction in service, we will be forced to sign with another mercenary company. This year's production cycle is too important."

"Understood, sir."

Sandiset nodded and signed off.

Colt, only too aware of his officers gathered around the table, kept his face still as he turned to them. The somber expressions that met his gaze reminded him that they shared his frustration. The usual morning brief had become a bad news roundup.

"At least we've still got the job," he said. "They could have tried to cut out early."

"I hate to say this, but I'm almost hoping the refinery gets hit, so we can earn the combat bonuses," Petrov said. "We need every credit we can get."

Repair costs for the ship were still coming in, but the tally looked bleak. By Colt's estimates, the repairs might cost more than the refinery job paid, which would put the company even deeper into debt. He hoped Weep could massage the numbers to keep them afloat.

"I don't blame you," Colt said. "In the meantime, I've sent Weep to meet with Grennis Bredge. I'm hopeful she'll have some friends who can use mercs."

"Wealthy friends, I hope," said Captain Granger. The Charlie Company commander's nanites had already erased the purplish bruise she had received during her harrowing thrill ride aboard the spin ring, though she still seemed jumpy.

Thankfully, Rooysot, FMT's resident Jeha engineer, had managed to get the ring back up to speed over the last several hours, allowing the crew to return to their stations. And not a minute too soon. With everyone crowding *Uncanny's* main fuselage, space had been at a premium for most of the last day and a half. Tempers had flared, resulting in a near riot when several junior enlisted had come to blows over sleeping space. Colt could hardly blame them. They had just lost three members of their team, someone on board had sabotaged the ship, and they were forced to live cheek by jowl because the command staff didn't want anyone leaving the vessel for fear of letting the perpetrator escape.

Colt turned his attention to Petrov and Levin. They looked careworn and sleep deprived, signs they had been working hard on their assigned project. "How goes the investigation?"

"We've narrowed the suspect pool down to four." Petrov tapped his slate and four images appeared on the table's Tri-V.

Colt stared at them for a long moment. Three he knew in passing, crewmembers he rarely had occasion to speak with. But that fourth...

"None of these are new hires," Colt said.

"No, sir." Petrov blinked a command to his implants, and a new set of images appeared beneath the first four. "Of the seventeen people we hired at Karma Station, none had access to engineering. They're all infantry, aside from two, and they are destined for admin positions."

"And the other four?" Colt tried in vain to ignore the ache in his stomach.

"They all did." Levin looked at Colt, and while her face betrayed no evidence of her affection for him, she managed to convey deep sympathy even he couldn't miss. She knew his history with the fourth individual. "It was Sloan."

Colt wanted to argue, to deny. Levin and Petrov hadn't seen the look of gratitude on Sloan's face when Colt had offered to send his pay home to Sloan's family. They hadn't experienced the man's sincere thanks when Colt canceled Sloan's public beating at Yardley's hands.

"He is our chief suspect," Petrov said.

"I took our evidence to an independent detective on Spimu last night," Levin said. "He concurs with our assessment. The other three had access, but none of them went near the target compartment in the last several days."

"I take it, Sloan did?"

Levin nodded. "Not only does his implant log show him in the vicinity during the time we think the bomber left the package, the shift schedule shows that Sloan traded his duty with one of the other three, Corporal Little of Bravo Company."

"Have you interviewed either of them yet?"

"That's our first order of business after this meeting," Petrov said.

"Why wait?" Colt used his pinplants to open a channel to security.

"Hello, Colonel," said the disembodied voice of Staff Sergeant Wayne Iverson, the company's security chief. "What can I do for you, sir?"

"Sergeant, I need you to send details to pick up—" Colt consulted his implants to find Little's first name—"Corporal Bill Little and Private First Class Brandon Sloan. Tell your people to be discreet but to bring them to Wardroom One-Alpha as soon as possible."

"You're certain you want to do this in front of everyone?" Levin's tone said Colt certainly did not want to do such a thing, that he was stepping on her job, and he knew it.

"Yes." Colt couldn't hide the sudden, seething anger welling up inside him. "I trusted Sloan. I helped him every way I could. And he did this?"

"Sloan might be more forthcoming if we interview him in a smaller group," Petrov said.

"No." Colt sliced a hand through the air in front of him as if he were cutting off the argument at the knees. "I want him to face the people he's let down. Captain Granger, he's in your company, how do you feel about that?"

"I agree. If he's guilty, he should face all of us and confess. If he's innocent, let him tell us that."

Colt stole a glance at Torres who gave him an infinitesimal nod. Then he turned back to regard Levin and Petrov. She was staring lasers at Colt while Petrov looked mildly agitated.

"I'm not trying to steal your investigation," Colt said. "I simply want the perpetrator caught, so we can put this entire thing behind us. You've done good work, and you did it fast. Thank you. Now we can finish it together. I'll leave the initial questioning to you two. I want you to find out what Little has to say, then we'll have a chat with Sloan."

That seemed to mollify Levin a bit, though she still looked pissed off beneath her no-nonsense business expression. Colt worried he had just ruined their relationship.

"Yes, sir," Petrov said, his expression easing minutely at Colt's words.

It took less than five minutes for the security detail to arrive with Corporal Little and PFC Sloan. Colt ordered them to hold Sloan outside while Little faced the command staff. Contrary to his surname, Little stood over two meters tall with a barrel chest and hands the size of small dinner plates. A shock of red hair, cut into a buzz, framed his melon dome and freckles covered his pale cheeks. He braced to attention before the gathered officers.

"At ease," Petrov said, and the big man settled into a stiff parade rest. "Do you know why we called you down here, Corporal?"

"No, sir." Little kept his eyes fixed steadfastly on a point across the room above the seated officers' heads.

"We'd like to know why you traded guard shifts with PFC Sloan two nights ago," Levin said.

Little's green eyes momentarily shifted to her then back to the wall. An expression of sudden panic washed across his face, there and gone in a flash. "I don't know, Sergeant."

"I think you do, Corporal," Levin pressed. "You took him up on the offer. Did he give you something in exchange for trading places on the schedule?"

"No, Sergeant."

"Then why did you trade?"

Little swallowed, making a squeaking sound in the near silent room. "Is PFC Sloan in trouble, Sergeant?"

"Should he be in trouble?" Petrov leaned forward in his chair, hands splayed on the table. He looked like a guard dog ready to pounce on a would-be thief.

"I don't know, sir." The corporal sounded unsure. "All I know is Sloany wanted to trade shifts with me on the night that bomb went off. He didn't give a reason, and I didn't need none. He's good people. We've known each other since our freshman year, ya know? Er, sir."

"So, you've already made the connection between the schedule change and the bombing?" Levin's gaze could have flash frozen a medium-size star.

"Yes, Sergeant."

"And you told no one?" Petrov stood up, his lips drawn back from his teeth in a snarl.

Corporal Little looked like someone had smacked him in the face with a shovel. He physically rocked back on his heels though he maintained his rest position. "It wasn't Sloany, sir. The schedule change was a coincidence. He'd never do that sort of thing. Never. That's why I didn't tell. It didn't matter."

"I'm afraid it does," Petrov said gravely. He looked at Colt. "I think we should see Sloan now, sir."

"Am I in trouble?" Little asked.

"Yes, Corporal," Levin said. "But probably less than you think. Loyalty isn't a crime." She motioned to the two guards standing behind the big man. "He's restricted to his bay until we have time to deal with him. Have Sloan brought in on your way out."

The guards took Little by the arms, and though the big man could have tossed either or both of them across the room without breaking a sweat, he hung his head and let them lead him away.

Sloan looked like a cornered rat as he entered the room, his guards pacing behind him. His gaze briefly met Colt's, and his face fell. Until that moment, Colt had hoped Sloan was innocent, but that one look shattered his hope like a glass slipper.

"Do you know why you're here, PFC?" Levin asked.

Sloan trembled. He drew a long breath, his chest heaving, then lifted his gaze to look at the first sergeant. "I did it."

A collective intake of breath followed the confession as the company commanders looked around at each other in stunned disbelief and horror.

Captain Granger started to rise, her face livid as she stared at her trooper. "You sorry son of a—"

"Please, Captain, don't." Petrov held up a hand to forestall the Charlie Company commander. "Let us question him."

Though flushed red with anger, Granger nodded at the major and sat down.

"Just for the record," Petrov said. "You did what specifically?"

Sloan's gaze dropped back to the ward room floor. "I planted the bomb in engineering two days ago."

"Why did you plant the bomb?" A muscle tremored in Levin's cheek, the only sign of her inner anger. Otherwise, she looked and sounded perfectly calm, though Colt knew her too well for her outward façade to fool him.

"Money." Sloan rubbed his nose and cheek with the back of one sleeve.

"Money from whom?" Levin asked. "Styver?"

"No, sir. Mountside."

* * * * *

Chapter Twenty-Eight

Reluctantly, Colt had allowed Sloan a seat. The dishonored PFC gripped the arm rests with both hands, his gaze on the floor.

"They found me at the Merc's Delight on Karma station." He spoke in a monotone, as if he had practiced this speech a thousand times, uttering the words by rote. "There were two of them. Both Human. They bought me drinks after most everybody else had already headed back to *Uncanny*. At first, I thought they were a couple of mercs. I guess they were, but they were working for Mountside."

"Any idea what company they were with?" Captain Sampson asked. Of all the company commanders, she looked the least scandalized by Sloan's tale.

Sloan shook his head. "No idea, ma'am. I just know what they offered me."

"Which was?"

"Twelve million credits plus complete debt forgiveness. They wouldn't ever come after my wife for the money we still owed Mountside. I'd be off the hook."

"Did they give you the bomb or did you build it?" Colt asked.

"They gave it to me. Told me where to put it, so it would damage the ship's maneuvering thrusters."

"Why are you confessing?" Levin asked. "Why not lie?"

Sloan remained silent for several seconds before he cleared his throat. "I never meant to harm anyone. They told me the bomb would just knock out the orbital thrusters—strand us where we were. Afterward, when I heard—" Sloan broke off as tears leaked from his eyes. He mopped them away with a handkerchief Captain Butler handed him. "When I heard I had killed people, it broke me inside. I had set the timer to go off three hours earlier. When it didn't, I tried to go back and collect it, but there were too many people around. I assumed the thing was a dud, and I'd be able to remove it that night. But—"

"—but it went off in the morning and killed three people." Colt drove each word home like a hammer.

Anguish creased Sloan's face. He nodded.

"And the spin ring. Did you know your attack would cause it to slow?" Captain Sampson asked.

"No, ma'am. I swear I didn't." Sloan rubbed his neck with one hand as if he could wipe away his guilt. "I wanted to turn myself in, but I kept dithering about it. I did what I could to help. I volunteered for the rescue teams every time they let me."

"He was one of those who dragged me off the ring," Captain Granger said. Though her rage seemed to have abated, her throat and ears remained red, her voice low.

"How did Styver connect to the bombing?" Petrov asked. "Did the two of you coordinate the attack?"

"No, sir. I didn't know about Styver. The Mountside guys must have hired him after me, or before, I don't know."

"But you crippled us just in time for his attack," Colt said. "You must have signaled him somehow."

Sloan shook his head. "I promise I'm telling you everything I know. I never had any contact with Styver. I saw him in The Merc's Delight on Karma station, but I never spoke with him."

Colt stared at the PFC, trying to read his face. He certainly sounded convinced of his own words. And why would he lie about signaling Styver after he had already confessed to planting a bomb aboard *Uncanny*?

"I think he's telling the truth," Colt said.

"So. Operatives working for Mountside hired him to blow our maneuvering thrusters, then separately hired Styver to wait for that explosion and attack." Levin looked as though she was trying out the ideas as she said them. She nodded slowly. "Yeah, that would make sense, if they didn't wholly trust Sloan. Let's say he lost his nerve and leaked the plan before he planted the bomb. We'd have him and his connection to Mountside, but we'd know nothing about Styver. They could have used him to attack us, or not, at their leisure."

"This entire setup makes no sense," Petrov said. He shook his head. "Mountside owns us, almost literally. One look at our books, and they'd know we're nowhere near paying off our entire debt before the deadline. If they wait a few months, they'll be able to legally press every member of FMT into indentured servitude, and they'll have received all those monthly payments in the meantime. So why risk killing us? Sounds like a bad investment on their part."

"They weren't trying to kill us." Colt looked Petrov in the eyes, mounting fury at the situation overcoming his natural anxiety. "They meant for Sloan's bomb to make us a walkover for Styver. He was supposed to traipse in here and capture us, not kill us."

"With all due respect, you can't know that for certain, sir." Petrov met Colt's gaze evenly. "It was still a major risk. Whoever orchestrated it couldn't have predicted how we—you—would react. In fact, I think it's obvious you dashed their expectations when you destroyed Styver's ship. So why do it? They'd be killing the goose who lays the golden eggs."

That was what made Feliks Petrov such a good officer. He didn't back down from giving his commander advice, even when it ran counter to said commander's thinking. He considered his arguments, marshalled them like an old-world general, and marched them out when needed. Angry or not, Colt had to consider Feliks's point of view, if for no other reason than it made such good sense.

Colt turned to Captain Torres who had remained quiet all this time. The big merc looked decidedly uncomfortable under the command staff's scrutiny, but he didn't flinch or falter.

"You send Mountside weekly updates on everything we do, correct?" Colt asked.

"I do."

"And that includes our financials?"

"Everything." Torres rolled one shoulder in a half shrug. "Almost everything. I didn't tell them it was I who brought you to Karma the first time."

"But you did tell them we were going there?" Colt asked.

"I had no choice. They would have found out eventually."

"So, that's how they knew they could find Sloan on Karma station." Levin said. "I hadn't put that together before now."

"They didn't warn you about the bomb?" Colt hated asking the question. He had come to trust Torres despite the big man's role as hired overseer aboard *Uncanny*.

Torres' ample brows drew down in annoyance. "If I had known about the bomb, I would have told you, Colt. I'm paid to observe. That's my job. But my integrity is worth more than credits. I wouldn't let innocent people die for money. I hope you know that about me by now."

"Do you have any idea why Mountside would sabotage our ship?"

"No. If I did, I would tell you." A hint of anger touched the big merc's voice, but that was all. The look in his eyes was more hurt than angry. "I have no reciprocal contact with my employer. I send them weekly updates. They send me nothing. I swear to that."

Colt held Torres' gaze for a moment longer, then nodded. "I believe you."

"Sir?" Sloan said. "I think I might know why they wanted to cripple *Uncanny Valley*. At least, I have a good guess."

"Why's that?" Colt asked, wary.

"It was something one of the Mountside agents said. Sort of an offhanded comment I don't think he meant to let slip. I had told them I didn't want to hurt any of my crewmates, and he said, 'we don't want to hurt them either, just to keep them from coming back to Zion.' His partner gave him a scathing look, and he clammed up after that."

It felt as though someone had smashed Colt's breastbone with a hammer. He turned from Sloan to the command group, the air knocked out of him. "Onishi. They know we're due to pick her up next month, and she warned us there were odd ships coming into the Zion system. Could those be mercs hired by Mountside?"

"You think Mountside is massing a merc fleet to attack the Mormons?" Petrov sounded incredulous. "What for? We've seen their planet. It's got nothing anyone would want. That goes for the whole system."

"Does it matter why?" Levin glanced back and forth between Petrov and the rest of the command group. "One of ours is there. If Mountside is planning an attack, Onishi will be caught in the middle. Her contract is almost up, but for now, she's fighting on the Mormon side. She'll do her duty no matter the odds."

"Problem is, we don't know those odds." Captain Sampson placed her hands on the table. "And our numbers are down. We've got almost two companies of troopers working garrison jobs on Spimu. If we rush into a fight, we might find ourselves overwhelmed."

"An expeditionary force." Petrov looked like a man who had just solved a particularly taxing mathematical equation. "We send a couple of squads into Zion to gather intel. They can reconnoiter the situation on Brigham and send us what they find."

"That will take weeks." Levin looked pained at the idea. "It's obvious Mountside doesn't want us returning, because they know we won't like what we find there. That's enough to make me think Onishi's in danger. Like you said, Feliks, they were willing to risk killing us to make us stay away. That alone makes me want to go down there, guns blazing."

"I know that's right." Captain Butler smiled, but there was no mirth in his expression.

"Okay then," Petrov said. "If we're going back, I suggest we nix our current contracts and pull our people back. We don't know what we might face in Zion, either spaceborne or on the ground. If we're going to do this, we can't do it shorthanded."

"Do we really want a reputation as a company that burns contracts?" Captain Samson asked.

No, Colt certainly didn't want that. But burning contracts was one thing. Letting a member of FMT burn was another.

"We do what we must," he said, then opened a channel to the bridge. "Zorn."

"Go ahead, Colonel."

"I know we're still recovering, but we've got an emergency. Contact Yardley. Tell him it's time to come in from the cold. Same goes for our people at the Nexvar refinery. We need everyone. After that, you're to get us underway for the Zion system with all haste. Do whatever you see fit. Just make it happen."

"Roger that, Colonel."

"Weep," Colt called over an open channel so the staff could hear.

"Yes?" The Flatar sounded out of breath, which made Colt wonder what she did in her time off, but he dismissed that thought immediately.

"You're not going to like what I'm about to ask of you."

"Oh, joy."

"We need a replacement dropship, immediately. Think you can speak with the guys at the shipyard where they repaired *Hermes*, and maybe get us a good deal?"

A long period of silence passed during which Levin lifted her eyebrows and Captain Butler shook his head.

"It doesn't matter how well I negotiate, we don't have any credits." Weep sounded like a teacher trying to explain a tough concept to a particularly slow student. "We can't buy a new ship with air."

"How about extra RATs, spare CASPer parts, and whatever credit anyone will grant us?" Colt realized how desperate he sounded and didn't care. "We need a dropship to replace the *Doubleday*, and short of robbing someone, I really don't care how you get it."

"I suppose I could call in a favor with Grennis Bredge. She really was taken with us after we saved her life, but that doesn't mean she'll just give us a ship. It's still going to cost us."

"Understood."

"And, you did say I can get it by any means short of theft?"

Colt hesitated a second. Weep hadn't always been the most scrupulous financier in her time. Then again, they really needed a ship. "Short of theft, yes."

"Okay, I'll do my best."

"Oh, and Weep," Colt said before the Flatar could break the connection.

"Yes, Colonel?"

"We're going to need that ship within the next two hours."

Weep uttered a word Colt's implants refused to interpret.

* * * * *

Chapter Twenty-Nine

Colt floated at the center of *Uncanny Valley's* bridge, his command group around him, as the ship transitioned back into real space and the Zion system. A moment of disconnection with reality passed through him, then the sublime whiteness of hyperspace disappeared from the forward Tri-V, replaced by the all-encompassing depth of space filled with stars.

The last one hundred and seventy hours had been pure hell for Colt, and he knew the same went for his entire command. They had all lived on a razor's edge, wondering what they would find when they finally arrived. A black field of stars was almost disappointing.

"You know your orders," Zorn told Benwarst. "Push for Brigham at max accel." The K'kng officer turned to Colt after checking the small holo display on his personal slate. "We came out of the gate in a good position, sir. We'll need only minor adjustments to reach the planet. I haven't run the numbers yet, but we should be there in about eleven hours."

"We've got something interesting showing up on sensors." Benwarst folded his millipede-like body almost in half to inspect the Tri-V set into his console. "The range is long, but I'd say there are at least two ships parked at the system's L4 Lagrange point."

"Put it up on the main display," Zorn said.

While indistinct, the image clearly showed the silhouettes of two cruisers parked close to one another, outlined more by the absence of stars behind them than Zion's light, though the nearer one enjoyed a narrow strip of illumination from the star. Beyond that, Colt could tell little.

Hope made Colt's heart beat just a little faster. Had they arrived before Mountside had launched their attack? Or, even better, had his command group's hypothesized attack been nothing more than overactive imagination?

One look at Levin told him she was thinking along the same lines. Petrov too, though he looked more concerned than happy, which made sense. If they had made a mistake, they had burned two contracts for no good reason.

"Correction," Benwarst said, interrupting Colt's racing thoughts. "I'm detecting too much mass in that area. It looks like two ships and a spreading cloud of debris that was a third."

Colt spun in place to look at Benwarst. "Any way to tell who those ships belong to? Are they Mormon or someone else's?"

"Mormon. The intact vessels are emitting automated distress calls."

"If I'm not mistaken, that was the entire Mormon navy—three heavy cruisers." Petrov stared at the zoomed in holographic display, a pained look on his face.

"Try hailing them." Zorn swiveled his command chair to face the comms tech.

"Yes, sir," said Private Reskins. "But at this range, we'll have a lag of about eight minutes, give or take."

"Let's send a longer message then," Colt said. "Ask them to advise us of the strategic situation in-system and if they need rescue."

"Roger that, sir." Reskins worked her fingers along a holo display on her console, then sat back to wait.

Colt chaffed at the idea of altering course, but he wasn't about to leave people to die in space if he could help it.

"This is why I didn't go into the Navy." Captain Sampson nodded at the ships on the Tri-V. In a CASPer, your troops either heard you or they didn't. There was no time lag.

"Can we tell anything about Brigham?" Petrov asked Captain Zorn.

"I was just checking," Zorn said, consulting his slate. He shook his head. "No, sir. Not much. We're not detecting missiles or particle accelerator fire anywhere within sensor range. And no fusion drives either."

"I'm choosing to take that as good news."

"What about other ships?" Colt pointed at the Tri-V. "Somebody attacked those cruisers. Do we have any way of tracing who did it?"

"Not quickly, sir." Benwarst turned and looked at Colt with his insectile eyes. "I would need to inspect the battle area to make a reliable guess. But I can speak to the timing. From the size of the debris cloud spreading from the third ship, I'd say it was destroyed about eight hours ago. Perhaps as little as six. Whatever ships attacked it have left the immediate area."

"So they could be at Brigham by now?" Colt fought the shiver that tried to breeze down his spine. He didn't relish the idea of meeting heavy cruisers in orbit around the planet. *Uncanny* wouldn't stand a chance.

"Without a doubt, sir." Benwarst spread his many arms in a complex gesture of mild condescension—a Jeha's equivalent of saying, "Duh!"

"With that much time, they could be just about anywhere in Zion system." Captain Catlett waved at the Tri-V as if to take in all of space. "Or they could have transitioned. We're in the dark."

"Not completely." Yard, who had kept mostly to himself since Colt had ordered him and his sentries to return to *Uncanny*, looked around at the command group. "We know one thing for certain. There is a shooting war going on in Zion. That means we didn't come here for nothing."

"Sir, I'm getting a message back from the Mormon ship, *Zelph*."

"Let's hear it, Private," Zorn said.

"Uncanny Valley, this is Apostle Admiral R. Victor Becker of the LDSV *Zelph*. I can't tell you how sweet it is to hear a friendly voice in the system. Yes, we are in need of assistance, but I'm afraid New Nauvoo needs you more. We've managed to save all we can from the *LDSV Effulgent Light*, which was destroyed. Not many survived the attack.

"As for the strategic situation, I'd deem spaceborne ops nominal despite our sorry state. The four cruisers that attacked us were MinSha. They made immediately for the stargate, once we were out of the fight. My guess is they weren't paid to do more. We marked three frigates headed in-system shortly after that. Those belong to a different company, according to their registries, a KzSha outfit called Armored Star. I believe they plan to land forces and take New Nauvoo, though I'm not sure if they plan to hold it or simply make off with our resources.

"Either way, as an apostle of the church and officer of our navy, I hereby authorize you to interdict these aggressors. We may not have much of a fighting force, but I assure you the Latter-day Saints can and will pay you to protect our people and our holdings. Please, we need your help, and may God speed you on your way."

"Three frigates," Sampson said in the silence that followed. "That doesn't sound good."

"I'm sorry, sir, but we can't take on one armed ship in our current condition," Zorn said. "It's going to be a challenge to get this behemoth into a stable orbit."

Though FMT's engineering crew had been working day and night to get *Uncanny's* orbital adjustment thrusters functioning at one hundred percent, there hadn't been enough time or resources to make it happen. According to Rooysot's last report, the ship could currently provide an estimated thirty percent of its usual maneuverability.

"If we can't maneuver in orbit, we're not going to play hide-and-seek with these guys or go toe-to-toe," Yardley said. "But maybe we can do the opposite. If we get close, we can try to deploy a CASPer team to attack them directly. We've done it in the sims."

Colt nodded absently, his gaze on the bridge's padded bulkhead, his mind awhirl with ways to approach the problem. "That's not a bad idea."

"It's not?" Petrov looked mortified. "Sir, we don't know what sort of point defense these frigates have. We could be setting our troopers up as target practice."

"That's why we need to get close." Yardley threw up his hands. "We don't give them a chance to pick us off. We deploy a dropship to race in and spit us out like seeds. We attach and go to work breaking their ships down from the outside."

Petrov turned to Colt. "Colonel, you can't—"

"Sir, I'm sorry to interrupt, but we've got another message coming in," said Private Reskins. "This one originated from Brigham."

"Play it," Colt said.

"Attention Fulcrum Mercenary Tactics. This is Tory Howard. As a duly-appointed representative of Mountside Financial, your credit holder, I am ordering you to leave the Zion system immediately. You have no business here. Obey this order or you will be considered a hostile by mercenary agents in our employ. This is your first and only warning."

"To hell with that," Levin said, her nostrils flaring.

"Orders? This guy thinks he gets to give us orders?" Butler looked offended. "I say we go in hot, pull that sorry sack of stupid out of his frigate, and see what he's made of."

Colt held up a hand, and the group fell silent. "That's it."

"What's it?" Levin lifted her eyebrows at him in confusion. "We're going to grab Tory? I doubt that will be easy if he's hired mercs who can field three armed frigates."

"No. What Yard said. Fast insertion like spitting out seeds." Colt pulled himself up so he could address the entire crew. "Yard's idea isn't impossible, even with *Uncanny* in its current state. I believe it can work, and it solves both of our insertion problems. But it's going to take some planning."

* * *

Colt checked his guidance program for perhaps the hundredth time since the armor team had strapped him into his CASPer. Everything checked out, but that didn't stop his thoughts from wandering through every possible worst-case scenario that might occur in the next—he checked his chrono—five minutes.

"How are you holding up?" Levin asked over a private channel.

"So far, so nervous." Colt cleared his Tri-V to avoid checking the program one last time and looked over at the CASPer cradled next to him in *Osmosis'* main bay. Though he couldn't see Levin inside her suit, hearing her voice and knowing she was there stripped away some of his fear and worry. There were fifty other suits crowded around hers, all secure in their cradles, but hers felt special.

"Rooysot went over the numbers," Levin said. "Your plan is going to work."

"We'll know for sure in four minutes."

"Look on the bright side. If it doesn't work, there'll be no one left to blame you."

It felt good to laugh. Colt flipped the Tri-V feed to show him Levin's face. That felt good too. "Thanks. I needed that. Truly."

"Colt, if things go bad down there—"

"Nichol, don't."

"If they do, I just want you to know these last few weeks of sneaking dates has been fun. I really like you."

"I'm in really like with you too."

She made a rude gesture at the camera. "You know what I mean."

"Yeah, I do. And I feel the same."

"Colt," Torres said over a separate channel. "Are you ready for this?"

"The HALD or the assault?" Colt asked sardonically. A HALD, or High Altitude Low Deployment insertion, allowed CASPers to drop onto a planet's surface without riding a dropship the entire way down. At about sixty kilometers from the surface, Lieutenant Brindle, *Osmosis'* pilot, would abruptly reverse course and open the ship's external doors. Momentum combined with the planet's gravity would haul the CASPers from the bay like salt from a shaker.

"Both."

"Ready or not, I'm going. Onishi's down there because I sent her, and there are innocent people in danger—people who were willing to help me and mine when we were on the verge of enslavement." Colt smiled inside his CASPer. "Question is, are you ready? Seems like attacking mercs hired by your employer might be a conflict of interest. How's Triple T going to take this?"

"I think, once he sees what Mountside's up to, Tom will shake my hand. He's not the type to back two-faced, backstabbing jerks like Tory Howard."

"And if he doesn't, you've always got a place at FMT."

Torres chuckled over the comm. "Thanks kid. Don't tempt me. I might take you up on that offer."

"If we live, I'll have Weep draw up a contract."

"Listen, Colt." Torres' voice sobered. "We didn't get much time to talk in the last few hours. These KzSha, they're tough. And their company, Armored Star, it's got a bad reputation. Not the sort that keeps them in good standing with the Mercenary Guild, if you know what I mean. They've been caught slaving at least three times. I don't know how they're still incorporated."

"Hopefully, between us, Onishi, and the Mormons, we can beat them," Colt said. He wished for the thousandth time they had been able to contact Onishi, but the KzSha frigates were jamming all signals emanating from the ground. As far as Colt knew, everyone on the planet could already be dead.

"Remember, keep calm and keep your mind clear. Levin and I will have your back."

"Thank you, Captain."

"One minute to deployment," said LT Brindle.

"Here we go," Levin said. She sounded excited and not the least bit afraid.

"See you in the air," Colt said, to both Levin and Torres.

"Everyone hang on," Brindle yelled into the channel, his voice exultant. "We're away!"

The dropship's bay spun violently. Colt's stomach clenched and his eyes tried to roll back in his head as *Osmosis* pin wheeled away from *Uncanny Valley*.

A few troopers voiced their surprise or fear over the common channel, but Levin returned them to disciplined silence as *Osmosis'* rear deployment doors split apart. Beyond them lay a black vista pin-pricked with stars and the bright curve of the planet, Brigham. The feeling of freefall increased as the ship plummeted toward the ground like a ten-ton stone.

Colt thought he glimpsed *Hermes* flash past, but it was probably his imagination. If all went according to plan, Yardley and Team Fortress had already covered at least half the distance between *Uncanny Valley* and the first of the enemy's frigates. They had ejected from *Uncanny's* main docking bay thirty-five seconds before *Osmosis* and her escort, *Bleakend*—the dropship Weep had procured on short notice—boosted for the planet.

Using his pinplants, Colt switched to an outside feed. It took a moment to adjust the angle before *Uncanny Valley* appeared before him. Having dropped its cargo, the converted freighter had fired its main system thrusters at max acceleration, its bulk pointed at an oblique angle that would take it near enough to Brigham to skip off the atmosphere, but not close enough to cause damage. Or so Colt hoped.

With so many targets suddenly in view, the enemy frigate crews appeared confused about which ship they should attack. The nearest one fired three missiles at the departing *Uncanny Valley*, but the freighter's point defense lasers picked them off easily. The other two frigates sprayed laser fire at *Hermes* for about five seconds before some intelligent gunner realized that every time they missed the dropship, they hit their sister frigate.

The aliens fired at *Bleakend* as well but came nowhere near hitting it as the dropship sped away. It raced toward Brigham on a matching trajectory with Colt's own *Osmosis*, the atmosphere making its hull glow orange.

"Nearing HALD point," LT Brindle called over the comm. "Ten seconds."

Osmosis rumbled, and its engines screamed as it fought to reverse course. The resulting g-forces smashed Colt down inside his suit like a thousand tons of water dropped on his head. His vision went gray at the edges, and he struggled for breath. Remembering his training, he tightened his calves, thighs, and shoulders in an effort to squeeze blood back to his brain. The cradles holding the CASPers whirred into motion, moving their charges out from the wall and turning them around so their feet, and therefore their jumpjets, faced the open doors.

"Initiating HALD." LT Brindle's voice sounded strained but controlled.

A light above the bay doors turned green and, like high velocity ammunition fired from a machine gun, the CASPers shot from the back of the dropship in sets of two. The bay emptied in less than five seconds, and Colt found himself plummeting toward the surface, the sphere of the planet beckoning him onward.

* * * * *

Chapter Thirty

The simulators aboard *Uncanny*, while impressive, hadn't done the HALD justice. The screaming of the atmosphere passing over Colt's suit and the heartrending, panic-inducing fear were completely new to him. Though the CAS-Per's computer handled the first portion of the drop via a preprogrammed sequence, Colt couldn't help obsessing over the readouts flashing across his Tri-V. Everything looked fine, but he kept worrying the program would glitch or his Mk 8 would malfunction and crash into the surface like a meteor.

He also expected to see, or maybe feel, antiaircraft fire from the surface, but none came. That wasn't too surprising. From the little intel his people had collected on their headlong run for the planet, the KzSha mercs Mountside had employed for this incursion hadn't left any protection forces outside the city. Why bother? Until *Uncanny* had arrived, there were no ships or ground forces in the Zion system to challenge them. At least, none other than those they were already attacking.

Before launch, the ship's armorers had fitted each of the HALD CASPers with a heat shield that covered its legs. At about sixteen kilometers, the explosive bolts on Colt's shield blew, sending it winging away from his armor. At the same instant, his weapon systems came online as they had crossed the Union's free weapons altitude limit.

Colt engaged his jumpjets to slow his fall for the last eight kilometers of the drop. He and his fellow troopers touched down in a cloud of red dust in a landing zone six kilometers from New Nauvoo's largest dome, which twinkled in the afternoon light.

"I don't see a welcome wagon." Levin maneuvered her CASPer to get a better view of the city. "Looks to me like our friends entered on this side. See there? The burns around that airlock."

Colt zoomed in on a spot she had emblazoned on the battalion feed. "Yeah, looks melted."

"Where are these people's planetary defense systems?" Levin asked over a private channel with Colt while the squad leaders formed up their people. "How could they let Armored Star get a lander down here? They should have blown it up in space. Those frigates too."

Colt shrugged inside his suit. "I think they trusted their three-ship navy to keep them safe."

"That's insane."

"Maybe," Torres said. "But imagine growing up in a system where everybody's the same and no one fights. You become complacent. How many non-Mormon ships do you think pass through here in a year? In ten years? This place is self-sufficient. They don't trade much except to sell some resources on the open market. And since Brigham doesn't have anything especially interesting to the galaxy, nobody cares about it. The only reason you and I heard about it was because Belknap tried to steal their armor shipment."

"That's odd, isn't it?" Levin said. "This place is peaceful. Why, all of a sudden, did the Mormons buy all those suits, then hire us to guard their city?"

"No clue." Colt said. "But I have a feeling Tory Howard knows."

"We waiting for Petrov's group? Or are we heading in on our own?" Levin's tone made her choice clear.

Since Colt had sawed the *Doubleday* in half with an overamped laser, FMT lacked the dropship capacity to transport all of their troopers in one run, even with the addition of *Bleakend*. That meant Lieutenant Brindle and Kit, once she had delivered Yard and his Fortress Team to the enemy frigates, would have to rendezvous with *Uncanny* to pick up the remainder of their force, a trip Captain Zorn had estimated would take over an hour since the freighter had gone screaming away from Brigham at top speed.

FMT currently had ninety-one CASPers and two hundred and thirty-four RATs in working order. Yard had taken twenty-six of the CASPers for his spaceborne fight, which left fifteen CASPers under Major Petrov's command aboard *Uncanny* along with all of the RATs, which couldn't make a HALD jump. That left Colt fifty in his reduced platoon, though in the unlikely event Onishi still had her full complement, Colt could count on an additional twenty-seven CASPers and thirty-eight RATs inside the city.

Unfortunately, with the jamming signal still in place, he knew almost nothing about conditions under the domes, though the melted doors weighed on him. He remembered New Nauvoo as a gorgeous oasis in the middle of Brigham's dead plain. The people who lived there had worked hard to make it so. And though he found their choice of lifestyle strange, he couldn't fault their work ethic or their generosity. They had given him and his people a chance at freedom when all had appeared lost. Colt knew he could never repay that debt, but perhaps today he could make a start.

"No, we're not waiting. Organize your squads. We're going in."

Without RATs to slow them, Colt's fifty CASPers crossed the six kilometers in less than five minutes. They might have traveled faster using their jumpjets, but Colt wanted to approach cautiously. No need to lose troopers for lack of patience.

As they neared the high wall surrounding New Nauvoo's main dome, Colt could make out tracks in the red dirt where Armored Star's forces had landed. From the scorch marks on the ground and those around the airlock, it looked like the Mormons had fought a pitched battle to keep the invaders out. And lost.

Colt had seen the powered armor the Mormons used in combat the first time he had come to the planet. It was formidable. That meant the KzSha attackers were more so, or they had landed a force big enough to overwhelm the defenders. Given the number of tracks he could see leading from the LZ to the wall, maybe both.

This close up, Colt's exterior mics caught the explosions and deep rumbles emanating from somewhere inside the city dome. Tremors ran through the ground into his armor.

The melted gap in the airlock wouldn't accommodate a CASPer. Two sergeants began widening it with arm lasers until one of them could pass through.

"Williamson take point," Levin said. "Colonel?"

"Yes?" Colt stood at the back of the formation, his heart racing as he prepared to follow his troopers into the city.

Levin switched to a private channel. "Please keep this position as we move inside. I can't give you an order, sir, but if you leave the back of the formation, I will drag your ass back *into* formation."

"Yes, Sergeant."

"Glad we have an understanding."

The KzSha invaders had blown a much wider hole through the inner airlock. No doubt, tons of breathable air had escaped. Colt figured that had been part of Armored Star's infiltration plan. They didn't give a damn about human life. Suffocating the entire population meant less work for them in taking the city.

Fortunately, someone had thrown an improvised stasis membrane across the gap. The three-micron-wide, semi-permeable barrier constructed of nanites prevented more air from escaping. Staff Sergeant Patton Williams tentatively pressed an armored hand against, and then through, the surface which reformed around his hand. He quickly passed through the membrane, and the remainder of the troopers filed through behind him.

The sounds of battle intensified as Colt pushed through the barrier, Torres right behind him. Along with the echoes of distant explosions, chemical-propelled artillery, and the unmistakable crack of rounds impacting came sudden chatter over Colt's radio. The computer-modulated system detected three distinct network trunks carrying comms across the city. Two were set aside for civil use, and the third was dedicated to the 'Mormon Militia.' All three buzzed with interference from the KzSha jamming device and the nearly incoherent voices screaming orders. On the civil comms channel, the voices seemed to be mostly screaming. No FMT-marked chatter appeared on Colt's Tri-V.

Levin flicked an armored hand at three of the troopers. "Merkel, get our eyes up. You two advance with Williams two hundred meters to that first dome scraper. We need to know what we're facing."

Corporal Merkel, whose CASPer sported a large box on one shoulder that looked like a launcher without missiles, turned to face the city. The box engaged, flipping up and over her shoulder with a whine of servos so the blister packs lining the business end were aimed upward at a forty-five degree angle. A staccato series of compressed air blasts sounded as she fired thirty palm-sized drones toward the sky. The buzzing craft zoomed upward on their precisely controlled fans and took up a box formation above the team's heads.

New data popped up on Colt's Tri-V as the drones' digital network engaged and some of the jamming signal disappeared. The enhanced tactical display showed a smattering of activity four blocks from their current position—mostly groups of two or three Humans in civilian clothes armed with anemic laser rifles or, in a few cases, bricks and knives, standing on street corners trying to look menacing while wearing oxygen masks.

"Calling Captain Alice Onishi, this is First Sergeant Nichol Levin. Do you copy?" Levin broadcast her voice over all channels. If Onishi was alive, and in range, her comms system should pick up the drone-boosted call.

But no answer came.

Colt fought down despair. Any of a million reasons could explain the lack of response, and he didn't have time to waste contemplating them.

"Who is this?" asked a deep voice over the Mormon Militia channel.

"First Sergeant Nichol Levin of Fulcrum Mercenary Tactics. We are a relief force, here to defend the city. Whom am I addressing, please?"

"This is Bishop General P. Oscar Lund, commander of the Mormon Militia. How many are in your group, Sergeant?"

"Fifty CASPers in this initial drop, sir, but we have more armor on the way within the hour."

"Fifty CASPers?" General Lund sounded surprised and immensely pleased. "That's good news."

"Bishop, this is Colonel Colt Maier from FMT. We're inside the city near the western airlock. We've encountered no hostiles as of yet. Where are you, sir? And what is the situation on the ground?" As he spoke, Colt motioned for Levin to get their force moving. He needed to find the enemy if he planned to engage them.

Levin gave the order, and Williams moved forward with Kirkenall and Baker flanking him. The remainder of the company moved in an ordered arrow formation behind them.

Bishop General Lund barked orders to people for several seconds before answering Colt. When he did, he sounded exasperated. "Our situation? We're being overrun in our homes, that's our situation. All of our sensible civilians are sheltering in atmospherically controlled buildings since the KzSha bled off most of our breathable air before we could stop the venting. There are a few crackpots on the streets trying to fight, but otherwise, our people appear safe. The enemy is engaging us street by street. If you've come to help, I'll gladly accept. Bring your fifty to the following coordinates and attack these monsters from the rear."

Latitude and longitude numbers appeared on Colt's display, and he did his best not to sigh in frustration over the open circuit. This was their general? Who had trained this guy? Did he think the Armored Star mercs weren't monitoring their comms? Now they knew where Colt was supposed to hit them, which meant he couldn't. And Lund hadn't provided Colt a force estimate. He had no clue what sort of resistance he might find when he reached Lund. "Bishop General, how many enemy combatants are in the city?"

"We don't have hard numbers, but we think there are at least three hundred."

"Three hundred?" Colt's heart sank into his stomach. He had known a figure that high was possible. Armored Star had brought three frigates after all. But he had hoped the invaders had fielded fewer and kept a reserve in orbit—a reserve that would have been too distracted by Yardley's Fortress Team to attempt reinforcing their brethren on the ground.

"Yes. Three hundred. Perhaps more. And they're near impossible to kill. I'm afraid we're losing ground to them."

Levin started down a narrow street between tall residential buildings, but Colt waved her off, quickly sending her an encrypted message via his pinplants. For the briefest instant, a feeling of deja vu overcame him, and he recalled sending the same sort of messages to Yardley, except this time he was in charge.

Ever the professional, Levin said nothing as she passed the order along, and the platoon reversed course and followed a wider thoroughfare called Alger Way. The sounds of battle intensified as they double-timed up the street. They passed a group of lightly armed Humans who cheered them as they hustled by.

"Bishop General," Colt said as he silently ordered the platoon to turn right, completing a long detour around the coordinates Lund had given him. "One of our people was detailed to work as a guard here some months ago. Her name is Alice Onishi. Is she with your forces?"

"Onishi? Yes! She is the tip of our spear. We wouldn't be holding like we are if it wasn't for her."

"Contact!" Williams, who had rounded the next corner, walked his CASPer backward, his guns blazing. Laser fire repeatedly scored his suit until he pulled out of range behind a building.

"How many?" Levin asked.

"Thirty-four on the street." Williams said. "More in the park beyond."

Colt cursed himself for dividing his attention. He should have been watching his heads up display. He switched to an overhead view provided by the drone network and cursed again. The system marked enemy combatants in red, Mormon Militia in white, and FMT members in blue. The street Williams had just vacated contained so many red dots it looked like a kid with chickenpox.

"Hold fast and open fire!" Levin shouted over the comm as a dozen KzSha warriors spilled into the intersection, laser rifles flashing red death.

The wasp-like KzSha stood just under a meter and a half tall. Though shorter than an average Human, no one who had met them in battle would underestimate the eight-limbed creatures' ability to fight. Thick chitin covered their bodies, which they augmented with combat armor. While they employed their four lower limbs for locomotion, the other two sets consisted of an upper pair capable of fine manipulation like firing a gun and a lower pair that looked for all the galaxy like serrated swords.

To make things worse, they had wings.

Though incapable of sustained flight under one standard gravity like that found on Earth, Brigham's 0.75G presented little hindrance for the KzSha. Dozens of them buzzed into the air, some opting for direct attacks, others rebounding off adjacent buildings into sharp dives toward the Humans, guns blazing.

Colt scanned the situation, sent orders to his platoon with designated targets marked for concentrated fire, and activated the over-the-shoulder laser on his left side. The team, their pinplants feeding them Colt's commands, followed his orders without hesitation, and though the KzSha's armor provided a substantial barrier against attack, it could not withstand the concentrated fire of fifty CASPers for any length of time. Missiles, lasers, and bullets turned the KzSha into paste as Colt's troopers fired on target after target.

Unfortunately, the CASPers couldn't maintain that rate of fire for long, not without resupplying. And unless Colt got word from Yardley that the frigates were no longer in play or from Petrov, confirming his people were dropping planet-side, he had to assume his current ammo supply was it.

Colt ordered Levin to fall back while continuing to lay down covering fire. He designated six more targets as his people withdrew, placing buildings between them and the alien force.

A group of twenty-four KzSha raced after the Humans. The enemies' antennae lit up in a complex array of lights and colors, mimicked by the surface of their armor. The light show raced along their ranks from farthest to nearest until it reached those on the verge of overrunning Colt's position. As one, they froze in place, executed a synchronized spin, and retreated back the way they had come.

Colt's platoon split left and right, seeking cover behind a couple of apartment buildings nearly as tall as the dome.

"Colonel, you got any idea why they called off pursuit?" Levin asked.

"Nope. They were taking losses, but they have us beat on numbers. They could have overrun us easily."

A voice attracted Colt's attention. At first, he couldn't place it. He turned to find eight men and two women, most dressed in plain clothes, and all wearing rebreathers, approaching from the west.

The man in front, a thin, old guy with bushy gray hair that poked out around the breathing apparatus strapped to his head, waved a small, energy-only, laser rifle over his head, trying to get Colt's attention.

"Hey! Where is your leader?" he asked. "Tell him we're here to help. Where do you want us?"

Colt flicked on his external speakers. "Sir, you need to get off the streets. This is a battle zone."

"You think we don't know that?" demanded the old man. "These infernal demons have come to destroy our homes and profane our temples. Let us thrust them back to hell together."

The rabble behind him put up a muffled cheer through their oxygen masks. Some, Colt noticed, carried hard, plastic table legs and rolling pins.

"Colonel, you'd better take a look at the tac." Levin's voice rose slightly, but that minute change was enough to set off alarm bells in Colt's head.

He turned his attention back to the Tri-V and blanched. No wonder the KzSha leaders recalled their impetuous subordinates. Streams of red icons flowed north and south for three or four blocks to either side of Colt's position as Armored Star troops hastened to surround his people. At least three groups of twenty-five had already crossed streets parallel to the one Colt's platoon occupied. In less than a minute, they would round the corners and pounce on the gathered Humans.

And Colt had civilians on his hands.

It took him less than two seconds to analyze the situation and spot the best course of action: fly out and regroup at the wall. Unfortunately, that would mean abandoning the well-intentioned citizens to the mercies of the KzSha, a fate Colt wouldn't wish upon the executive board of Mountside Financial.

Well, maybe not.

The next best option was heading for high ground. With plenty of dome scrapers surrounding them, it seemed like a good idea. Besides, Colt didn't have much time to make a decision. The KzSha were coming fast.

Colt blasted a message to his platoon as he seized the old man in one arm. The nearest nine troopers followed his lead, each grabbing a citizen in an armored embrace. The civilians protested and flailed against the suits. Not that it did any good.

KzSha mercs spilled into view from three different feeder streets. They converged like a river flowing in Colt's direction, legs and wings beating the air. With a cry of fury, and not a little fear, Colt fired his jumpjets, willing his five-hundred kilogram suit to somehow rise faster than its specs would allow. His troopers rose with him, screaming toward the dome.

* * * * *

Chapter Thirty-One

Colt realized his mistake the instant his CASPer's feet left the ground. He should never have picked up one of the civilians. That choice put him at the head of the rising column of troopers with no way to fight without putting their charges in harm's way. He should have remained behind to help shield FMT's retreat.

A curse, followed by a cry of pain over the platoon channel, grabbed Colt's attention. He switched to rear view and gasped. Forty KzSha had taken to the air in pursuit of his platoon. Though unable to rise straight up like the Humans' CASPers, their vertical leaps took them dozens of meters into the air before gravity obliged them to catch hold of a building, reset, and leap again. At least ten KzSha had managed to latch onto CASPers. Three had managed to slice through Sergeant Williams' armor.

Colt watched in shock and rage as Williams' CASPer spun erratically for a moment before losing power. It plummeted toward the ground—a dead, broken thing—and its assailants buzzed away from it to seek new targets.

By the time Colt had spun around to target their pursuers, three more of his people had fallen to the tenacious aliens. He placed his targeting reticle on the nearest clump of KzSha and sprayed them with high velocity machine gun fire. The old man screamed and tried, unsuccessfully, to cover his ears while maintaining a grip on his laser rifle. He would likely suffer hearing loss from the noise, but better that than getting torn to bits by KzSha mercs.

The creatures' armor, both natural and manufactured, was tough, but no match for the high velocity machine gun rounds. Colt killed four of the nearest pursuers, their blue blood filling the air as bullets cracked through their chitin.

Levin and several others fired rockets, further disrupting their pursuers' flight plans. The explosives devastated the front row of KzSha. Limbs and wings went spiraling away in all directions.

Unfortunately, the city's designers had never envisioned high explosives going off next to one of their buildings. Reinforced glass and portions of the walls shattered as the Earth-standard atmosphere inside outgassed in an explosive decompression. The resulting BOOM shook the building and reverberated through Colt's suit. Dozens of KzSha, and three CASPers were caught in the blast. They toppled end over end away from the detonation, some of them in multiple pieces. According to Colt's status board, Corporal Dennis and Sergeant Reynolds had died on impact. Private First Class Hoyer survived the explosion, but must have lost consciousness. Her CASPer plummeted into the rising mass of oncoming KzSha, its course uncorrected by its occupant. The flood of buzzing aliens swallowed her.

Colt bared his teeth, but refrained from expressing his rage over the comm. He wanted to reverse course, fly headlong into the enemy's line, and find his downed trooper, killing any KzSha in his way. But no, doing so would mean death for him and the old man in his arms. He could do nothing but watch as Hoyer's status indicator changed from green to red to gray—the color of death.

Compounding his anguish, he had no way of knowing how many residents had died when the building's air suddenly rushed out. Hopefully, it had airtight doors between levels.

The dome scraper rose a little over six hundred meters into New Nauvoo's thin air. Colt, his forty-five surviving troopers in tow, raced up its southern face, the building's ochre stone facets and dark windows flitting by like laser fire.

Their KzSha pursuers buzzed after them, undeterred by the loss of their fellows in the explosion. While they couldn't rocket to the top of a building like a CASPer, their wing-assisted jumps from one perch to the next carried them aloft far too fast for Colt's liking.

The instant Colt landed on the roof, he dropped his spluttering passenger on his feet and spun to take aim at their pursuers. Careful to avoid his own people, Colt fired a series of short bursts intended to force the KzSha to take cover in whatever recesses they could find.

"Levin, set up defenders to repel these monsters." Colt fired again, his rounds chewing through the carapace of a KzSha who had come within ten meters of the roof. Its antennae flashed a series of colors—azure, gold, orange, and finally a solid blue—as it fell.

"On it!" Levin began shouting orders to move troopers into key positions around the roof's perimeter.

One of the eerie things about fighting the KzSha was their silence. They didn't use a language Colt could hear, either externally or over any comms network his CASPer could pick up. As far as he could tell, their only form of communication was through the lights on their antennae, which were mimicked by the gleaming pixels on their armor like an amplifier. It was enough to make the hair on

Colt's arms stand up. And watching the colored messages wash back and forth across their line made it even creepier.

Torres took up a spot next to Colt and added his fire to the defense. Linking their targeting computers, they were able to bat down several of the creatures, giving the remainder of the troopers time to reach the roof and add their firepower. Soon, they had the KzSha at a standstill. Every time one of the aliens tried to climb any side of the building, a rain of bullets, lasers, and grenades would blow them to pieces or send them reeling downward. Most abandoned the chase or hung onto the walls below, afraid to poke their heads out.

The civilians armed with rifles wedged themselves in next to the CASPers and fired at the enemy. They were a pain in his side, but Colt couldn't fault their bravery. Though one or two sported light armor, most wore simple clothes. And yet, they fought.

With their pursuers' heads down, Colt backed away from the firefight to survey his surroundings. From atop the building, he could see the park where Armored Star's forces had massed. According to his Tri-V, they numbered three hundred forty-four. That number made Colt's stomach clench.

Luckily for him, whoever was commanding the enemy force had sent a mere fifty after the Humans. The bulk of the KzSha force surrounded a large building on a rise just beyond the city park. Gleaming white in the afternoon sun, its architecture reminded Colt of ancient structures from the European renaissance. The walls looked like marble, but he figured they were some sort of synthetic. Three towers, the center one a few meters taller than the others, fronted the building. A golden statue of an angel blowing a horn stood atop the central tower. Lush topiaries and flower beds surrounded perfectly groomed walkways that connected the building to the park below.

In better times, the place was probably awesome, but right now, a host of alien invaders squatted in the park and overran the walkways. Blackened scorch marks, cracks in the outer facade, and broken windows venting smoke like chimneys robbed the building of its grandeur. If the dome's oxygen mix hadn't bled so low when the KzSha breached the outer walls, the fire would have consumed the besieged building by now.

As he watched, laser and gun fire lanced out from the building's main entrance, tagging KzSha who had moved too close. The Mormons and Onishi must have set up a defense point there, but there was no way they could hold it for long. Not with that many warriors arrayed against them. The alien force returned fire, and dozens scrambled to gain entry, while others scaled the walls and punched out windows to slip in.

"What is that place? Why are the KzSha interested in it?" Colt turned to the old man he had carried to the roof and pointed at the gleaming building.

The old guy peered curiously at Colt as if he had asked a supremely stupid question. "That's our temple. Can't say why a bunch of hell spawn would want to get inside except to profane it."

Now it was Colt's turn to look confused, though the old man couldn't see his face. "You know those are aliens, not demons, right? They have their own planet. Or, at least, I think they do."

The man shrugged one skinny shoulder. "Course they do. You think demons pop up out of nowhere? The armies of Satan have their own thrones and dominions just like those of heaven."

Colt opened his mouth to say something more, then shut it so hard his teeth clicked. Now was not the time for a religious or philosophical debate on the nature of demons and aliens. "What's inside there that would interest a finance company?"

The old man rubbed his neck below his breathing mask. "Plenty of art. Some precious wood from Earth. Nothing much more than that. And from what I can see, the demons are wrecking that stuff." His face contorted with anguish under the plastic. "They're destroying the holy of holies. My God, we must stop them."

"We will if we can," Colt said and switched channels so he could talk to Levin. "How are we for ammo?"

"Good for now, but we'll begin to run low on high velocity in about half an hour defending this roof. Lasers will last longer, but not much. We can't stay up here forever, sir."

Abruptly, the jamming that had buzzed across all channels, ceased. It was like Colt's ears had popped, allowing him to suddenly hear things he hadn't realized he was missing.

"FMT actual, this is Team Fortress, do you copy?" Yardley's voice broke over the battalion channel like the first rays of dawn.

Colt couldn't suppress his grin as he keyed his mic. "Fortress, this is FMT actual. Good to hear your voice, Yard. You took a frigate?"

"We took two." Yard sounded supremely proud of himself, a feeling Colt couldn't fault. "These KzSha are nasty customers, but they come around once you start cutting their ships apart."

"What happened to the third?"

"Its crew managed a quick orbital adjustment before we could reach them. They're still evading, but we're in pursuit. *Uncanny* is on approach. She'll be in geosynchronous orbit within the hour, but

Petrov and his RATs have already launched. They're en route to you now. Kit's helping bring them down, so you should have the full complement minus my people in the next half hour or so."

Colt wrinkled his forehead. "Wait, are you driving those frigates?"

"No. None of my team can fly. But it's amazing how much a machine gun applied to the head can motivate pilots."

"Did you capture Tory Howard?" Colt couldn't hide the anger in his voice.

"Yes, sir! Already socked him into the brig."

"Good work. We'll come for you once we've secured things down here."

"Roger that."

"Bishop General Lund, do you copy?" Colt broadcast over the militia frequency. While speaking with Yardley, most of his mind had been trying to solve the KzSha problem. He had an idea.

Twenty seconds passed before the Mormon leader answered. With his voice came the sound of heavy weapons fire in the background, coupled with frantic voices shouting over an adjacent channel. "We copy, but we're getting overrun! If you're going to assist us, we need you now!"

"We can't take on three hundred with less than fifty troopers," Colt said. "I'm sending you encrypted instructions. Follow them, and I believe we can hold until my relief force arrives."

Several tense seconds passed before Lund's voice returned. "This is insane. And impossible. You expect us to blow out one of the temple walls?"

Colt ground his teeth inside his CASPer. Even if the fool disagreed with Colt's plan, why did he have to blab it over a possibly unsecure channel? Colt shook his head. Then again, it wasn't like the enemy could do much with the information if Lund moved decisively—or not much more than they were already doing. Better to fight than get ticked off the battlefield one soldier at a time. "A strategic withdrawal is only logical. Blow that wall and run. If the KzSha follow, it spreads their force. If they occupy the temple, even for a few minutes, it gives you time to escape. "

"I shall not abandon my assigned post! My soldiers and I are prepared to give up these fleeting mortal bodies to defend our sacred halls. Our prophet ordered us here, and here we will stay. We'll spend our lives like water if we must."

"But Onishi is with you!"

A series of explosions cut off whatever the bishop general said next. The alien force outside the temple surged forward, their front lines encroaching on the main entrance. For a moment, it looked as if Lund had suddenly changed his mind and decided to follow Colt's instructions. But, unless the general had made a field expedient door on the back of the temple, the walls remained intact.

In the next instant, a barrage of concentrated fire mowed down scads of KzSha, confirming Colt's fears. The Mormons, and therefore Onishi and her troopers, hadn't moved. They still defended the main entrance. Unfortunately, combining their fire did nothing to stem the tide. The KzSha had plenty of bodies to expend. They gained the front walk in seconds and began pouring into the building.

Levin cursed, and Colt felt his heart try to crawl up his throat. Helplessness leached through him like a fast spreading infection.

In desperation, he switched to FMT's common channel. "Onishi! Do you copy?"

Static and the sounds of battle answered his call.

"Alice!"

"Colt!" Onishi sounded frantic. "Can you assist? We're—" A boom that shook the thin air three blocks away interrupted her. She shouted orders for a few seconds before returning. "Colt, we need you in here. Now!"

Colt watched the invaders surge into the temple with fury. Even if they attacked them from the rear with perfect surprise, he couldn't see a way to victory with his CASPers running so low on ammo. But Onishi and Lund needed him. Could he stand there and listen to them die over the comm?

"Torres," Colt said. "You getting this?"

The captain, who remained at the roof's edge firing at whatever KzSha popped its head out, turned to face Colt. "Every bit of it, kid."

"What should I do?" Colt's throat tightened, and his sinuses stung the way they did when he was a child on the verge of tears.

"I can't tell you what to do, Colt. You're the commander."

Colt started to say something hot and despondent, but Torres cut him off.

"But I can tell you that nothing's more important to a good commander than the people who serve under him. The troopers on this roof are feeling exactly what you feel right now. They understand the consequences of fighting and they understand the consequences of doing nothing. Both suck. But they'll follow you either way. And so will I."

Colt considered the veteran's words. Remaining on the roof while the aliens slaughtered his people and the Mormons with them was out of the question. He needed a way to get his people inside without alerting the KzSha outside. And he thought he saw a way to do it.

"Levin," Colt said, his jaw set like steel.

"Orders?"

"We're going down there, but we're going to do it smart." Colt scrutinized the temple and the aliens' lines, deconstructing the problem the way Torres had taught him. He saw an opportunity. "Lund refused my plan. But it can still work, just in reverse."

"What do you need us to do, Colonel?"

"See if you can get that door open." Colt pointed at a roof exit with the image of a stairwell painted on it. "We need to get these people to safety."

Before Levin could act, the old man, following Colt's finger, hurried to the door and pressed his hand to an activator plate affixed to its frame. It opened without releasing pressurized air, and Colt could see a small airlock behind it. The old man beckoned to his compatriots who reluctantly left their posts and followed him inside.

"Thanks for the lift, merc! Give those demons hell!" the man called just before slamming the door shut so he and the others could cycle through.

Accessing his implants, Colt quickly designated an empty stretch of grass on the south side of the building as a landing zone on his Tri-V, highlighting it in silver brackets. "Get everyone to that position in the next thirty seconds. We're heading in."

* * * * *

Chapter Thirty-Two

Despite Levin's protests, Colt led the way. He fired his jumpjets and shot straight up toward the dome before rolling over and cruising along its inner surface at breakneck speed. Crosshatched steel braces raced by a meter from his cockpit, their interlayered translucent sections blurring as he gained speed. His troopers raced after him, maintaining a tight formation as the KzSha who had chased them to the roof opened fire with a barrage of laser blasts.

More than twenty of the aliens bounded after the platoon. Though they couldn't remain airborne for more than a few seconds due to the weight of their arms and armor, they made a sport of flitting from one building to the next in pursuit of their prey. Several of Colt's troopers rolled to fire at them, but Levin called them off.

"We're faster, and we're not going far. Get to the LZ, then we'll take care of our tail."

Colt reached the area he had designated and killed his jets. His CASPer dropped like a five hundred kilo ball of steel. Timing it just right, he fired his jumpjets ten meters above the grass and landed with flexed knees next to the temple's southern wall. His troopers did likewise, blowing up leaves and loose gravel from the adjacent walkways.

"Form a fire line!" Levin pointed at the wave of enemies bounding toward them. "On my targets!"

Colt turned his back on the fight. His people could handle the handful of pursuers who had managed to keep up. But the KzSha assaulting the front of the temple couldn't have missed a platoon of CASPers passing overhead. He likely had less than a minute before they would dispatch reinforcements to overwhelm the interloping Humans.

"Sergeant Wimberly, I need an entrance through this wall. Now."

"On the double, sir." Sergeant Wimberly detached from the gathered troopers. He pulled four gray breaching charges from a sling attached to his CASPer and affixed them to the wall.

They appeared harmless—octagonal metal discs two hand widths across—but Colt knew better. Inside, each carried fifteen programmable shaped explosives whose directional yield could be altered according to the user's desires.

"We'd better back off, sir."

"Roger that." Colt maneuvered back and to one side until he nearly bumped into Levin who was still orchestrating the platoon's fire.

"On your command, sir," Wimberly said.

"Do it." It really was a shame. The building was beautiful. But sometimes, when you've got an infestation, it takes harsh measures to root it out.

The charges produced a surprisingly low-key thump. Though all four delivered their stored energy without a hiccup, the energy focused directly into and through the temple's ivory-colored wall with little blowback. A few puffs of dust, insulation, and pulverized rock jetted into the air leaving behind an outline of a rectangle large enough to admit a CASPer.

"Inside, everyone!" Colt went first, using thermal imagining to mark the KzSha warriors through the debris cloud. The creatures were warm-blooded, but not as hot as Humans. They looked like cool, blue wasps on the display.

Locking his reticle on a target rushing at him, Colt fired the high velocity machine gun on his left arm, hitting the creature in the chest. The rounds sent the KzSha hurtling backward, his armor glowing in a furious array of colors that shouted his alarm as he died. Others must have seen his lightshow of distress. Twelve more appeared out of the smoke, laser rifles ready. They opened fire, concentrating on Colt.

Shooting pain, feedback from his haptic suit, raced along Colt's arms, chest, and legs. He grimaced and returned fire while moving to one side to make room for his troopers to follow. A cacophony of gunfire and explosions rose steadily and filled the building as more and more armored Humans pressed through the gap. Rockets and K bombs lit up the opposing side like a fireworks display. Laser fire and high-velocity rounds did the rest. In less than thirty seconds the KzSha had either died or run. Either suited Colt just fine.

Though Colt had feared he might have led his platoon into the bulk of the enemy and essentially flanked his own people, the KzSha inside the wall turned out to be a small attack force, fewer in number than the ones outside. Whoever was in charge of the KzSha had probably dispatched them offhandedly to take care of the Humans. By the time Colt and those with him had dealt with them, Levin and the rest of their platoon had turned the others into a heap of fallen bodies.

"Excellent work, Top."

"Thank you, sir." Levin entered the temple last after making sure all her people were inside. The next time she spoke, her voice came over the private channel between her and Colt. "Seriously, stop running ahead like that. You might not realize it, but you could have died just now. Remain at the back and let my people handle point. Please."

"I will. And Nichol..."

"Yes?" she sounded pissed.

"I'm sorry."

As the dust and smoke settled, Colt saw they had entered an auditorium, though it was far smaller than he would have expected considering the temple's size. Hand-carved chairs and benches, most of them overturned, broken, and scored with burn marks covered the floor. A thick burgundy carpet lay beneath the detritus, burned through in places to reveal the wooden floor beneath. Even in the heat of battle, Colt couldn't help thinking about how expensive it must have been to import that much wood.

Now that they were inside, Onishi's position, along with those of sixteen of her troopers, appeared as faint telltales on Colt's holographic display. Though he had no blueprints for the building, the CASPer's computer could make logical assumptions based on exterior dimensions as to the place's layout. But it seemed to be suffering some kind of existential crisis. Onishi's icon, along with those of her troopers, kept disappearing and reappearing on the screen, sometimes above ground, sometimes below.

"Captain Onishi, do you hear me?" Colt called.

"Can't talk. Dying!" Heavy fire nearly drowned out Onishi's voice though Colt's external mics were only picking up a dull thrumming carried more by the building's floor than the thin air.

"We're in the temple! Give us your position, and we'll assist," he said.

"East! Head east and look for heavy blast doors. We're downstairs, and so are all of the KzSha!"

"This way!" Colt headed toward a set of double doors at the other end of the room, kicking bits of broken wood and fallen plaster aside as he went. Though one of the doors had been blown off its hinges, which made the entrance wide enough to accommodate a CASPer, the passageway's frame hadn't been constructed for armored suits over two meters tall. Colt ducked as much as he could, but was forced to shatter part of the frame, along with the connected bricks and drywall, to squeeze through.

"Colt!"

"Did it again, didn't I? Someone had to clear a path for us. Come on."

There was a wide hall leading directly to the temple's entranceway on the other side of the door. That and a gaggle of KzSha who had been left behind as guards. Colt could tell by the way they jumped he had caught them off-guard. They must have assumed their buddies in the auditorium had taken out the pesky Humans.

Good. That meant they were underestimating Colt and his troopers. No commander could ask for more than that on the battlefield.

He fired three rockets into their midst before most of them had turned to face him. A dozen KzSha warriors went flying, their bodies slapping against the temple walls. Tough or not, the sudden explosions rang their bells. Those who survived the impromptu flight died under a hail of bullets and laser fire that took them before they could get their bearings.

Colt scanned the hall. Though many doors led off to the right and left, none looked like the blast door Onishi mentioned. He thought he must have missed it and started back toward the main entrance when he finally figured out what he had seen behind him.

The door, which he had taken for a wall due to its sheer size, stood opposite the temple's entrance. It was painted brilliant white and inscribed with three perfect circles. Made from the same sort of alloys as Colt's suit, it stood at least three meters high and was wide enough to admit two CASPers abreast. It loomed over Colt and his people like a titan from ancient Earth.

Onishi's location icon resolved as Colt approached the door. She was clearly beyond it and deep below Brigham's surface. The sounds of fighting, though still muted, grew as he approached.

Colt pressed an armored hand to the door and felt dull vibrations. There was a major battle going on beyond it. He scanned the walls as his troopers crowded in behind him and found a burned out activation switch on the right. It looked as though someone had melted its innards with heavy laser fire.

"They sealed themselves in," Levin said when she saw the switch.

"Now what?" Colt asked. He searched around, but saw no further switches or manual emergency releases.

"Check the floor." Levin squatted low, her CASPer precariously close to the tipping point. "Look here, the top layer, just below the carpet, is made of wood."

She slammed one armored fist into the floor directly in front of the blast door. The sound of splintering oak filled the hallway. She did it a second time and managed to get both of her armored hands underneath the lip of the blast door. "A little help, sir?"

"Top, you're a genius!" Colt quickly followed Levin's example. He moved as close to her as possible.

"Lift on three," Levin said. "One...two...three!"

Servos whined in both CASPers as Colt and Levin strained their muscles, augmented and real, to the absolute limit. The floor cracked under their feet, and the power stress meters on Colt's Tri-V display clicked over into the yellow warning zone. But heavy lifting was in a CASPer's design. The first models created for battle had been little more than walking forklifts converted for martial use. Their designs had evolved substantially since those days, but they were still capable of heavy lifting.

Something inside the walls sheared apart with a screech of tearing steel. The door rose an agonizing half meter and stopped cold.

"It's not enough," Levin said. "I think we tripped an emergency brake or something."

"Don't stop lifting," Colt said. The sounds of intense battle had increased the moment the door rose, making his heart race. His people could be dying on the other side of the door.

"I would help if I could," Torres said. He stood just behind Colt, but couldn't squeeze in to add his lifting power.

"Fire your jumpjets at half power on my command."

"Are you sure about that, sir?" Levin sounded skeptical.

"Yes. Everyone else back off. Levin, now!" He fired his jets, obliging her to follow suit.

The jumpjets roared, their sound overwhelming the explosions and the whip crack of supersonic gunfire from the other side of the blast door. The carpet directly below them caught fire as did the walls to either side.

The door rose slowly at first, then faster as mechanisms inside the wall broke apart from the strain. Colt and Levin stood erect and pressed their arms straight up so the blast door disappeared into a recess above them. It clicked into place with an echoing thump.

At a sign from Colt, they cut their engines and stepped back. Everyone cheered when the door failed to drop back into place, but their elation was cut short when a beam of blue-white light shot out of the open doorway. Part of it struck Levin's knee which exploded in a shower of sparks. She screamed as the afflicted joint gave way and tumbled forward out of sight.

"No!" Without thinking, Colt reached for Levin, missed his footing, and went rolling down a flight of stairs. Fortunately, the fall saved his life, as the next high intensity blast sizzled the air where he had been standing a second before, but that did nothing to soothe the pain of tumbling ass over elbow in a metal suit.

Colt rolled down the stairs, laser fire strafing his CASPer as he went. The fall seemed to last forever, his suit clanging after Levin's like a tin pot parade. Just when he thought it would never end, he hit bottom and bowled into Levin with a hollow, metal-on-metal screech.

Colt gritted his teeth as several lasers scored glancing hits against his armor, but the angle must have been too acute for the KzSha to get a good bead on him. He hunkered closer to Levin in an effort to assess the damage to her leg. He didn't have time for proper triage, but he saw enough to know whatever had hit her had melted that part of her CASPer and likely Levin's flesh with it.

Colt got to his feet. They had fallen into a vast warehouse thirty meters tall and half a kilometer long. In the distance, two forces traded fire, but he could make out little else. A group of twenty-three

KzSha had taken up defensive positions facing the stairs. They hid behind enormous metal packing crates and unidentifiable machinery to take potshots at the Humans. Three of them dressed in heavier armor than their fellows had set up a crew-served heavy laser at the front of their squad. They had it trained on Colt, but to his relief they seemed to be having trouble fitting a replacement chem-pack magazine into its undercarriage.

"Colt!" Torres said. "Take cover behind the stairway. We're coming!"

CASPers flew into the warehouse from the top of the stairs, firing guns and lasers, forcing the KzSha mercs to pull back or get shot. They landed in twos and threes, laying down continuous fire as Colt dragged Levin's CASPer to safety.

"Nichol, can you hear me? Are you conscious?" Colt hissed through his teeth as he inspected her leg. The laser beam had burned through the upper mechanical joint and into Levin's leg. Though he couldn't tell how serious her wound actually was, it looked like she had lost her foot.

"I'm here." She spoke in an anguished whisper.

"Stay down. We've got heavy contact."

"I don't think staying down will be a problem." She lifted her left arm machine gun. "Just lead the little scumbags over here in a line, so I can get some payback."

Colt smiled. Even wrapped in a CASPer she was beautiful. He started to say so when the world turned red. A continuous laser beam as big around as his forearm sliced through the stairs above his head, then the steel wall behind him. For all he knew, it punched straight through the building above, the city's dome, and headed off into space. It made a sound like a guitar string strummed by the hand of God.

Colt cursed and bent down to shield Levin, not that his suit would do much good. The laser fire had turned the stairway and the warehouse wall into slag. If it touched either of them, they would fry.

"Scatter!" Torres shouted, his voice carried over the battalion channel and his external speakers.

As abruptly as it had begun, the red laser beam disappeared. Colt breathed a sigh of relief and peered around what was left of the stairs to assess the fight in time to watch the KzSha crew blast Staff Sergeant George King into oblivion. One moment George was running for the stairs, the next his CASPer burst like a melon, burning parts flying in all directions.

Troopers scrambled every which way, some of them taking to the air in a desperate bid to escape the laser. Some tried to return fire, but the gunners' armor stopped their attacks as if they were nothing. Undeterred, their commander methodically designated targets like a bored ride operator at an amusement park. The gun fired again and again in half second bursts, each one maiming or destroying one of Colt's people.

"No!" Colt fired his jumpjets and leapt toward the enemy's front line as he activated his shoulder rocket launcher.

The gun tracked him, and Colt found himself staring into a barrel big enough for him to reach inside with room to spare. A red glow appeared deep within it, and Colt's breath caught. He triggered a rocket without much hope. It would never reach the gun before its beam turned him and his CASPer into molten chunks of refuse. An instant before oblivion could take Colt into its white hot embrace,

Torres flew into the gun's path, his jumpjets roaring. A flash of red light cut through his CASPer like a whip slicing through fog.

The ensuing explosion sent Colt flying into the melted stairs, alarms blaring in his ears. He could feel the heat through his CASPer.

Where Torres had been, there remained nothing but fire and lumps of melted metal glowing red.

* * * * *

Chapter Thirty-Three

The sounds of Torres' death were still echoing off the warehouse walls as Colt gained his feet. He zeroed in on the gun crew, purposefully ignoring the flaming wreckage between him and his target. His jaw clenched so tightly the muscles in his neck screamed with strain, Colt ran at the gun, all thoughts of plans and problems and drilling down to solutions gone from his mind, and with them his fear and anxiety. He possessed a single, driving urge.

Destruction.

Colt reached the cannon before the crew could fix their aim on him. The nearest KzSha tried to raise a laser rifle, but Colt rammed him into the cannon's alloy mount with chitin-crushing force. Lights flared across his suit and long antennae as the alien slumped to the floor, thorax crushed.

A second KzSha sprang at Colt, its serrated middle limbs poised to slash at whatever vulnerable points it could find on a CASPer. But Colt didn't give it time. Using his pinplants, he extended a blade from his right arm. Almost as long as the KzSha was tall and propelled by an arm made for lifting by the ton, the sword's edge sliced through the creature's armor and the KzSha inside as if both were made of butter. Blue blood flew from its separated halves in long arcs that covered the floor and the adjacent warriors.

The third gunner, having watched his buddies so quickly dispatched, fled, though others from his team fired incessantly at Colt.

Colt ignored the laser fire, though warning signals appeared on his display, telling him some of the beams were striking vulnerable sections of his CASPer. None of that mattered. These monsters had killed Torres.

"Everyone back off!" Flashing a savage grin, Colt tossed three K bombs at the cannon. He backpedaled as fast as he dared, his troopers moving with him, to put the ruined stairs between himself and the KzSha. Most of the aliens recognized the danger, or at least the Human's reaction to it, and likewise dashed for cover. A handful attempted to save their doomed weapon by picking up the bombs, probably in hopes of tossing them Colt's way before they could explode.

Idiots.

With grim satisfaction, Colt triggered the bombs. The concussion rocked him, even with the stairs blocking most of its power. Surprisingly, the cannon remained largely intact as it rose into the air, flipping end over end. The KzSha standing near it did not. Oversized wasp-like appendages flew in every direction.

Those still in possession of their lives and limbs scattered, buzzing away in long leaps. Most headed for the fighting in the distance. Some ran for the stairs and escape into the building above.

Colt wanted time to mourn as he stood watching them flee. He wanted time to gather his wounded and see to their injuries while no one was shooting at them.

He couldn't.

"Corporals Banderghast and Stevens, remain here with Top. She's injured, and I don't want any KzSha finding her defenseless."

"Roger that, sir," Banderghast said.

Colt checked his display; he had thirty-nine troopers remaining. He firmed his lips, his features set like steel under the harsh light of his Tri-V. "The rest of you are with me. We're taking back our own."

"Sounds grand," came a new voice over the battalion channel, one that made Colt jerk in shocked surprise. "Why do it on your own?"

Five CASPers dropped from the head of the stairs—Colt's four company commanders with Major Petrov leading the way. With them came all the functioning RATs left in FMT's inventory: seventy-six total, each of them armed with a laser or high-velocity machine gun. Lacking jets, they bounded down the steps as nimble as mountain goats and leapt over the ruined sections and onto the floor.

"Thank God you made it." Colt turned and looked at his entire company. Quickly, he shot orders for two RATs with medical experience to relieve Banderghast and Stevens. "She was shot by an oversized laser. Treat her in place if you must, but evac her if you can."

"I'd like to tell you where to stick your evac orders, *Colonel*," Levin quipped over their private channel, her voice hoarse with pain. "But seeing as I'm indisposed at the moment, I'll settle for saying you had better be careful."

"I will, if you promise to do what the medics tell you."

"Yes, sir."

"Orders, Colonel?" Petrov asked, unaware of his private conversation with Levin.

"We attack. You're in charge of the main battle. Company commanders, take charge of your assigned RATs and assume a basic assault formation. Our goal is to break the enemy force. They know we're here, and they know we're coming, which means this won't be easy. I expect heavy resistance. But we've got the advantage. They're pinched between us and whatever's left of the Mormon forces and Onishi. Form up and head out." Colt switched to the Mormon Militia channel while his officers got their people into formation. "Bishop General Lund, come in."

"I read you." Lund sounded stressed. "Things are looking pretty grim. Any chance you'd like to join our little party?"

"We're enroute. Where do you need us?" Colt sent the command and his troopers headed off, the CASPers running ahead of the RATs at top speed. Despite his suit's damage, he was pleased to find he had little trouble keeping up with the others.

"Everywhere. Anywhere. The central part of this facility is empty. We've managed to build a barricade, but it won't last much longer. You'll see when you get here."

"Colonel," Petrov said as he ran for the opposite end of the warehouse.

"Go ahead."

"Have you noticed the fuel tanks built into the walls of this place?"

"Negative." Colt looked toward the eastern side of the cavernous room. Petrov was right. A series of white, lozenge-shaped fuel tanks blanketed the wall from floor to ceiling. According to his pinplants, each was three meters tall and a hundred meters long.

"I could be wrong, but I'd lay down a credit to a stick of gum there's F11 in those tanks."

Colt took a second, longer look at the storage devices. "How do you figure that?"

"There are heavy duty, double redundant feed exchangers on each valve. That means whatever's inside is under extreme pressure, and the people storing it are willing to go the extra nine meters to make sure nothing gets out. Also, those tanks are too thick to waste on storing natural gas or petroleum. They're made for extremely high tolerances. Not to mention they're buried a hundred meters underground behind a blast door."

"Point taken. I guess we now know why Mountside hired mercs to take this place." Colt switched his view back to the enemy. "How much do you think they've got down here?"

"Hard to say, but if I had to hazard a guess, I'd put it at about twenty million gallons. Maybe more."

Colt nearly choked. "That's worth more than this entire planet."

"Probably the entire system," Petrov amended.

"But it belongs to the Mormons, not Mountside," Colt said through clenched teeth.

"Yes, sir. That's why we're here. I say we show them what happens to thieves when they come up against FMT."

"Death before default!" Colt roared over the battalion comm, and his troopers echoed him.

As he had anticipated, the KzSha split their force as his CASPers drew near. Luckily, they had no crew-served lasers this time. They must have expected the defenders at the stairs to wipe out Colt and his platoon. This was the second time they had underestimated him. He didn't plan to give them a third shot at it.

A wave of twinkling lights flared across the KzSha's bodies as more than half of them performed a synchronized about face. The forward ranks crouched, clearing the firing lanes for those behind. A second later, laser fire began jumping the gap between them and Colt's battalion. It wasn't the one strike kill scenario they had faced with the heavy laser, but with more than one hundred and fifty individuals firing at once, the strikes accumulated quickly.

Scads of new damage icons appeared on Colt's Tri-V as his front line CASPers took hits. He sent a quick order for Alpha and Bravo companies to slow and split apart, opening their formation like a flower to allow Charlie and Delta the room to fire as they continued forward. He waited for a count of ten, then sent Alpha and Bravo into the air to give the battle a third dimension.

This tactic worked as planned. Confused about which targets to engage, the alien host shifted from a concentrated unit into a gaggle of individuals, each firing at a different target. Some launched themselves into the air to meet the foe while others held their positions, trying to pick off the advancing horde piecemeal. Not only did the KzSha hit rate drop significantly, the confusion reduced the effectiveness of their strikes.

Colt fired his jumpjets. He rose above the fray to a stable position about twenty meters off the ground, which gave him a crow's nest view of the fight raging below. He wished he had ordered his drones to enter the building with him. He couldn't hang out near the roof all day. Sooner or later the KzSha would get their fire under control, then he would be a sitting—flying—duck.

But it didn't take him long to assess the situation. As Lund had said, the Mormons, aided by Onishi and her twelve remaining CASPers, had set up a hard point in the center of the massive warehouse. They were using spare cruiser parts—hyperspace engine housings, ten-meter-long sections of fuselage, and several defunct particle beam cannons—as cover from the attacking aliens. From the way they conserved their fire, allowing the enemy to close to a dangerous distance every time they attacked, it was obvious to Colt the Humans were low on ammunition. As he watched, one of Onishi's people fired a rocket that exploded a couple of meters from a KzSha squad, killing two or three. The rest backed off, but they didn't go far. They, too, sensed their enemy's weakness and were eager to take advantage of it.

That eagerness gave Colt an idea. He reduced power and dropped to the ground, furiously sending commands to his officers just as the platoon's RATs arrived. They filtered between the bigger CASPers to aid in the fight, moving with agility and grace.

The timing couldn't have been more perfect.

Colt waited until Major Petrov and each of the company commanders acknowledged, then sent the command to execute. It took a moment for the orders to filter from the commanders to the mercs, but in less than ten seconds the Charlie and Delta CASPers took to the air in near perfectly synchronized leaps that positioned them in the midst of the KzSha force. In the same instant, Alpha and Bravo charged forward on the ground, the troopers carrying rockets and high velocity machine guns leading the way. The RATs trailed after, zigzagging toward the suddenly bewildered enemy to avoid fire.

The KzSha lines lit up like a Christmas display. Colt, who had joined Bravo Company in the ground charge, ran full tilt into a cluster of aliens, all shooting in different directions in their confusion. A couple of laser beams sizzled against his armor, but he paid no attention as he slammed into the enemy like an orbital strike. Bodies flew. Those that didn't receive a slice from his arm blade felt the brunt of his laser. One brave KzSha tried to shoot him pointblank, but Colt struck first. He cut the alien's rifle, and the alien, in two with a vicious diagonal slash.

"Onishi!" Colt shouted over the comm.

"I hear you."

"Press forward! Rally your people and attack. Advise Lund to do the same. If he refuses, to hell with him. You've got to aid Charlie and Delta!"

"Copy that! We're on the move."

Though surprised by the Humans' sudden aggression and confused momentarily by the furball of battle, the KzSha hadn't earned a reputation for ferocity by avoiding a fight, and close quarters was just the way they liked it.

Lights flickered across their armor and antennae as the eight-limbed creatures passed orders across their unit. All at once, Colt found himself facing a pocket of determined KzSha mercs that turned their combined fire on him. Blood roared in his temples as the sudden realization of what he had done hammered home with lasers scoring telling hits on his CASPer. Without any cover he, like the rest of his troopers, was forced to charge forward or flee. And he wasn't about to flee, not with Torres' death fresh in his mind.

Colt leapt toward the nearest group of KzSha, blade ready, his rounds pinging off their armor and chitin. They fired at his right leg where the CASPer's thigh met its torso, just below the cockpit. A heat warning blared, followed immediately by a servo failure alarm. Colt's haptic suit registered the damage as a stinging sensation that ran down his hip into his thigh. He stumbled and would have fallen except he got a hand down on the warehouse's metal floor.

Just as he regained his balance, one of the KzSha mercs chucked its rifle and pounced. It latched onto the cockpit, sinking one of its serrated blade arms into the CASPer's shoulder joint, triggering yet another alarm. Colt had a feeling he wasn't going to enjoy whatever came next.

The KzSha brought its arm down, again and again, while it held on tightly with its other seven limbs. Nothing Colt did could shake it. He tried bringing his arm cannon to bear, but the joint wouldn't bend that far. Nor would the arm blade. He tried spinning in place, but the creature held fast and continued slashing at the CASPer's armor. Though he managed to push it a bit with an armored hand, the angle was wrong, and he couldn't dislodge it.

Colt's Tri-V flickered. The KzSha must have sliced through something important. A slew of critical failure lights blazed across its oscillating display. The alien slashed again, and its blade cut through the cockpit, passing mere inches from Colt's right shoulder. He had to ditch his hitchhiker quickly, or it was going to peel his armor apart like an orange.

"Colonel!" Petrov shouted over the comm, though Colt had no idea where the major was.

"Shoot it!" Colt wailed, his voice desperate.

"I can't risk it. I might hit you."

Colt knew Feliks was right. With his armor compromised, whatever weapon the major used to take out the alien would likely kill Colt as well. He had to think fast.

Sending a quick command to his failing suit, he fired his jumpjets enough to lift him and the hapless KzSha five meters into the air. The alien tried to leap away from the CASPer, but Colt flung his arms about the creature in an Oogar hug. Red, green, and turquoise lights flashed urgently across the KzSha's armor as it struggled to free itself.

Colt belly flopped onto the warehouse's steel floor. Almost half a ton of metal came down on the KzSha's abdomen, shattering it like glass. Blue blood and other viscous fluids splattered the floor and everything within a couple of meters. Some of it even struck Colt through the gap the KzSha had opened in his suit. He grimaced as he stood up. The stuff smelled of rotten eggs and the lighter fluid Colt's dad used to start his charcoal barbeque.

The KzSha gathered around Colt stared at him in silence. Some of them flickered muted lights at one another, but most remained dark. Behind them, Onishi's troopers fought side-by-side with armored Mormons to cut their way through the remaining KzSha on the front lines.

Colt lifted his gun and pointed it at the seemingly frozen aliens before him, but he didn't fire. They no longer seemed interested in fighting. One of their number, a particularly short specimen, carefully laid his weapon on the ground. When he straightened up, his armor began to flash a rapid sequence of lights. Others picked up the pattern and passed it along their ranks.

"Humans," said a translated voice over the comm. "We, the Armored Star, yield. We no longer wish to pursue this contract. Our losses are too great." The aliens fighting Onishi drew back and dropped their weapons.

"Please allow us to gather our fallen and return to our vessels."

Colt wasn't sure if he was hearing one KzSha or the entire group. He had found so little information about them on the GalNet, they could be a group mind for all he knew. He wasn't sure how to respond. Torres would have known the right answer. Thinking of him sent a fresh pang of loss through Colt. He switched to the officers' command channel. "Do we let them walk? That doesn't feel right."

"No way." Onishi's voice cut through the ensuing silence. "These jerks attacked us—they killed our people."

"And we killed theirs," Petrov said. "That's what happens when merc companies fight. We take our losses and we move on."

"I'm with Onishi," Captain Butler said. "These guys owe us and the Mormons restitution."

"Maybe so, but how are we supposed to make them pay?" Colt asked. "Until about a minute ago I wasn't sure we were going to survive this fight. I think letting them go is our only real option unless we want to involve the Mercenary Guild. And I don't see us holding these guys for weeks while we wait for a reply that may never come."

"It's up to the Mormons," Petrov said. "It's their planet."

"Bishop General Lund," Colt said over the militia channel. "The KzSha have yielded. They want to gather their dead and leave. What do you say?"

A tall figure dressed in pearl white armor that had seen better days approached the KzSha lines, his darkened face shield cracked in several places. He slung a rifle over one shoulder, holding it by the butt, and regarded the aliens for several seconds before he finally spoke.

"Our place is to always forgive. Take your wounded and your dead and never come here again."

* * * * *

Chapter Thirty-Four

From the outset, it was clear to Colt that Tory Howard's preliminary hearing was little more than a formality. The Merchant Guild had sent a Buma called Graven Ulroos, as their representative to Brigham. The alien looked something like a meter-and-a-half-tall owl with its outrageously large eyes and brown feathers, though Graven Ulroos had more neck than the Terran bird. Sitting at the head of a judge's bench in a courtroom provided by the Mormons, Ulroos looked down on those gathered before him from an impressively high perch. According to Bishop General Lund, who had confided in Colt before the trial, Mormon carpenters had been forced to provide Ulroos with a booster seat so he could see over the ornate bench, otherwise all of him except his triangular ears would have disappeared behind it.

Everyone in the courtroom held their breath as the corporate representative sent by Mountside Financial, Edward Allwell, Vice President of Public Relations, took the stand. He had kept mum since his arrival in the Zion system, and no one knew what he would say about Howard's exploits.

A pair of MinSha guards who were part of Ulroos's entourage flanked the witness compartment. They moved aside as Allwell approached. A Mormon bailiff swore him in, and he took a seat on the cushioned chair next to the judge's bench.

"Vice President Allwell," Ulroos intoned, his voice melodic, his words clipped and precise. "You have heard the testimony of many witnesses against your employee, Tory Howard. The question stands, did he represent Mountside Financial's corporate will when he attempted to sabotage *Uncanny Valley* through bribery, hired disreputable mercenary units to besiege the city of New Nauvoo, and attempted to steal its lawfully obtained property?"

Ulroos and all the lawyers and other representatives involved in the trial referred to the Mormon's vast F11 supply as property, resources, or in one case, stockpile. No one ever said F11, or fuel for that matter. Colt understood. The government had insisted he and all FMT employees sign a binding non-disclosure agreement that prevented them from divulging the secret hidden under the Mormon city. Though Colt intended to keep his promise, he didn't see how they could enforce such a stupid demand, but he had asked his people to sign anyway to keep their hosts happy.

Allwell, a hale fifty-year-old with blond hair graying at the temples and a wide, muscular neck, focused his green eyes on Tory Howard who sat almost directly across from him at a table with his court-appointed lawyer. "No, sir. Definitely not."

"Yes!" Yardley, who sat next to Colt in the courtroom's audience area, pumped a fist by his side. Several others joined him with a smattering of applause or exclamations.

Though Colt didn't cheer, he couldn't fight the smile on his lips, especially when he saw the look of utter dismay cross Howard's face. Had the guy imagined Mountside would back him after what he did? Even if they had sanctioned every move he made, it wasn't likely they would admit it to the Merchant Guild. They'd be out of business the next day, and that would be the least of their problems. The guilds weren't to be trifled with.

"Quiet!" Ulroos could be quite loud for such a small creature. "No outbursts. This is a hearing, not a gambling pit." He turned his attention back to Allwell. "Am I to understand that your company disavows Tory Howard's actions in these matters?"

"Correct. The board has directed me to formally disavow all knowledge, participation, and sanction of Mr. Tory Bartholomew Howard and his actions."

Ulroos sat quiet for a moment, his gaze settled on Allwell. "If you disavow Tory Howard's actions, how do you explain his ability to secure payment for two mercenary companies, the MinSha space interdiction units and the KzSha shock troops? How could a single employee of your company amass enough wealth to pay their retainer fees?"

Colt smiled at Yardley on his left, then at Levin on his right. They had hoped the Merchant Guild envoy would call Mountside out, but they hadn't been sure he would. Colt had worried Ulroos would lay the blame solely on Howard even though he clearly had help organizing his attacks.

"Honored Envoy," Allwell said. "Our independent representatives like Mr. Howard are afforded broad executive powers in the course of their duties. That includes access to funds, sometimes in quite high amounts, necessary for their work."

"Are you saying Tory Howard illegally used Mountside's money to hire these merc crews and to bribe Mr. Brandon Sloan to sabotage Fulcrum Mercenary Tactic's ship?"

"Yes, sir."

It was no great surprise to anyone in the courtroom. Sloan, who had testified earlier in the day, had told the story of his recruitment into the Mountside plot. Ulroos had then remanded him to Mormon custody since he had committed his crimes aboard *Uncanny*, which was their salvaged property.

Howard jumped to his feet, knocking his chair over in the process. He pointed an accusatory finger at Allwell. "That is a lie! I dealt directly with you, Edward. You gave me the order to secure those mercs. You—"

"Tor'ett!" Ulroos boomed.

The MinSha nearest Howard leveled a wicked-looking rifle at the Human. Something inside it whirred in the sudden silence as Howard's lawyer clapped a hand over the idiot's mouth.

"Do you deny these charges?" Ulroos asked Allwell.

"Of course, sir. Obviously, Mr. Howard is looking for a way to excuse his horrific actions against the people of Brigham."

Ulroos made a low, contemplative sound in his throat as he stroked the small feathers running down his chin onto his throat. "You are a liar, Edward Allwell."

Allwell's eyes widened. Obviously, he wasn't the sort of man accustomed to having someone question his word. He looked like he might retort, but thought better of it.

"Nothing to say?" Ulroos looked out over the audience of Mormon Militia and members of FMT. "I'm sure we're all glad to hear your silence. You see, Mr. Allwell, after I got the invitation from President Talmason to hear his government's grievances against Tory Howard and Mountside Financial, I did a little digging. No, that is a lie. I had my staff do that digging. And do you know what they found?"

Allwell's complexion had steadily leaked color as the envoy spoke; it now looked completely bleached. "No."

"I'm certain you don't want to hear it, but I'd wager you can guess, eh? They found conclusive evidence that not only did Mountside Financial authorize Mr. Howard to commit his crimes, they endorsed them wholly. In fact, my team even uncovered courier ship files linking you, sir, directly to the team hired to suborn a member of the FMT crew."

More cheers erupted as the audience could no longer contain themselves. This time Colt joined them in clapping.

Ulroos indulged them for about ten seconds, then slammed a feathered hand on the bench, bringing the court to silence.

"Envoy," Allwell said, his lips drawn back in a grimace, "I want a lawyer."

"And you will have one when we arrive on Capital for your formal trial. I'm sure Mountside has a veritable stable, which is good. You're going to need them. In the meantime, as of this moment, I am dissolving Mountside Financial and revoking its right to operate under Merchant Guild sanction. I'm further issuing a summons for the company's executive board and the seizure of all its current assets until this matter is resolved."

"Your Honor?" President V. Ronald Talmason, who sat in the front row surrounded by guards and deputies, stood up, and everyone in the room, especially the Mormons, fell quiet. The sort of reverence they showed the man made Colt uneasy, but their people, and Talmason in particular, had treated him well.

"Yes?" Ulroos sounded put out by the interruption but appeared willing to accept it.

"If you are dissolving Mountside, what does that mean for our friends in FMT? The company currently holds quite a bit of debt from each of them."

Ulroos made a sound that was something between a cough and a laugh. "With all Mountside put them through, consider it absolved. You are forgiven your debts."

This time Ulroos could do nothing to contain the cheering, nor did he try. Colt and his team rose from their seats, clapping, shaking hands, and slapping each other on the shoulders.

Yardley pulled Colt into the tightest hug he had ever endured. And though it triggered his anxiety, it felt good. When he let go, Yard shook Colt's hand, his smile a meter wide. "We did it!"

"Yes, we did!"

Levin spun Colt away from Yard and kissed him.

The room erupted in a second wave of cheers mixed with cries of astonishment. Colt didn't care. He kissed her back for all he was worth, his heart pounding in his ears until he could no longer hear the crowd.

In that moment, he didn't care if it burst.

* * *

They gathered in the staff conference room aboard *Uncanny Valley*, still giddy from the trial and the relief it had brought them. Two weeks of repair work had seen the ship almost put back to rights, though some of the outside structural damage would require a shipyard. Colt figured they could handle that once they worked two or three more contracts. The old bird was holding up well enough to make transits, and that would do.

"I propose a toast to FMT," Levin said, holding up a snifter of scotch she had rescued from Belknap's old bar.

"To the company!" Colt raised his glass of red wine. He had no desire to get trashed, and he figured there would be less chance of that happening if he drank wine.

"And to the troopers." Petrov was drinking scotch as well. He had already sampled three glasses, and his speech was a bit slurred.

They cheered the troopers, and they all drank.

"So, how many times did the Mormons invite you to church?" Yardley raised his eyebrows at Onishi who, like Colt, had opted for red wine.

"Only about ten thousand. I swear, every guy in that place between the ages of fourteen and forty-five asked me out. They all want an outsider, but they want to make her an insider first." Onishi shivered. "It's like the galaxy's biggest fish bowl down there. I'm glad to be home."

The word home made Colt glance up and smile. He had never thought of *Uncanny* as home, at least not in his conscious mind, but the concept fit. Though he missed his parents and his little brothers, he certainly didn't feel the same sort of affinity for their house in Stanford as he did for the old converted freighter.

The doorbell chimed.

"Come!" said everyone in the party, and they all laughed, a sure indicator of their tipsiness.

Staff Sergeant Mona Flowers strode into the conference room, a barely contained smile on her full lips as she surveyed the gathering. "Celebrating, are we?"

Seeing her made Colt melancholy as she reminded him of Captain Torres. "Yes, come have a drink with us."

"Can't." She looked genuinely disappointed. "My ride's here. I'm expected aboard the *Drake* in an hour. I thought I'd say goodbye first, and—" Flowers hesitated, her gaze focused on Colt who did his best to meet it. Then she looked around the table and nodded once. "I'm glad you're all here. I have a message for you from Enrique. I found it in his personal effects."

Colt sat forward in his chair, the warm flush of alcohol seemingly burned away at the mention of Torres. "What is it?"

Flowers produced a data chip from her hip pocket and inserted it into a slot on the desk's main Tri-V. In an age when all media could be hacked with a thought or a wave, hard memory was the last, unassailable bastion for safeguarding information.

"I'm afraid he hadn't finished it yet. He was probably going to surprise you with it when you returned from freeing Brigham. That's how much he believed in you."

Enrique Torres appeared above the desk in perfect 3-D. He wore his everyday Triple T uniform with the T³ embroidered over his heart. "Hello, Colt."

Colt's breath caught, and his nose stung. He hadn't realized how much he had missed Torres' voice.

"I'm not too good at making these sorts of things. My mother always said I was terrible at surprises, so I'll probably never show you this recording. I'll just end up blurting the secret some time." Torres rolled his eyes and shook his head. "Well, that's just crap. Computer, stop recording."

The playback ceased only to be replaced by Torres a second later. "Okay. I suck at making Tri-Vs. Live with it!"

Everyone gathered about the table laughed. Colt chuckled through barely contained tears, and Levin took his hand under the table. She squeezed it, and he gave her a nod of thanks.

"I'm just going to blurt it all out, and maybe when I do this in person, it will sound urbane and smooth like I'm an officer in a legit merc company. Colt, Yardley, Levin, and Petrov, what happened to you, to all of FMT, was a true FUBAR situation. Especially considering your ages. You could have folded the instant you found out your school was a sham, but you didn't. You rose up. Death before default! Damn, I smiled the first time Levin said that."

Levin smiled now, her eyes glassy with tears.

"Cut to the chase, Enrique," Torres said and gave himself a soft slap on the cheek. "Point is, as you well know, you impressed me these past few months. Through everything that befell the company, you kept marching on. Because of that, I think you deserve a chance at the education Belknap and his people stole from you."

Yardley turned to look at Colt, an expression of utter shock and eagerness creasing his features.

"So," Torres said matter-of-factly, "I contacted one of my school buddies, a woman named Nancy Yaleman. She oversees a scholarship board called the Order of the Cadre. That's O-O-T-C, pronounced OOT-SEE. OOTC runs a program called VOWSelect, where they choose deserving young people with high enough VOWs scores to warrant interest from the big merc universities, but not enough money to foot the bills. It's a donation-driven program that pays tuition and living expenses. Past graduates fund it top to bottom. VOWSelects get a full ride, including a food and clothing stipend and tuition. In return, they sign on for no less than eight years with a willing merc company and pay back three percent of their annual income for five years. A lot of us elect to keep paying for the remainder of our careers or make charitable donations to OOTC periodically."

Torres shook his head and reached for the Tri-V. The display went blank.

Colt started to speak, but Flowers shook her head. "Hold up, there's a little more. He comes back."

Torres reappeared. "Okay, I thought I was meandering off topic, but I just watched that first part, and it was pretty much what I wanted to say about OOTC, except that we're a great community. There's a comradery you gain by becoming a member. It's built on what we call the Ladder of Hands. We help out the next generation, so they can help others. There I go off topic again. Point is, I sent Yaleman a message detailing everything you've done over these last few months, and she was impressed. Majorly impressed. Bottom line, she's offering VOWSelect status for you, Colt, as well as for Levin, Petrov, and Yardley. She'll want to see your actual VOWs scores, of course, but I think that's just perfunctory. All four of you can attend the university of your choice, once you've cleared everything with Mountside. Hell, you all could end up with one of the Four Horsemen if you play your cards right!"

Torres cocked his head to one side and stared intently into the camera. "You all deserve it. Truly. I've never seen a group of kids— no, scratch that, a group of people—come together the way you have. I've been honored to *observe* you these past few months." Torres grinned before going on. "Colt, you made a joke a few days ago. You said after FMT had cleared its debts, I should sign on as an officer. You don't know how tempting that is. In fact, I think I'll do it. But I'm not going to tell you that 'til the time comes."

A lump formed in Colt's throat as the Tri-V cleared. Levin squeezed his hand again and smiled at him, though her own expression was a little fragile. He squeezed back, wishing he never had to let go.

# # # # #

ABOUT THE AUTHOR

David Alan Jones is a veteran of the United States Air Force, where he served as an Arabic linguist. A 2016 Writers of the Future silver honorable mention recipient, David's writing spans the science fiction, military sci-fi, fantasy, and urban fantasy genres. He is a martial artist, a husband, and a father of three. David's day job involves programming computers for Uncle Sam.

You can find out more about David's writing, including his current projects, at his website: https://davidalanjones.net.

.

The following is an

Excerpt from Book One of the Earth Song Cycle:

Overture

Mark Wandrey

Now Available from Theogony Books

eBook and Paperback

Excerpt from "Overture:"

Dawn was still an hour away as Mindy Channely opened the roof access and stared in surprise at the crowd already assembled there. "Authorized Personnel Only" was printed in bold red letters on the door through which she and her husband, Jake, slipped onto the wide roof.

A few people standing nearby took notice of their arrival. Most had no reaction, a few nodded, and a couple waved tentatively. Mindy looked over the skyline of Portland and instinctively oriented herself before glancing to the east. The sky had an unnatural glow that had been growing steadily for hours, and as they watched, scintillating streamers of blue, white, and green radiated over the mountains like a strange, concentrated aurora borealis.

"You almost missed it," one man said. She let the door close, but saw someone had left a brick to keep it from closing completely. Mindy turned and saw the man who had spoken wore a security guard uniform. The easy access to the building made more sense.

"Ain't no one missin' this!" a drunk man slurred.

"We figured most people fled to the hills over the past week," Jake replied.

"I guess we were wrong," Mindy said.

"Might as well enjoy the show," the guard said and offered them a huge, hand-rolled cigarette that didn't smell like tobacco. She waved it off, and the two men shrugged before taking a puff.

"Here it comes!" someone yelled. Mindy looked to the east. There was a bright light coming over the Cascade Mountains, so intense it was like looking at a welder's torch. Asteroid LM-245 hit the atmosphere at over 300 miles per second. It seemed to move faster and faster, from east to west, and the people lifted their hands to shield their eyes from the blinding light. It looked like a blazing comet or a science fiction laser blast.

"Maybe it will just pass over," someone said in a voice full of hope.

Mindy shook her head. She'd studied the asteroid's track many times.

In a matter of a few seconds, it shot by and fell toward the western horizon, disappearing below the mountains between Portland and the ocean. Out of view of the city, it slammed into the ocean.

The impact was unimaginable. The air around the hypersonic projectile turned to superheated plasma, creating a shockwave that generated 10 times the energy of the largest nuclear weapon ever detonated as it hit the ocean's surface.

The kinetic energy was more than 1,000 megatons; however, the object didn't slow as it flashed through a half mile of ocean and into the sea bed, then into the mantel, and beyond.

On the surface, the blast effect appeared as a thermal flash brighter than the sun. Everyone on the rooftop watched with wide-eyed terror as the Tualatin Mountains between Portland and the Pacific Ocean were outlined in blinding light. As the light began to dissipate, the outline of the mountains blurred as a dense bank of smoke climbed from the western range.

The flash had incinerated everything on the other side.

The physical blast, travelling much faster than any normal atmospheric shockwave, hit the mountains and tore them from the bedrock, adding them to the rolling wave of destruction traveling east at several thousand miles per hour. The people on the rooftops of Portland only had two seconds before the entire city was wiped away.

Ten seconds later, the asteroid reached the core of the planet, and another dozen seconds after that, the Earth's fate was sealed.

* * * * *

Get "Overture" now at:
https://www.amazon.com/dp/B077YMLRHM/

Find out more about Mark Wandrey and the Earth Song Cycle at:
https://chriskennedypublishing.com/

* * * * *

The following is an

Excerpt from Book One of the Salvage Title Trilogy:

Salvage Title

Kevin Steverson

Available Now from Theogony Books

eBook, Paperback, and Audio

Excerpt from "Salvage Title:"

A steady beeping brought Harmon back to the present. Clip's program had succeeded in unlocking the container. "Right on!" Clip exclaimed. He was always using expressions hundreds or more years out of style. "Let's see what we have; I hope this one isn't empty, too." Last month they'd come across a smaller vault, but it had been empty.

Harmon stepped up and wedged his hands into the small opening the door had made when it disengaged the locks. There wasn't enough power in the small cells Clip used to open it any further. He put his weight into it, and the door opened enough for them to get inside. Before they went in, Harmon placed a piece of pipe in the doorway so it couldn't close and lock on them, baking them alive before anyone realized they were missing.

Daylight shone in through the doorway, and they both froze in place; the weapons vault was full. In it were two racks of rifles, stacked on top of each other. One held twenty magnetic kinetic rifles, and the other held some type of laser rifle. There was a rack of pistols of various types. There were three cases of flechette grenades and one of thermite. There were cases of ammunition and power clips for the rifles and pistols, and all the weapons looked to be in good shape, even if they were of a strange design and clearly not made in this system. Harmon couldn't tell what system they had been made in, but he could tell what they were.

There were three upright containers on one side and three more against the back wall that looked like lockers. Five of the containers were not locked, so Clip opened them. The first three each held two sets of light battle armor that looked like it was designed for a humanoid race with four arms. The helmets looked like the ones Harmon had worn at the academy, but they were a little long in the face.

The next container held a heavy battle suit—one that could be sealed against vacuum. It was also designed for a being with four arms. All the armor showed signs of wear, with scuffed helmets. The fifth container held shelves with three sizes of power cells on them. The largest power cells—four of them—were big enough to run a mech.

Harmon tried to force the handle open on the last container, thinking it may have gotten stuck over time, but it was locked and all he did was hurt his hand. The vault seemed like it had been closed for years.

Clip laughed and said, "That won't work. It's not age or metal fatigue keeping the door closed. Look at this stuff. It may be old, but it has been sealed in for years. It's all in great shape."

"Well, work some of your tech magic then, 'Puter Boy," Harmon said, shaking out his hand.

Clip pulled out a small laser pen and went to work on the container. It took another ten minutes, but finally he was through to the locking mechanism. It didn't take long after that to get it open.

Inside, there were two items—an eight-inch cube on a shelf that looked like a hard drive or a computer and the large power cell it was connected to. Harmon reached for it, but Clip grabbed his arm.

"Don't! Let me check it before you move it. It's hooked up to that power cell for a reason. I want to know why."

Harmon shrugged. "Okay, but I don't see any lights; it has probably been dead for years."

Clip took a sensor reader out of his kit, one of the many tools he had improved. He checked the cell and the device. There was a faint amount of power running to it that barely registered on his screen. There were several ports on the back along with the slot where the power cell was hooked in. He checked to make sure the connections were tight, he then carried the two devices to the hovercraft.

Clip then called Rinto's personal comm from the communicator in the hovercraft. When Rinto answered, Clip looked at Harmon and winked. "Hey boss, we found some stuff worth a hovercraft full of credit...probably two. Can we have it?" he asked.

* * * * *

Get "Salvage Title" now at:
https://www.amazon.com/dp/B07H8Q3HBV.

Find out more about Kevin Steverson and "Salvage Title" at:
https://chriskennedypublishing.com/imprints-authors/kevin-steverson/.

* * * * *

Made in the USA
Columbia, SC
15 December 2020

28358387R00213